The author was born near Middlesbrough in 1954. He attended Eston Grammar School and then joined the Army, serving in Public Relations, Field-Force and Intelligence units. Foreign travel began with bivouacking in Kenya. The Americas, Far East and Europe followed.

Post Army Colin worked as a financial consultant, freelance journalist and security officer. Until recently, he was employed as a driver for children with special-needs. Charity work has involved The Captain Cook Museum and taking aid to Romania. He is currently writing a seafaring novel.

Colin lives with his partner Sarah in North Yorkshire. He has two sons, Andrew and Robert.

IN THE SHADOW OF THE KESTREL

Colin Farrington

IN THE SHADOW OF THE KESTREL

Vanguard Press

VANGUARD PAPERBACK

A CIP catalogue record for this title is
available from the British Library.

ISBN 978 1 84386 836 1

*Vanguard Press is an imprint of
Pegasus Elliot MacKenzie Publishers Ltd.*
www.pegasuspublishers.com

First Published in 2012

**Vanguard Press
Sheraton House Castle Park
Cambridge England**

Printed & Bound in Great Britain

ACKNOWLEDGEMENTS

My thanks go particularly to Mrs. Hanne Barton, headteacher, The Dales School, for having assisted with Danish geography and nomenclature; my chess partner Dan O'Sullivan for having provided invaluable advice on matters literary and historical over many years of friendly competition; Stephen Bosomworth for having shared his considerable insight into the nuances of the English language; Ian and Viola Nau-Berry for their unwavering friendship and intellectual stimulus; and to my partner Sarah Horne, without whose support in all manner of fields this book could not have been written.

This book is dedicated to the memory of my parents, June and Jim Farrington: they always did their best for us.

Chapter One

Hambleton Village – 2010

What will people think, I wonder, when they learn the truth that puts paid to an amazing lie? Will friends that have known me for years, decades even, shun me for my wife's and my great deception, shall the neighbours refuse to pass the time of day, shall the authorities come at dawn to ask questions, shall the police then come to arrest me? This being my ninetieth year, I have no fear of the latter, particularly now that it's been over a year since my beloved Martha died. Nevertheless, I would be sorry to lose the esteem of those with whom I have twice shouted myself hoarse supporting England at Twickenham, of those with whom I have regularly enjoyed a couple of pints in the local pub on a Friday evening after work, and of those with whom Martha and I used to go dancing. My eyes begin to fill as I remember how much Martha loved to waltz; but those days were over at least ten years before the cancer took hold eventually to take her from me. Of course she went to a better place. Indeed, I only make this revelation on the basis that I believe my wife would want me to meet my maker with a clear conscience, and even though I'm far from certain as to whether that will be possible for me to achieve, I can but try.

Taken in more youthful years, and looking like a film star, Martha's image smiles at me as I wipe up a few drops of milk I've managed to spill on the table. Her expression as I perceive it at this moment seems to be imbued with greater love and pride than it was only moments ago. Once you have been made fully aware of the imposture we perpetrated, and have learnt not only all the facts, but also those often overlooked nuances and subtleties which usually reveal themselves to be the most important elements in our human behaviour, I would ask you to keep in mind that our actions were motivated ultimately by love. I say 'ultimately' with good reason, for our lives together began in a world, and at a time, when hatred abounded, and the evidence as depicted in the mounds of rubble where buildings once stood was plain to see. Some of those burnt-out shells of buildings I helped to create. There can be no doubt that, as is possibly the case when every man and woman meet, get to know each other, and finally experience that whirlpool of emotion which is one kind of love, the role played by fate was pre-eminent. My personal feeling is that in Martha's and my initial encounter, the mystery of its workings manifested itself more dramatically than is likely to have been experienced by the majority of couples, regardless of the fact that we, along with millions of others, lived in, and had to endure, destructively turbulent times.

The vast majority of people alive today and going about their business in this relatively prosperous and harmonious Europe of ours at the very least disparage the swastika, and of this great number the preponderance are likely to despise the symbol under which I flew and fought. Today the few that wear the distinctive armbands are more than likely to find themselves being ridiculed as fools or madmen rather than feared as potential tyrants.

Decades ago things were different. I was impressionable at a time when the emblem which was hoisted and carried aloft in the great torchlight parades was a symbol of hope. Now, of course, I wonder how could so many be so easily beguiled, aware that I too, at least for a time, could be counted amongst the ranks of those whose naivety proved to be so dangerous. The strange and unsettling fact is, however, that the zeitgeist (and forgive me for falling back on my native tongue, but no word in English with such a concise and potent meaning comes to mind) symbolised by the swastika brought me to the love of my life. Indeed, there are times, particularly when in recent months I've woken in the dead of night feeling dreadfully alone after years of reaching out for and finding Martha's warm female presence beside me, there are times when I've entertained the thought that all those cities were bombed, all those lives were lost, simply so that we could be together. I know it must seem an insane thought to a rational mind in the light of day, but I ask you to be tolerant of the thoughts an old man has after midnight, for come the dawn, be they harmless or otherwise, the delusions fly.

Don't get me wrong on this point. I am not seeking to expurgate the heinous crimes perpetrated in the shadow cast over Europe and beyond by that infamous cross, nor do I seek to resurrect the swastika in accordance with the meaning attributed to the Sanskrit word, specifically, 'Conducive to well-being'. No other symbol in history has come to signify a meaning so diametrically opposed to that which was originally intended. Notwithstanding the many negative connotations, however, I can think of no other symbol which so clearly depicts the hand of fate and the mystery of its workings. To my mind, and to the minds of my friends and colleagues as they began to feel a resurgence of pride in the fatherland as we scanned the newspapers for stories about how heroically our forces were fighting in Spain, about how effective they were in keeping the hordes of republican atheists at bay, the 'armed cross' was nothing less than a sign from God, and depicted perfectly the phrase which I had learned in English before I arrived by landing, metaphorically speaking not unlike Icarus falling to Earth after the wax holding in place his wings had melted, abruptly in your midst.

You have to understand, just as I have had to learn to understand how wrong we were, that after the humiliations and ignominies inflicted upon us in that infernal railway carriage at Compiègne, after the hardships of the twenties summed up by the epithet 'Weimar', we Germans needed a hero, a modern Siegfried capable of slaying the dragon Fafnir before going on to subdue and claim fealty from the Nibelungs. We needed to celebrate a victory; and for we that were too young to do our bit, that's exactly what the bombing of Guernica was – a resounding victory, a victory of German ingenuity and organisation over those that would, as I then believed, deny God. Indeed, it was after I had been watching newsreel footage of our brave bomber crews returning from that raid, and others like it, that the seed of an ambition began to grow, for I too wanted to be a dashing 'flyboy' just like them. My male friends and I believed that pilots got the prettiest girls.

I watched these films in a hall which my friends and I called 'the fleapit', but a more inappropriate misnomer would be hard to find, for Gunter the caretaker kept the place meticulously clean. Nevertheless, on more than one occasion we took great delight in scratching at our non-existent infestations as we walked past Gunter to leave the building after a show had ended. I watched the footage of crews returning from the Guernica raid with Bertha, my girlfriend of those years, seated beside me. That was to be the last summer in Streisund, a small town near the Baltic coast where I lived with my parents from the day I was born until I left home to return only for a few short visits when granted leave. Yes; I had succumbed to the big-screen propaganda that life in the air force would be one long adventure, to that and to Bertha's influence when she let it be known that she would feel immensely proud to walk arm in arm with a man wearing a Luftwaffe uniform, particularly if that uniform were emblazoned with pilot's wings. She could not know then, as I reached round her back to cup her breast farthest from me in my eager hand, how much her words were to resonate in the not too distant future. We didn't pay much attention to the fact that our heroes with smiling faces had just killed hundreds of people, civilians mostly, women and children included. I wouldn't become concerned about such matters until I had changed my name, my complete identity.

Chapter Two

Aarhus, Denmark – 1942

"Do you have to fly tomorrow Hans? Can't you get somebody to take your place?"

About as inane as you can possibly get, these questions were posed by Hanne as she snuggled into me. With her left hand she was absent-mindedly stroking the hairs on my chest. We lay in bed together naked. Since arriving back shortly after midnight at the apartment in Aarhus I had rented for the weekend, we had made love three times. Now, rather than curling up together and sleeping until a respectable hour, I was mentally preparing myself for this morning's mission.

"Must you smoke those wretched things?" Hanne asked, referring to the cigarette I had just lit whilst peering up at me affectionately with eyes which, in the intensity of their blueness, could turn the beholder into a fawning acolyte.

Their coolness had the power to burn. The point is I found them to be irresistible. She knew that she only had to look at me in a certain way to test severely my Teutonic self-discipline, often making me forget for several consecutive moments that I was a Hauptmann in the mighty Luftwaffe. I looked down into Hanne's lovely eyes and smiled; and then, like a boy who has just lost his virginity in a brothel and in consequence smugly perceives himself to be an all-conquering hero who can do no wrong, I blew smoke into them. Her natural reaction was to recoil from me, withdrawing the hand that had been stroking my chest, and her other hand from where it had lain at rest on my thigh, to waft the polluted air away from her face. There proved to be considerable method in my playfulness, for the violent reaction caused by my girlfriend's alarm and disgust caused the bed linen to fall asunder. My treat was to behold the exaggerated movement of Hanne's breasts, those almost twin objects of desire and beauty which in their perfection were so attractive to at least four of my senses.

"If you ask me another question you'll make me suspicious," I said in return, stroking with one hand Hanne's golden tresses as they came to rest on the taut flesh of her shoulder nearest to me. My words may have sounded a little harsh, perhaps somewhat threatening, but by my actions I meant to restore calm, to soothe.

"Why should you be suspicious?" asked Hanne, her question motivated not so much from an attitude of defiance, but I'm sure simply from not having listened properly to what I had said.

"Very well Miss Hjelmsleve, how long have you been working for that bunch of wankers you call the Danish Freedom Council? Come on, we have ways of making you talk you know."

"Please don't Hans, you know how much I hate it when you start talking like a policeman, even when you don't mean it. It's just that soon you will walk out the door to do something so dangerous you could easily be killed or badly injured, and…"

Hanne didn't finish the sentence. Overcome with dread, the emotion of fear, for a few moments she buried her face in both hands.

When she finally removed them I noticed a tear trickling down her left cheek, and I was moved to think that if I were to be shot down over England on the morrow, at least somebody other than my mother and sister back home in Streisund would miss me. I was glad that Hanne was weepy at the prospect of my leaving perhaps never to return. It gave me strength for the job I had to do. She made me feel more like a hero.

I tilted my head backwards so that it rested on the garish, flower-patterned wall behind the elegantly carved bed-head. Against a white background, though it was impossible to distinguish colour in a room presently illuminated only by moonlight, I knew there to be rows of pink roses. The room which I rented from Friday night until Monday morning, on average twice a month for a hundred kroner per weekend, was hardly decorated in a style which I would have chosen, but it was undoubtedly comfortable enough for our needs. Being young and virile – I had just turned twenty-three – my needs were mainly carnal. Hanne, whose age I didn't know because she persisted in keeping it from me, was youthfully lissom, nubile. I estimated her age to be a few years nearer to thirty than mine, and I knew for certain that she was possessed of a sexual appetite equal to my own. Enabling us to express our mutual desire as we wished, the status of the bed in this enclosed weekend world of ours was pre-eminent. It was a fine piece of furniture, but being old, and in recent times well-used for activities not nearly so passive as sleeping an embarrassing squeak had developed which, at the height of our passion could be heard, I imagined, in the nave of the cathedral on the opposite side of the Great Square, or 'Stor Torv' as Hanne would say. If the noise of our love-making didn't in reality penetrate Aarhus Cathedral walls to disturb the Bishop's sermons, I am sure that several of our nearer neighbours were not so oblivious. We didn't receive any complaints, but perhaps that was because none of the other residents in the apartment block wished to antagonise a German officer, and for obvious reasons. Nevertheless, even in Hanne's and my opinion the situation had become intolerable. It wasn't that I particularly cared about what others might think, it was simply that the creaking, being a noise which became progressively louder as I became more vigorous, in the end was quite off-putting, if you know what I mean. The fact is it made us both laugh, and laughter, I discovered, is not an essential requirement for, and may even be detrimental to, pleasurable experience.

On the basis that the problem would have to be solved, and being a man not without practical skill, I turned up a month ago with a few blocks of wood, a hammer and nails, my intention being to put matters to right. There's a widely held belief that officers are hopeless at practical tasks involving manual work, and with good cause. This lack of ability, however, is not universal, as I intended to demonstrate. Moreover, I wasn't particularly snobbish about artisans and their trades. Paradoxically you might think, this kind of snobbishness is more common in the Army.

Hanne suggested that I first obtain the landlady's permission before I set to work. My immediate reaction was to scowl. I didn't think that such a request was at all necessary, but for Hanne's sake I agreed to accede to her wishes. Hanne can speak German. The landlady, knowing only a few words of the language which I believed was destined to become the European lingua franca, was content to remain in ignorance. I had no option, therefore, but to let Hanne explain my creak-eradication plan to the matronly woman who in her face and somewhat neglected figure, a figure created by over-indulgence, bore a striking resemblance to a favourite aunt of mine. My aunt's doppelganger smiled her approval at me, before turning to speak warmly to Hanne in Danish, a language which at the time was Double Dutch to me. Our landlady's delight at the prospect of quiet nights to come was obvious to behold. Secure in the knowledge that we had obtained verbal agreement, in just over an hour one Saturday afternoon I completed the task essential for, as a submariner might say, silent running, and after a series of vigorous tests I am able to report on a job well done, in all respects.

The only other items of furniture squashed into the space provided by the room's small dimensions was a rather squat leather armchair positioned in the corner nearest to me, and a writing desk, together with, at the other side of the window in the corner opposite, a chair designed for straight-backed sitting. On the desk was an oil-lamp, presently unlit. Hanging from the wall adjacent to the door which led on to the landing was an oval mirror. That was it, and even that was a superfluity as neither of us had sat at the writing desk to write a letter, or, to my recollection, anything else. The armchair, however, was a different proposition, for I gained great pleasure from sitting in this remarkably comfortable item of furniture of a morning reading a magazine or a newspaper in the natural light which streamed through the window. The chair's broken springs didn't pose a problem provided I didn't make any sudden leaps of the type which, as I once discovered to Hanne's amusement, would see me land bottom-first too heavily. At such times the relaxed voices rising from the street, and the sonorous chimes of the cathedral bells on a Sunday, convinced me not so much that there wasn't a war on, but that despite our having suffered a number of reversals of late, the war would soon be over, and unlike the last time, this time we would win. We would win because what we believed in was right, and in the end right always prevails. The contented voices speaking in Danish beneath the window were proof of that if proof was needed, and didn't the church bells proclaim it? All we had to do to establish order completely was to eradicate the malcontents, eliminate undesirable sects. I stubbed out my cigarette in the glass ashtray balanced a little precariously on the arm of the chair.

"I suppose you're going off to bomb the British," commented Hanne in a tone which invited me to interpret her statement as a question.

Reluctantly, I extricated myself from Hanne's embrace, and the bed linen, and closed the curtains prior to picking up my cigarette lighter in order to light the lamp. After removing the glass cover this I managed to do at the first attempt. The lamp's radiance grew in intensity, but nonetheless illuminated the far reaches of our room only dimly.

"You look really sexy standing naked with the light falling down one side of your body, the near-silhouette of the other side leaving more to my imagination, which at this moment is fertile to say the least. Your muscles on the side nearest the light are so beautifully defined. Well are you?"

"Am I what?" I asked, attempting to ascertain precisely which question in the enfilade she had fired at me she was in earnest for me to answer.

"Are you going to drop bombs on the British?"

"I'm not going to tell you where I'm going, but I can tell you that I'm not going to drop bombs on anyone, at least not in the next few days," I replied, hoping that my answer would put an end to Hanne's questions about the mission, and at the same time ease her anxieties.

My answer was truthful, but if anything the forthcoming sortie was likely to be far more dangerous than a raid involving the entire squadron. My orders were to fly over the North of England taking photographs, specifically of the dams holding back the water in an area of rugged country north of Leeds. Somebody paid to think back at headquarters in Hamburg thought that it would cause the British war effort a setback if the dams were destroyed, thereby releasing the pent-up waters of Gowthwaite, Grimwith, and nestling side by side, Angram and Scar House, Fewston and Swinsty Reservoirs. The prospective targets had probably been reconnoitred on the ground by one of our agents working undercover in that part of the world. I surmised this because the mission had been ordered by Das Abwehr, the secret intelligence service. The job was simple enough in theory, and involved finding and then flying over the reservoirs with cameras running. The fact that we would not be carrying bombs enabled us to take an additional crew-member to see for himself with a practised eye, and to ensure that the cameras functioned properly. This fourth person was as yet unknown to me, and as I buttoned up my shirt I wondered to which service, if any, the stranger belonged. Once again Hanne broke my train of thought as I reached for my trousers folded neatly over the less comfortable of the two chairs.

"I'm glad you're not going to bomb the British tomorrow," she said thoughtfully, thinking of tomorrow as being merely the daylight hours.

"Before we were told to think differently," she added, looking at me sternly as if I were to blame, "My friends and I, in fact almost everyone I know, thought of the British as our friends. What's more it's highly probable that more than a few of them and us are related bearing in mind that Cnut was King of Denmark and England."

"That was a long time ago," I rejoined, my attention now focused on pulling on my boots.

I wasn't surprised at all by Hanne's ability to educate me, particularly on matters relating to Danish history. For all the importance of sex between us, I'm certain that I would not have been nearly so attracted to my Danish beauty if, between our love-making, conversation had been non-existent. I admired her for her brains as well as her body.

"It was not the Führer's intention to go to war with Britain, but they forced our hand. They are an admirable race, but they persist in behaving towards the rest of the world with outmoded attitudes. Every Briton, it seems to me, believes that he or she has a God-given right to protect the weak. Despite being advocates of democracy, they control their colonies like patronising emperors. The one important thing they forget in their pathetic crusade, however, is that in order to be in a position to be able to protect the Poles, the Czechs, or whichever people you care to mention presently learning to accept Teutonic efficiency and discipline, a country and its people must first be strong. Didn't our armies drive them, along with the decadent French, into the sea at Dunkirk? Only with American help have the British been able to survive for so long in this war."

I could feel myself getting hot under the collar as I turned my back on Hanne in order to inspect my image in the mirror. I never allowed myself to forget that I had standards to maintain. In the reflection I watched as my girlfriend got up off the bed and put on her dressing gown, the garment which had been lying on top of the bed where our feet had been. Her clothes she kept in a small suitcase under the bed.

A car pulled up in the street just beneath the window. Judging by the sound of the engine, it was the 'Merc' we had 'borrowed' from the motor pool on Friday. I checked my watch. It was just after one. I knew that the car's driver would be Ernst, the navigator in my crew, but I drew back the curtain a fraction to look and make sure. It was Ernst sure enough, and I watched him get out of the car to stretch his legs. He had spent the weekend with a young woman from Hortens, a town about half an hour's drive south of Aarhus. Conscious of the fact that we had a two hour drive back to our quarters located near the perimeter of Aalborg Airfield, and then, after a few hours' sleep, a hazardous mission to undertake cooped up in the 'flying pencil' that was our Dornier 17, Ernst was obviously taking this opportunity to enjoy a few unfettered moments. He was leaning on the car with his back to me when I tapped on the window. He turned towards the sound, smiling acknowledgement when I held up four fingers to indicate how long I would be.

After putting on my jacket Hanne and I embraced. We kissed each other passionately, both aware that there was a distinct possibility that this would be the last time we would touch. It was she who broke off our kiss to lean back at arm's length and look at me intensely, as if at that moment she were trying to fathom my soul. Then, with an affectionate lightness of touch she began to dust off a speck or two from my jacket, as if she were a good wife ensuring that her husband was looking at his best for an appointment with destiny. At that moment my feelings for Hanne were deep, and I wanted to share more of my inner self with her than I had done to date. Compelled, therefore, by an invisible force rising from within, I blurted a snippet of information which I hoped would make Hanne think, and when she had thought, act.

I said, "We've heard a few rumours of late. I have no specific dates, but if you have any Jewish friends tell them it would be best to leave Denmark as soon as possible, certainly within the month."

Before Hanne had a chance to respond, Ernst demonstrated that he was becoming impatient by tooting the horn a second time. My time with Hanne was up, and after kissing her bemused face lightly on the forehead, tip of the nose, and lips, for the last time I walked through the door.

Chapter Three

River Ebro, Spain – 1937

George Gilbert had come a long way, literally. From his rustic cottage a short walk from the centre of the village of Hambleton nestled in the North Riding of Yorkshire to a trench protected by rubble and sandbags overlooking the River Ebro about a mile north of the town of Fayon, was, he estimated, about a thousand miles, but the journey his soul had travelled in the eighteen months since he had said goodbye to hearth and home, and to Martha, his stoical wife standing at the garden gate, was, if such a journey could be measured, much greater. He had, it seemed, compressed more of life into that short period of time than he had in the preceding twenty-eight years, and for reasons both moral and personal he was glad that he had made the decisions which had led ineluctably to his present location and current circumstances. This being the twenty-fourth of July, the sun was beginning to make its presence felt as the intractable disc rose once again above the distant, featureless hills, apparently from out of the sea somewhere east of Tarragona. In an hour or so the heat in the trench would become almost unbearable, and George would long for the cool of evening. When the sun was approaching its zenith George and the other occupant of this hole in the ground measuring no more than the surface area of two coffins placed side by side, would take it in turns to keep watch whilst the other sought refuge in the shade of an olive tree a few yards to the rear. Each trench along this stretch of the front was manned by two men, each of whom had been given an arc of fire covering the approach uphill from the river below. George's comrade-in-arms and fellow legionnaire was a pugilist from East London called Osborne, Harry Herbert Osborne to give him his full name, and Harry was making the most of the relative coolness of these early hours by fetching a sizeable block of stone, the third he had purloined that morning, from the dilapidated walls of a disused farmhouse situated between them and the next trench in the line. He was sweating profusely. His aim was to improve the protection along the parapet directly in front of the trench. Encumbered also by the machine-pistol slung over his left shoulder – standing orders stressed that personal weapons should be carried at all times – Harry appeared to be exerting himself to the limit of his strength. Indeed, he had to drop the block several paces from its intended position. Temporarily exhausted, he sat down on the dry earth behind the trench, allowing his legs to dangle freely as he reached for his water bottle. He had left it propped-up against a sandbag. He drank copiously, and after drinking wiped the moisture from his lips with the back of his hand. There being, within easy walking distance, a stream flowing down the hillside to merge with the river coursing languidly towards the sea, maintaining a regular supply of drinking water wasn't a problem.

Looking across at George with a broad grin which revealed the gap from where he had lost two front teeth during a fight in Cáceres, the town to which the two Englishmen had been taken soon after their arrival in Spain, he said, "Do me a favour mate, and move those couple of sandbags a little to the left so I can plonk this blighter where it'll do the most good."

Harry, being a man in his forties, and a Londoner to boot, was usually able to bring his greater experience of the world to bear in the daily discourse and undertakings involving the two men, even though they were of equal rank in the Legion. Leaning his Mauser rifle against the trench wall in order to free his hands, George hastily complied with his friend's request. After George had completed the reorganisation of their defensive position to Harry's satisfaction, the latter handed George the water bottle, beckoning him to drink whilst he set about completing his own self-appointed and much more strenuous task. Incongruous as it might have seemed to a stranger, the two men really had become good mates over the past eighteen months in each other's company.

Notwithstanding their different backgrounds and the gulf between their respective ages, the empathy the two men shared had much to do with the way in which they viewed the world, and it was that view which had brought them together in the first instance. They both admired the political movements which were, at the time when George was packing a small suitcase at home in preparation for the journey south, beginning to flex their muscles in Europe. Their opinions of Hitler and Mussolini were that these were the men of the moment, the leaders whose strength and vision would lead the peoples of Europe, Britain included, into a golden age of prosperity. This new age, they reasoned, would be achieved by demonstrating a clear sense of purpose in all fields of human endeavour, and by a resolve, a strength of will which had not been seen since the emperors of Rome had sent forth its mighty legions. Indeed, in his role as a teacher, George had more than once taken a party of school children to explore the forts and excavations along Hadrian's Wall, and on each occasion he had spoken like an orator, like a man inspired as he described what the Romans had to endure in this remote corner of their empire, and as he went on to explain what a civilising influence, therefore ultimately what a power for good, was set in motion by Julius Caesar's invasion of these shores. On the morning of George's departure for London, which happened to be the second of October, our apologist for the hegemony of Rome provided his wife with some amusement as she entered their somewhat chintzy bedroom to find her husband standing in front of the mirror practising a fascist salute.

George Gilbert's plan had been to travel to London to take part in the big march organised by Sir Oswald Mosley and his followers through a predominantly Jewish area. In our now erstwhile teacher's opinion this was an opportunity for true Britons, Britons that were prepared to fight for their birthright, to be counted. Pride of place in George's suitcase was allocated to his black shirt and trousers, the uniform of the British Union of Fascists. Incidental to his true sense of purpose and motivation for leaving at this juncture was the fact that, following accusations and rumours of an inappropriate dalliance with a girl of fifteen who had been a pupil in his class, a girl who, it has to be said, had the beauty and wiles to charm a man into trouble, Mr Gilbert had resigned his post. Of course, being the man that he was George denied any impropriety, and ultimately it was his word against the word of his accusers, they being the parents of the girl involved. There had been no evidence to prove, or witnesses to testify, who was in the right and who was in the wrong. On the basis that he had saved up enough money to keep Martha and himself going in the short term, he had thought the best course of action to placate wagging tongues was to leave the village. In the course of his travels, though he had mentioned the idea only in passing to Martha, George hoped to get a job elsewhere. The job he hadn't expected to land, though in reality it was undoubtedly a calling rather than a mere exchange of time, energy and whatever talent an individual possesses in exchange for money, was to be a combatant in the Army commanded by Generalissimo Francisco Franco Bahamonde, to be up to his neck in the Spanish Civil War.

Chapter Four

East London – 1936

Of the two friends it had been Harry who had first mooted the idea of going to fight in Spain, and that had been just after he had been blooded in a fight in his home town, an event which took place soon after the two men had met for the first time in an old warehouse near the river.

The building, which was partially empty and, apart from a few broken windows, quite sound, had been converted into an accommodation block for members of Mosley's gang that had travelled into London for the march planned to take place the day after next. Being a Londoner born and bred, Harry wasn't a visitor, as it were, but his job was to organise those that were. The inner walls consisted of bricks painted a sickly cream colour. The floor was concrete. A sparse array of bare light bulbs hung from the ceiling. This was high, a feature which reminded George of the school he had attended between the ages of five and eleven. To his knowledge, however, there had never been pigeons nesting in the upper reaches of school. A couple of them were cooing merrily here. The furniture in the area set aside as a temporary dormitory consisted of four rows of camp beds, two rows of fifty beds along the lengths of facing walls, with a similar number placed back to back down the centre, making exactly two hundred beds in total. At the outset on each bed two grey Army blankets had been placed neatly folded. Between the rows of beds were little enclaves, each of which was made up of a table surrounded by four chairs. Of these enclaves there were six, three in either aisle. Other amenities available were two toilets situated near the entrance. Originally they had been for either sex, but in this uniformly male context the demarcation no longer applied. All but one of the toilet bowls were without seats. The washing facilities were equally spartan and consisted of two sinks with taps which released, irrespective of whether it was the tap marked hot or cold which was turned, water which made the pores of the skin close abruptly. At least the toilets flushed, and they were kept spotlessly clean.

The austerity of the accommodation suited George as, an hour after his arrival, he stripped to wash. There were at least forty other men in the room at this time. Some were writing, some were reading, and a few were sprawled on their camp beds staring up at the antics of the pigeons. At this point George had exchanged only a few words with Harry as the latter had shown the new arrival what was where. On first meeting George was struck by two aspects of Harry's dress and manner, one of which he determined to put right at the earliest opportunity. George, who at the time was dressed in civilian clothes, was impressed by the insignia sown on to Harry's shirt sleeves at the top of each arm. This was a rectangle with a red background containing a blue circle in the centre which in turn was encircled by a white perimeter joined by a white zigzag flash. George's black shirt was yet to be emblazoned in such a manner. More difficult to replicate even if he had wanted were the mannerisms and speech of this individual compared to those revealed and expressed by the people at home in Yorkshire, and no doubt to those projected by himself. At this time of year the smallholders and farmers that lived and worked in and around the village of Hambleton would be rounding up the crop of lambs which had been born in the spring and taking them to market, or to be slaughtered. Presently embedded in the heart of the great metropolis, he wondered if the likes of Harry had ever set eyes on a cow or a sheep in the flesh when that flesh is standing on, and indeed comprises, four legs. No; Harry's world could not have been more different. It was a world filled with the teeming hustle and bustle of humanity compressed into narrow streets, streets that were pungent with the smell of exhaust fumes from buses, vans, and in ever increasing numbers, privately owned cars. Down by the river it was a world of wharfs, jetties and cranes, installations and equipment necessary to unload from ships the produce of an empire, an empire which was the legacy of Rome, but, as the countries coloured red on the maps in the books at school indicated, far greater in size, in power. From leaving the train at King's Cross, the sights, sounds and smells which greeted George on his first day in the capital were a world removed from the bucolic paradise which he had left under a cloud.

George's first words to Harry as he was being shown around were to enquire if there were rats in the building. He had come across rats in outbuildings at home, but he had dealt with them without mercy, and they had never come into the house. He didn't relish the prospect of a creature which he found more disgusting than most crawling over him as he lay sleeping. Harry, like a man with a dark secret at first chuckled to himself, but then responded in earnest by saying that after putting down poison a number had been found dead. He expressed the hope that the problem had been 'sorted', but he couldn't be absolutely certain that it had.

George's second question of Harry was to ask where it would be possible to get hold of a couple of shoulder flashes, a needle and some thread.

"If you give me your shirt I'll take it home with me tonight," Harry had replied. "I've got a few spare insignia somewhere. It'll just be a matter of finding them. Mum'll sew them on for you. She likes to make herself useful for the cause when she can; not that she's much interested in politics mind you: it's just that she dotes on me. You know how mums are."

"That I do," replied George, removing the carefully folded item from his case before handing it over so that the embellishments might be made.

"Does she live far from here?" asked George as he pulled out a second shirt from the case, the most remarkable feature of which was that it wasn't black, but a military-style, khaki-coloured garment which he sometimes wore when walking across the moors. "I only have the one black shirt," he commented as he fastened the buttons of the shirt he intended to wear that evening.

"Don't worry about that," said Harry, "as long as you have the right gear on the big day. Mum and I live about ten minutes' walk away, in Swedenborg Gardens, though what, if anything, the gardens have to do with Sweden beats me."

"I should think they're named after Emanuel Swedenborg, the Swedish mystic whose followers founded The Church of the New Jerusalem," commented George, revealing for the first time to his interlocutor that he was a man of some education, a fact which instantly made an impression on Harry, the kind of impact which only superior knowledge can make. Indeed, in the weeks and months ahead, Harry's worldly experience and street-fighter instincts often gave ground to the arguments posited by the mind which revealed a keener intelligence for having accumulated a greater store of abstract learning.

The initial meeting between this reputedly errant Yorkshireman and the Londoner had gone well, but it wasn't until the day of the march that the relationship between the two men deepened as their respect for each other grew, a consequence of contending with, and, in their eyes, overcoming, shared adversity. The fact of the matter was that the march which Sir Oswald – known affectionately to a number of his subordinates as 'Oz' – had organised to be a show of strength, didn't go according to plan. It was estimated that as many as three thousand Blackshirts turned up for the march to find themselves confronted by much greater numbers of people whose sole intent was to prevent Mosley's followers making progress. Moreover, the great throng was made larger by the presence of thousands of policemen, a small number of whom were on horseback. The riders sought to clear passages through the crowd so that omnibuses could travel along their normal route, but as soon as each bus moved forward the crowd surged back into the space the vehicle had momentarily left in its wake. Cable Street, the name by which the riots became known to posterity, was heaving with people whose conflicting ideologies inevitably led to scuffles, fights with fists. It was during one of these outbreaks of violence that George had felt compelled to get involved in the fray.

Attired in his smartly pressed shirt now adorned with the shoulder flashes which Harry's mother, Edna, had dutifully sown on for him, George, in the early afternoon of the fourth of October, and in the company of approximately sixty fellow fascists that had been denizens of the warehouse dormitory, had marched along Dock Street in three ranks. They were making for Royal Mint Street, the area designated as the forming-up point. Like a seasoned Army drill instructor – which he had never been – Harry called the step. Those that knew the words sang the fascist anthem as they marched. Their hearts were stirred, by the significance of the words, and by their tuneful resonance.

> *"Comrades, the voices of the dead battalions*
> *Of those that fell that Britain might be great,"*

Marching in the centre of the second row, despite his being able to hear Harry calling left right left right clearly, George was finding it difficult to keep in step. His legs and arms didn't seem to be working in quite the same way as those of his comrades. He knew the words of the first verse only, and these he sang with gusto as he struggled with his wayward limbs.

> *"Join our song, for they still march*
> *In spirit with us,*
> *And urge us on to gain the fascist state…"*

"Left, right, left, right," called Harry, his voice becoming more stentorian by the minute.

> *"We're of their blood and spirit*
> *of their spirit,*
> *Sprung from that soil for whose*
> *dear sake they bled…"*

By this time George had managed to get the hang of marching in step, but what he gained on the swings he lost on the roundabout, because also by now he was only able to mumble sounds which he thought might resemble words known to the others by heart.

Suddenly, shouts of, "Fascist bastards!" could be heard above the martial calls and singing, the verbal hostility emanating from a group of anti-march protesters appearing from the right as the marching column was about to turn into Royal Mint Street. The insult echoed several times, along with many other choice expressions indicating that these name-callers owed their political allegiance to anyone but Sir Oswald Mosley. The crowd which had gathered at the western end of Cable Street, and which was distinctive for not wearing a uniform of any description, was huge. The anti-march protesters outnumbered the Blackshirts by several to one. At that moment, its driver struggling against the odds to maintain a sense of normality, a bus appeared. Tooting the vehicle's horn almost continuously, the driver steered manfully out of Leman Street to make a left turn into Cable Street. He was way behind schedule. The bus's arrival on the scene was significant, for it caused the fascists to break ranks, at which point a few of the men that had been at the head of the column, Harry and George included, found that they had become separated from the rest. The crowd around them looked menacing. The singing had stopped. Now the only voices to be heard in unison were chanting. From the direction of Royal Mint Street could be heard, "We want Mosley! We want Mosley!" Sounding much louder in the ears of the little isolated group of fascists came the reply, "So do we, dead or alive!"

George turned his back on those elements of the crowd which appeared most threatening to look in the direction of Royal Mint Street. Aware that there is safety in numbers, he was eager to be where, judging by the sound, the Blackshirts had gathered in strength. His thoughts were disturbed when he had to side-step quickly so as not to be trodden on or knocked flying by a policeman mounted on a grey mare standing sixteen hands high at least. The policeman was gently edging his horse into the crowd in an attempt to keep the junction clear for traffic. It was an impossible task. On recovering his balance George turned around to observe that the mounting tension had erupted into violence, and though he would not have previously condoned such acts, he felt that he had no choice but to assist a fellow Blackshirt, a man with whom he had had some rapport. About twenty yards away Harry Osborne was being set upon by three anti-march demonstrators. George thought the odds unfair. George Gilbert's instincts were hardly pugnacious. In fact, when discussing the events of that October afternoon at a later date, he was hard put to remember the previous occasion he had been involved in fisticuffs. It had been, he concluded, twenty years ago in the playground at school. In the present melee he bounded towards the burly Londoner and his opponents with the ferocity of a lion. From the experience he had gained at Passchendaele in the 'war to end all wars', and in numerous civilian occupations an essential qualification for which was an ability to twist arms whilst demonstrating a potential for further violence, there was probably no man in London who was more capable of looking after himself than Harry; but he was glad of the assistance nonetheless. Up until that moment he had been taking more punishment than he had been giving. Following George's lead, a fellow Blackshirt also set off in haste in Harry's direction, and in turn the fascists were followed by two policemen, whose job, of course, was to keep the peace. With a final salvo of blows to Harry's head and body, for which one individual received a couple of hefty thumps in return, the anti-march enforcers made good their escape. Two more police reinforcements arrived. Between outbursts of laughter the three fascists shook hands and slapped each other on the back. Without a word being said on the matter, by this act they hoped to demonstrate to the watching policemen, and other onlookers, their unbroken solidarity. Neither the jeering crowd, nor the policemen, were impressed by this show of bravado. One or two civilians mocked the blood dripping from Harry's nose down the front of his shirt. The police presence had put an end to the violence, and they took no further action other than to inform the Blackshirts that they might as well go home, for Mosley had called off the march.

In response to George's plea to be escorted away from the mayhem, the four policemen ensured the safety of the three Blackshirts until the threat to their persons had become negligible. That place of relative safety was in one of the quieter streets linking Cable Street with the parallel thoroughfare to the south known as The Highway. The policemen left their erstwhile likely victims in order to return to the scene where the potential for trouble was greater. By a route known only to Harry the fascists made their way back to the dormitory. Shortly after entering the building George was hit on the head by a dollop of excreta seemingly aimed by a crack-shot pigeon. The incident, though undoubtedly unpleasant for the individual concerned, served to lighten the atmosphere created by the sombre scene of approximately a dozen fascists going about their business in various states of undress as they licked their wounds, so to speak, prior to changing into clothes which were less conspicuous, less provocative to those outside the Union. Evidently the day had not gone well.

"It must be a communist," said George wryly, referring to the pigeon cooing mockingly as the bird strutted along a girder supporting the roof.

Until that moment the man targeted had managed to survive the day's events unscathed.

"Not at all," responded Harry. "Don't you know it's supposed to be good luck to be dumped upon, at least by a bird."

Rather glumly George replied, "I don't feel particularly lucky."

He was thinking back over all that had happened to him over the past several weeks as well as the past several hours.

The fascist who had set off with George to render Harry assistance in his moments of greatest need left their company to attend to his 'personal administration' as he described it. Seeing that George's spirits were at a low ebb, and thinking that his disappointment was mainly due to the failure of the march to go ahead as planned in the face of formidable resistance by real communists, Harry invited George to have a drink with him in a pub which he had in mind. George readily agreed, and that evening, after both men had had a bath, and then eaten a meal cooked by Edna, they sat in the bar of 'The Prospect of Whitby', which, as Harry informed his new drinking partner, is reputedly the oldest riverside inn in London. Harry chose the venue because he thought its name would make George feel more at home. Perhaps the person who had named the pub centuries ago felt similarly inclined in respect of the Yorkshire coal ships which used to anchor nearby. Over pints of London ale the two men discussed the march that never happened, the weather, football, politics – in Europe as well as in Britain – women, life in London, life in Yorkshire, and which side was likely to win the war in Spain. After their fifth pint – or was it their sixth – Harry and George shook hands on their decision to go and fight on the side that was destined to win.

Chapter Five

Denmark 1942

I jumped into the front passenger seat of the Mercedes with an alacrity which was in marked contrast to the languid movement demonstrated by Ernst as he climbed in to position himself behind the wheel. It also struck me that from the little I could see of his features in the moonlight that my navigator, who on this occasion was also my driver, was not in the best of moods. Oberleutnant Ernst Eckener and I had flown on twenty missions together, one of which had nearly ended in disaster when, having flown home on the proverbial wing and a prayer, we crashed on landing. Fortunately we had both been able to make good our escape from the wreckage prior to the fuel tanks exploding. Our gunner, who by all accounts, his own included, had been an exceptionally good footballer before the war, had not been so lucky and had perished in the explosion. In the time that we had been together in the squadron Ernst and I had got to know each other as well as any two men could get to know each other, and our relationship was essentially based on mutual respect. Most of the time Ernst was cheerful in the extreme, and his youthful face would be creased with the broadest of smiles at the slightest stimulus, sometimes even when that stimulus might be expected to create a frown. On features which were regular when expressionless, the smile which was Ernst's normal demeanour created a peculiar asymmetry. The lines created by the broadening of the mouth and the revealing of an even row of white teeth were definitely more pronounced on his left side than the right. It was the same with the so called crow's feet at the corner of the left eye. It was as if throughout his life Ernst had smiled more with one side of his face than the other, and so the indelible impressions had been made. My friend and colleague's intelligence was revealed in a forehead which appeared worry-free beneath a head of thick black hair, and in the beady brown eyes which he admitted were his most unattractive feature. A hand which looked as if it would not have been out of place holding a violin took hold of the steering-wheel, whilst the other slammed shut the heavy car door. I surmised that my companion's low spirits were the consequence of an unsatisfactory weekend with his girlfriend in Hortens. I had yet to meet the young woman, but from all that Ernst had said about her in the Mess and on the journey south from Aalborg on Friday, I was left in no doubt that he considered her to be something special. I knew that she was about the same age as Hanne, that she was called Margareta, and that she was a brunette. I was also aware that she worked as a teacher in a kindergarten in Hortens. The only other reason for Ernst's morose demeanour that I could think of was that he had become anxious about the forthcoming mission. We didn't need anyone to tell us that flying is a risky business, and we would have been unbelievably foolish not to realise that those risks increase a thousand-fold when there is the likelihood of a Hurricane or a Spitfire shooting up your ailerons. Being the men we were, however, and at the age we were, our natural defence mechanism when giving due consideration to our passing, to the possibility of our meeting a violent end, was to make jokes. It probably didn't need an expert psychologist to gauge how much our jocularity was based upon fear. Most of the time, however, we managed to keep the idea of our own deaths and its contingent emotion at a distance. Predominantly in our minds death was a shadow suppressed below our personal horizons. Of course, we knew it, whatever 'it' was, would one day appear on the skyline moments before it seemingly rushed to meet us, but in our delusions so far off was that day that in the present we considered ourselves to be immortal, this despite the fact that more than a few of Ernst's and my friends had gone to meet their maker.

"What's the problem?"

Ernst was pulling on his leather gloves when I asked the question, a question which I hoped by its brevity allowed him the greatest scope in answering. Perhaps it was the perspicacity of my realising that there was indeed something gnawing at Ernst from within which caused my friend to look at me quizzically, in the first instance at least, to look at me as if I were a fool to think that there could possibly be anything wrong. His doleful expression, however, was all the proof I needed that I was on the right track. Using exactly the same words I repeated the question.

"Was ist denn los?"

"It's nothing really," replied Ernst as he leaned forward slightly to place and then turn the key in the ignition. Despite the coldness of the clear autumnal night the powerful eight cylinder engine immediately sparked into life. Subsequently the sound produced was a gentle purr. On pulling away from the kerb I had the presence of mind to turn my head and look up at the window where I imagined Hanne was watching. I saw no sign of her but I waved nevertheless. There wasn't a chink of light to be seen. I would have been ill at ease with myself for the entire journey if, by being focused on Ernst's state of mind, I had forgotten to bid Hanne goodbye with a final gesture. My vanity may have wished it otherwise, but I convinced myself that it didn't matter if she wasn't taking a last peek through a gap in the curtains. I had done my bit for love. Ernst drove out of the square and soon we were speeding along the wide road leading north out of the city, the detached houses of prosperous Danes, many of which I imagined belonged to Jews, looming out of the shadows either side. They were destined to be lost in darkness just as quickly, for the power which had been cut after the heavy drone of unfamiliar aircraft had been heard around midnight, evidently had not yet been reinstated. We were heading in the direction of Randers. Needless to say the only traffic on the road at that time of morning was comprised of military patrols. At a checkpoint in the suburbs at the edge of the city we were requested to stop by a sentry waving a torch, but he gestured for us to go through once we drew close enough for him to be able to read the insignia on the side of the vehicle. I am sure that the smartness of the salute he gave us was due to the fact that he believed the car's occupants were of higher rank in the military hierarchy than we were. Our progress was good, and I was looking forward to getting at least three hours' sleep before the morning briefing at 0700. With luck we might make it into our beds by three, but that would only be possible if Ernst were to drive with a sense of purpose equal to my desire for sleep. In the meantime my colleague had begun to divulge what it was that had wiped the smile from his face.

To my surprise the cause of the man from Bonn's pensive melancholy had nothing to do with Margareta, nor was his unhappy frame of mind directly influenced by the forthcoming mission. The story Ernst told to me was that earlier that evening he had fallen asleep – for no longer than half an hour – and during his nap he had dreamed a dream which had been unsettling, a nightmare from which he had woken with a start. The culmination of the seemingly real experience, the unreal happening which had jarred him into a conscious state, had involved the fate of his brother in the desert at a point in time when it was uncertain whether the latter was to live or die. I knew that Ernst's brother was a pilot in the Luftwaffe, just as I was, and I also knew that his job was to fly in support of the Africa Korps in its struggle against Field Marshal Montgomery's Eighth Army, the so-called Desert Rats. In Ernst's dream his brother's lone Heinkel – a machine with which I was not unfamiliar – was attacked in quick succession by three Spitfires descending from above and behind with machine guns blazing. The outcome was inevitable, and before the last of the attackers had begun to fire his guns, the Heinkel had become engulfed in flames and smoke. In his dream Ernst had seen his brother bale out, the only crew member to do so before the aircraft plummeted to crash into the cliffs of a wadi, cremating the occupants dead or alive in a final dramatic explosion. At this point it seemed to me that Ernst should have been relieved to observe, in the war being waged inside his head, that his brother was as yet unscathed. The parachute had opened fully and appeared a thing of beauty in the tranquil scene which had followed the carnage, the billowing white silk of the canopy contrasting serenely with the cloudless, and now deathless, sky. Indeed, my friend informed me that for a time he was reassured to the point of experiencing a great joy, but the feeling didn't last long. In the moments prior to waking he had observed one of the attackers swoop down towards his brother. The problem for Ernst was that he had no idea whether the triumphant Spitfire pilot was about to act with a total disregard for chivalry and open fire on the helplessly dangling figure, or whether he was intending to indicate to his foe that he had made a note of where he was about to land with a view to his being picked up by one side or the other rather than being left to die a slow, painful, and lonely death. At this point in the narrative I decided to interject. Perhaps it's not to my credit that as soon as Ernst told me that the cause of his being down in the dumps, so to speak, was about as insubstantial as you could possibly get, I began to feel less concerned for his well-being. More than once I had allowed my mind to wander, back to Aarhus to consider what Hanne might be up to presently, and forward to when I might finally get to bed, this time to sleep. My comment to Ernst informed that the problem with dreams was that they rarely provided a satisfactory ending. In this regard, I added didactically, they compared unfavourably with a good film. Ernst's final comment on the subject was that if this were true, and on balance he believed it was, then perhaps dreams were more true to life than one might at first imagine.

Following this statement we drove for the next twenty miles in silence.

Thinking that it would be wiser not to travel through an area of forest called the Rold Skov without an escort vehicle, we opted to take the secondary route north of Randers, intending to cross the Mariager Fjord at Hadsund. Any wisdom inherent in our decision was based on the fact that a number of vehicles not travelling in convoy had been ambushed by members of the Danish resistance movement whose area of operations ranged between the towns of Hobro in the south and Svenstrum in the north. The Rold Skov provided perfect cover for terrorists to mount an ambush and make good their escape. Personally, I couldn't understand why anyone in Denmark should resist so stubbornly, so pig-headedly, the inclusion of their small country in the great Aryan Empire, in the Reich we were told would last a thousand years; but I suppose the reason we were fighting this war was to convince people of our cause. The minor road between Hadsund and Aalborg is fairly straight, and though by taking this route we would drive through a number of villages, we didn't anticipate losing much time in getting to our destination. How wrong we were.

We had just driven through the village of Lundby when we almost wrecked the front of the car by nearly crashing into a tree which was blocking the entire width of the road. Ernst stopped the vehicle with only a metre to spare. In an attempt to make us less of a target than we were, he switched off the lights. Towering like sentinels in impenetrable darkness, still growing arboreal specimens flanked the road on either side. Half expecting to see muzzle flashes as British Sten guns in the hands of Danes opened up from the protection of the forest on one side of the road or the other, I ordered Ernst to switch off the engine and get out of the car. We crouched by the side of the vehicle, Ernst on the driver's side, I on the other. Depending on which side the rounds were likely to come, at least one of us had a chance of surviving the opening bursts of fire, and having survived those, that person would at least have a chance of getting away unscathed, bearing in mind that the attackers would probably want to make good their escape as quickly as possible. We referred to these tactics as 'shoot and scoot'. We kept low for what seemed like an age, but in reality our time spent in the limbo of anticipation had probably been no more than a minute. Nothing happened. No shots were fired and nothing stirred in the trees save for the hoot of an owl which at first called several times from its perch nearby before flying off to resume its hauntingly plaintive performance on the branch of a distant tree. In terms of human activity everything may have been as quiet as the grave nearby, but I was certain that I heard a noise, a barely audible metallic scattering which I couldn't identify specifically. My impression was that it came from the direction we had just travelled. In a voice not much louder than a whisper I enquired of Ernst if he had heard anything.

"Nothing but that damned bird," he replied, his aspirant voice matching mine in tone and volume. Then, in his normal voice, he asked, "What do you think?"

Evidently the longer the time without incident the greater his confidence grew that we were not about to die.

"I'm not sure," I replied, and matching each other's movements, slowly, warily, we rose to our full heights. My heart was beating rapidly. The pistol-grip which had felt so cold on my first drawing the weapon from its holster, now felt clammy. I was aware that I was holding the gun too tightly.

Feeling so tense, any shots I might fire would probably miss the target. Moreover, my hand was beginning to ache. By an effort of will I composed myself sufficiently to relax my grip slightly. Whilst trying visually to penetrate deep into the forest for signs of clandestine activity, we left whatever cover was provided by the car to inspect the obstruction. We could have switched on the engine and turned on the headlights, but we were both disinclined to make our presence obvious again after the minutes of silence. Besides, the sudden noise and brightness would severely diminish our general awareness. Ernst had found a torch in the Mercedes' glove compartment, and was using it to good effect, shining its beam along the line of trees prior to bringing it to bear on the sizeable trunk blocking our progress. I could tell merely by looking that the damned thing was too heavy and unwieldy for two men to remove manually. The question which came to mind at that moment was whether the tree had fallen as a result, for want of a better way of putting it, of an act of providence, or had it been chopped down deliberately. If the latter, the question then was had it been done specifically to impede our progress, or to hinder the movements of the German military machine generally. Upon inspecting the couple of feet of trunk protruding from the ground by the right hand side of the road when left and right is determined by the direction in which we were heading, it became apparent that the deed was malicious and involved the use of a saw worked by human beings. There being no sign of movement other than our own, we put away our pistols. A quick survey of the ground at either end of the tree's extremities revealed that there was no way round for a car. A tracked vehicle could have circumnavigated the tree for certain, and I'm sure a tractor would not have been defeated by the rough terrain, but of course no such vehicle was to hand. The thought occurred that a rope might do the trick, but this was followed immediately by a contrary notion which warned that the use of a rope might damage the Camp Commandant's car horribly, making any trouble we might already be in for borrowing his pride and joy seem like a bequest from a favourite aunt to her favourite nephews by comparison. After imagining that the dead-weight of the tree would prove too much for the car to pull, and that some difficult to replace mechanical part would break irreparably in the attempt, for the mission after next I envisaged our being sent alone and with just enough fuel to reach the target, to bomb Biggin Hill in broad daylight, that or one of half a dozen other hornets' nests. We were, as it turned out, unable to ascertain if the car was capable of pulling such a heavy load, for not a fibre of hemp could we find. The question now was what to do next.

"Come on Ernst," I said with as much good humour as I could muster. "You're an officer trained to use his initiative in situations requiring resourcefulness and initiative, what's the plan?"

By this time we had returned to the improvised roadblock where Ernst, like a schoolboy or a member of the Hitler youth eager to test his strength in front of his peers, tried to push the obstruction out of the way. Needless to say he failed. I didn't offer any assistance. Following his exertions, Ernst sat on the trunk to rest. After removing his cap with his left hand, he raised the other forearm to wipe his brow with the sleeve of his jacket. In the cold, night air, I didn't think there was much perspiration to wipe.

"You forget my dear Hauptmann Hebbel," said Ernst, emphasising the alliteration in my rank and name for a reason only he knew. "As the senior officer here, the responsibility for getting us out of this predicament is yours. In these circumstances, I, a mere Oberleutnant, am not paid to think, merely to obey," although after a momentary pause he added, "And to assist. How may I assist?"

"You can start by passing me the torch," I said peremptorily, thinking as I spoke that Ernst was still smarting from having been passed over for promotion last time round.

I doubt whether he would ever say so to my face, but he might think that I was in some way responsible, when in fact I wasn't. That decision had been made by Krupp, the Station Commander.

Without demonstrating any of the haste which by his own appraisal of the situation might be considered appropriate, Ernst replaced and straightened his cap. In his own good time he reached forward to pick up the battery-powered lamp from between his feet. The beam, the torch being still switched on and illuminating the surface of the road to no purpose, had become perceptibly dimmer. In order to prevent the batteries from being drained of power further, I switched the thing off as I strode the few paces back to the rear of the car. I found the map I was looking for folded neatly on the back seat. It was where we had left it after our last scrutiny of its lines and symbols in Randers. Of course, in trying to ascertain where we were and how we might find a route around the obstruction, I needed all the light the torch could provide. I hadn't overlooked the fact that in the event of it failing, we could forget about drawing more attention to ourselves than I had originally thought wise and make use of the headlights. Perhaps I used more power switching the beam off and on than I would have done otherwise, but whatever the merits of either course of action – the actual and the hypothetical – in attempting to lead by example that's what I did. Ernst came to join me as I began to make a two-dimensional study of the three-dimensional options available to us. Not so far back, no more than four hundred metres, we had passed a road leading off to the right, and this I managed to identify on the map without difficulty. In the hope of obviating the need to look at the map again, I tried to imprint the configuration of the roads and the villages they linked on any available space in my brain. In this exigency I was undermined considerably by Ernst's untimely request for information.

"Who do you think is responsible for chopping down the tree?" he asked, turning his head to survey the obstruction from left to right, effectively from bottom to top, from roots to leafy crown.

I didn't think it necessary to point out that the tree had been sawn and not chopped. I was a little irritated by the interruption, and as I made a mental note of the names of the villages we would need to go through before we reached the road running parallel to the inlet from the sea known as the Langerak, I also answered Ernst's question as succinctly as possible.

"The Churchill Gang," I responded. "If it had been any of the other groups we would have been shot dead by now."

In fact, having satisfied myself that I knew where to turn left and where to turn right, I gave serious thought as to who had been responsible, and how they had learned of our movements. It wasn't that I had sought to mislead my friend by blaming the 'Churchill Klubben', the name by which the gang was known, it was simply that my answer had been more instinctive than reasoned, more spontaneous than considered. After my rumination I saw no reason to change my opinion as to who had perpetrated the misdemeanour. If the assassins of the Hvidsten Group had been involved, in all probability our bodies would have been found lying – each in its own pool of blood – by a mobile patrol in the morning. Operating in and around Aalborg, the members of the Churchill Gang were not so infamous, their deeds being much less violent. Acts of sabotage in this area to date had been small in scale and had not resulted in the deaths or permanent injury to a single serviceman. Indeed, the worst incident to my knowledge was the prank played upon a motorcycle dispatch rider who came off his machine after speeding into a rope which had been pulled taut across the road at body height. He sustained fractures to his leg, arm and collarbone. At least he wasn't shot where he lay, but lived to tell the tale. Mainly the acts of sabotage carried out by this group were more of an annoyance to the authorities than a danger. In this regard they really did resemble schoolboy or student pranks rather than the deadly games of kill or be killed played by the more ruthless elements of Holgar Dansk. Despite the name of the Aalborg saboteurs being common knowledge, as yet, or so I had been reliably informed, none of the members had been identified by the authorities, and so they remained, anonymous to outsiders, free to roam at large, and by simple methods bring a little misery into the lives of German officers such as Ernst and myself. Beckoning Ernst to get into the car, I considered the puzzle of how the perpetrators of this nefarious little deed had come to learn of our route, our timings. The puzzle was made more intriguing by the fact that we hadn't made a decision to come the way we did at the beginning of our journey back in Aarhus. Confident that I would be able to navigate and drive after memorising the relevant square of the map to the best of my ability, I had climbed into the driver's seat, and as Ernst clambered in beside me I held out my hand for the key to the ignition. After rummaging through the pockets of his pants for seemingly an age, he at last found the item and placed it in the palm of my hand. I detected a look of relief in his eyes, a look engendered by the realisation that he had not lost something very important after a few nervous moments when he thought he had. His only comment as he made himself comfortable was to agree with my answer to his question and my subsequent analysis. Then, as I started up the engine and switched on the lights, he adopted a position indicative of a person intending to sleep, a posture of course determined in this instance by a leather-upholstered seat rather than a bed. By way of confirmation he pulled his cap down over his eyes.

The thought occurred to me as I turned the car about that the Churchill Gang may have tried to make fools of us, but really, when all was said and done, what was an hour's delay in the scheme of things? There could be no doubt that if we had failed to see the obstruction in time Ernst and I would have been in considerable trouble for the damage done, and for which, in the first instance, we were responsible by 'borrowing' the car. That obviously didn't happen, and I wondered if it had really been worthwhile for the gang to have risked being caught in the act and shot, or their suffering the same fate by firing squad some time after capture. Responding to the conclusion I came to, I shook my head from side to side.

"The turning we're looking for can't be that far down this road," I said aloud, careless of whether or not I received a reply. None was forthcoming other than a sleepy hum of agreement.

We hadn't gone more than two hundred metres down the road when Ernst's slumbers and my thoughts were disturbed abruptly as an ominous succession of pops and hisses indicated that things were not going according to plan. Before the realisation dawned that more than one of our tyres had been punctured, I kept my foot on the accelerator as my weary brain collated, and then analysed, the information fed to it by my no less weary senses. Our forward motion was no longer a smooth experience. In fact far from it, in consequence of which I had the distinct impression that our wheels were no longer round but square. Eventually, but only a matter of seconds after my first becoming aware that we were not out of the woods yet, I realised that once again we had no alternative but to stop the car.

"Um Gottes willen Hans! What's happening now?" called Ernst, adjusting his position to that of a man prepared for flight or fight.

"I think we've been well and truly scuppered this time," I replied laconically.

We set about confirming my suspicions. I didn't bother switching off the headlights as I got out of the car to inspect the damage, though I did switch off the engine. There didn't seem much point in being concerned about the battery. Neither did I take the precaution of drawing my weapon, for if I had shone the torch in the direction of Aalborg, I might just have been able to make out the severed tree with the torch beam when at its brightest, and as we didn't come under fire there, it was unlikely that we would be attacked now. Ernst more or less mirrored my movements on his side of the vehicle as I inspected first the front wheel, and then the rear. Both tyres were completely deflated. Ernst informed me that those on his side were in a similar condition. From off the road we both picked up one of the devices which had caused the damage. The device was cunningly simple but effective, consisting of three nails ranging from eight to ten centimetres in length. Each nail had been bent into a shape forming two sides of a rectangle. The lengths leading to the heads normally hit by the hammer had been tightly bound with string in such a way that the pointed ends were splayed at different angles. When scattered it was inevitable that two of the points would come to rest on the road, whilst the third would point upward menacingly. There must have been thirty to forty of these anti-pneumatic tyre mines lying around, and it was obvious to me now that the vaguely metallic sounds I had heard earlier had been the sound of their deployment. A certain amount of care was needed as to where we stepped. The last thing we wanted was to puncture the soles of our feet, particularly now that there looked to be a long walk ahead of us. There could now be no doubt that we had been specifically targeted, and that the saboteurs were indeed members of the Churchill Gang, for these three-pronged weapons had been deployed by the group on a number of occasions in the recent past. This kind of thing was typical of them. It was their modus operandi.

"Come on," I called to Ernst as I set about securing the vehicle, more from force of habit than for any practical purpose. "We'll walk into Aalborg and hopefully get a lift with a military police patrol."

"Beggars can't be choosers," replied my friend philosophically.

He was feeling the point of a nail with the tip of his finger. Then he threw the object away in disgust as we set off walking in the direction of town. I thought it would be a good idea to retain one of the sinister tripods as proof of what we had had to contend with, and as evidence. I therefore picked up a 'mine' and, after cushioning the points with my handkerchief, put it in my pocket. I estimated that it was about ten kilometres to the suburbs of Aalborg, and assuming that we would have to walk the entire distance, I also estimated that the journey would take us between ninety minutes and two hours. Clearly the amount of sleep we were likely to get before the briefing had reduced from hours to minutes, and there was a distinct possibility that we would get no sleep at all until our return from the mission. Striding manfully, it didn't take us long to arrive at the point where our problems had begun, and as we stepped over the fallen trunk we heard a prolonged cry emanating from the trees near to where we had left the car. More human than animal, I thought the sound was a triumphant cackle of laughter.

Chapter Six

River Ebro

One of the men from the trench located on the far side of the ruined farmhouse, approximately the same distance from the crumbling walls as the trench occupied by George and Harry, was following Harry's example and walking away from what was left of the building with a block of stone. The Englishmen knew him to be a Dutchman who spoke English perfectly. George noted that by being stripped to the waist, and by working out of reach of his personal weapon, their fellow Legionnaire was either blatantly defying 'standing orders', or was ignorant of their significance. Knowing him to be the adventurer he was, the Yorkshireman's opinion was that the Dutchman had little time for rules and regulations if he could get away with disregarding them with impunity. Colonel Astray, the founder of the Legion, would not have approved, nor would any of his junior officers if they had appeared at that moment. The Dutchman's name was Dick van Loon. Such a name was bound to attract a certain amount of derision from English speakers within the unit, though being hailed as 'Looney' no longer perturbed the man with the ever so predictable sobriquet. He was a tall, rangy specimen of humanity who, because of his fitness, made the work he was about look effortless. Dressed in a grubby pair of khaki trousers tucked into boot-polish blackened gaiters of which barely a square centimetre was not caked in dried mud or covered in dust, and wearing boots which were in a similar state, van Loon was hardly parade ground material. Seemingly precariously, probably because it was a size too small, perched on his head of dark hair was a kepi. At some time or other in the dim and distant past this item of military headgear must have been uniformly white, certainly when first issued to the Frenchman from whom van Loon had bought the hat for a pittance in a bar in Marseille. In this attire the Dutchman looked as if he was about to fend off a band of warrior tribesmen in the desert. Even from a distance the kepi looked as if it had seen better days. The same could not be said of the Dutchman's smile, a feature of which Harry was more than a little envious. Not only was van Loon, unlike Harry, in possession of all his teeth, but they appeared remarkably white and even. Set in a face which had been tanned for months by the Iberian sun, they contributed a charismatic, film-star quality to the Dutchman's appearance. On his second trip to the farmhouse he called across to the Englishmen to inform them that he would be test-firing his gun in a few minutes, and that there was no need to be alarmed. Including himself three men occupied van Loon's trench, so naturally it was a little bigger than the others. The light-machine gun manned by van Loon and his number two – the man whose job it was to feed in the belts of ammunition – provided the main protection along this section of front against enemy infantry were they to be so fanatical as to attempt to advance up the slope after crossing the river.

"Would you like me to pass that on to the chaps on our left?" shouted George, putting a hand to either cheek in order to create, to the best of his ability, the effect of a megaphone.

Notwithstanding the volume, his manner of speaking was typically middle-class, typically English, and as such was redolent of his meeting with the mother or father of one of his pupils outside school, when he might have asked the parent if he or she would like him to pass on the news that little Johnny had just achieved his twentieth merit badge at cubs, or that little Johnny was taking two weeks off during term time to visit his grandparents in Scotland, to the headmaster.

"Of course!" replied van Loon. "Though I'm not sure you'll be able to make yourself understood. They're former civil guards and don't have a word of English."

Whether the two Spaniards in the trench at the base of a rocky outcrop about fifty metres to the left of George and Harry's position were unable to speak a single word of English was a debatable point, but van Loon knew that the Englishman's skill in Castillian was as yet limited to asking for food and drink, and obeying, along with a few other simple instructions, the order to march. He took it for granted that it would be pointless trying to communicate to anyone other than a fellow citizen of the Netherlands in his own vernacular.

Communication was bound to be a problem in an organisation which comprised individuals from at least twenty countries, many of whom were barely literate in their respective mother tongue. Learning Spanish was obviously strongly encouraged, but operational expediency invariably took priority over tortuous language lessons. Formed on the instruction of the War Minister of the day, none other than the Viscount de Eza, the Spanish Foreign

Legion formerly came into being on the twenty-eighth of April, nineteen-twenty. Modelled on French lines, the Spanish counterpart had been the brainchild of Lieutenant-Colonel Millan Astray, a personal acquaintance of the Generalissimo. The Legion comprised the usual mixed bag of lost and desperate men searching for a family of a different kind from that which gathered of an evening to listen to the radio and bathe the children in front of the fire. These were men eager to begin a new chapter in the books that had been, and would be, their respective lives. Such men may not have been able to forget the past, but in the ranks of the Legion they were certainly able to put that different country behind them, and apart from being pricked on occasion by conscience, escape the consequences of whatever crime or disreputable act they had committed within its nebulous borders. The exchange made by new recruits was to forsake many of their erstwhile wicked ways for a life regulated by bugle calls and discipline. Of course, those in command did not expect their men to give up on dissipation completely. That would have been unnatural. Warrior monks the Legionnaires were not, as many a woman could vouch after responding passionately to a Legionnaire's amorous advances in a secluded al fresco location, say on the river-bank after a naked swim around midnight, or in the fragrant air of an orange grove. A warm climate has many attractions, and all work and no play makes Pablo and Pierre, Karl and Luigi, Felix and Jack, dull boys.

The ethos of the unit which had adopted George and Harry for the duration of the hostilities could be summed up in the portentous words of its founder, a copy of which had been given to the Englishmen in translation. Where appropriate the following text was also distributed in French, Italian, German and Arabic.

> *You're here to die! Yes, to die! Now that you've*
> *crossed over, you've lost your mother, your sweetheart,*
> *and your family. From today the Legion is everything*
> *to you. Service comes before everything, in the honour*
> *you have taken on, which is to serve Spain and the Legion.*
> *There's still time left to consider whether you really*
> *are ready to make the sacrifice. When you've thought it*
> *over, you may tell your Captain what your final decision is.*

George didn't want to die, so despite there apparently being no imminent danger along that stretch of the river for which they were responsible with regard to deterring crossings, incursions, or even full-blooded attacks by large formations, he made it his practice to dash as fast as he could between cover provided by rocks, trees, and of course, purpose-built defences. In this way, he reasoned with himself and others, he would be difficult for the best of sharpshooters to hit. There could be no faulting his logic. Placing the palms of his hands flat on the ground either side of the dugout, he demonstrated admirable athleticism as the strength in his arms combined with the thrust from his legs to catapult himself, as it were, out of the ground, ending up crouched with both feet together ready for the dash. In the next instant he grabbed his weapon and launched himself into a sprint across the sun-baked, sparsely vegetated, exposed terrain, resembling in his dynamism, notwithstanding the fact that he was carrying his Mauser rifle 'at the trail', one of the larger primates making good his escape from the hunter, be it man or beast, the latter in the shape of a leopard perhaps. In short, instinctively he kept his head low, his shoulders stooped forward in the direction he was heading. In addition to his speed of movement, the posture he adopted was also aimed at achieving a longer life than he might otherwise have by making himself as small a target as possible to the opportunist sniper. Harry didn't take any of this seriously. After watching George's hasty departure, he couldn't help but grin at his friend's zealous precautions. He was still grinning as he turned his head through one hundred and eighty degrees to see his own gaping smile reflected perfectly in the Dutchman's gnashers. Contrasting with the apparent effortlessness he had shown on his first foray to the farmhouse, languidly van Loon retrieved yet another building block for his parapet. His actions on this occasion bore signs of the weariness a labourer might be expected to reveal at the end of the working day. It was as if the energy generated by the Englishman had drained him, van Loon, of his dynamic power.

The fact that no sniper had taken aim and fired on the outward leg of George's little enterprise didn't convince him that there was no need to do the return leg in a similar style. Once again he ran to cover the intervening ground as if his life depended upon it. He pulled up a yard from home, which was fortunate because the Londoner had just laid the working-parts of his machine-pistol on top of one of the blocks of stone forming the heightened parapet, and undoubtedly he would have been less than pleased if George had kicked up any amount of dust to negate the cleaning work that Harry had already done, or making worse the preponderance still to do. George was also smiling broadly as he dropped down into the dugout to pick up his pack from where it lay in one corner. He had only been away five minutes. His smile, which imparted to his face a look of youthful freshness and innocence, so that his expression more closely resembled that of a ten-years-old boy who has just received the gift he was hoping for on his birthday than the countenance of a soldier in the Spanish Legion, was a smile of satisfaction at having accomplished his mission. In its physical manifestation it more closely resembled van Loon's than Harry's, but that was because he had managed not to get involved in fisticuffs whilst training in Cáceres.

"What are you looking so pleased with yourself about?" asked Harry, cleaning the breach-block of his machine-pistol as he spoke.

George was struggling to release the straps securing his pack.

"I was just thinking that I would have been a good mime artist given the chance," he replied.

After undoing the first of two straps he put the pack down again for the time it took to give a repeat performance. He worked through the sequence of gestures he had made in order to convince the Spaniards that the firing they were about to hear was merely a test, and therefore presented no danger, unless of course a Legionnaire was foolish enough to put himself directly into the line of fire. The mainly silent enactment did involve some vocal renditions. In one instance this involved imitating the rat-a-tat-tat of a machine-gun being fired. This unmistakeable soundtrack accompanied the mime of clenching his fists with the thumb knuckles uppermost, and with fingers curled tightly so that the nails dug into each palm, he positioned his hands about four inches apart and about two feet away from his chest. Moreover, he leaned his head forward a little as if he were taking aim. Then he traversed his body through thirty degrees, pointing the imaginary barrel of the no less imaginary gun he was firing in the direction of the river. After a lengthy imaginary burst, he completed the charade by holding up the splayed digits of one hand, pointing with the other in the direction of van Loon's trench. His intention was to communicate that he expected the firing to commence in five minutes, though he realised as he gesticulated that the information which he had received had not been so precise.

"Didn't you say anything to them?" asked Harry, carefully placing the part of the firing-mechanism he had just cleaned on to a surface that was relatively free of dirt.

"Of course I did," replied George, whilst peering into his pack. "Ah! There it is," he said in answer to a question which he had posed silently inside his head.

George extracted a writing pad and a wad of envelopes. Then he repeated the procedure as he searched for his pen. The whereabouts of the latter remained a secret for several frustrating minutes. He found it only after rummaging blindly through the contents of clothes and other necessities.

Success was tactile as his fingers brushed against and then curled around the writing implement. His intention this morning was to write to Martha.

Resuming his conversation with Harry he reiterated what he had said earlier in Spanish. "I said 'Hola and no problemo'," he said, grinning broadly.

"And did they say anything to you in return?"

"'Si'."

"So what did they say?"

"No you idiot; what they said was 'Si, and entiendo'."

"What does that mean?"

"I understand," answered George.

Harry was well aware that George had provided the answer to his question, but in order to pass the time in trivial banter he continued by pretending to be more obtuse than he sometimes looked.

"I know you understand, but what does 'entiendo' mean?"

Equally George realised that his comrade was attempting, in a good-natured sort of way, to make an ass out of him, but he was having none of it. He placed pen and paper on top of the parapet and came to the conclusion that as they were at chest height when he was standing up, this was a good position in which to write. For a time he deliberated as to whether to wait for van Loon to fire his maschinengewehr. The decision he eventually made was to extend his deliberation until firing had ceased. This pause in his own activity allowed him to give utterance to what he perceived to be a serious flaw in their defences, a flaw created by the supposed improvements. Neither George nor Harry had as yet been forced to contend with the unnerving experience of being shot at, at least as far as they were aware, but that didn't prevent an intelligent mind from trying to foresee avoidable danger, and subsequently taking action to eradicate the threat. Right action now would provide a much greater chance of survival once the bullets began to fly. It seemed to George that the improvements they had intended to make by building up the parapet with stone taken from the farmhouse wall, needed to be taken one stage further for the situation not to be counterproductive, and, therefore, mortally dangerous. George pondered over these concerns as he waited for the peace of a beautiful Spanish morning to be disturbed by the Dutchman's German bullets.

If we imagine George, and Harry for that matter, to be at the centre of a circle, then just out of reach and bisecting the top left quadrant, is where a creature which had scurried into view was now perfectly still. The lizard, which was no bigger than a man's forefinger, was basking in the increased warmth of the sun. George identified it as a Moorish Gecko. In the acquisition of knowledge the natural history lessons he had taught at school had been of just as much benefit to him as they had been to the children. In some subjects he had worked on the basis that all that was necessary for effective teaching was to stay one step ahead of the kids. George studied the lizard for several minutes, focusing intently on the creature's right eye, which in turn kept a watchful gaze on the human beings. No doubt the gecko thought the men to be a potential source of danger. A bowshot away the river flowed without haste in a southerly direction towards Fayon, and beyond that settlement its gentle waters turned in the direction of the rising sun towards the village of Ribarroja. Directly below, the course of the river had formed a loop which in time would become an ox-bow lake. The vegetation along the river banks consisted of bushes small and large. This verdure was appealing to the eye, and made for a striking contrast with the predominance of sunburnt colours beyond. The land stretching to the horizon from the opposite bank was sparsely covered with trees. Formed by a slope rising gently from the river to meet the sky's concavity with a convex curve, that horizon was relatively near, and was broken by the crowns of Spanish chestnut trees. The nuts of similar trees growing behind their lines were added to normal ingredients to make the Legion's bread. The scene was profoundly peaceful, and for a few treasured moments, moments which George thought would pass to become a memory he would treasure until he died, the former teacher felt at peace with the world, that there was no place he would rather be. Eventually his contemplation was disturbed not by the anticipated sound of gunfire, but by Harry questioning why the firing had not begun. Whatever the cause, the Dutchman's maschinengewehr seemed prone to malfunction. His reverie broken, the Yorkshireman, after a brief look along his friend's line of sight in van Loon's direction, once again turned his mind to practical matters to do with their safety in the event of an attack.

"It would appear that they haven't got the thing to work as yet," commented George with mounting concern, not so much for what was happening or not happening in the trench to their right, but because of the confusion he had probably sown in the minds of the Spaniards in the trench to his left.

"Forget van Loon for the moment. I think we should pay some attention to our own situation, for as things stand we may be assisting the enemy."

Harry hadn't taken the slightest offence at George having called him an idiot, but upon hearing that inadvertently they had been treacherous towards themselves, and sensing that the morning's hard labour was about to come in for some criticism, he felt an emotional reaction which made it unlikely that he would respond to any suggestion George might make with enthusiasm. Determined not to be undermined completely by the Yorkshireman's greater imagination and raw intelligence, the hard man from London felt his resolve stiffen. In this regard he was like a king trying to stem a tide of greater perspicacity.

"In what way do you think I may have assisted the enemy?" asked Harry.

There was a waspish tone to his voice. This was particularly pronounced in the emphasis he placed upon the personal pronoun.

George, noting the incipient asperity in his friend's words and demeanour, spoke as if his own words were daggers to be handled with caution.

"Well it seems to me that if a volley of shots were to hit these blocks of stone head-on, we wouldn't have a problem. The good work that you did earlier would have saved our lives, and when the war is over – no doubt by Christmas – we'll be able to return to dear old Blighty with our heads held high. Of course by then Mosley will be occupying Number Ten."

The last sentence brought a barely perceptible smile to the Londoner's former stern expression.

"So what the heck's wrong with that then?" asked Harry, imitating a Yorkshire accent which was considerably broader than George's normal intonation.

"Not a bleedin' thing mate," the Yorkshireman responded in kind, though his mimicry was hardly convincing in that he sounded more like an Australian bushwhacker than a man brought up on jellied eels in the East End. Disappointed with his feeble attempt at speaking Cockney, returning to his normal voice George expressed his concerns.

"But imagine what would happen if a bullet were to hit the stone at an angle. The round would be deflected in the direction of one or other of us, and then it would be goodnight and God bless."

To illustrate his point George followed with his finger the possible trajectory of an incoming round to its hypothetical impact point on the exposed surface – the gable end as it were – of the stone nearest to Harry, and then, after quickly estimating the angle of deflection, he directed his finger into the big man's sternum.

"There you have it; a bullet that would otherwise have missed has killed you."

"But what if…"

"What's more," continued George, effectively cutting short Harry's interruption, "A round striking in such a way is likely to unloose splinters that would almost be as dangerous as the bullet itself."

By now Harry had cast aside the blinkers of negativity, and was totally convinced by the logic of what he had heard. The fact that he was rarely capable of making imaginative leaps himself didn't mean that with an open mind he was incapable of responding positively to the mental powers demonstrated by a more agile brain, particularly when that brain is a friend.

"What do you suggest?" he asked, tacitly indicating that he was ready to respond to his friend's recommendations to rectify the problem as if they were direct orders from Franco himself. "Do you think we should get rid of them?"

"What I think we should do is pack earth, or sand, at the front and in-between to form a rampart that would absorb incoming rounds without any chance of ricochets. Imagine the rounds going into the bank of earth behind the targets when we were training on the ranges."

Harry's recollection was instant. George's words had created a convincing image, for in every case as soon as the bullet had hit and entered the mound of earth that bullet travelled no farther.

"What we need is a bucket and spade," said Harry, turning his gaze towards the river.

His response may have sounded as if he was talking to a small child at the seaside, but now that he was convinced that this was a matter of life or death, he was being completely serious. Once he had been shown the way forward in theory, Harry was more than capable of working out the practical means to achieve results. Compressed by boots and baked hard by the sun, the ground thereabouts was almost as hard as concrete, as the Legionnaires had discovered when the unit had been ordered to dig-in in this locale. It had taken the best part of a day to hew out their trenches, and that was when there was a pickaxe to hand. In view of the fact that the nearby spring-water that provided their drinking water trickled over rock, undoubtedly the best place to obtain the now essential building material was from the banks of the river, or from the river bed. It was about half an hour's hike back to where the battalion's support vehicles had laagered, and it was in their direction that Harry set off walking to fetch a bucket and spade. In the meantime George decided that he would wait in limbo no longer for van Loon to disturb the peace, and putting pen to paper he began to write.

The correspondence which he began by addressing the intended recipient, "My dear Martha, my love," was his sixth letter home. This didn't amount to an avalanche dropping through the addressee's letter-box, nor even a ream of paper sent to Hambleton in the months he had been away, but it did compare favourably with the news from home he had received in return, which was no news at all. The words of the Legionnaire creed came to mind each time he put pen to paper: "Now that you've crossed over, you've lost your mother, your sweetheart, and your family," and it was only by bribing the sergeant with either money or an object of some value which Fernandez could sell quite easily – a watch for example – was he able to send his epistles on their way. The system, such as it was, didn't inspire the kind of confidence that George had experienced whenever he had posted letters via the Royal Mail. Indeed, the problem for George was that he had no way of knowing whether a single letter had dropped through the letter box to land on his Hambleton doormat. In fact he didn't even know if he still had a wife. Despite the indoctrination as manifested in the Legionnaire creed, despite the inculcation of a sense of loyalty to a brotherhood of adventurers, idealists, rogues and vagabonds, the ache of missing his partner in life gnawed at him from time to time, and this he countered by directing his energy towards some more or less pointless manual task; pointless that is other than for the fact that physical activity, be it work or exercise, cleared his mind. In the act of writing to Martha, however, he had no choice but to confront his demons of remorse and guilt, and come to terms with his suppressed longing for the people and landscape he had left behind. George Gilbert's sensibilities illustrated perfectly how the equanimity of a man with emotional baggage is always susceptible to subversion, and if this can be said of any man, no doubt it can also be said of any woman.

Uncertain that Martha was apprised of anything he had written thus far, the Yorkshireman invariably began the second paragraph with a synopsis of how they had arrived – Harry and he – in their hole in the ground. In the first paragraph he had always expressed his love for the woman whom he had not seen for the best part of a year, rationalising his absence by confirming that cliches are invariably true, the relevant truism in this instance being, 'Absence makes the heart grow fonder'. In his first letter to Martha, and repeated again with less detail in the second and third, he had described how the two fascists had travelled first to Dublin to join a ship which was scheduled to leave for Spain with several hundred Irish blue-shirts on board. These were led by an unkempt individual by the name of O'Duffy. Their port of entry into Spain was Vigo, in Galicia, and it was from here that George managed to send his first letter. George, Harry, and the band of Irish warriors – many of whom were Catholics from the north of the island of Hibernia – may have come to Spain to fight on the same side, and for the same cause, but that didn't prevent a certain amount of internecine strife from developing. Some of this strife was centred on Harry. The Londoner was not the type of man to turn the other cheek and walk away from a fight, so when baited by a recruit from Armagh who was worse the wear for drink, it was inevitable that the two men would come to blows. Out of consideration for Martha and her female, ergo more gentle, perspective on life, in his second letter, in the letter he had sent from Cáceres, George kept details of the aggressive debate to a minimum. Salient facts which he did include were that both pugilists had retired from the contest wounded, Harry missing a couple of prominent teeth, and the Irishmen bleeding from his nose profusely. Neither of the two Englishmen knew Harry's opponent's name, and if asked the morning after the night before what all the fuss had been about, neither would have been able to provide a sensible answer. The news which George had been keen to impart to Martha was that thus far he had managed to stay out of trouble, and that as yet he remained unscathed. He also expressed his delight that Harry and he had been sent to a unit which was deployed a long way from O'Duffy and his men.

George had just completed the first page of his latest letter, wherein he reiterated his innocence regarding the accusations which had driven him from his chosen profession, and ultimately from wife, hearth and home, when he noticed a large animal emerge from a thicket on the far bank of the river. The wild boar, or jabali as it is referred to in Spanish, approached the water's edge to drink. The presence of the mammal was of much greater interest to the eye of the would-be naturalist than a mere gecko. By this time the little lizard had disappeared from George's view. Believing itself to be safe from predators, the large boar lapped at the water as if its life depended on it. In a little while a second boar appeared, drawing alongside the first so that it too could quench its thirst. In watching the animals drink nature's most commonplace elixir, the erstwhile casual observer had become transfixed, and being the teacher that he was at heart, if not in fact, he watched in order to learn.

At that moment the Englishmen's attitude may have been to live and let live, but the same could not be said of van Loon, and the other Legionnaires in the Dutchman's trench. For them the appearance of the wild boar presented an ideal opportunity to test their gun whilst providing food for a feast. To this end van Loon broke the spell cast by the sudden appearance of the animals, and with the butt of the machine-gun pressed into his right shoulder, with the forefinger of his right hand he squeezed the trigger to send half a belt of 7.92 millimetre ammunition, fired in two distinct bursts, hurtling towards the unsuspecting beasts. Static at a distance of approximately two hundred and fifty metres, and being quite big, the wild boar didn't make for a difficult target, although because of a problem with the weapon's sights it was necessary for van Loon to adjust his aim as he, along with everyone else watching, saw the first rounds hit the water yards in front and slightly left of the mark. Sensing imminent danger, the loud report of the first few rounds was all that was needed to alarm the animals, and they had just turned their heads in the direction in which they were intending to run when the first deadly bullets hit. They penetrated flesh and bone in the region of the head and neck, and both animals fell without having heard the percussion of the shots that killed them.

The effect of van Loon's hunting had more repercussions than he or anyone else had bargained for. At least forty minutes had elapsed since George had tried to communicate with the Spaniards to his left, and although they had interpreted his body language and somewhat pathetic Spanish correctly initially, they became increasingly unsettled by the fact that nothing had happened within the time-scale indicated. The longer the passage of time without the anticipated event taking place, the more their perplexity grew. Once the firing did start the effect on George was startling. Unable to see the wild boar from their position, the effect on the Spaniards was even more dramatic, and believing that they were under attack from an enemy force of unknown strength hidden in the bushes by the river, aiming in that general direction they opened fire. In next to no time the crackle of small arms could be heard as Legionnaires opened up all along the line, at least as far north as the scarp of a hill which on the side facing the river was as sheer as a cliff. This rugged feature in an otherwise gentle landscape was about a kilometre away from George Gilbert's position, and in that distance the Englishman estimated there to be ten trenches similar to his own, and judging by the furore it seemed that the occupants of every one of those trenches were shooting at what they thought was a clandestine enemy, when in reality the targets they were hitting were nothing more menacing than leaves, twigs, and branches. In the trenches beyond van Loon's, those in the line leading towards the town of Gandesa, the shooting was more sporadic, as if a number of individuals had joined in the enfilade for the hell of it. Perched on top of the promontory a kilometre distant was an observation post, and it was from this position that upon hearing the first shots being fired that the Company Commander had searched the horizon for signs of an advancing enemy. With cool deliberation he scanned with binoculars from left to right and then right to left, working his way down methodically from far to middle distance, until, with a final close scrutiny, he surveyed the river. Finding nothing untoward, simmering with anger, he ordered runners to be sent to relay his order to, 'Alto el fuego'. A descendant of a prominent conquistador who had served with Gonzalo Pizarro in the conquest of Peru, el mayor was a man not likely to let his authority be easily undermined. The order having been given, the officer regained his composure by stroking his moustache.

Van Loon, the man who had started the proceedings, and one of only a few individuals who were aware of what he was firing at and why, had removed his finger from the trigger long before he heard the command to stop wasting ammunition. In due course the pastoral scene returned to normal as slowly the smoke cleared to reveal a landscape which gave no real clues to the events which had recently taken place. The river continued to meander slowly. Apart from where the sun's influence dazzled, the sky continued to be uniformly blue.

Of course, the exception to earlier perceptions of normality was the presence of two dead boar lying on the bloodstained river bank. After half an hour of relative silence he thought it safe enough to venture down to the river to retrieve his kill. By this time Harry had returned with a shiny new spade and an old metal bucket which had a hole in the bottom the size of a half-crown. He explained to George, who had discovered the defect before Harry had had a chance to point it out to him, that it was the only bucket he could get. He expressed the opinion that it would be good for carrying anything but liquid over the distance involved, and George, applying the logic with which he had earlier convinced Harry of the need to reinforce their rampart with earth, was forced to agree.

"I heard gunfire so I got back as quick as I could," said Harry, jumping down into the dugout. "I didn't want to miss any of the action," he added, before stating in conclusion, "but it would appear that I have."

Harry looked about him to see what had changed. Not surprisingly he was unable to distinguish which bushes had been damaged by gunfire from those which had been allowed to flourish unmolested, but he did in due course spot the carcasses.

"That was an awful lot of shooting to kill a couple of pigs," Harry commented wryly, having quickly mentally grasped at least a part of what had taken place in his absence.

"Come on, grab your weapon and the bucket, I'll carry the spade," said George, eager to get the job done.

The enthusiasm he communicated in his speech didn't wholly translate into vigorous action, for he clambered out of the trench with much less agility than he had demonstrated earlier that morning, and it was with genuine weariness from the hike he had just completed laden with weapon, bucket and spade, that Harry also hauled himself on to the parapet.

"No peace for the wicked," he said, picking up the bucket by the handle with one hand while slinging his machine-pistol over his shoulder with the other.

The two men set off walking towards the river more or less side by side. In their advance they were soon joined by the Dutchman and his number two, both of the latter being keen to retrieve their prey before the meat began to putrefy in the mid-morning heat. Van Loon and his side-kick had already discussed and agreed that the best course of action would be to take the jabali back to the laager for the cooks to do with as they saw fit, but only after obtaining a verbal assurance that the meat when cooked would be sent back to the front as part of that day's rations. Despite his lowly rank, as the killer of the animals van Loon felt he had enough authority to say as much. It was obvious that this reasonable man was neither a hoarder nor a glutton; nor was he a mind-reader, and the sight of the Englishmen ambling down the slope laden with gardening accoutrements (or were they builders' tools), baffled the Dutchman sufficiently to prompt him to ask the obvious question.

"Ah, the eccentricity of the English!" he exclaimed in response to Harry's explanation.

Without expressing any of his recent thoughts on the Anglo-Saxon element with whom he was more or less happy to serve, van Loon had suspected that George and Harry were about to perform deeds considerably more eccentric than their stated intentions. He had surmised, because he had heard that the English loved and respected animals, that they were going to bury the dead. In this regard he hadn't worked out what the bucket was for.

The unhurried advance of the four men did not go unobserved, for el buen mayor from his observation post on high had spotted their movement in line abreast across open ground, and had trained his binoculars on the group. Despite being a man who took pride in the fact that he always looked for, and usually found, the best in people, he couldn't prevent that most extreme of negative thoughts from crossing his mind, specifically that four of his men were deserting to the other side. El mayor had not read any of the works of Pyrrho of Elis, but his training and observations of life had led him to put into practice theories similar to those propounded by the philosopher who had lived in ancient Greece. These were that it is a wise man who can suspend his judgement, and that the fool is more likely to be the individual who acts with naive spontaneity, and, therefore, often jumps to unfounded conclusions.

Messrs Gilbert and Osborne started work digging into the bank on the side of the river nearest to their own defensive positions whilst van Loon and his chum stripped completely naked in order to wade into the chilling Ebro. When the water was waist-high both men began to swim, van Loon settling into a seemingly effortless crawl, whilst his friend bobbed through the water using the slower breast stroke. George placed a flat stone over the hole in the bucket, which he then proceeded to fill mainly with soil, but adding also a little water. The mud he had made looked as if it would provide the perfect solution to their problem, once, that is, it had been baked by the sun. After having filled the bucket, the Englishmen held a discussion about which of them was going to carry what was likely to be the first of several such loads uphill, but their conversation was interrupted in the most emphatic way imaginable when, following the whine of shells passing overhead, a series of explosions shook the earth. The artillery barrage was remarkably accurate, for the shells were falling within a band no more than thirty metres wide along the line of the nationalist trenches. For George, Harry, and their Legionnaire friends, the Battle of the River Ebro had begun.

Chapter Seven

Aarhus

Hanne had waited for what seemed like an age for Hans to make his parting gesture from the car parked in the square below, and for that length of time Hans' attentions were focused elsewhere. Only as Hanne straightened up with the intention of extinguishing the oil lamp, which in turn would allow her to open the curtain and look out upon the world without fear of reprimand, did she observe from the corner of her eye that Hans had not forgotten her. By then it was too late for the Danish beauty to respond in kind, for being caught in two minds, for a pivotal moment she hesitated, deliberating on whether to put out the lamp as she had intended, or return once more to her unsatisfactory perch by the window. Upon hearing the Mercedes pull away, she returned the room to darkness.

Hanne's earnest wish now was to sleep, but as she fluffed up the pillows to support her head, she sensed that the state of repose would be elusive. Her mind was too active to allow her body to be still for long, for after attaining a measure of comfort on her right side, within a few minutes that feeling had gone, and she turned over on to her left side. She alternated her position several times. In short she tossed and turned.

Eventually she made a conscious decision to postpone trying to get to sleep and lay on her back, raising her right knee beneath the bedclothes. She found that in this position she grew calm, and was able to give her thoughts free rein as she pondered the circumstances of her life, past, present, and how they might unfold in the future. For Miss Hjelmsleve thus far the war had not been an ordeal in the way that it had been for thousands of people in other occupied countries, or indeed in those countries which as yet remained unoccupied, but which, by being heavily engaged in the war, were suffering as a consequence. A depiction of the British Isles came to mind, quickly followed by the more disturbing images she had seen of London burning. No;

the problem for Hanne in this time of near global conflict had little to do with her physical security, and everything to do with her mental and emotional equilibrium. For a young woman who had not been abused in any way, and who had not seen any of her family suffer other than in a manner that might be expected of any patriotic Dane having to endure the impositions and restrictions imposed by their Teutonic masters, the occupation posed a number of dilemmas. First and foremost of these was her relationship with Hans, a relationship which had endured for the best part of a year, and which had deepened in that time, certainly on Hanne's part, although she believed the feeling was mutual, into something resembling love. Hanne's feelings for Hans, indeed his very existence, remained a secret to her parents, and as far as she was aware, to other members of her family. She didn't believe that her parents would think less of her for consorting with a German officer, but she was reluctant to test the water, as it were, by making revelations with a view to arranging introductions. Life for the Hjelmsleve family may not have been harsh, but neither was it normal. Hanne's parents owned a mixed farm near Skanderborg, a town approximately twenty kilometres south-west of Aarhus, and being farmers – people noted for their close affinity to the earth and to the seasons, and therefore to the flux of life – they had no enmity for anyone. Hanne knew that if asked to vote on whether Denmark should become a fully independent state, as it obviously was before the Wehrmacht poured over the border and dropped from the skies, her parents would have no hesitation in casting their votes in favour of a return to full autonomy, but meaningful democracy within the present system was a forlorn hope. In consequence they kept their heads down and their shoulders to the wheel, so to speak, activities befitting practical people. They would plant their crops and rear their pigs just as they had done before the war, striving to make the most of an unsatisfactory situation. The fighting they would leave to those members of the resistance movement who felt sufficiently aggrieved by the presence of foreign troops in their towns and villages to take up arms. The pragmatism demonstrated by Hanne's parents, a pragmatism which went so far as to provide the German garrison in Aarhus with fresh supplies of pork and eggs, might not be so accommodating as to welcome her daughter's lover with warm handshakes, even less with hugs and kisses. Hanne had decided not to tell her parents about Hans days after they had first met in a night-club located just across the square, but which was hidden from view from the window of the room wherein Hanne and Hans made love by the cathedral. The longer the secret had remained locked within her psyche, the more damaging it was to her state of mind. Mr and Mrs Hjelmsleve, and most of Hanne's other relations, lived far enough from Aarhus to make it unlikely that she would bump into any of them in the places Hans and she frequented, but a potentially embarrassing encounter was not impossible. To be able to spend the amount of time that she did with her handsome pilot, she needed an alibi, an excuse for being away from home every other weekend. A credible alibi was provided by Hanne's best friend, Astrid Aakjaer. The friends had first become acquainted on their first day at school, during the morning break to be precise. Over the ensuing weeks the girls had discovered that they had much in common, and their acquaintanceship had developed into the sort of friendship which withstands life's vicissitudes and the test of time. In wartime Aarhus Hanne had arranged to meet Astrid later that morning for coffee.

With a suddenness which was unexpected for the fact that the power had been off for so long, Hanne's love nest was flooded with light emanating from the electric bulb suspended through a pink shade in the centre of the ceiling. The power had been cut hours ago, at an instant in the lives of the Danish beauty and the German officer which, depending on one's point of view, may or may not have been appropriate. From one moment to the next the couple had been making love with the light on only then to be plunged into darkness which was total. The impact which this had on their lovemaking had been profound for reasons they were aware of, but which they would have been hard put to explain. It was as if the blackout, which had occurred a minute before the drone of aircraft engines in flight could be heard from the direction of the Kattegat, that body of water which, along with the Skagerrak, links the Baltic to the North Sea, had heightened the olfactory and tactile senses to the enervation of the other three. The aircraft were too far away even for a pilot of Hans' experience to be able to identify, although he was certain that the lights had been switched off either as part of an exercise, or as a precaution, and that there was no cause for concern. The Royal Air Force had dropped bombs on Danish territory in the past, but never on Aarhus (that was to happen later, in 1944 when RAF Mosquitoes bombed Gestapo headquarters), and besides, he had reasoned at some point in the amorous proceedings, if the aircraft had been British bombers they would surely have been heard initially approaching from the opposite direction, from the west. Latterly Hans had been unable to see the expression on Hanne's face, a face which in the instant before the power failed had revealed two intensely blue eyes gazing up at him with all the tenderness that a woman with a healthy sexual appetite, and who was in a rapture of physical ecstasy enhanced by love, was capable of showing. Once the darkness had become absolute, and before his eyes had become adjusted, those moist eyes and the image of Hanne's cheeks glistening with tears of joy, her lips, her nose, naturally disappeared from her lover's view completely, though her face was only inches form his own. The couple had remained conjoined, and in their sightless conjunction it was as if their psyches had merged, so sensitively, so altruistically did they respond to each other.

The drone of the aircraft engines had died away long before power was restored. Reluctantly, clearing her mind of flashbacks to events so deliciously recent, presently Hanne willed her body to get out of bed. She knew it would be impossible for her to get to sleep with the light glaring in her eyes.

With a sense that the world had been returned to some kind of normality – though to that statement must be added the caveat that what might be considered normal today would have been thought distinctly abnormal a couple of years before – upon returning to bed Hanne lay on her side and fell into a recuperative sleep which lasted till morning.

The slamming of car doors in the Stor Torv awakened the sleeping beauty, and almost immediately she thought of Hans driving off into the night for an encounter with danger. The voices which accompanied the opening and shutting activity spoke Danish. Hanne quickly put things in their true perspective, and turned on her back to contemplate the phantasmagoria which had pervaded her mind prior to her becoming fully conscious. She tried hard to remember the dream which had almost been supplanted by wakeful associations, and gradually the images she had created in her seemingly unconscious state became more vivid. These images were a little strange, but they were hardly surreal. In the drama of her dream she had been sitting eating breakfast at the kitchen table in the familiar setting of her parents' house when she noticed a worm crawling across the floor. Her mother was in the enclosure at the back of the house feeding the chickens, of which there were about two dozen. Her father was conspicuous by his absence from the scene, from the somnolent workings of Hanne's mind. Thinking that it would be a good idea to remove the worm, she returned her cup to its matching saucer and dropped down on to the carpet in order to approach the creature on her hands and knees. This was the first strange feature of her dream, for there was no carpet in the kitchen at home; the second was that sensing that it was about to be captured and subjected to a fate which it would not have wished for itself, the creature sped across the floor at an amazing speed, but not so fast as to be able to evade being grasped by two of Hanne's deft digits – her thumb and forefinger to be precise. At that moment Mrs Hjelmsleve appeared at the door holding a basket. Hanne was unable to see what the basket contained, but knew that the contents were that morning's collection of eggs. In the flesh Mrs Hjelmsleve was a tall, well-built woman, and her depiction in Hanne's dream was true to life. On the basis that she spent more time with a smile on her face than not, this was her most remarkable feature, and made the fact that her countenance had a somewhat lived-in look about it seem inconsequential by comparison. Initially the mother was puzzled to see her daughter up to something mysterious on 'all-fours', so to speak, but she smiled her customary smile as soon as the realisation dawned that her only child, though now a young woman, was chasing a worm. She put down her basket of eggs on the kitchen table as Hanne rose to her full height, the captive creature dangling helplessly from her gentle grip. With hand forming a pincer similar to that demonstrated by the worm's captor, Mrs Hjelmsleve reached out to take the worm, gripping it in a like manner to her daughter, but a centimetre lower down its body. About seven centimetres in overall length, this wasn't a fat, juicy earthworm, but one of those yellowish, thin jobs that loves to bore its way through potatoes, a pest known by different names in different locales. Hanne followed her mother as the latter stepped outside to feed the unfortunate specimen to the chickens.

"It's a cruel world," Hanne muttered to herself as she reached down by the side of the bed to find the clock she had brought with her. She found the little time machine by touch rather than sight, but when she eventually looked upon the clock-face, she was alarmed to discover that the hour was later than she had imagined. After throwing back the covers, like a woman who is likely to be late for an appointment, Hanne thrust her legs energetically over the side of the bed in order to be rid that morning of all further temptations proffered by the mattress. From beneath the bed she pulled out the small suitcase she had brought with her for the weekend, extracting from it her last items of clean underwear. She dressed hurriedly, periodically checking the time to see how late she was going to be. At two minutes to ten she estimated than she was going to be ten minutes late for her rendezvous with Astrid, but that didn't prevent Hanne, after she had visited the bathroom across the landing, from spending a couple of minutes preening herself in front of the mirror. Her initial reaction upon seeing her reflection was to frown. In the main her gloomy expression was caused by beholding the creases in her skirt and blouse. She realised there was little she could do about her sartorial fault-lines before she stepped out into the world. Other aspects of Hanne's appearance which gave her cause for concern this Monday morning were the condition of her hair and an unusual heaviness around the eyes. Hanne was grateful to her parents for the genes she had inherited and which were manifest in her lithe body and handsome physiognomy, but she was acutely aware that presently she was not looking at her best. The features for which she was grateful were a porcelain complexion which revealed not a blemish; eyes so intensely blue that any man that beheld them was immediately, albeit temporarily, spellbound, for they had the power to transport the male from his own little world of pleasures and privations into the depths of a universe measured by light years; a nose which was finely chiselled and in perfect proportion to the shape and dimensions of a face that was oval. A balanced regularity was the overriding characteristic of Hanne's appearance, and one didn't need to resort to a rule and take meticulous measurements to appreciate that everything was in proportion to everything else. Despite having such a lot going for her, there was an aspect of her visage which Hanne thought she could improve upon, given the opportunity. The focus of her slight disapproval was her mouth, particularly when she smiled. Her lips in their fullness were enticingly sensuous, but the imperfection in that area was a set of teeth which were not perfectly straight. Naturally she had grown accustomed to the feel of them, but whenever she gave the arrangement of her incisors and molars some thought, she came to the conclusion that they were a fraction too big for her mouth. Regardless of an opinion which to date Hanne had not revealed, nobody else thought her appearance, including her smile, was anything other than that which could be measured on a scale the opposite extremes of which could be designated 'divinely beautiful' and 'merely attractive'. With a final tug of her skirt and flick of her hair, she turned away from the mirror to make a token effort of tidying the bed. Her actions prior to departing the love-nest involved opening the curtains and switching off the light. In between she studied the scene in the Great Square through the window. Bathed in autumnal sunshine, the Stor Torv beckoned. Astrid beckoned.

The friends had arranged to meet in the Café Kobenhavn, a small establishment run by an acquaintance of Astrid's on the side of the square facing the cathedral tower and the main entrance to the place of worship, on the side which off to her right was at a right-angle to Hanne's viewpoint. She had noted in her quick survey of the scene that a couple of German Army trucks and a motorcycle and sidecar were parked approximately midway between where she was and where she intended to go. Five or six soldiers were loitering, seemingly without purpose. At least two of the men were smoking. Only one of the soldiers was carrying a gun. It was slung over his shoulder. Evidently the soldiers believed that they didn't pose a threat to anyone, and their easy-going manner also indicated that they themselves didn't feel threatened. In that instant, however, Hanne decided not to take the shortest route to her rendezvous, a route which would have seen her steering a path along an imaginary hypotenuse in the direction of the men in field-grey uniforms, and then having to contend with the unwanted attention that would no doubt ensue. Instead she would take the longer route along two of the edges of the square.

The sound of Hanne's footsteps on the stairs reached the landlady's ears, prompting the kindly businesswoman to project her head and ample torso into the hallway from the doorway of her private living room. She made an appearance for no purpose other than to say goodbye in as friendly a manner possible, for the landlady wasn't a fool. Hanne, after checking that Hans had paid for the room in advance (and she knew that he had), and that there was nothing more to pay (even though she was certain that there wasn't), made towards the door that was the main entrance and exit to the house with conspicuous haste. Not only was she constantly aware of her tardiness in respect of her friend, but in the moral maze she was also eager to escape the landlady's scrutiny and judgement, and in the spatial world configured by walls and objects, the confined space within the hall. The feeling she experienced at that moment was a mild form of claustrophobia, and in response to the landlady's parting question as to when the charming couple would return, Hanne, her face flushed with embarrassment at what the question implied, was only able to mumble, "Soon." Breathing the fresh air blown on shore from the Kattegat made Hanne feel good, and upon stepping on to the pavement, after gently closing the heavy, wooden door of the apartment block behind her, she stood for a few moments to fill her lungs. Turning her head slowly from left to right she surveyed events in the square from ground level, and what she saw wasn't dispiriting. People were going about their business much as they had done before the war, although now they were perhaps less in number than had been usual for a Monday morning. Hanne tried to gauge whether the individuals, couples, and little knots of people that she saw, citizens of Aarhus emerging from or going into shops and cafés, people cycling or simply walking along, mothers holding young children by the hand, or elderly folk making tentative progress in the manner of old people everywhere and at all times, looked different in any way under the occupation, whether they were more downcast in their demeanour than of yore. She didn't reach a conclusion. The thought crossed her mind that perhaps the best way forward for the Danish people was to accept integration into the Third Reich so that eventually, by intermarriage and the mixing of genes, they would be considered equals and not merely as a subjugated people. The thought occurred to her that when all was said and done, if the group of soldiers leaning against their vehicles and joking amongst themselves had been Danish instead of German, she would still have been deterred from running the gauntlet of their lechery.

Hanne was wise enough to realise that her thoughts of appeasement had been largely influenced by Hans, but she was surprised by how quickly they could be expurgated, how adroitly her attitudes could change. The transformation towards a greater sense of who she was and where she belonged, towards a greater sense of pride in her national identity, occurred when she focused her attention on the impressive Romanesque structure that is Aarhus Cathedral. Inspired by the sun glinting on the spire of the tallest church in the country, she cast her mind back to the great figures of Danish history she had learned about at school. First in line was Svein Forkbeard and his son Cnut, the king who had, apocryphally it has to be said, found it impossible to hold back the sea, but who certainly, in addition to maintaining two wives, had effectively ruled the English. Coming forward in time she remembered the amazing reign of Queen Margrethe, who was styled, 'All powerful lady and mistress of the Kingdom of Denmark', she who by virtue of the Treaty of Kalmar gained control over Norway and Sweden. In her pantheon of heroes Tycho Brahe appeared, a man dedicated to the power of the mind to make discoveries rather than with matters pertaining to temporal power. Like ghosts of time past, the philosopher Soren Kierkegaard presented a far from clear image, as of his person but not in his work did Hans Christian Andersen, the great storyteller. Hanne's final mental apparition was that of Wilhelm Ludwig Johannsen, the famous geneticist. The very names of these individuals were prominent symbols of Danish genius. The irony was, however, that the building which had prompted Miss Hjelmsleve to bring these great Danes to mind, Aarhus Cathedral, was replete with examples of German genius and endeavour. The cathedral's wonderful altar piece was carved by Bernt Notke of Lübeck, the pulpit by Michael van Groningen, and the baptismal font was a fabrication in copper by Peter Hansen. Kaspar Fincke had created the Golden Door.

With her mind torn between acceptance and rejection of the status quo, Hanne turned sharply right to walk under the awning of the Café Danmark on her way to the Café Kobenhavn. What she desired more than anything in the world at this moment was breakfast. Her stomach had begun to rumble. Upon approaching the café entrance, through the large window to the left of the door she saw that Astrid was sitting with her back to her reading a book. The only other customers were a man and a boy sitting with their backs to the wall as far away from Astrid as it was possible to be without being somewhere else. The man was in his thirties, moderately handsome, and smartly dressed. The boy, who was about twelve or thirteen years of age, looked a little tired as he put down the glass which he had just drained of milk. By the side of their table was a large suitcase. Hanne quickly formed the impression that the man was a travelling salesman visiting Aarhus on business, and had brought his son with him to gain valuable experience. The boy's father was gazing vacantly through the window, his expressionless eyes focused on the soldiers and their vehicles for no apparent reason. On the table in front of him was an empty cup and saucer. In his right hand was a spoon which he fondled aimlessly. Dressed in a white shirt beneath a black waistcoat, Astrid's acquaintance, the proprietor, was polishing glasses behind a bar which took up approximately one fifth of the café area visible to patrons. The remainder was given over to the polished wooden benches and tables in a seating area that was L-shaped. A little bell attached to the door tinkled as Hanne entered, causing Astrid to look up from her book with an expectation which, in defiance of logic, somehow managed to be both eager and restrained. Upon recognising her friend standing in the doorway Astrid beamed. Immediately she placed the piece of paper that served as her bookmark onto the page and closed the book. Astrid rose to her feet in order to embrace her friend as Hanne drew near.

"I'm sorry I'm late," apologised Hanne, inevitably.

"No you're not," responded Astrid sharply, but without any hint of acerbity. "Whenever we arrange to meet, you're the one who is always late, and each time you say, I'm sorry I'm late. If you really were sorry you would make an effort not to be late in the future, and until the miraculous day arrives when you are within five minutes of being on time, I will assume that you are merely paying lip service to being sorry, and that you don't really mean it."

A chastened Miss Hjelmsleve didn't take offence at the unexpected criticism, mainly because she knew that her friend was absolutely right. At the same time the thought crossed her mind that Astrid ought to get out more often, that she ought to get a man rather than spending so much time with her head in a book.

To judge by her appearance there was no obvious reason why Astrid didn't have a boyfriend, apart perhaps from an earnestness of character which was reflected in her demeanour. Whereas Hanne's normal expression was like the sun radiating warmth and light, Astrid's countenance was inclined to be saturnine. Her eyes, which were brown, looked out upon the world with perceptible sorrow at the madness which was being perpetrated, in her opinion, by male oligarchies lusting for power. At heart Astrid was a feminist, and although the idea of being in love was not anathema to her, romantic ties and responsibilities were not what she presently craved. What Astrid craved more than anything was peace, for the world to return to a mind-set which was not at odds with her own, which was not at odds with sanity. Her dark hair tied behind was collar-length, framing an open and honest face which projected her vulnerability, a vulnerability which diminished considerably in Hanne's company, or whenever she became immersed in the literary lives of others, be they fact or fiction.

In an attempt to steer the conversation away from her lack of punctuality, Hanne enquired of Astrid as to what she was reading. The attempt was successful.

"Shakespeare's Hamlet, Prince of Denmark," Astrid informed.

"In Danish?" asked Hanne.

"In English," the play's reader replied.

Hanne knew that her friend was as fluent in English as she herself was in German. Both now seated, the women were facing each other. There was a handwritten menu which Hanne, working her way down from top to bottom, scanned methodically. Before she had time to fully digest the contents, however, Astrid suggested that they order the house speciality – omelette made with more eggs than can be counted on the digits of two hands. Without answering, and with a view to making up her own mind, Hanne was about to resume deciphering the proprietor's scrawl when her friend acted unilaterally and called to the owner by name. The owner's Christian name was Hanning. Hanning obeyed his summons and appeared with a notepad and pencil. In her normal voice Astrid asked Hanning to make them one of his specials, and then, in a whisper, she asked if there was any real coffee to be had. Initially Hanning smiled and nodded, but he either didn't hear, or pretended not to hear, the more aspirate part of Astrid's request. Instead he looked over his shoulder in the direction of the commotion being made by his other customers as they prepared to leave.

"Excuse me ladies," the owner apologised, "I'll just see to these people," and so saying, in order to take payment, he left the two women temporarily in limbo.

There followed an exchange between the two men consistent with a minor business transaction. Hanne had followed the proprietor with her eyes, and suspected that Astrid's friend was a Nazi, either that or he was in league with the Resistance. The furtiveness of his movements suggested he was privy to secret information upon which, to some extent, the outcome of the war depended. With little to go on to enable her to fathom Hanning's likely allegiance, Hanne kept these thoughts to herself. Her observations were disturbed by Astrid's playful comment.

"It's no use ogling him," she said. "He's happily married with two teenage children."

Turning to face Astrid as Hanning deposited the money he had been paid into a small, metal box which he kept locked and out of sight behind the bar, Hanne smiled as she answered, somewhat predictably, "He's not my type. In fact," she continued, once again lowering her voice so that only Astrid might hear, "I think he's a bit creepy. How long have you known him?"

"Since the early days of the occupation," replied Astrid. "Although I only got to know him because I was friendly with his wife, Pia. She and I became friends when we worked at the egg factory together."

"I thought eggs were produced by hens," interjected Hanne flippantly.

The doorbell tinkled, and the man accompanied by the boy bade everyone good-day as he was about to depart the premises. The proprietor responded by returning the compliment. The seated young women merely smiled as the man struggled to get his suitcase through the door. The boy had preceded him. Astrid began to explain that the eggs which the hens had laid needed to be graded and packed, but broke off her conversation in this vein when she realised that an explanation wasn't really necessary.

"It was she who told me that her husband ran this place, and what's more, that he has a secret supply of coffee. That's the reason I come here so often. That's right isn't it Hanning?" asked Astrid, raising the volume of her voice as she posed the question.

"What's right?" retorted Hanning, returning to the table occupied by the women with pencil poised in one hand and notepad in the other.

He regarded his female patrons benignly, but in that look of kindness there was also a hint of smugness born from an assumed male supremacy.

"That this is one of only a few places where a person in the know can get a cup of real coffee."

Hanning scribbled on his notepad and then glanced through the window at the German soldiers. The soldiers appeared to be grooming themselves. They were occupied in straightening their uniforms and combing their hair. In this respect the lorry wing-mirrors were proving to be of invaluable assistance. Hanning, turning his attention back to the young women, placed his index finger vertically in front of his lips and winked at Hanne. This rapid closing and opening of one eye made her cringe, she hoped not visibly. Without further comment Hanning disappeared from view into the kitchen at the back of the building, no doubt to make coffee, and break more than a few eggs.

"Where does the coffee come from?" Hanne asked, and although the subject matter of her enquiry wouldn't, under normal circumstances, engender such a feeling, at this point in time she felt as if she were probing into a world of shadows and illicit, clandestine dealings.

"I don't know," replied Astrid, "and I thought it wise not to ask."

"I was merely wondering whether it was smuggled in under the cover of darkness from Sweden, or whether it was supplied by our lords and masters."

The answer to a question which was implied rather than expressed explicitly, would have been, without providing hard and fast confirmation that Hanning was involved in subterfuge of any kind, in no small way revealing. For a fleeting moment Hanne wasn't sure whether to believe Astrid when she claimed not to know the source of Hanning's secret supply, but then she inwardly remonstrated with herself for doubting the word of a friend whom she had known for the best part of twenty years. She rationalised her doubt by blaming the war. The greatest casualty of life as lived under the Nazi occupation was trust. Even trust between members of the same family, as well as between friends, was not immune from the contagion of doubt which erected unseen barriers between people, compelling them to speak guardedly. In this polity, under this regime, it was difficult not to believe that behind every wall was a pair of friendly or unfriendly ears, and the consequences dependent upon the difference between ears that belonged to a friend and those that belonged to a foe were more significant, more potentially dangerous, for the individuals involved than at any other time in the nation's history. Hanne resolved not to doubt her friend's word in the future, unless, of course, Astrid gave her a reason so to do.

"How's your relationship with Hans progressing?" Are you going to marry him?" asked Astrid, gently disturbing Hanne's train of thought.

(The disruption was gentle indeed, for the question which Astrid had been tempted to ask initially, but in the nick of time had thought that she had better not, rather crudely was, "Have you slept with any German pilots lately?")

"Our relationship is fine, but I'm not going to marry anyone until this mess of a war is over," informed Hanne, and in thinking of Hans she realised that he would probably be facing great danger in the skies above England even as she and Astrid were chatting. "He's on a mission as we speak, but if it's all the same to you, I would rather not talk about it. There's always a chance in his line of work that he'll be shot down and I'll never see him again."

Hanne realised that she was stating the obvious, and although it made her feel good to apprise Astrid of how anxious she was in respect of the dangers her lover faced, she didn't want to go into too much detail. From her perspective Astrid could see by the way her friend's face clouded over at the thought of losing Hans that it really would be better to steer a new conversational course.

"Well what shall we talk about?" enquired Astrid enthusiastically.

"There is something I want to discuss," Hanne replied. "It was something Hans said just before he left this morning, and it's been on my mind ever since."

"Go on!" commanded Astrid, delighted that she would no longer have to prompt Hanne to reveal her innermost thoughts. To show that she was 'all ears', so to speak, she firmly pushed 'Hamlet, Prince of Denmark' farther to one side and leaned forward, her folded arms resting on the table in front of her. This keen interest in her friend's affairs had an obvious and beneficial effect on Astrid's spirits. Of the two, it was the usually carefree Hanne who now seemed the more vulnerable.

"I'm not sure whether this is the right time and place," she said, with some trepidation.

"For heaven's sake!" exclaimed Astrid, irked by her friend's reticence. "We're the only two people in the room at present. How can there be any danger? When Hanning brings the food," she continued, raising her head and voice as she focused on the door which led into the kitchen, "we'll talk about something completely different; a conversation about our respective periods should see him make a hasty retreat. Of course, if your periods, or lack of them, are really what you want to discuss, we'll have to switch the conversation to discussing suitable locations for hiding explosives, or when and where the next canister of Sten guns is to be dropped. Besides, I'm sure Hanning wouldn't betray us to the authorities. He would be losing a couple of customers."

At that moment Hanning appeared bearing a tray laden with a huge coffee pot and the requisite means to imbibe the aromatic stimulant the pot contained. With all the finesse that a sommelier might bring to opening and pouring a bottle of excellent vintage wine, Hanning, having laid out the cups, saucers and spoons, poured each of his customers a cup of real coffee.

"A special delivery from Colombia via Sweden," whispered Hanning.

"Mmm," mumbled Astrid, as she savoured the unmistakable aroma.

"That really is good," commented Hanne after sipping the hot, dark liquid.

She liked to drink her coffee black. Pleased that his patrons were pleased, Hanning disappeared with the empty tray only to return moments later with what looked to be the perfect omelette.

"Enjoy your breakfast ladies," wished Hanning as once again the doorbell tinkled, and in trooped five German soldiers.

Chapter Eight

Hambleton Village – 1938

The village of Hambleton, nestled snugly between the River Seph and the River Rye, and surrounded by woods and hills, would have been an ideal location for the first Cistercian monks, on their arrival from Clairvaulx, to establish a monastery. Instead, having been granted land by Walter L'Espec, Lord of Helmsley, the austere followers of Saint Benedict set up their monastic house in an equally tranquil setting at Rievaulx. The monks, and their army of lay brothers, by keeping thousands of sheep on the common near Hambleton for example, made a significant impact on the land, a land the beauty of which had been enhanced and not diminished by the onset of civilisation, by farming.

Standing at her garden gate on a bright morning in October, Martha Gilbert wasn't really aware of how much the scene she surveyed had been influenced by the industry and intelligence of the Cistercian monks toiling so diligently so far back in history. Presently, in keeping with the season, Martha observed that the trees in the valley through which flowed Ladhill Beck were beginning to change to autumnal tones. The anticyclone which had been forecast for that morning was expected to be in place over much of the country for the entire week. Martha savoured the scene like a person who is about to lose something precious, something that she loves. Despite the BBC's prediction that in the short term the weather was set fair, as a woman who had lived in rural Yorkshire for several years, she knew that a hard winter was just around the corner. Moreover, the news that she listened to over breakfast sounded more ominous each day, not in the sense that Hitler and Mussolini, in the context of the Nazi alliance they had formed in 1936, were doing dastardly deeds, for in Martha's rather naive opinion the two leaders were merely taking back what rightfully belonged to their respective countries, but in the sense that certain influential voices were calling for

Britain to re-arm in readiness for war. Being a woman of some intelligence, she realised that if war did come between Britain and Germany, she and George would be put in a morally difficult position. The upheavals that they had experienced in their marriage over recent years might not seem so great in comparison to the changes that might be forthcoming. She was thankful indeed that her husband's and her political leanings and affiliations were not known locally, and that in his absence she had lived a quiet life.

Martha had come to the garden gate of the solidly built stone cottage she rented from a local landowner to admire the view. The full panorama was not available to her from within the house because of the spreading branches of a mountain ash planted in the garden by a previous resident. She had often considered getting rid of the tree, the topmost twigs of which had grown as tall as the guttering along the roof line, but as yet had not found the will to wield the axe, neither literally nor metaphorically. A more altruistic reason for her coming to the gate was to save the postman, who was usually punctual, from having to walk down the path to deliver any mail he might have for her.

Mrs Gilbert had received only one letter from her husband in the entire length of time that he had been away fighting in Spain. That letter, received so long ago that she had forgotten exactly when it had arrived, had alarmed her more than a little. An incongruous aspect to Martha's logic led her to accept with equanimity the possibility that her husband might be killed in action, yet at the same time caused her to be distraught at the prospect of his being beaten up in a brawl, as evidently had nearly happened. Regarding the accusations which had been made against her husband two years ago, and whether he really did have a lascivious eye for young girls, she was, as yet, not sure one way or the other. She believed, however, that she knew her husband sufficiently well to be certain that he would be the last person on Earth who would get involved in fisticuffs if he could at all help it. She had never met George's friend, Harry Osborne, but upon reading between the lines of her husband's letter, her instincts told her that the Londoner had probably been to blame for the fight, that he was a rough sort, the sort likely to get involved in, and indeed cause, a fracas.

No matter how sublime the view, there's probably not a person alive that doesn't feel compelled to take action after contemplating a scene of natural beauty, otherwise one might as well be comatose. Bearing in mind that this view, and this air, were elements in her life she could savour often, it didn't take Martha long for her to begin attending to her garden and the encompassing wall. She didn't apply herself to the task of pulling up a weed here, a clump of grass there, with gusto. Her actions were those of a perfectionist making fine adjustments whilst whiling away the minutes as she waited for the postman to appear on his bicycle from around the bend at the bottom of the hill. Time and again she stooped to insert her fingers into the cool soil in order to extract an unwanted interloper by the roots, and each time that she straightened her back and rose to her full height, she turned her head in the direction of the village, the direction from which any visitor, whether welcome or not, would be likely to come. She couldn't help her feelings of expectancy. Nonetheless, if experience was anything to go by, her excitement at the prospect of receiving a missive from George was unfounded. The weeks that had turned into months since she had last received news from her husband had, up until this morning, dulled her hopes of ascertaining for certain whether or not he was safe from harm and terrible privations. Insistently this morning, however, her intuition had driven her from the house to wait by the garden gate on a day she felt was destined to be remarkably different from the long retinue of days that had gone before. Unable to find any more weeds to extract from that particular border, Martha stepped through the white, wooden gate into the road. Closing the gate behind her, she noted that the wood was rotting badly in the bottom right hand corner. Then, after moving a few paces to the left so that her view wasn't so restricted by the rowan, she cast her eyes up to the nearer second-floor windows of her marital home, noting that they too were in need of more than a fresh coat of paint. In the past these would have been jobs which George would have attended to at weekends or during the school holidays, but now she would either have to cajole the owner of the cottage to allocate one of his hired hands to do the remedial work, or do the work herself.

"Good morning Mrs Gilbert," called a voice from halfway down the hill. "And what a fine morning it is to be going about God's work."

The voice belonged to the vicar, who, dressed in his normal working attire, was striding manfully in Martha's direction. A tall, rangy figure with a stride to match, the gentle incline which led down towards the centre of the village didn't present much of a challenge to the man of God walking uphill, and subsequent to his greeting he covered the intervening stretch of road between himself and Mrs Gilbert in next to no time. Martha had been surprised to hear her name, so occupied had she been latterly in scrutinising the decaying fabric of her home. The identity of the caller was, initially at least, a disappointment. She had nothing in particular against the Reverend Jeremy Strang, in fact she quite liked the man, but it was unlikely that he would be bringing news of George. Or was it? When the thought crossed her mind that she had not heard from her husband because he had long since been buried in the ground, and that in the chain of messengers relaying the bad news, the vicar, in keeping with his position in the parish, had been chosen to deliver the news in person, Martha's heart missed a beat. She observed the approaching figure closely. Strang had the look of a man who has just placed a bet on a horse and won. The smile on his face was smug, though nonetheless genuine for that. It was hardly the expression of a man about to deliver a mortal blow.

Martha began to relax, sensing that the worst scenario she had allowed herself to imagine was not about to happen. Eventually, as the vicar drew near, Martha became convinced that she was not about to be the recipient of bad tidings, at least not from Reverend Strang. With the passing of one anxiety, however, another followed, and she began to feel guilty that it had been an age since she had last been to church.

Now standing within an arm's length of Martha, the Reverend Strang held out his hand to share in the customary greeting. Aware that her hands were grubby from the impromptu gardening session, the prospect of making physical contact flustered Martha a little, and she hastily wiped her hands on the apron she was wearing in the hope of transferring as much of the grime as possible on to the already stained flower-patterned cloth rather than on to the vicar's palm.

"Don't worry about a bit of harmless muck Martha," warmly advised reverend Strang as he grasped the small, frail hand in his. "Many of my flock are farmers as you know, and a more down-to-earth group of people you cannot meet. What I'm not saying, of course, is that farmers are unhygienic in their ways, but when I call in person unexpectedly, the timing of my visit may be inopportune to say the least. That has certainly been the case previously, and on more occasions than I care to count."

Martha wasn't sure what to do with her hand once the vicar had relinquished his grip. He placed his in the pocket of his trousers and drew out a neatly folded handkerchief. This was completely white save for the initials of the owner embroidered in blue ornate lettering on the corner of the square that was immediately visible. The vicar had no intention of using the handkerchief for its normal purpose, but instead reached up to his temple to remove his spectacles. He set about wiping the lenses, peering up at Martha to scrutinise her with eyes that looked peculiar for being uncovered, in a sense naked. For the first few moments the lids opened and closed rapidly, and Martha wasn't sure whether this flickering movement was at the vicar's conscious behest, or whether the eyes were making their own adjustments to the change in focal length. From the perspective of both parties order was only restored when the Reverend Strang replaced his spectacles, when for one individual the world was once again brought into sharp focus.

"That's better," he said as he looked about him, surveying objects near and far like a man whose vision was blurred, and who has just been blessed by the miracle of perfect sight. "Mrs Strang says that I should wash my glasses in warm, soapy water daily, but unfortunately I fall well below the meticulousness of her suggestion in this regard, even though when I do clean my spectacles properly the effect is remarkable, and frequently marvellous. I say," uttered the vicar suddenly, without giving Martha an opportunity to comment on matters optical, "your garden gate looks as if it is about to disintegrate."

After returning the handkerchief to his pocket he bent down to give the rot his full attention. He did this by probing the open wound with his hand. Several fibrous fragments broke off, and he rubbed his thumb and fingers together to be rid of the contamination. Then Strang began to press an area which still looked sound, but in fact wasn't. The fact that it wasn't soon became apparent as new cracks appeared in the paintwork. The vicar's actions resembled those of a doctor gently pressing a patient's skin to ascertain the extent of any swelling, and whether the inflammation is painful.

"Please don't make matters worse than they already are," instructed Martha, observing the vicar's intervention with some concern from her vantage point which was slightly behind and to one side: in effect she was standing over him.

From this position Martha was able to look down upon the vicar's bald pate, noting how tanned and shiny the skin was where it was drawn tightly over the cranium between flanks of grey hair on either side. Conscious that he may have stepped over the line between propriety and impropriety by meddling, the Reverend Strang ceased what he was doing at once and peered up at Mrs Gilbert over his shoulder. Perhaps it was because she was standing upright, whilst the vicar was as yet still crouched, that enabled Martha to speak with such authority. Regardless of how she came by her resolve, with arms folded in readiness to defend against any verbal thrust the vicar might make, she continued in the same vein.

"It's always a pleasure to see you vicar, but I doubt that you've come all this way to show me how you go about cleaning your glasses, and I'm sure I'm right when I say that neither did you come here with the sole intention of inspecting my gate."

The Reverend Strang and his wife, along with their two teenage daughters, lived at Saint Anne's House, a remote property to which there was no access by metal road. Had the vicar walked to Martha's cottage directly from home by the shortest practical route, he would already have walked two miles, but by calling first at Arncliffe Hall, the manorial residence in the

76

opposite direction from Saint Anne's House when the ultimate goal was to pass through Mrs Gilbert's gate and door, he had extended that distance by at least a mile.

"That's very astute of you my dear," said the Reverend Strang, in a patronising manner, before adding, with a greater sense of purpose than he had demonstrated thus far. "Do you think we might be able to go inside and talk?"

Glad to be over the small talk, the preliminaries and pleasantries, Strang was clearly expecting the woman for whom he had walked so far to visit, and for a specific reason, to accede to his stated wish in this regard, and without further comment or ceremony he opened the garden gate and beckoned Mrs Gilbert to lead the way. After an initial pause, a matter of seconds during which time Martha's worst fear returned to cloud her face by transforming her features, she did indeed do as had been suggested, leading her reverend guest up the garden path and on through the front door which the visitor dutifully closed behind him, along the corridor running parallel with the stairs, and into the kitchen. The kitchen was warm from the fire in the range which Martha had laid and lit whilst still in her dressing gown. That had been two hours ago. Without asking the Reverend Strang whether or not he would like some tea, she set about heating a large, blackened kettle by hooking it in position directly over the hottest part of the fire. The vicar, meanwhile, had sat down on one of two matching chairs which were positioned either side of a rarely polished table, the leaves of which, for the sake of space, were folded. The backs of the chairs and the table that separated them were hard against the interior wall, and seated as he was, the vicar sought a kind of visual escape from the austere dinginess of his new surroundings by peering through the small panes of the Georgian window into the bright sunlight falling upon the shed at the bottom of the garden. At that moment the shed looked as if it would be a brighter and better place to be.

"I'm sorry about the washing," said Martha, nodding in the direction of a pile of clothes in a basket on the floor next to the mangle, "but I wasn't expecting anyone to call but the postman. Monday is wash-day in these parts you know."

"That I do know," responded the vicar, mindful of how effectively his wife drove him from the house each Monday by tending to the family's laundry.

Judging by the contents of Mrs Gilbert's basket, Strang thought it remarkable how little the amount of laundry a person living alone produced in comparison with his own family, a family of four. Upon entering the kitchen Martha had, as surreptitiously as possible, quickly adjusted the pile so that neither she nor her visitor would be embarrassed. The kettle, having boiled once already that morning, soon began to steam. After wrapping a cloth around the handle otherwise too hot to touch, Martha removed the blackened container from the heat and poured a little of the water boiled therein into an earthenware teapot. Eventually, with as much adherence to correct procedure as might be observed at an oriental tea ceremony, but with less solemnity, the beverage was ready to be imbibed. Equally, just as between sips Martha was now seated and ready to listen, the Reverend Strang was ready to talk.

"Have you heard from your husband lately Mrs Gilbert?" asked the vicar, thinking that the best course was to maintain a polite formality between himself and a woman who, though in the prime of her life, was living in a state of enforced celibacy.

"It's funny you should ask," responded Martha, though there was nothing in the least bit amusing about what she was about to say, "but this morning I awoke with the feeling that I would be hearing from him."

The imprecision of Mrs Gilbert's speech tweaked the vicar's grammarian sensibilities, for as there was no telephone in the cottage, to be heard Mr Gilbert would have to be within human earshot. For the present Strang allowed Mrs Gilbert to continue without interruption.

"The last letter I received from George was way back in August, and in that he seemed undaunted, quite cheerful even, at the prospect of going to the front. The war is lasting much longer than I imagined it would, and I suppose it must be difficult to send letters home. I understand there has been much devastation and loss of life as a result of aerial bombardment," she said, turning to look directly at the Reverend Strang with eyes which sought either confirmation or denial.

After a lengthy pause, with sadness in his voice the vicar said, "Wars usually last longer than people expect my dear. It was the same in The Great War, the war to end all wars. We were told that the boys would be home for Christmas as they marched off to fight for King and country, and like millions of others, having made the ultimate sacrifice, my boy didn't come home at all."

In memory of his fallen son the Reverend Strang allowed his head to drop forward a little so that he looked down at his hands now clasped together, seemingly in an attitude of prayer. At first he had been able to focus only with difficulty, for his eyes had misted over. It wasn't long after she and George had arrived in the village that they had heard the story about how Lieutenant David Strang had been killed in action somewhere in France, and her heart went out to the deceased soldier's father as she allowed him a few quiet moments of reflection. Eventually, as the Reverend Strang reached for the handkerchief he had used earlier, Martha broke the silence by asking if he would like more tea. After wiping the moisture from his eyes the vicar nodded his acquiescence. Martha poured.

The Reverend Strang's normal emotional state was one of quiescence, the foundation for which was an unwavering faith. Feeling more than a little disappointed with himself for having shown weakness in front of a person who was almost a stranger, the vicar made an effort of will to regain his composure. He did this by clearing from his mind all thoughts of self-pity, and in the process he realised that he had been in danger of abrogating his role as a spiritual leader.

"You must miss your son a great deal," said Martha solicitously.

"More than you can imagine my dear, but despite the pain we as a family have suffered at losing David, given the opportunity I would encourage my son to fight the good fight again and again, to be a Christian soldier. That's why I admire you and your husband; Mr Gilbert for having volunteered to stand up for democracy, to fight the evil tide of fascism which is threatening to engulf Europe, and you for keeping the home fires burning with such forbearance and devotion."

Martha could do nothing to prevent herself from reacting nervously to the Reverend Strang's mistake. A tremor ran the length of her arm to her hand, there to erupt in a spillage of tea. She had sunk her top teeth, albeit rather gently, into her bottom lip. Setting about wiping up the mess, she decided to say nothing for the time being.

"And I'm sure that your pride in your husband's heroic deeds will increase immeasurably when you hear my news."

On her way to the sink to wring out the cloth she had used to wipe the table, Mrs Gilbert stopped in her tracks. Realising that this was the pivotal moment, the moment when she would learn the real purpose of the vicar's visit, Martha looked at God's messenger intently.

"What news?" she asked directly, managing to impart in two words more than a hint of impatience.

"It would seem that those allegations made against your husband by that... how should I describe her... by that young lady," articulated the vicar through the difficulties imposed by a sudden bout of coughing, "were entirely without foundation."

Without completing the task as she had intended, Martha threw the damp cloth into the sink and returned to her seat. The news she had just heard was not what she had been expecting, although other than her husband having been killed or injured, she hadn't really considered possible alternatives. Nevertheless, the information which she had just received, though welcome, was numbing, so that the effect upon Martha's psyche, and in consequence her body, was probably not dissimilar to the effect she would expect to experience were she to be informed of George's death.

"By all accounts she is with child by a man whose name I am unable to disclose at this juncture, though I can say that the father is somebody close to her, a relative if you grasp my meaning. The individual responsible has been arrested and under questioning has absolved Mr Gilbert of any impropriety towards the accused party's niece. It would seem that he was responsible for encouraging the girl to make those allegations in order to deflect suspicion from his own wicked deeds. 'Foeda est in coita brevis voluptas et taedet Veneris statim peractae'. Do excuse my little foibles my dear," said the vicar apologetically immediately after his Latin outburst, "but I was quoting Petronius." He continued by providing his listener with an English translation, "Delight in lust is gross and brief and weariness treads on desire. Doubtless the police will be paying you a visit in due course, but merely to assist in their present line of enquiry, so there's nothing to worry about there. Given what you and your husband must have been through together, the future couldn't be brighter for the Gilberts of Hambleton Village."

The names of the residents and the emphatic enunciation of the place where they resided resonated like a clarion call informing the world that a number of those that had been thought guilty were innocent. Martha wept tears of joy, and the Reverend Strang, being a helpful man in more ways than one, loaned her his handkerchief.

Chapter nine

River Ebro – July 1938

Perched prominently upon the hill, it didn't take long for el buen mayor's observation post to be blown almost to smithereens. The direct hit by a republican shell caused the more than likely unmourned deaths of several legionnaires, but not that of the man who had earlier given them their orders. At the time of the explosion in question he had been relieving his bladder among an outcrop of boulders, and as he turned in mid-flow to gain a visual impression of an eruption that might have killed him, he was hit on the head by a chunk of debris which merely knocked him unconscious. His legs crumpling beneath him, he fell to the ground in a manner which neither he nor his illustrious antecedents would have been proud of, for in what would be his resting place for the next half hour he lay on his back with not only his now hatless face and head exposed to the sun, but also his forlornly flaccid penis.

To the men watching the spectacle from what initially was the relative safety of the river, the devastation taking place before their eyes was stunning, literally in the sense that they looked on transfixed by the violent upheavals taking place where minutes before they had been discussing the best means of improving their position. The two Englishmen, Harry Osborne and George Gilbert, stood watching for a considerable time longer than van Loon and his chum. The latter, having been caught in the open completely naked by the surprise attack, reasoned that whatever action was going to be necessary in the immediate future would best be undertaken with their nakedness covered, and to this end, having given up on retrieving the jabali, they swam back across the river to regain their respective garments. Van Loon was just about to fasten the belt which kept up his shorts when the fatal bullets hit, his now suitably attired number two being killed almost in the same instant. A burst of automatic fire penetrating the upper torso and neck had done for the Dutchman. When he dropped to the ground he fell in two stages, collapsing first to his knees and then head-first into the river, so that his body was half in and half out of the water rapidly turning red with his blood. Van Loon's friend, who had remained anonymous to the end to George and Harry, fell in such a way that his lifeless head bounced off the Dutchman's heels. The sudden supremacy of death over life striving to be decent was sufficient motivation for those in imminent danger of suffering a similar fate to take evasive action. By this time the smell of cordite was noxious, and though the noise of the artillery barrage had been loud in the extreme, between detonations could be heard the other gruesome sounds of battle. In the act of diving for cover and searching for a safe place to hide, the Englishmen could not cut out the screams of dying men. In addition, above the low rumble of heavy armour approaching the Ebro from the Republican Army's positions, could be discerned desperate voices, some shouting in Spanish, others giving orders in English. All were heard against a background of fire from smaller weaponry. To the men hiding in the narrow crevasse of a dried-up creek, to George and Harry, the sound of this shooting was unfamiliar because the weapons they could hear being fired around them had come from Russia, not Germany.

Crouching one behind the other, George turned around in order to ascertain by a look how Harry was coping with the situation, a turn of events which was perilous to say the least. Harry, responding to George's quizzical scrutiny with an expression which was commensurate with the seriousness of their shared predicament, placed the forefinger of his left hand in front of his lips in the time-honoured and ubiquitous fashion. Needless to say the cross formed by finger and lips indicated that silence should be maintained, on this occasion at all costs. Their lives depended on it. George, reassured by his friend's composure, returned his attention back to the river, the disturbed waters of which he could just make out flowing beyond their cover of moderately dense foliage. More than likely that was the direction from which danger would come. All around them the light was dappled, a remarkable contrast of brilliance and shade. A form of camouflage, the broken patterns formed by nature and illumined by the sun worked to their advantage. Both men pressed their bodies into the sandy bank, their intention being to make themselves as inconspicuous as possible. Each man held his weapon with the butt pressed into his shoulder, each with his trigger-finger curled around the trigger-guard. They had cocked their weapons, and apart from having to release their respective safety catches, a task able to be completed by a flick of the thumb in the blink of an eye, they were ready to open fire.

The artillery barrage stopped as suddenly as it had started, and to Harry and George, notwithstanding the fact that the roaring engines of the enemy's armour were now more prominent, that was a welcome development. Ensconced in their leafy hiding place, seemingly from all points east and for what seemed like an age, the relentless din informed of a formidable, but not yet, at least for two particular pairs of eyes, visible menace. The stutter of machine guns and the crackle of rifle-fire continued. Forced by the sequence of events to cower ineffectually, George sensed that the battle was not going well for their side. Harry was of a similar opinion.

During this rather precarious phase in Harry's and George's earthly existence, had they been able in these moments to give voice to their thoughts, the listener would have learned that they were ruminating upon different, but not unrelated, subjects. Harry, having been witness to van Loon's and the other jabali hunter's death from a viewpoint an arm's length from George, from a distance of no more than thirty yards, re-enacted the scene in all its gory detail several times, with one crucial difference. In his imagined scenes, repeatedly he saw himself lying face-down in the water instead of the Dutchman. It was a sight to make a man's blood run cold, an image which almost inevitably led him to think, 'There but for the Grace of God go I', the 'I' referred to being flesh and blood. He also had time to consider that if God, the gods, the workings of fate, or pure chance, allowed him to get out of his present predicament unscathed, he would think twice about embarking on a similar adventure. By contrast George's mental machinations were not so hauntingly vivid, for in him at this time the sense of fight or flight was more acute. In this regard he was not unlike a fox which, believing that it has outfoxed the hounds has gone to ground. He was all ears and eyes.

Alert to the prospect of coming face to face with the enemy at any moment, the skulking pair sought to become even less conspicuous when a tank's engine roar grew to a crescendo as the tracked vehicle broke through the bushes a little downstream on the opposite bank. George, being slightly forward of his comrade-in-arms, had the better view of the fighting machine, but not a clear view. By being able to see several of the tracked wheels, the turret and part of the forty-five millimetre gun, he was able to identify the tank as a Russian-made T-26. The Englishmen in hiding stirred not a muscle as the turret began to traverse, and with it the main armament, from pointing directly to the front in line with the tracks. Turret and gun turned first to the right, stopping in that direction when the barrel seemed to be pointing directly at the men in hiding. Fortunately for George and Harry no round was fired, and after a few seconds the turret proceeded to traverse through one hundred and twenty degrees so that the gun ended up aiming downstream, at nothing in particular. The tank had been stopped in its tracks by the river, and consequently the noise of its engine had diminished to a persistent growl. Thwarted in their advance by an obstruction which everyone involved in the attack must have known about, the pause seemed to indicate that the unseen crew were uncertain as to what to do next. At this juncture George was startled by a noise from behind which almost made him jump out of his skin, despite the familiarity of the sound and its cause. Harry had sneezed. Alarmed by the possibility that they might be killed or captured simply because his friend was unable to control his nasal eruptions, George himself risked giving away their position by turning around to glare at the offender, thereby silently expressing his admonishment. He need not have bothered, for as inevitably as night follows day, a second sneeze followed. Yet again the Englishmen were fortunate for their antics were neither seen nor heard, unlike those perpetrated by the enemy. Evidently a section of the opposition's infantry had arrived on the scene, and the individual who appeared to be the section-commander – a burly, barrel-chested figure of a man who sported a beard, and around his forehead, a red bandana – was giving instructions to one of his men. The chosen man dutifully removed his boots and socks, and after placing the latter inside the former, deftly tied left and right boot together by their laces. The soldier then placed the laces around his neck, thereby allowing his footwear to dangle, seemingly in perfect balance and hopefully not so low as to get wet. Now ready in a literal sense to test the water, holding his rifle aloft, the barefoot soldier stepped into the Ebro. It didn't take long, no more than two strides, for the water to cover the wader's thighs. He was watched in his aquatic explorations not only by his scruffy and rather intimidating superior officer, but also by the tank-commander. Dressed in black overalls, he had opened the turret to emerge from the tank's interior, but only to the extent that his head and torso were visible. His first act upon greeting the sun was to rub his bedazzled eyes. The actions of this little battle group suggested that they thought it unlikely that they would come under accurate fire at that moment. From their place of concealment George and Harry tried to make sense of the proceedings, particularly when they heard the noise of laughter. The enemy commanders were seen to join in the guffaws, demonstrating a sense of humour no more subtle or refined than that of their men. George, being privy to more information than Harry, formed the hypothesis that the man ordered into the river had been sent forward to gauge the depth, probably with the security of the tank and the safety of its crew more in mind than what might happen to his infantry colleagues were they to attempt to ford the Ebro at that point. George's suppositions, as far as they went, were correct in every detail.

They were less than comprehensive in the sense that for a time he was totally perplexed by the enemy's careless laughter, although eventually the reason for it became obviously apparent. The human depth gauge had returned dripping water from every part of his body, and those items of attire and equipment which he had intended to keep dry if at all possible were completely saturated. Not even the hapless soldier's rifle had escaped immersion.

"Idiota de mierda!" shouted the fellow in the red bandana.

"No sirve para un carajo," came the spluttered reply. The speaker turned towards the man perched in the turret to add, "Como se puede ver, el rio es demasiado hondi alli."

George was unable to understand all the words, but, as he observed the derided enemy soldier turn to point to a particular spot in the river, he knew perfectly well what was being said. All further conversation audible to the secreted listeners ceased as the cracks, plops and thwacks of bullets breaking twigs, striking the water, or kicking up clouds of dust where they hit the ground, served to remind the republican attackers that resistance in the area had not been silenced completely. While shouting at the driver to get moving, the tank commander hastily closed the hatch over his head as he dropped down to take advantage of the protection offered by Russian steel. Once again the tank's engine roared as the driver spun the vehicle around ninety degrees before speeding off to search for a likely crossing point farther downstream. Keeping the tank between themselves as potential targets and the Legionnaires that had been shooting at them, the Republican infantry also appreciated their metal shield.

Against the background of the battle which was being waged all around them, but no longer in the immediate vicinity, the Englishmen were able to 'stand down' without breaking cover.

"Let's get out of here," suggested Harry, daring to speak in a voice louder than a whisper.

"Let's wait a few minutes longer," advised George, holding out his hand with the palm facing down, a gesture designed to indicate to Harry that he should refrain from making any sudden movements.

Harry complied by repositioning his legs and allowing the blood to flow more freely. His right foot had been numb for what seemed like an age, but the truth was that it had only been a source of discomfort for a few minutes. He felt sufficiently secure to lay aside his machine-pistol, thereby freeing both hands. These he applied to massaging his lower limbs, paying particular attention to each calf and the topmost part – the part of each ankle not protected by the boot – of his Achilles tendon.

"Ah! That's better!" exclaimed Harry with a sigh.

George, wondering what it was that had improved so remarkably, turned around to look at the events unfolding behind his back. His observation that Harry had allowed himself to relax completely had a positive effect on his own nerves, and imitating his friend he too sat with his back supported by the bank of earth, his legs stretched out in front, the toe-caps of his boots pointing at the sky at equal and opposite angles from the perpendicular. The Mauser lay at rest across his thighs.

"That was close," said George, tilting his head in Harry's direction.

Harry nodded his agreement, but his attention was focused elsewhere. He appeared to be preoccupied with his thoughts, and continued to stare directly ahead with a vacant expression. George was too emotionally drained by recent events to enquire about the cause of his friend's distraction.

"I'm parched," said George at last, realising that neither he nor Harry had brought their water bottles with them when they had set out on their mission with bucket and spade. "I think it's safe for us to move now. Do you think it's safe for us to move now?"

Harry, having dismissed dark concerns pertaining to his own mortality, reached for his weapon and rose to his feet. George did likewise, and this time it was his turn to follow where Harry led. The taller man threaded his way between the bushes with shoulders forward and head bowed, following the course of the river in the opposite direction to that which had been taken by the enemy. Occasionally losing sight of the Ebro altogether, and sometimes almost stumbling upon it, like stalked animals they crept warily over the rough terrain for about a hundred yards. Their senses were acutely primed for a possible second confrontation, be it with friend or foe. Eventually they emerged into a small clearing where there was a beach of sorts. Baked hard by the sun, the patch of bare ground curved down to the water's edge. This looked like an ideal place for the parched pair to slake their thirsts. In the heat of the sun near its zenith it seemed that numerous trigger-fingers had grown weary of trying to kill their fellow human beings, for the sound of gunfire, having become merely sporadic, had diminished in intensity. During a prolonged lull of not less than two minutes, not a single shot was heard. This created an ephemeral illusion to those in search of respite that the citizens of the world were once more at peace with each other. It was during these illusory minutes that George gave way to temptation, and, after placing his Mauser on the ground by his side, knelt forward on his knees to dip his cupped hands into the water clear at this point for flowing over a bed of rounded pebbles. The effect of the sunlight dancing on the ripples was therapeutically hypnotic. George was reminded of the River Rye at the height of summer. Harry, meanwhile, had remained in the bushes crouched on one knee, machine-pistol at the ready. His willingness to provide cover for his friend as the Yorkshireman drank his fill demonstrated a remarkable, though probably necessary, degree of military discipline, but unfortunately only for a short while. Between gulps George had commented on how delicious the water tasted, and without his fully appreciating that the Londoner was being cautious for a reason, had unthinkingly invited Harry to join him. Assessing that the coast was clear, even where there was no coast in sight, Harry responded to the invitation positively. Kneeling upon the shore side by side, their weapons discarded but within easy reach, their bottoms in the air a perfect target for a Corporal's boot, they knew that they had been more than a little careless when a burst of automatic fire made spouts in the water almost a foot high not that far from Harry's left shoulder.

"Levanten! Arriba las manos o disparo a matar!" called a voice from behind the Englishmen, and with just enough knowledge of Spanish to realise that the better course of action was to do as they were told rather than be killed, they rose to their feet with hands held high above their heads.

With backs to their captors they were facing the river. For several moments nothing happened, and the longer the interlude of inertia, the more the Englishmen began to suspect that they would be shot in the back where they were standing. There was no point in trying to take a few of the enemy with them, for their guns might as well have been at the bottom of the river for all the use they would have been at that moment. Both men knew that they had only themselves to blame for dropping their guard and allowing themselves to be taken by surprise, for their naivety.

George's thoughts at this time were not so much concerned with seeing his life flash before his eyes as he considered the prospect of his death occurring imminently, but somewhat incongruously with why it was that their one and only captor to have spoken thus far had such a peculiar, albeit familiar, accent, bearing in mind that he had been speaking Spanish. Harry, mesmerised by the play of light upon the water, had resigned himself to whatever fate had in store. The pad of approaching footsteps preceded a sharp prod in Harry's rib cage with a gun barrel. The violence of this action forced the Londoner to stumble into George, and when both men had regained their balance and composure they were out of reach of their weapons. A consequence of this upheaval was that of their own volition they had turned to face their captors, and what greeted their eyes was hardly surprising. Arrayed in a semi-circle were seven men dressed in a style of uniform which the captors had not previously seen. Each of the soldiers facing them was wearing a soft cap the most remarkable feature of which was a red star in the centre. The uniforms were buff-coloured, and in that regard reminded Harry of manila envelopes. Three of the soldiers facing them were wearing ammunition belts over their tunics. These crossed at the sternum. Harry and George had turned around to discover that the barrels of seven guns were pointing in their direction. Neither Englishman thought it necessary to determine which and how many guns were pointing at whom. If only one of their captors were to open fire death would be a certainty. The eighth man, the soldier who had poked Harry in the ribs, bent down to retrieve first Harry's machine-pistol, and then George's rifle. In so doing he was given additional orders by the shortest man present. The flame-haired individual was standing on the extreme left of the group when viewed from the Englishman's standpoint. It was he who had instructed the unsuspecting pair to raise their hands in surrender. Of considerable surprise to the prisoners was the fact that these latter instructions had been spoken in English with a Scottish brogue.

"Unload the weapons and clear them," had uttered the man in charge. "We don't want these two trying anything desperate later."

Still with their hands raised, George and Harry looked at each other in astonishment. A glimmer of hope that their lives might be allowed to continue shone from two pairs of eyes.

"I know what to do," replied the soldier carrying out the orders seconds ahead of their being enunciated, and sure enough he did what was required of him quickly and efficiently.

"Come se llaman y que es el nombre de su regimento?" asked the man with the Scottish accent.

"There's no need to speak Spanish to us mate," Harry replied. "We're British, just like you if I'm not mistaken."

Eager to garner what benefit he could from their common birthright, Harry beamed as much goodwill as it was possible for him to beam at the men holding the guns. In his enthusiasm to generate this life-prolonging empathy, however, he made the mistake of stepping over the mark by lowering his hands. Like many a person seeking to express himself with conviction he held out his hands in front palms uppermost, a gesture by which he was instinctively pleading for greater understanding and tolerance. Needless to say he wasn't allowed to make free with his gestures for long, for to a man the men holding the guns made it blatantly obvious that as yet the fact that they had met up with fellow Britons in the battle for the soul of Spain counted for little.

"You were fighting on the side of the fascists," said the officer whose rank wasn't obviously apparent. "And as my men and I are all volunteers in the British Battalion of the XII International Brigade, you are our prisoners."

After a pause for thought the officer added, "You can rest assured that unless you do something stupid we'll not be your executioners."

Words which were meant to be reassuring failed to convince George and Harry that they had a long-term future.

Chapter Ten

Approaching Aalborg, Denmark

In my later teenage years there was nothing I liked better than to get up early on at least one of the weekend mornings and put on my walking boots in preparation for a long, lonely hike along the sometimes calm, but more often wild and windy, coast near to my Sreisund home. Despite enjoying my own company, invariably on those solitary excursions I would dream of there being someone like Hanne by my side, a young lady whose hand I could hold as we laughed at our failed attempt to dodge an incursion made by the tide. At that age I used to savour the romantic melancholy of pining for love, and the act of walking alone along the Baltic shore proved to be an irresistible combination of angst and solace. Moreover, I once spent a week of the school holidays in the south of the country, in Bad Reichenhall to be precise, a small town of considerable charm in the Bavarian Alps. I don't think it was possible for me to be farther from home and still be in Germany, and the effect on my psyche was as dramatic as the Alpine scenery. On my forays into the mountains I frequently felt inspired in ways that I had not experienced previously, as if I were destined to be an artist or a great composer. My heart used to pound with the effort of ascent, my lungs fill with the purest German air imaginable, and to think that I was only a few kilometres from Herr Hitler's retreat. More than once I have thought it not inconceivable that I might have met the Führer as he stretched his legs in the valleys and mountains north of Berchtesgaden, his mind pondering the next move in the political game that would once again make our country great. If our paths had crossed I'm sure I would have been at a loss for words. Adolescent holidays and weekends aside, however, by contrast the perambulation which Ernst and I were making at present was no fun at all. Indeed, the experience was proving to be more painful than either of us had imagined when we had decided that there was no alternative but to walk. Mainly our problems stemmed from being improperly dressed. Our uniforms had been designed to impress the locals by cutting a swagger in town rather than for serious marching of the kind regularly undertaken by columns of troops. It had been years since I had walked more than five kilometres in one go, and as a consequence my feet had lost whatever toughness they had had. Add to this the fact that my boots didn't fit so well after we had been walking for about an hour, probably because the feet inside them had begun to swell, and you can begin to imagine my discomfort. I was particularly aware of the pain emanating from the heel of my left foot, certain that when the time came to remove my footwear – and that moment couldn't come soon enough – I would discover an area the size of a five-mark piece on my heel which had been chafed red-raw. Looking askance at Ernst I could tell that he was also in some difficulty, and judging by his limping gait I gained the impression that the source of his pain was his right foot. I knew from our previous conversations that walking was anathema to him, and that as a cosseted boy from Bonn, before the war he had travelled everywhere he possibly could by one form of wheeled transport or another. Since the onset of the war, and since our respective roles in the conflict had become clearly defined, most of the kilometres he had travelled had been by aeroplane, and many of those in my company. In short, insofar as walking any considerable distance was concerned, flying had made us soft. This lamentable state of mind and body was expressed emphatically when Ernst broke the vocal silence.

Somewhat predictably he said, "If I had wanted to get from A to B on foot I would have joined the bloody Infantry."

"With comments like that I'm sure you would have fitted in rather well," I rejoined severely, before enquiring less harshly, "How are the feet?"

"The right foot is painful, but it's nothing I can't cope with," Ernst replied, his beady eyes fixed on the lights of Aalborg beckoning from the distance of a few kilometres. "If they ever catch the culprits that did this," he added, referring to the roadblock and the scattering of tyre-deflating spikes. "What did you say the organisation more than likely responsible was called – the Churchill Club was it? – well if they ever fall into our hands I would like to make it known here and now that I would be more than willing to command the firing squad. Nothing would give me greater pleasure than to see those ungrateful bastards piss themselves as they're led to the execution posts."

"What about having to put a bullet into the head of one of the condemned terrorists if he's still breathing after the riflemen have done their work, would you be happy to do that?" I asked, surprised that my friend was prepared to be so ruthless for the sake of a few blisters and four punctured tyres.

"Do you think that might be necessary?" asked Ernst, the vehemence with which he had just spoken giving way to a tone expressing unease, a growing apprehension.

"I don't claim to be an expert on the subject of firing squads, but as I understand the procedure it may be necessary for you to draw your pistol and perform the coup de grâce."

"Keine probleme!" he responded emphatically.

I wasn't totally convinced that Ernst would relish the task if indeed he were nominated to take command of the firing squad, but I also knew that our discussing the matter was more or less an irrelevance, as there was little chance of Ernst commanding anything other than his slide rule and charts.

"We had better keep our voices down just in case there are miscreants in the vicinity eager and able to inflict the coup de grâce on us."

"At least then I wouldn't have to contend with this blister on my little toe," rejoined my navigator.

I was about to make a comment about that being my point, but thought better of it, so letting Ernst have the last word. For another ten minutes we walked on in silence, our thoughts returning to their former introspection. Of course I had no idea as to what my colleague was thinking at this juncture, but I was beginning to experience an upsurge of anxiety on account of the reprimand I could expect for borrowing and damaging the Commandant's car. I tried to dispel these thoughts by replacing the image of the bespectacled, table-thumping Commandant with the more pleasing vision of Hanne, naked. In my fantasy I was climbing into bed to be next to her. For the time that I was able to keep my lover in mind not only did my concerns about being called to account for my unsanctioned actions recede, but the pain in my foot also diminished to a point where it was merely negligible. I realised this with regard to the latter only when the pain returned soon after Ernst and I stepped onto the road running from the coast more or less parallel with the stretch of water known as the Langerak. Despite there being a minor road directly opposite, a road which would have led us eventually and by a more circuitous route to where we wanted to go, the direction we needed to take at the crossroads was immediately apparent.

Over to the east, in the direction of the sea, and beyond that neutral Sweden, the sky above the horizon was beginning to lighten to a deep turquoise. The road leading into Aalborg, however, mainly stood out from the land on either side because its asphalt surface was better able to reflect the silvery light as the moon appeared briefly, and seemingly specifically for the purpose of illuminating the way ahead. Just as we were about to turn sharp left to head into town, from the opposite direction we caught sight of headlights approaching, a single beam followed in quick succession by a number of pairs as the vehicles to which they belonged were driven over a slight rise in the ground. Heading directly for us, they were approximately two kilometres away when we first saw them. I surmised that the single headlight in front belonged to a motorcycle.

"This looks as if it might be of interest to us," commented Ernst, no doubt hoping that we would be able to return to base in style rather than having to complete the journey ignominiously on foot. "What do you think Hans?"

"Well... they're unquestionably military vehicles, and in this part of the world that means they're undoubtedly on our side," I replied. "I would hazard a guess that it's a convoy bringing troops back to barracks after they've spent the night on duty guarding the coast between the mouths of the Limfjorden and the Mariager Fjord. Whatever they've been up to, you can at least look forward to a good breakfast in the next half hour," and without considering the possibility that we might be perceived to be members of the Resistance and shot without ever having been given the opportunity to identify ourselves, I stepped forward a pace in order to be able to gesticulate freely for the convoy to stop. I did this by repeatedly crossing my arms above my head. Approximately fifty metres from where we were standing the lead vehicle – the motorcycle – came to a halt followed in turn by the trucks. All the vehicles kept their lights on and their engines running, which made it difficult for Ernst and I to make out what was happening, and rendering it impossible to hear what, if anything, was presently being said. It became apparent that at least one order had been given, however, for I had the distinct impression that a number of troops had alighted to take up defensive positions either side of the road. No doubt their guns were pointing at us. Evidently we had been seen, and although the convoy commander was suspicious of ambush, for the time being he was prepared to give us the benefit of the doubt. The bedazzling effect of peering into the headlights was nothing compared to the instant when a searchlight fixed atop the lead truck was switched on to catch us in its beam. This event was quickly followed by a direct order for Ernst and I to raise our hands above our heads in an attitude of surrender, and having done so, to keep perfectly still. Our life or death instructions had been amplified by megaphone. Needless to say we complied with these instructions without equivocation. By this time, the convoy commander must have realised that he had been waved down by a couple of comrades-in-arms rather than by a marauding band of terrorists, for Ernst and I were summoned to approach the vehicles. We kept our hands aloft just in case, lowering them only when we were asked to confirm our identities. Our identity cards were checked by a tall, lanky Army officer who looked as if he hadn't been long out of school. On one side of his face the freshness of the Leutnant's complexion was plain to see as he inspected first Ernst's and then my photographic images in the glare of the leading truck's headlamps. The soldier operating the searchlight had put his more powerful beam to use scanning first one side of the road ahead, and then the other. I had noticed in passing that the motorcycle was 745cc BMW with sidecar. I could see out of the corner of my eye that the soldier occupying the passenger seat was still pointing his machine-pistol in our direction. Only when the young Leutnant, who was also the convoy commander, satisfied that we were whom we had said we were, clicked his heels and performed a punctilious, parade-ground salute, did we gain an impression of weapons being relaxed, that we were no longer in anybody's sights. The Leutnant, after listening with a barely suppressed smile to my description of the events which had led to our present predicament, and to our immediate requirements, gave an order for the section which had disembarked to get back in the truck. The searchlight was switched off, and the motorcycle rider revved his engine, the latter being an act calculated to express impatience with the delay rather than the serving of any practical purpose. The officer in charge led us along the line of trucks, three of which had canopies over them. The same three were occupied by weary soldiers, which meant that the number of soldiers in the convoy was about Company strength, quite a responsibility for an erstwhile schoolboy to command. We were led to the rear of the last vehicle in the convoy, a truck which was different from the others in the fact that its sides were metal. On the side we passed was painted a large cross inside a circle, a display which was presumably matched on the side opposite. A smaller indication of the vehicle's role was displayed on the rear doors. In the shadows I could just about discern that the crosses were red and the circles white. We were being offered a lift back to base in the back of an ambulance. The shape of the vehicle was unusual, and following my enquiry regarding the truck's provenance, the Leutnant eagerly explained that it was British in origin, and had been captured intact in Belgium prior to the Tommies being driven into the sea. With a tone of impatience in his voice the officer instructed the driver to get out of his cab and open the rear doors for their Luftwaffe guests. The driver apologised, albeit with more than a hint of sarcasm in his voice. Despite his muttering something about not being psychic, dutifully he did as he had been instructed. Our friendly Leutnant took out a torch from his pocket and shone the light inside to reveal the means that would allow two tired airmen to travel in style, and be able to get a few minutes rest to boot, specifically two perfectly acceptable beds.

With a slightly dumbfounded expression I looked first at Ernst and then at the Leutnant. I was playing for time, for my mind was working assiduously at thinking of a plausible reason as to why we shouldn't allow ourselves to be transported as if we were patients, as to why we shouldn't allow ourselves a cat-nap. It would mean relaxing our guard completely, of course, but why should that be a problem in the company of friendly troops. Being an ambulance, not only did the doors open in a civilised manner, but the vehicle was possessed of a step which could be extracted from beneath the chassis when needed, and then slid back again after use. On this occasion the driver contradicted his former negation of possessing psychic powers, pre-empting his superior by extracting the step to assist Ernst and myself in climbing aboard with, on our part, the least possible effort. With considerably more effort he managed to push back the metal platform as Ernst and I seated ourselves on our respective beds. There didn't seem to be anything to choose between the mattresses.

"You might be interested to learn," informed the Leutnant, "that when we captured this vehicle from the Tommies, there was a wounded soldier occupying each of these beds. They were being attended to by a Belgian nurse. Unfortunately for the wounded men neither of them made it."

"What happened to the nurse?" I asked, hoping to conclude our conversation on a lighter note.

"I don't know for certain, but quite possibly she's working in the hospital in Brussels, or Liege perhaps; unless, of course, she happened to be Jewish."

With this rather sinister comment the Leutnant saluted as smartly as he had done previously, and then ordered the driver to close the ambulance doors. Before the doors were slammed shut I managed with a shout to delay proceedings, and I did this simply because a scintilla of doubt had crossed my mind that we hadn't made it absolutely clear where we wanted to go, and how important it was to get to our destination as soon as possible. I wanted to get the message across that although we may have looked like a couple of strays with all the time in the world to be rescued, this wasn't actually the case.

"You do realise Leutnant..." I said, pausing after stating the Army officer's rank as the thought crossed my mind that it would perhaps be useful at some point to know his name; subsequently, therefore, I asked, "What's your name by the way?"

"Schultz, Hauptman, Otto Schultz from Stuttgart," he replied.

The answer to my question confirmed my opinion regarding Leutnant Schultz's accent. Without having been able to place him by his pronunciation of certain words specifically to Stuttgart, I knew that he hailed from the south of the country.

"You do realise that we want to go directly to Squadron headquarters at Aalborg Airfield," I said, being as specific as I thought was necessary bearing in mind that shortly after setting off we would be in ignorance of where we were at any given point in time, and as time was getting on, there was no room for error.

"My men and I are more than happy to take you to the airfield," said Schultz, and without more ado he nodded to the driver to close the doors.

The sound of the doors being secured on the outside was unnerving. The darkness which then surrounded seemed total.

Chapter Eleven

If there were presently a source of artificial light that worked inside the body of the ambulance, the Leutnant had failed to mention it. The Luftwaffe officers had accepted without question that no such light was available. Hauptman Hebbel had expressed his regret at having left their own torch in the car, but immediately excused the failing by pointing out that the batteries were all but dead. Upon their first becoming enclosed inside what was little more than a metal box, for both men the darkness had indeed been absolute, but that was because their eyes had needed time to adjust to the fact that only a minimum amount of light available to the world outside was able to penetrate the interior. Nonetheless, that world was gradually becoming lighter, and eventually, as their eyes slowly became accustomed to the deeper more pervasive darkness within, the passengers were able to discern a few shapes vaguely. The supine Oberleutnant Eckener was able to make out the rectangle formed by the base of a cupboard positioned above his head. Presumably the cupboard had been, and perhaps still was, a repository for bandages and medicines. The Oberleutnant's visual awareness may have been assisted by the fact that he had, and this was before his organs of sight had fully made the adjustment, accidentally given himself a glancing blow on the head. With his temple he had hit the bottom corner of the cabinet. Fortunately the impact had not been so severe as to break the skin. Ordinarily an ambulance is a good place for an injured person to be, but in this context, left to their own devices, that more than likely wouldn't have been the circumstance. Eckener's immediate response to the sudden, sharp pain had been to emit an expletive followed by the first four numbers of his count to ten. By the time he had reached four the pain had been assuaged sufficiently for him not to need to complete the exercise. Hauptman Hebbel had smiled at his friend's misfortune, and from his own supine position, once his friend had settled, he was able to perceive, or so he believed, two pairs of boots pointing to the ceiling. Without a word on the subject, because of the short length of time both officers expected to be incarcerated, they had thought it not worthwhile to take off their boots. For that reason Hebbel wasn't as comfortable as he could have been, mainly because there was an aspect of his upbringing which deterred him from lying on a bed with his boots on, and so from his calves down, his far from clean footwear extended from the end of the bed solely to prevent the mattress from becoming more sullied than he thought necessary. From the vehicle's initial lurch forward as the driver, after grinding the stick to find first gear, clumsily.let out the clutch, the ambulance progressed less than steadily towards its preliminary destination. Leutnant Schultz had decided to turn right on to the minor road heading north at the crossroads rather than go into Aalborg by the Luftwaffe's chosen route, and the right turn had been obvious to the unsighted officers in the ambulance, so much so that Ernst was almost thrown out of bed.

With an escorting Company of soldiers to wake them as soon as they arrived at Squadron Headquarters, there was no reason at all to stay awake for the thirty minute journey. Notwithstanding the short period of time available for rest, however, Ernst couldn't resist a little pillow talk, so to speak. In the absence of real pillows both officers had removed their jackets to use as head-supports.

"Were you ever afraid of the dark Hans, as a boy I mean?"

The timing of the question was uncanny, for seconds before the articulated sound-waves resonated in his ears, Hans had been meditating on the gauntlet that he used to have to run (although seldom literally) in the company of his mother. The journey in question was from his grandmother's house on Bismarck Strasse to home, the most direct route being through the cemetery, a distance of approximately half a kilometre from gate to gate, with not a single lamp between the gates to reveal the way. Hans was more than willing to describe his minor ordeal to Ernst.

"Sometimes we would take the longer, well-lit route home, but when mother was in a hurry for whatever reason, she would urge me to summon up my courage, as no doubt she had to summon her own, to venture through the gate into the forbidding darkness. Invariably I would take a last look over my shoulder towards the security of the illuminated street we had left behind. There is a large and fairly solitary Gothic house just inside the gate – the home of the cemetery superintendent – and I used to think of it as the last place on Earth I would choose to live. On reflection though, I may be merely echoing an idea originally expressed by my mother. Are you sure you want to listen to this?"

In order to ask this question Hans had raised his head a few inches above his improvised pillow, straining the muscles in the back of his neck as he turned to face the man who was only too willing to be the audience of his personal history, at least this aspect of it.

The squealing of brakes indicated that the convoy had arrived at another junction. Soon after the column had got under way again the sound of vehicles travelling in the opposite direction could be heard at intervals, and Hans noted how their headlamps flashed briefly through a number of holes descending from the ceiling in no recognisable pattern. In a time-scale determined by how long it took for the mobile source of illumination to pass, Hans concluded that there were five such holes, all the same size, and that not much bigger than a pfennig coin. The lowest of the holes was half a metre above Ernst's jacket-supported head. When the shadows returned, and Hans once again found himself looking into an apparent void, the realisation dawned that the holes which had let in light had been made by bullets.

"Go on," encouraged Ernst, a clear image of a haunted house in mind as he listened with his eyes closed.

"Well, as you can imagine, we didn't have to go too far into the province of the dead before the gravestones began to take on living forms in our fertile, and some might say febrile, imaginations. To bolster her own courage sometimes my mother deliberately tried to frighten me by suggesting that a bush or a headstone was something other than it really was, only then to attempt to dismiss the fear which she had helped to instil by telling me not to be silly, transmogrifying say the bush which I had begun to perceive as a man – and not just any man, but a mad axe-man – back to the bush which, had my own thoughts been left unmolested, I might have considered throughout to be a perfectly innocent example of one of nature's specimens pruned to a pleasing shape. Once or twice we did meet a human being walking in the opposite direction, but not once were we threatened with decapitation. On the contrary, then the hardly hospitable environment through which we were passing like souls in transit produced an hospitable effect as my mother separately bade each stranger, 'Guten Nacht'. I have to admit though, that when my imagination did get the better of me, in those nerve-tingling moments fear became a physical manifestation, the sensation being not unlike a disembodied finger running down the length of my body from the back of the head to the base of the spine. There you have it my friend, a brief description of one of my more fearful tenebrous experiences to date. What about you, Ernst, were you ever so scared in the dark that the hairs on the back of your neck stood on end?"

Initially the silence in response to the Hauptmann's question was deafening, a silence which from the direction of the person who was meant to reply was soon replaced by nasal sounds indicative of sleep. Hans wondered how much of the latter part of his narrative Ernst had heard, but he didn't wonder for long, for soon, soothed by the motion of the vehicle, he too drifted into the realm ruled by Somnus, the god which in Roman mythology was the god of sleep.

Asleep in the back of the ambulance, the Luftwaffe officers were ignorant of the convoy crossing the bridge over the Langerak, just as they were oblivious to its passing close by the Viking settlement of Nørresundby, where the cremation graves of seven hundred of Hanne's and Astrid's ancestors are marked by stones placed in the form of a triangle, an oval, or a ship, and where also may be found the charred remains of one hundred and fifty Viking boats and ships. The aircrew were also oblivious to the slanting rays of the sun, as it rose above the horizon, falling upon the white-washed walls of Aalborg Cathedral, or Budolfi Domkirke as it is called in Danish, primarily because the church is dedicated to Saint Botolph, patron saint of sailors. From an operational perspective, more important was the fact that Hauptmann Hebbel and Oberleutnant Eckener were oblivious to the ambulance passing through the gates of Aalborg Airfield.

The driver of the last vehicle in the convoy was waved through the main gate without ceremony, and with only a cursory glance to check that he wasn't an infiltrator with sabotage in mind. The personnel manning the guard-room were a mixed bag, comprising men that had served in Luftwaffe Field Divisions on the Russian front, and that had been given, relatively speaking, a soft posting to allow them to fully recover from their wounds. The clock fixed to the guardroom in the centre of the wall which formed the apex supporting the roof informed all that cared to look that it was ten minutes before seven. If they had been awake to notice, there would have been every reason for Hauptmann Hebbel and Oberleutnant Eckener to be confident that they would be in time for the briefing after all. Pulling up adjacent to the wreckage of more than one Blenheim bomber piled up as scrap awaiting disposal just inside the gate, Leutnant Schultz got out of the cab of the leading truck in order to give specific instructions to the ambulance driver relating to his passengers and what he should do after dropping them off, instructions which led, upon the convoy arriving at the first road junction on the base, to the ambulance and the other vehicles going separate ways. The Leutnant had thought that it wouldn't be a bad idea, if they could be catered for, for his men to have breakfast here rather than at their own barracks, and with that aim in mind had set off in the direction of the canteen. The ambulance driver found the building which had been designated Squadron Headquarters without difficulty, although less efficiently he demonstrated a lack of forethought by parking the ambulance in such a way that it was impossible to open the rear doors effectively. A wall of concrete prevented their being opened more than an inch. The driver, who was a Private soldier, noticed his mistake as soon as he approached the rear of the ambulance, and berating himself for being such an idiot, turned about with the intention in mind of driving forward a metre to rectify the situation. Unfortunately for all concerned, just as he was about to clamber up to get behind the wheel, the air-raid siren began to wail, and moments later he noted several figures running for the nearest shelter, whilst others were running just as fast towards a gun emplacement. The events unfolding presented the lowly Private with a singular moral dilemma. The decision he needed to make was either to complete the task in hand and risk being caught in the open, the most drastic consequence of which would undoubtedly be to be killed for doing his duty so conscientiously, or alternatively leave the Luftwaffe officers to their fate and run for cover. Needless to say he didn't spend long in thought, and having decided long ago that in principle his primary responsibility was to survive the war, he opted to save his own skin by making a beeline for a shelter some seventy metres away. The shelter in question was a simple construction. It was essentially a tunnel built in the shape of the letter E minus the bit in the middle. The walls surrounding the tunnel supported a mound of grass-covered earth, which meant that those seeking safety inside were well protected from strafing. The siren continued to sound as the driver made himself as comfortable as possible within the cramped confines of the shelter. He did this by sitting on the cold concrete floor with his knees drawn up in front of him, allowing the left and right patella to rest in the hollow of its matching elbow. The soldier made a number of discoveries as he waited for the sequence of whines and crumps that would have been indicative of bombs falling from the sky and detonating across the airfield, as he sat waiting for the battery of 88 millimetre anti-aircraft guns to engage the enemy. His first discovery was to realise that he was not alone in the shelter. Three individuals whom he took to be Luftwaffe ground crew had entered the shelter before him, and like three wise monkeys they were seated in a row with their backs to the wall. The second spark to ignite with apparent spontaneity and flash across the Private's synapses to end in a thought distinct from that which had gone before it, brought about the realisation that the keys to the ambulance were not on his person. That didn't prevent him from patting in turn each pocket of his uniform just to make sure. In due course he surmised, correctly as it transpired, that the keys in question were dangling where he had left them, in the ambulance ignition. This oversight caused him more anxiety than the prospect of imminently being bombed. He had signed for the ambulance, and didn't want to lose it, though he wouldn't have minded, assuming that his passengers had woken up and left by this time, if it were to be obliterated. If, on the other hand, the ambulance were to be merely stolen, the punishment he envisaged of being sent to Stalingrad in time for Christmas caused him to shiver involuntarily. The odd-man-out in the shelter remained silent for the duration of the alert, whilst the others made either caustic comments about life in what they considered to be the back of beyond, or why it was that they never ended up in the same shelter as the Frauleins from the communication centre.

Ten minutes had elapsed since the siren signalling the onset of the raid had died away, and still no explosions or guns were to be heard. In point of fact the alert was either a drill or a false alarm, for not a single Allied aircraft attacked the airfield that morning. This lack of aggression was eventually signalled by the siren sounding the all-clear, the wailing of which penetrated Hauptmann Hebbel's subconscious mind to wake him from his slumber. For a few moments he lay in a semi-conscious state. He sought to differentiate dream from reality, but was confused by the fact that they seemed to be progressing in tandem. He was vaguely aware that the black, open-top carriage he had been driving around the park was in danger of being attacked by a swarm of mosquitoes. His concern for the safety of the pair of Holstein horses in harness, gave way to the realisation that he wasn't really in a carriage, but in the back of a captured British ambulance which might, in the ensuing minutes, inadvertently be attacked by a Mosquito not of the order Diptera, but of the fighter-bomber order of entities.

Hans swung his legs over the side of the bed and reached across the aisle to shake the still sleeping Ernst by the shoulder. By now there was sufficient light being filtered through the holes and cracks for Hans to be able to see the Oberleutnant open his eyes.

"Are we there yet?" asked the navigator upon waking, aware that a siren was wailing quite close by, though he didn't immediately register its significance.

"There's an air raid in progress," informed Hans mistakenly, unaware that he had slept through the alarm that had sent everyone not on essential duty running to the shelters. "What can you see through the holes, anything that might tell us what's going on?"

These days, as an adult of some considerable experience, Hans didn't mind being in dark surroundings, but figuratively speaking he hated being in the dark with regard to plans and events appertaining to him.

"Well, we're certainly back where we belong, and although that damned siren would seem to indicate otherwise, the view from this side of the truck reveals nothing out of the ordinary," Ernst reported, having closed one eye to gaze with the other at the uninspiring scene of a runway flanked by grass. "In fact the only signs of life that I can see are a few crows sitting on the perimeter fence. They don't seem to be concerned about anything in particular. Besides, the thought has just occurred to me," the Oberleutnant added, turning his head to look up at Hans as the latter tried the door handle, "being inside an ambulance with huge red crosses on the roof, back and sides isn't such a bad place to be. It's more comfortable than a shelter, and not nearly so smelly."

"You may well be right," replied Hans, his frustration at not being able to open the doors clearly discernible. "But how can you be absolutely certain that we're about to be attacked by the British?"

The rhetorical nature of the question had no influence whatsoever on the fact that the speaker almost spat the words, as ineffectually he rattled the door handle backwards and forwards several times. Finally, exclaiming, "Verdammt!" he gave up.

"Do you think that it's designed not to open on the inside so that delirious patients can't jump out while the truck's moving?" asked Ernst, only half seriously.

"Come on!" exhorted Hans, ignoring Ernst's enquiry completely. "Let's see if we can get the thing open by the application of a little more force than can be applied with bare hands," and leading by example he sat with his back against the end of the bed on which he had slept longer than he should have, and with feet together thrust his legs forward with all the muscle power he could muster. He struck the door with the heels of his boots.

Despite the violence of the impact the doors failed to open at this first attempt at using brute force. The second attempt should have been successful but wasn't, for on this occasion Oberleutnant Eckener had imitated the actions of his superior, but unfortunately without the necessary syncopation. For the third attempt the Hauptmann took command, and after counting, "Eine, zwei, drei," the officers kicked the doors simultaneously, their boots striking the metal panels centimetres from each of the handles. Under normal circumstances the doors would have flown open with such momentum that they could have caused serious injury to any unsuspecting individual passing by; not so this time, however, simply because the force applied proved easily resistible as almost instantly the doors came into contact with the presently immoveable object that was the concrete wall. The clattering of hard things sounded ominous for Hauptmann Hebbel's plans not to be ridiculously late for the briefing. Checking his watch, the Hauptmann thought that when eventually he was called upon to give an account of the night's proceedings, which was inevitable, his superior officer would be just as likely to laugh with derision as allow his physiognomy to show signs of rage. For Hans the prospect of being laughed at was more annoying than the chastening experience that he had thought, up until this alternative outcome had presented itself, was in store for him. The officers raised themselves to their feet to inspect at close quarters why the doors wouldn't open. Ernst placed his hand on the dented metal and pushed it gently until the door was pressed firmly against the unyielding obstruction.

"Der Tolpel!" he exclaimed.

The driver had acquired the status of a dolt in the Oberleutnant's eyes because his deeds, whether mindless or mischievous, had just become apparent to the trapped officers, and with that awareness came the realisation that there was nothing they could do to escape their predicament but call for assistance, or wait. Hans commented that they might as well save their energy for the time being for the simple reason that nobody was likely to be passing in the middle of an air raid.

Meanwhile, concerned about the security of the vehicle he was meant to be in charge of, the driver of the ambulance was delighted to see that the machine, the peculiar shape of which left him in a quandary as to whether it was ugly or handsome, was where he had left it. He was just about to jog across to assuage his anxiety completely by confirming that the keys were where he supposed, when he was deflected from his purpose by a restraining hand placed firmly on his shoulder. The hand the Private caught sight of was big and gnarled, with skin that resembled the bark of a tree. The soldier turned round to find that he was confronting one of the three wise monkeys from the shelter, to discover that the man who had detained him was a Stabsfeldwebel in need of another minion to assist with a specific task he had in mind. From shelters strategically positioned in relation to the aerodrome's buildings, people were returning to their routine duties, though none of this activity was visible through the holes in the ambulance's side.

"Come with me Private," ordered the Warrant Officer. "There's a small job I want you to help us with. After all, you can't expect to enjoy Luftwaffe hospitality and not give something in return."

"But sir, I've got to…" began the soldier, in a state of some confusion as his eyes flitted from the rugged features of the man standing close by to the more youthful countenances of the airmen standing slightly behind and at either side of the man in charge.

"No buts," interrupted the Stabsfeldwebel. "Let me put it to you this way, if you don't volunteer I'll put you on a charge."

Once again the hapless soldier brought to mind an image of a winter scene far removed from the quiet, almost friendly, snowfalls blanketing the pine forests at home, where, as promised by the lights shining from many a cottage window, his own included, comfort beckoned. By way of contrast he knew for certain that opportunities for eating bratwurst and drinking Glühwein in the rubble of Stalingrad would be extremely limited. With the sharpness of mind possessed by a great many, if not all, of life's born survivors, the Private also reasoned that if the trapped Luftwaffe officers had been awakened by the furore generated by the siren, and being eager to stretch their legs in the sun, were becoming restless, the Stabsfeldwebel had just provided the soldier with another reasonable excuse for the delay in letting them out by his absence. In the instance of being admonished, he would, with resounding sincerity, be able to pass on the blame so that responsibility rested squarely on the shoulders of the Stabsfeldwebel whose name he didn't wish to know. Dutifully he followed the Warrant Officer to perform the special task.

The task which required his assistance involved the positioning of a dilapidated car which had been transported to the airfield earlier that morning atop a flatbed lorry. The airmen and soldier made their way towards the main gate where the driver of the recovery vehicle was awaiting instructions regarding where to take his load. On their way, acting in the manner of Warrant Officers in armies, navies and air forces the world over, the Stabsfeldwebel sought to impose his authority over anyone of inferior rank whose present role in life looked to be somewhat aimless; and so it was that by the time the little band of vehicle retrieval operatives arrived at the guardroom, yards from where the flatbed was parked, their numbers had swelled from four to eight. Not many in the Stabsfeldwebel's line of sight had managed to get away. Those that had succeeded in eluding his summons had either shouted something suitably vague back at the Warrant Officer whilst demonstrating a recently acquired sense of purpose in respect of something crucially important, or had simply turned a deaf ear.

"Don't worry about them," commented the Stabsfeldwebel to his band of followers. "They might think that they've got one over on me at the moment, but I have just the job in mind for those idlers later."

Nobody in the work party was really convinced. On arrival at the lorry transporting the car the airmen and soldier gathered round to inspect the damage to the vehicle all but one man recognised as being Major Hofmann's formerly plush Mercedes, the Major being the Camp Commandant. Clearly obvious was the fact that the erstwhile beauty of a car had not been involved in a collision. It was equally obvious, therefore, that the damage sustained had been malicious. The evidence for this was visible in the scratches which ran long and deep along the vehicle's sides from the engine to the boot, scratches which looked as if they had been gouged by a rake. In addition there were numerous indentations in the body-work which, according to the consensus of opinion, had been perpetrated by a man with a grudge in possession of a hammer. Compared to this damage the four flat tyres seemed insignificant, but none of those gathered, apart from the ambulance driver, and his knowledge amounted to little more than an accumulation of snippets of overheard conversation, was aware of the circumstances leading up to the act of vandalism. The Private was about to blurt out all that he knew about the matter, but at the last moment thought better of it and checked his urge to speak. His caution emanated from unresolved concerns, and he held his tongue now so that he didn't provide verbal ammunition for persons that did not wish him well to use in evidence against him later. In short, he didn't want to incriminate himself.

"Dumm Banause!" exclaimed an airman standing at the back of the group, a man evidently aggrieved that anyone in his right mind could perpetrate such wanton damage, and he proceeded to let it be known that it had long been an ambition of his to own a Mercedes, one that was in better condition than the model presently on display.

After a brief exchange of words with the driver of the lorry, who all this time had been waiting patiently in his cab, the Stabsfeldwebel ordered his men to climb aboard. Standing on the few centimetres of lorry space available either side of the chained-down Mercedes, with each man taking responsibility for his own safety, to a man the group held on to the sides of the car for the short journey to where the Stabsfeldwebel had said it was to go. Able to look down from their newly elevated position into the interior of the Commandant's car, what became immediately apparent to every member of the group was how much damage had been done to the upholstery, the consensus of opinion on this occasion concluding that a knife had been the weapon of choice.

Whilst the truck was in motion everyone holding on to the Mercedes was delighted to see, appearing from the right, a mobile crane arrive at the junction they were about to pass.

After giving way, the vehicle with the heavy lifting capability turned to follow their tail-lights. Initially the thoughts of the Private upon first seeing the damaged car were that he and the others were going to have to tackle what seemed like a Herculean task manually, though he hadn't quite worked out how they were going to get the Commandant's pride and joy off the lorry without causing further damage. The appearance of the crane was a godsend, and led the soldier to surmise that the task they were about to undertake wasn't going to be so difficult after all. Within a few minutes, either deliberately to provide a little excitement, or with little thought for those aboard, the lorry driver swung the flatbed round in front of the captured ambulance, his intention being to reverse into position. He applied the brakes when the rear of the flatbed was level, though obviously to one side, with the front of the ambulance. These manoeuvres were performed less than smoothly, causing several of the work party to lose their balance. Fortunately, however, nobody lost his footing completely. This disturbance to the general equilibrium was treated almost as sport, and as the only injury to occur was trivial, there was much light-hearted humour. This one and only injury was sustained by an airman when he jarred his elbow. This individual, who had sought to soothe the pain by rubbing, was the same man who had earlier expressed his ambition to own a Mercedes car, and, as a friend and colleague pointed out to him, his injury was probably caused by his having given offence to the god in the Danish pantheon of gods which looked after the interests of peasants. Immediately after the flatbed lorry came to a halt, the mobile crane drew alongside, the driver of the latter leaving just enough distance between the two trucks for him to be able to operate the jib effectively. The plan was simply to lift the car and lower it into position next to the ambulance. The driver of the mobile crane got out of his cab, and, after handing to the Stabsfeldwebel the straps needed to secure the car to the crane's hook, proceeded to release the chains which had kept the car in place on the flatbed. These he stowed in a metal box, which was an integral part of the flatbed behind the cab. Working with a sense of purpose which was spell-binding to watch, the Luftwaffe Feldwebel jumped down from the flatbed and climbed up into the cab of the crane to sit behind its array of levers. The crane swung into action. The Stabsfeldwebel handed the pair of straps on to the Private, giving him instructions to feed them through underneath the car just behind the front wheels and just in front of those at the rear, the intention being to ensure some stability when the crane took the strain.

Aware that there was a kerfuffle going on just outside the ambulance, the Luftwaffe officers imprisoned inside were at long last delighted to be able to observe some kind of activity, notwithstanding the fact that they were only able to see a fraction of what was happening only metres away. To do this the Hauptmann and the Oberleutnant demonstrated a blatant disregard for the state of the bed which had been occupied by Eckener, and clambered over it in their boots to take a peep at the first signs of life they had seen since arriving on the base other than for the coming and going of a few crows. Needless to say, the officers were optimistic that they would soon be released from their embarrassing predicament, and though they thought that the noise of the crane operating was perhaps loud enough to prevent their attempts to draw attention to themselves from being heard, that didn't prevent them from banging on the side of the ambulance with their fists and shouting for all they were worth. Their efforts were not in vain. The rumpus they made was heard just as the Stabsfeldwebel gave the crane operator the signal to lift, which he did by raising and lowering his hands, palms uppermost, three or four times. This followed hard upon his receiving the thumbs up sign from the soldier to indicate that the straps were securely in place.

The work party, the majority of whom had, as yet, done very little, turned towards the sound of the expletives, at which point the soldier decided that the time had come for him to take action. Without a by-your-leave he set off in the direction of the vehicle which he had come to think of as the ugliest thing ever made by Man, but his unilaterally determined progress was halted, albeit temporarily, by the Stabsfeldwebel's peremptory voice.

"And where do you think you're going?" the Warrant Officer asked.

"It's nothing to worry about sir," replied the Private confidently, "I'm the driver of that monstrosity, and this morning we gave a lift to a couple of your pilots."

The soldier turned his attention towards the centre of the group of airmen to direct his next comment.

"Wandering about like a pair of lost sheep they were," he said.

The reference to sheep was uttered at a volume slightly lower than the reference to his unit's act of altruism. Words which he considered to be the epitome of tact and diplomacy when aimed at getting a positive response from a bunch of Luftwaffe junior ranks would have more than likely backfired terribly if they had been overheard by the officers. In the Stabsfeldwebel's presence the Private was taking a chance, but he knew that he had got away with his jocularity, with making a remark which was tantamount to insubordination, when the Warrant Officer's smile reflected that of the others.

"Watch it lads!" ordered the Warrant Officer, effectively reasserting his authority over the men in the work party as the car began to rotate through several degrees three metres above their heads. Now was the time for concerted effort, and following the Stabsfeldwebel's example the airmen lined up with their arms raised ready to take a hold of the car while it was still in the air, their intention being to steady its descent and to ensure that when the flattened tyres came to rest, that the car was aligned properly in its designated position.

"Don't stand directly underneath the thing you dolt, Schmidt," commanded the Stabsfeldwebel addressing one of his men, an individual who had a reputation for being quite bright in the sense that he was able to quote lines from Goethe and Schiller, but who was thought to be lacking when it came to the application of that ubiquitous phenomenon referred to as common-sense. To a peel of laughter from his peers, Schmidt quickly got out of the way of the heavy weight dangling, not quite as precariously as the sword of Damocles, directly above his head, and slotted himself into a more sensible position next to the Stabsfeldwebel, a man for whom fate's tempter had considerable respect.

"Dummkopf!" exclaimed the Warrant Officer, though without really meaning it, for he had percipience enough to be aware that the man now standing to his left had a tendency to play the fool. "Steady there," the Stabsfeldwebel shouted to the crane operator as he and his men grabbed hold of the sills, and rear and front bumpers, when these parts were just above head height. "Bring her round at the front there," he instructed those men able to accede to his command.

Satisfied that the car was going to land, as it were, where he wanted, he called to the crane operator to lower away gently. Moments later the job was done.

While this had been going on, the soldier had turned the keys in the ignition of the ambulance expecting the engine to spark into life first time. This didn't happen, and neither did it happen at the second and third attempts. Just as he was thinking of giving up on trying to start the vehicle electronically, and was about to call upon the Luftwaffe to provide enough muscle power to be able to push the heavy truck away from the wall, seeing that the working party was now busy, he gave the engine one last try. To his surprise the engine began to splutter with the first signs of life, and to his subsequent delight, after a few uncertain moments when success or failure were in the balance, it settled down and began to purr. The Private was about to drive forward the short distance required when he noticed a group of Luftwaffe 'brass' approaching on foot from his left. They were about to cross in front of him. He made a decision to delay moving off until the group of three officers and an individual whose appearance made it difficult to determine what he might be had passed. The Private sat to attention, bolt upright so to speak, as the moustached figure a pace ahead of the others glanced his way. For the present the ambulance driver chose to ignore the din of one or more clenched fists striking the panel behind his seat, as well as the raised voices. He reasoned that the officers in the back couldn't be exacerbated further, whereas to move off at this juncture would be to test the patience of this second, higher-ranking group, and the officer leading the quartet looked as if he was already on the warpath.

To say that he was in a foul mood is an understatement. Major Hofmann had heard that his car had been recovered from a country lane in a damaged state as he sat down to breakfast in the Mess, and although the news had failed to spoil his appetite, he was abrupt to the point of rudeness with the pretty Danish waitress who had served him. The Camp Commandant certainly wasn't a man to cross swords with this morning.

Most of the personnel on the base were of the opinion that Major Hofmann wasn't a man to cross swords with at any time. This wasn't primarily because he strutted around the various offices and aircraft hangers hunting for minions to harangue; though as an observer of detail he was renowned for having an eagle eye, and although he wouldn't necessarily berate a young airman for walking with his hands in his pockets there and then, or question aircrew for being improperly dressed, he never forgot to mention these lapses in discipline to the duty officer at some point during the day. No; what people found to be most imposing, and somewhat disconcerting, about the Major was his uncanny resemblance to the Führer, a natural likeness which he accentuated to the best of his ability. Indeed, a casual observer couldn't help but notice that not only were Major Hofmann's facial features and overall physical demeanour similar to those of Herr Hitler, but he had also mastered many of the latter's more extravagant mannerisms. It was as if he had gone far beyond the mimicry performed by a mime artist, and had become his hero's, the Führer's, doppelganger. These aspects of the Major's persona were even a little intimidating to the higher-ranking officer following hard upon the Major's heels. A tall, striking figure of a man with a nonchalant manner, this was none other than Oberstleutnant Krupp, the Station Commander. He was followed by two men walking side by side as they engaged each other in conversation. One of the men was dressed in an ad hoc assortment of clothes.

His apparel may have been suitable for flying, but the totality didn't amount to a recognisable uniform. His interlocutor was dressed in the manner of Luftwaffe aircrew about to take part in operations. Not surprisingly, none of the members of the quartet passing in front of the ambulance was known to its driver, and the driver was disinclined to make their acquaintance. His present wish was for them not to take such a keen interest in his vehicle as they were undoubtedly taking. No doubt this was aroused by the fact that the object of their curiosity had obviously been captured, was British, and was therefore unusual. Fortunately, for the soldier waiting patiently in his cab, however, the interest of those at the top of Aalborg Airfield's hierarchy wasn't sufficiently aroused to ask him tedious questions. The officer leading the way had too much on his mind to be distracted for more than a moment by idle curiosity. When this officer and the group he was leading had passed, the Private drove his ambulance forward the short distance necessary. Hurriedly, after turning off the engine and pocketing the keys, he jumped down from behind the wheel and trotted around to the back to assist in whatever way he could, to show willing. Needless to say, having performed the one essential task, other than to assume the role of whipping boy his services were no longer required. For their part the Hauptmann and Oberleutnant were delighted to be face to face with the man whom they knew to be responsible for their enforced captivity, were gratified to have before them such a pathetic mass of protoplasm as the object of an enmity which had been bubbling up to boiling point over the past hour or so at last within their sights, and having jumped down from the back of the ambulance to stand almost nose to nose with the driver, the Hauptmann took a deep breath in order to be better able to release the pent-up tirade. At the point of delivery, however, curtailed from uttering a scathing word by hearing his own name, his need to express his anger was thwarted. Fortunately for the Private standing rigidly to attention and quaking in his boots in anticipation of having to contend with what he had known for some time was coming, the liberated officers were in much more trouble than he was, and the individual who had been most enraged by their high spirits, their japes and wheezes, their subterfuge, was standing in a state of high dudgeon only metres away.

"Hauptmann Hebbel... Oberleutnant Eckener... are you responsible for this... for this," the Major spluttered as he struggled to find the right word, "For this outrage?"

The rage he was feeling at the destruction which had been wrought upon his beloved car was almost palpable across the intervening space, and the trio about to become embroiled in a sequence of aggressive recriminations and defensive protestations in a ratio of two to one in favour of the attackers, were distracted from their relatively minor triangle of turbulence by the voice of higher authority, and as one they turned their attention towards the apoplectic Major. Oberstleutnant Krupp was standing behind Major Hofmann's left shoulder, and behind him stood the two individuals who looked ready for take-off. Krupp beckoned Hebbel and Eckener to approach as the Major took off his cap for no other purpose than to throw it down on to the bonnet of the car. The benighted officers did as they were bid, but not before Hauptmann Hebbel turned towards the Private to tell him to remain standing to attention precisely where he was. With a nod of the head the Private indicated his willingness to obey.

He did not inwardly rejoice at the plight of his former passengers, the 'schadenfreude' he had half expected to feel being overruled by an awareness of how hierarchical institutions and organisations work. He knew that the opprobrium he was presently witnessing would, in turn, unless the beneficent hand of his own personal god were to intercede, be meted out with greater malevolence to him.

"Hauptmann Hebbel," said the Major emphatically. "am I right in thinking that you took my car on Friday without permission so that you and your accomplice in crime," and at this point, by a fleeting glance, he indicated the Oberleutnant, "could spend a weekend of debauchery with a couple of tarts?"

The Major was leaning forward, the weight of his upper body supported by hands, one of which projected two tobacco-stained fingers, splayed upon the grey metal of the wreck. His questioning of the Hauptmann had begun in a tone which suggested that the Major had regained his composure, but by the time he had impugned the character of his subordinates' female companions, nobody was under any illusions, for nobody could doubt that his inner being was anything other than a cauldron steaming with emotion. Now it was the turn of the miscreant officers, both of whom were standing to attention, to experience a slight trembling in the knees, a queasy sensation in the stomach. The public nature of their humiliation added to their discomfort. The pair who had been engaged in conversation now stood quietly in the background in an attitude of respect adumbrated with embarrassment.

"I can't speak for Oberleutnant Eckener's floozie," replied the Hauptmann, "but I resent your calling the love of my life a tart."

To gild the lily (des Guten zuviel tun) wasn't Hebbel's normal mode of expression, but he was aware that he was doing so in describing his relationship with Hanne in such a high-minded manner, his rationale being that the best form of defence is attack. If, however, he thought that his attempt to placate the Major was going to be served well by the injection of humour, as exemplified by his oblique reference to Ernst's relationship with Margareta, and implying in this regard that the Major's comments might not be so wide of the mark, he was utterly mistaken. Not only did he notice out of the corner of his eye that his friend's reaction was to scowl rather than smile, but unmissably that the Major had hit new heights of ire. Thumping the car with such force that he hurt his hand (though he only became aware of the pain much later, when his ire had cooled), at the top of his voice Major Hofmann shouted, "I'll call your Danish whores what I damn well like!"

At this juncture an unexpected event occurred which altered the scenario dramatically. Occupying the sidecar attached to the motorcycle which had led the column, Leutnant Schultz arrived. After ensuring that his men had been fed and watered, so to speak, and this despite the interruption to breakfast imposed by the wailing siren, he had come to reclaim his missing Private. In this quest the distinctive livery of the ambulance was useful, and having seen the red cross on a white circle from far off, he had decided that the vicinity of the otherwise olive-green vehicle was the best place to begin his search. What he discovered there proved him right.

The arrival of the Army officer was a godsend to the Private who had been anticipating chastisement, and he saw in the person of Leutnant Schultz the hand of fate interceding. For his part Leutnant Schultz was astonished to find himself clambering out of the motorcycle sidecar under the watchful eyes of no lesser mortal than Adolf Hitler, or so he thought; and why wouldn't he? The black hair styled in such a way that it curved down from the right side of the head to sweep round in a continuous line around the left ear, incongruously revealing more of the forehead above the right eye than the left; the eyes that could pierce a person's skin in order to analyse their blood; and the moustache narrower than the mouth and seemingly stuck on half a centimetre above the upper lip; all provided, on the basis that imitation is the sincerest form of flattery, strong clues as to whom the Major sought to flatter.

What caused the Army Leutnant to pause for thought, however, was the dexterity with which the man who resembled Hitler used both hands, and the fact that he was wearing an Air Force Major's uniform. Perceptive to the slightest nuance revealing the state of mind of the individual whom he happened to be observing, Oberstleutnant Krupp smiled at the newcomer's confusion, the reason for which he had divined correctly. In due course, and it was only a matter of seconds, Leutnant Schultz dismissed the idea that he was standing face to face with the Führer, but he put a special effort into his normally impeccable salute just in case. Armed with a little prior knowledge as to why the group was gathered around the damaged car, the Army officer was able to quickly synthesise the diverse elements of the scene before his eyes. Sensing that emotions were running high, Schultz tentatively requested permission to speak.

"Yes, what do you want?" snapped Major Hofmann.

"I've come to collect one of my men... that soldier over there in fact," replied the Leutnant, turning his head in the direction of the individual whose fate was about to be decided.

"Yes, get your man and go," barked the Major.

"But sir, I was..." interjected Hebbel, aware and aggrieved by the probability that the Private who had been the cause of so much trouble to Ernst and himself was about to get away with his errors of judgement.

Hebbel's interjection was interrupted,

"If you dare to question my authority once more Hauptmann Hebbel, I'll put you on a charge and have you shot," the Major warned, glaring at the hapless Hauptmann in a decidedly sinister manner, and so seriously did the latter take the threat that he became immediately 'schtum'.

"And the ambulance sir... it belongs to us?" added Leutnant Schultz, eager to escape the maelstrom which threatened to engulf all that came too close and stayed too long.

"Yes! Yes! Take it! Take it!" ordered the Major, gaining some satisfaction from the thought that by letting the Army officer and his men go their own way he was spoiling Hebbel's and Eckener's plans in ways which he would be happy to imagine.

Conscious of the fact that he was being watched by the Stabsfeldwebel and his work party, as well as by the bevy of officers, directing his compliment specifically at the Oberstleutnant – he being the highest-ranking officer present – once again Leutnant Schultz saluted smartly. Rather insouciantly the Oberstleutnant returned the compliment. Then, with a succession of nods and gestures but no words, the Leutnant directed the ambulance driver to get into his vehicle and start the engine. Moments later, from his seat in the sidecar, without a backward glance, with a forward motion of his hand the Leutnant gesticulated for the two vehicles to move off, first to rendezvous with the others at the gate, and subsequently, many months later, for the motorcycle rider and his passenger to rendezvous with death. Schultz would meet his end in the cellar of a farmhouse a few miles inland from Cherbourg, his body burned to a cinder by an American flame-thrower. The man on the motorcycle would ride into the sunset after being shot as he sped along a quiet country lane, again in La Belle France, by a lone sniper from the Maquis. The ambulance driver was destined to survive the war, and helped to rebuild the new Germany by running a bar, which nightly showed pornographic films, in the British Sector of Berlin.

With the departure of the Army unit, Oberstleutnant Krupp, in his usual quiet manner, took command of the situation.

"I understand that you have good cause to be angry with these officers Major Hofmann, and they will indeed be called to account," he said, turning his attention from the Major to glare at the malefactors. "But you two have a mission to complete, a mission which is already over an hour behind schedule. I don't need to remind you Major that operational matters take precedence, and so the officers taking part and myself will go to the briefing room to make preparations for take-off at 0900 hours. Hauptmann Hebbel, Oberleutnant Eckener... you may relax gentlemen... allow me to introduce Leutnant Kaiser from Das Abwehr. Leutnant Katz you already know. Major Hofmann you may direct the work party as you see fit."

After Hebbel and Eckener had shaken the hand of their Abwehr guest, the officers left behind all concerns and considerations related to the damaged car in order to go over the details of their mission to photograph, with a view to bombing, the Yorkshire dams.

Chapter Twelve

Aarhus

If they had as yet to order their breakfast rather than it already having been prepared and brought to them, Astrid and Hanne would have excused themselves to Hanning and made a hasty exit coincident upon the arrival of the soldiers, but with coffee and omelette steaming in front of them, there was no possibility of not eating breakfast in the company of the Wehrmacht, that is to say five of its number. For their part, if the young women had got up and left, in all probability the soldiers would have come to the conclusion that the café they had chosen as a venue in which to unwind was lifeless, and gone elsewhere in search of female company.

Perhaps it was because on a bright day in autumn the war seemed so far away that the soldiers were in good spirits and on a mission to please; though not just anybody of course. Their collective demeanour was that of a band of warriors seeking to make conquests of a different kind, or alternatively that of a gang of boys just let out of school for the holidays. Dressed smartly in field-grey uniforms, the tunic of which, without exception, was tucked into a black belt with a silver buckle, each soldier, most following the example of the Unterscharführer at the front of the file, had respectfully removed his cap before he had taken two steps inside the café. The last man through the door had had his removed for him by the soldier directly in front, the latter having been eager to demonstrate the teaching of good manners by hands-on methods. An unprepossessing individual, the Unterscharführer attended to the knot of his tie as he approached Hanne's and Astrid's table. Slyly he looked down and askance to ascertain what effect his preening was having on the Danish women. Unaware in a conscious sense that they were imitating their leader, each soldier in turn did likewise as he sought to embed the black cloth of the most impractical item of clothing designed to be worn by humankind (aesthetic considerations notwithstanding), snugly into the stiff collar of his

116

shirt, which, in stark contrast to the tie, was white. The Unterscharführer couldn't help but notice the dish the ladies were eating and that one of them, he presumed the brunette, had refined literary tastes. He made the assumption as to the ownership of the book simply from the fact that the text on the front cover could easily be read from where the brunette, Astrid, was sitting.

The words in English, being also the right way up for the Corporal to be able to read with equal facility, were a stimulus to his senses, and were it physically possible his reaction would have been similar to that of a horse when, on being offered a slice of apple or a carrot as a reward for good behaviour, it pricks forward its ears.

"To be or not to be," recited the Unterscharführer, enunciating arguably the most famous words in English Literature with an accent which, although difficult to place in a specific locale, was clearly English and not German; "That is the question, ja... I mean, yes?"

Despite their unwillingness to have anything to do with the mating game over breakfast, and no doubt with the individuals in close proximity at any time, with her mouth filled with omelette, out of politeness Hanne, her lips closed tightly together, gave the newcomers a toothless smile. This gesture in recognition of the soldiers' humanity was not replicated by Astrid. Reaching for her shoulder bag slumped on the chair beside her, she was about to put away the book which had become the focus of attention, but was prevented from doing so by the Unterscharführer's outstretched hand. By this time, having grown a little impatient at the delay, the Corporal's comrades had squeezed past him to settle themselves at the table closest to that which Hanne and Astrid occupied, situating themselves between the women and the bar. Hanning bid his latest customers good morning as he waited to take their order.

"May I see the book please," requested the Unterscharführer, yet again speaking in English as he put the question which was really a command to Astrid.

Astrid felt under threat. She wasn't sure whether it was forbidden to read books in English, but though there might be no proscription of Shakespeare's plays, she could be absolutely certain that her seemingly harmless intellectual pursuit was not going to be encouraged, quite the opposite in fact. Consequently it was with a trembling hand that she picked up the book from the table. In acceding to the Corporal's request without question, however, Astrid had succeeded in putting him in two minds, and he was torn between acting with good grace in order to impress the ladies, or assuming the role of a fascist, book-burning bully in order to impress his men. Astrid and Hanne knew already that there wasn't the slightest chance of their being impressed by the creepy specimen of German manhood standing before them, and the more unctuous he became the greater were his prospects for failure, creating, the harder he tried, an inverse ratio of matching proportions. He was a small-framed man with a pug nose. In observing his features from the front rather than from below, it was impossible not to be aware that his nostrils were more visible than they are on most people's faces, and this, unfortunately, gave him the look of a pig. In all other respects he resembled a weasel, its head protruding from the neck of a uniform which looked to be more than a single size too big, though the Unterscharführer was certain that it wasn't. No matter how brazen his manner, his eyes revealed a soul riven with fear and suspicion. The most striking aspect of his appearance, however, was the peculiar way in which his left ear stuck out from the side of his head at an odd angle, an angle much wider than that achieved by his right, tempting the beholder to believe that the Unterscharführer's auditory antennae had evolved differently from the rest of humanity, and that though unattractive in their obvious asymmetry, his ears were able to hear sounds toward which people whose hearing was good had no choice but to turn a deaf ear. Working on the premise that he was still in with a chance of stimulating Astrid's romantic interest, the Unterscharführer flicked through the pages of the book like a secret-agent searching for a code, a few lines of blank verse underlined here, a stage direction encircled there. Finding nothing of the sort, he at last found the speech he had been looking for and began to read aloud, beginning at the line of Hamlet's second soliloquy where the Corporal's knowledge of text learned by heart expired. To his chagrin he got only as far as 'the thousand natural shocks' when his attempt to project himself as a man of some literary sophistication and learning was undermined, and from two directions. First Hanne began to cough and splutter, acting as if a morsel of food had become lodged in her wind-pipe, which it hadn't. The greatest disruption to the Corporal's impromptu reading, however, was the loud summons for him to come and decide what he wanted from the menu, a call made naturally by one of his men. Surprisingly to the three Danes present, this entreaty was in colloquial English. The intrusions were enough to put the reader off completely, and the Unterscharführer, seeking to disguise his embarrassment, replied tersely in German, the language he resorted to when projecting his iron-will, his strength.

"Ja, ja, Ich kommt, Dummkopf!" he exclaimed, and then, turning to look directly at Astrid, he said, "I ought to confiscate, 'The Tragedy of Hamlet, Prince of Denmark', as subversive material."

The Unterscharführer waited for a response from Astrid, but none was forthcoming. He continued with his seduction by fear.

"However, I would love to re-acquaint myself with the works of the bard, and if I were to borrow the play I could return it to you next weekend, though of course, to be able to do that I would need to know your address."

The Unterscharführer smiled, ambiguously.

Now that she was fully alert to the real threat posed by the Unterscharführer, namely her suitor's bullying style of courtship, Astrid lost all fear, and thinking on her feet while remaining seated, she asked the Corporal if he had a pen she might borrow. At the same time she assertively took the book from his hand. The Corporal, with a glance at his colleagues to ascertain whether or not they were about to learn something useful from his imminent success (his own sense of self-worth would be all the more enhanced if they were) took out a pen from the top pocket of his tunic and handed it to Astrid. Meanwhile Hanne, who had not allowed any of the proceedings to distract her from the serious business of eating her breakfast, helped herself to a second portion of omelette.

"Hey, save some for me!" scolded Astrid playfully.

She hadn't yet swallowed a mouthful of hers. Turning once again to look up at the Unterscharführer with a smile on her face which foretold of future delights, she wrote down a number on the book's inside cover. She informed that this was her telephone number at her place of work, and in respect of all but one of the digits this statement was true.

"If you give me a call on Friday we could perhaps meet to discuss the premise that Hamlet showed cowardice in failing to avenge his father's ghost, or whatever aspect of the play you fancy. Now if you don't mind, I really would like to get on with my breakfast before my friend here scoffs the lot."

Astrid was only too happy to relinquish the book for ever and a day to be rid of this particularly objectionable individual's attentions. The Unterscharführer, beguiled by his vanity into falling for the simple subterfuge, after taking possession of the book and his pen, abruptly bowed his head and clicked his heels together. Only when he had moved away to pull up a chair and seat himself comfortably in the midst of his cronies did Astrid think it safe to confirm by question the seemingly incongruous information Hanne and she had gleaned with their eyes and ears, information which had signalled that the five soldiers in German uniform were not members of the master-race at all, but British.

"Yes, we're members of the Britische Freicorps," replied the soldier sitting directly behind Hanne.

He turned his chair side-on to the table so as to be able to converse more easily. Then he thrust forward the sleeve of his left arm to show the insignia which had been immediately apparent to the Café Kobenhavn's female patrons in their close encounter with the Unterscharführer, insignia which had niggled at each woman's psyche, but not so significantly that either party was able to make an inference. To the stoical Danes these soldiers wearing uniforms adorned with badges indicating rank and unit, and a number of esoteric things besides, at present resembled grown-up scouts, an impression reinforced by the absence of weapons. On the sleeve presented to Hanne for her perusal, approximately halfway between elbow and wrist, was a black band with white edging. Inclusive of the edging the band was about two centimetres width. Sown on the band in white letters were the words, 'Britische Freicorps'. Between this band and the elbow was a badge in the shape of a heraldic shield, and this was emblazoned with the Union Jack. Unbeknown to the women, the soldier eager to show that he was a traitor to the nation which the easily recognisable configuration of red, white and blue on his sleeve symbolised, spoke with an Antipodean accent.

"We were all captured before Dunkirk, and rather than spend the foreseeable future rotting in a POW Camp for a cause we were dubious about from the start, when given the opportunity to transfer our allegiance and take part in the great crusade against communism, we jumped at the chance."

In his enthusiasm this propagandist for fascism spoke quickly, but paused in his narrative when he realised that Hanne hadn't fully grasped all that he had said, and had asked her friend to translate into Danish the expression, 'jumped at the chance'. When everything he had said was clear to everyone listening, the traitor continued.

"I wouldn't personally want to fight against our own people of course, but that's not going to happen. We were given assurances that our unit, as soon as it is fully formed and trained, will be put into the line against the Ruskies. We're going to give Uncle Joe his comeuppance."

"And how many others are there like you in the German Army?" asked Miss Aakjaer boldly.

"We're not actually in the Army," replied the traitor eager to inform, "We belong to the Waffen SS, an elite organisation. To you ladies the difference is probably academic, but to us it's important... you know, inter-unit rivalry and all that; and as for numbers, well..."

At this point in the conversation the Unterscharführer, for genuine security reasons and not merely in an attempt to impress either the women or his men, ordered his fellow traitor to desist from revealing any more information about a unit which numbered only twenty-seven disaffected souls, and which, throughout its pathetic existence, never exceeded thirty.

"Perhaps you would like to go out with me one evening?" the garrulous Freicorps man asked Hanne in hope, hope based on the premise that he had nothing to lose and everything to gain by chancing his arm.

Rejection may not have been inevitable, but it was highly likely.

"I'm sorry. I already have a boyfriend. He's a pilot in the Luftwaffe," responded Hanne apologetically, and following this failure to emulate his leader, Hanne's suitor broke off the conversation completely, and turned his chair around to join in the bonhomie enjoyed by his peers, his pride hardly dinted.

At long last Astrid and Hanne were left to finish their breakfast in peace. The presence of the soldiers had prevented Hanne from discussing the matter which she had wanted to get off her chest, and the women finished their meal in silence. Their restraint was in stark contrast to the shallow but animated conversation going on behind them, and between the soldiers' ribald comments there were howls of laughter. If they had been asked subsequently, the women would have denied that they had been driven from the Café Kobenhavn by the oppressively boisterous atmosphere, but they undoubtedly were, to the extent that after quickly settling the bill they left the premises without a backward glance, and without a word of encouragement to the Unterscharführer's parting words, words which were voiced as a reminder that he would be in contact with Astrid at the end of the week. Upon emerging once more into the clear air of Stor Torv, both women felt a profound sense of relief at having escaped the attentions of the Britons, most of whom were destined to survive the war only to spend between them decades in Wandsworth prison. Sentences of up to fifteen years were the price they paid for their wartime treachery.

"Let's go and talk inside the cathedral," suggested Astrid, and without waiting for Hanne to respond she set off in the direction of Aarhus Domkirke. "I don't think we'll be interrupted by the Army, the Waffen SS, the Kriegsmarine, or even the Luftwaffe, in there on a Monday morning," she advised once her friend had caught up with her.

"You've omitted," responded Hanne, "to mention the Gestapo."

Miss Hjelmsleve was wise to express her concern at the prospect of being overheard in saying what she had to say to Astrid, for Gestapo headquarters was located in the city, just off Domkirkpladsen. The reputation of the Nazi organisation infamous for its ruthless interrogation methods was more terrifying than all the others put together, at least as far as the Danes were concerned.

121

In crossing the square the women made a point of not making eye contact with the soldier left guarding the trucks, and made their way directly to the door at the foot of the cathedral tower. Astrid had just put her hand on the knob of the wooden portal set in brick arches when her progress was arrested, not by the heavy hand of one of Himmler's henchmen, but by the softer, but nonetheless determined, restraint of Hanne's fair hand.

"It's such a beautiful day, rather than go inside let's just walk and talk instead. I'm sure there's nothing to worry about inside, and it would be safe to talk freely, but I've been cooped up like a chicken kept safe from the fox all weekend. A little fresh air will do me good, will do us both good. Put your arm through mine to show that nothing can come between us, you know, like we used to do when we were children walking to school, and we'll take a turn or two around the building, friends enjoying a stroll and a chat in the sunshine."

Astrid smiled her agreement, and she and Hanne set off on their perambulation arm in arm, initially following a path along the side of the great church that was in shadow. The drop in temperature once out of the sun was marked, and Hanne made a noise by vibrating her lips together rapidly to register the fact.

"Now what is it that you so desperately want to tell me?" enquired Astrid.

Fatefully Hanne felt that she was able to give voice to the snippet of information which Hans had imparted to her, and she told Astrid that in her opinion a round-up of Jews was in the offing.

"Tell me what his exact words were," said Astrid peremptorily, her face expressing her concern.

"He said if you have any Jewish friends tell them it would be better to leave Denmark as soon as possible," said Hanne, unaware that she was guilty of elision, an omission that didn't much matter anyway, seeing as how the missing words, if quoted, wouldn't have altered the gist of the warning, nor provided an additional nuance of meaning.

"And you're sure this pilot of yours wasn't telling you this merely to set you and the people you told up for the chop?" asked Astrid, gazing at Hanne intently as she searched for the slightest intimation of doubt in the silent language which was either going to, or not going to, back up her words. She found no discrepancy.

"Without a shadow of doubt," responded Hanne unequivocally. "And because I don't come into contact with Jewish people that often, and there's nobody I know of that Faith whom I could call a friend, I could have quite easily dismissed Hans' warning as irrelevant; but no, I came to the conclusion that were I to do or say nothing, I would be behaving either in a cowardly manner or totally selfishly. Nonetheless, on my way to meeting you in the Café Kobenhavn, I did mildly imprecate Hans for having burdened me with what amounts to a state secret."

"It's not a Danish state secret," interjected Astrid, and after a few moments reflection she added, "Why did you single me out to share your burden?"

"I suppose for a number of reasons," replied Hanne as the friends turned the corner of Denmark's longest church to emerge once again into bright sunlight; the sudden warmth on their faces was as pleasant as a kiss bestowed by a lover upon first meeting after a period of absence. "I chose to tell you because I trust you implicitly, and believe that I can tell you anything that's of concern to me. They do say that a problem shared is a problem solved, don't they?"

"I think that mainly applies to married couples," commented Astrid.

"Well, as neither of us is married, I don't see why that principle can't also be applied to friends. In fact, as we can testify, it often is. Anyway, I needed to get this… this burden… this state secret off my chest… not only to prove to myself that I am neither a coward nor a selfish person, but for the fact that I know that your friend Sara is Jewish.

Hanne was referring to a close friend of Astrid's with whom she herself was acquainted, but only slightly.

"Although I haven't had much time to reflect on the significance of Hans' words," Hanne continued, "It's been long enough for me to imagine how I would feel if somebody I knew to be your friend were to be taken in for questioning by the Gestapo, and I hadn't done anything to prevent, when it was in my power to do so, such a nightmare event taking place. I wouldn't be able to live with myself."

"Then we had better do something about it," said Astrid, demonstrating her resolve as the pair arrived at the cathedral's Golden Gates.

Chapter Thirteen

River Ebro

After filling their water bottles in the river – each member of this small element of the British Battalion of the XII International Brigade carried two – the Scotsman ordered his men to move off. He hadn't thought it necessary to introduce himself to his captives, but George had overheard the man who was small in stature but big in presence being referred to as 'the Captain', at which point he had made the correlation, correctly as it turned out, between the rank that was mentioned and the man leading the way. Aware, in a linguistic sense, that everything he said was hardly in an indecipherable code to their captors, George nonetheless made the observation to Harry that the Captain didn't have many men to command. In saying this quite openly he half expected to be told to be quiet by the republican soldier bringing up the rear, that or worse; and though the man at the back would have had to have been deaf not to have heard, he kept his mouth shut.

"Perhaps," said Harry, prior to cursing under his breath as he stumbled upon uneven ground, and then adding upon returning to his train of thought, "He's managed to get the rest of his men killed, or perhaps this lot have simply lost contact with the others."

With their hands tied behind their backs, ground which was relatively easy to cover for individuals able to coordinate the movement of all four limbs, proved problematic for the pair whose arms were thus restricted.

"Perhaps they're a commando unit on a special mission," retorted George, allowing his imagination to wander.

"What's the score mate?" asked Harry, risking losing his balance completely by turning around to address the last man. "Where's the rest of your unit?"

The last man pondered for a few moments over whether he should answer the question honestly.

In the end he decided that it would be unwise to give anything away, particularly as he had been given specific instructions to let the prisoners talk freely in order to glean what intelligence he could. This didn't imply that there was to be an equal exchange of information.

In response to Harry's question, the republican soldier, after adjusting the position of his weapon in the crook of his arm, smiled benignly and said, "I would watch where I was going if I were you mate."

Before stumbling for the second time, and this time so demonstrably that he managed to lose his balance completely, Harry was able to note a look in the features of the soldier whose advice he should have heeded, a look which he recognised to be that of a friend rather than a foe, not insofar that it was likely that his guard's ideological views had changed over the last half hour, but in the bond created in the longer time-line of their shared ancestry. He saw in the strong jaw-line and the long, straight nose, all of which were evenly tanned, the admirable strength of the island race to which he himself belonged, and he gave a smile of acknowledgement to that recognition. In return, the soldier smiled upon helped Harry to his feet.

At the edge of the boundary formed by the trees and bushes which followed the line of the river, the Captain ordered his men to halt, spread out on either side of him, and stay in cover. There were no words of command, merely hand gestures. The exceptions to this meagre deployment were his prisoners and the soldier keeping an eye on them – Harry's newfound friend. The Captain took from the side-pocket of his trousers a small pair of field glasses and proceeded to scan the positions which had previously been occupied by troops of the Spanish Legion. This defensive line, which had been the primary objective of the republican attack on that first day of battle, incorporated the trench which had been dug and then modified by the captive Englishmen. Many of the Legion's fugitives from justice in their country of origin had been killed, a greater number, el buen mayor included, had retreated. Only four had inadvertently advanced. Now half that number were dead, and the other two – George and Harry – were prisoners of an uncertain fate.

Seated on the ground with a rifle pointing in their general direction from somewhere close behind them, a position from which it was nigh on impossible to fire and miss, George Gilbert and Harry Herbert Osborne found themselves directly behind the man in charge. After scanning his objective for the second time, the Captain turned around to speak directly to George.

"Are there any mines or booby-traps that I should be aware of?" he asked.

George's first thought was that here he was dealing with a cautious man, and as such it was highly unlikely that he would have needlessly sacrificed the rest of his command. This hasty assessment of the Captain's character was immediately followed, however, by a contradictory thought which suggested, as he remembered the adage, 'Fortune follows the brave', that perhaps the Captain had been over-cautious, and the majority of his men had been annihilated as an unexpected consequence.

"Well!" exclaimed the Captain with impatience. "Are you going to answer my question?"

If George had required assistance in coming to a decision as to whether or not he should respond, it was aptly provided by the jolt of a gun barrel placed directly between his shoulder blades. Not wishing for there to be the slightest confusion, George was precise in his response.

"Yes, I will answer your question, and no, there are no mines or booby-traps, at least as far as I'm aware."

Attempting to gauge the sincerity of the Yorkshireman's reply, the Captain's cold, penetrating eyes gazed at Legionnaire Gilbert intently. He believed his prisoner, but he warned him nonetheless.

"If any of my men are killed or wounded because one of your fascist friends has left a nasty surprise, I'll overrule what I said earlier about our not being your executioners and shoot you myself."

At that moment the Captain received a tap on the shoulder from the soldier kneeling almost at his side. The officer turned his attention away from the captives to follow the line of sight indicated by his subordinate's index finger pointing to the left along the uneven line of dense vegetation. Soldiers were emerging into the open to make their way up the slope towards the lifeless fascist lines. It was amazing how many men of the British Battalion of the XII International Brigade the trees and bushes along the banks of the Ebro had hidden. In the middle distance a number of republican soldiers were taking no chances by following in the tracks made by a tank. It was probably the same machine that had appeared to threaten George and Harry so menacingly. The Captain, whom the captured Legionnaires had heard referred to as, 'Captain MacDonald, sir', rose to his feet and stepped out from cover. He held up both arms, his right hand still holding his weapon. The signal indicated was for the small band of warriors with whom, by dint of circumstance, the officer had the closest rapport, to advance in arrowhead formation. Slowly but surely they, and everyone else in the battalion able to march, narrowed the distance between themselves and their objective. Captain MacDonald and his personal bodyguard did not proceed on a line of march directly ahead, for the diminutive officer had decided to traverse the slope at an angle, directing himself and his men towards the ruined farmhouse, the walls of which were more dilapidated now than they had been before the recent barrage. Gradually these remnants of the British battalion began to relax in their minds, to lose the sense of alertness necessary to take the correct immediate action were they yet again to come under fire. They had been on the move since first light, and now, towards the end of a day in which they had sweated buckets, so to speak, a day in which they had absorbed into their lungs air pungent with the smell of cordite, a day in which they had heard men curse, and had heard men scream, and ultimately seen men fall never to get up again, they needed to rest. Being soldiers whose job is to do or die, however, rest was not immediately forthcoming, for the first job on the unwritten agenda after taking over the fascist positions was to prepare for a counter-attack. This necessitated reinforcing each dug-out so as to be prepared to repel an onslaught from the direction opposite to that for which they had been prepared initially. Secondly, a sizeable number of corpses had to be disposed of. The good news was that there were considerably more live souls than dead bodies waiting to be organised. The bad news from George and Harry's standpoint was that although they were prisoners of war, they could be used as slave labour if Captain MacDonald so wished. From the perspective of their continued survival, the prisoners were thankful that so far there had been no indication that any of MacDonald's men had fallen down a hole to be pierced by a spike, or that a hand-grenade cunningly hidden had blown up in a volunteer's face. In this regard they really didn't want to test their captor's resolve. They didn't want to be shot for the dastardly deeds of others.

Between sixty and seventy per cent of the Battalion had survived the attack, and under the direction of their surviving officers, the men worked into the night and all the next day to clear the lines of corpses and bury them. In effect the soldiers created a cemetery in an open area of ground which, in less turbulent times, had been the farmhouse garden. Two pits were dug about twenty yards apart and running parallel with each other. Into the communal grave which had been the first to be made ready to receive occupants were placed the bodies of fallen comrades, into the other, the corpses of the Legionnaires. Arranged neatly in rows with their feet pointing uppermost, if for one last time they had been able to stir, friend and foe would have risen to stand shoulder to shoulder as they prepared to face the enemy, perhaps just as they had done when their hearts had pounded with excitement and blood had flowed through their veins in a continuous cycle. After ceremonies of equal duration and simplicity, short orations conducted consecutively by Captain

MacDonald, the rows of dead mothers' sons from here, there, and everywhere, were covered with the dry earth of Spain.

Demonstrating remarkable grace the Captain had first asked George if he would like to say a few words over the grave of his fallen brothers-in-arms, but without stating a reason why, Legionnaire Gilbert declined the invitation, as did Osborne when he was asked. The prisoners had spent an uncomfortable first night in captivity, not only because of the hard ground that was their mattress, but also because of the cold, a cold which was all the more penetrating because the temperatures during the day were high. In these conditions, their heads and backs supported by the only section of wall to survive to a height above three feet, sleep was fitful. More than once George, and at other times Harry, had wakened to find that the guard watching over them was a different person, though each of the sentries adopted the same position, seating himself on a couple of empty ammunition boxes stacked on their sides. On each occasion that one or other of the prisoners awoke shivering, and in rearranging the position of his limbs, discovered also that parts of his body were numb, he was immediately aware that the constellations had seemingly cranked forward a little in the otherwise inky darkness above his head, and though George and Harry were each aware that the changes in stellar scenery were caused by their own planet's relentless motion, they thought it a strange phenomenon nonetheless. The silent beauty of the night was not only, as one might expect, conducive to abstruse contemplation on the nature of existence, but also to more meaningful conversations than had hitherto been sustained by captives and captors as the latter appeared individually in compliance with the duty roster.

Despite their objections, but hardly contrary to their expectations, the captives had indeed been made to toil, guarded in the first instance by Harry's friend, the soldier who had earlier given the Londoner such apposite advice. Under different orders than those obeyed by the rank and file among their captors, George and Harry's first onerous task had been to retrieve for burial van Loon and his mate, and they had discovered that a lifeless body, particularly a body as big as van Loon's, is a heavy weight to carry on the level, never mind uphill. Harry's friend had made his prisoners work without respite until darkness had descended fully, when he himself was desperate to take the weight off his blistered feet. This lanky individual with an insouciant manner, obviously hailed from the North East of England, from County Durham to be precise, and after leaving the pit village where, because of his height, he had banged his head too many times for the sense which had been knocked into him initially not to be in danger of being knocked out of him again, he had come to Spain with the conviction in mind that he would be fighting not merely to prove the supremacy of every form of Government you could mention compared with fascism, but for the rights of the ordinary working man in his seemingly perpetual struggle against capitalist-supported tyranny. If asked the question, he would have answered unequivocally that he hated fascists and the ideology which engendered and then nurtured the belief that might is right, and if asked subsequently what might be considered the first question's natural corollary, he would have said that George and Harry were misguided fools, and had, simply because of their misguided foolishness, chosen the wrong side. Feelings of hatred towards the prisoners in his charge, insofar as they were living, breathing proponents of an evil creed, had dissipated with knowing. His attitude towards the knavish pair was that of a preceptor, a rather more forceful teacher than is ever likely to be found in a school. Without the slightest idea as to where his attempts at persuasion might lead, he took it upon himself to try to teach the fascist Britons the error of their ways. None of this high-minded intent had any bearing on the fact that when consulted by Captain MacDonald, he had volunteered to take the first stint of guarding the prisoners through the hours of darkness. His spell on duty was from eight till ten. There was much method and no madness in the Geordie's (he had given up telling people that he wasn't really a Geordie and responded to being hailed by his sobriquet without question) wily decision, for it didn't take a genius to work out that the first and last two-hour spell of guard-duty permitted a long period of unbroken sleep. It was during Geordie's time on duty, after an unexpected supper of roast jabali had been devoured hungrily, that the men with fascist beliefs and the man with communist leanings learned more about each other, and under the pacifying influence of the shifting stars and gibbous moon, the conversation began in quiet, wistful tones, without recriminations or bitterness.

"I suppose our situation, yours and mine, was probably a common occurrence in the civil war, our own civil war I mean, ya know, the scrap between the roundheads and cavaliers, the parliamentarians led by Oliver Cromwell and the royalists led by King Charles," commented George and Harry's self-appointed mentor as he made himself as comfortable as possible on the empty ammunition boxes.

Despite the fatigue which he felt in his sinews, and in his eyes, it was George, conscious that he really was a teacher at heart, who felt most inclined to engage his guard in conversation. He realised that it had been a long time since he had been involved in any form of intellectual discourse, and the man who had begun the exchange of ideas had a certain look about him, a look which revealed sensibilities underscored by keen intelligence. In the light of an oil lamp casting all three faces in an eerie glow, the Geordie gave to George the impression that he would be a worthy sparring partner in a bout wherein the left and right hooks would be words.

"Forgive me if I'm being obtuse, but would you mind pointing out the similarities to me, just so that we're not speaking at cross-purposes?" retorted the thwarted teacher.

There was no mistaking the fact that Legionnaire Gilbert's interest had been aroused, and he surmised that the man seated directly opposite was largely self-educated and probably well read.

"Well surely here's an obvious similarity in that we are all three of us Englishmen fighting on opposite sides in a civil war," replied the Geordie from Durham without bothering to differentiate by numbers who had been fighting whom. "I know we're in Spain and there are those that would argue that this is not our fight, but that aside, imagine what it must have been like after the Battle of Edgehill or Naseby: there were bound to have been prisoners watched over by guards that spoke the same language and ate the same kind of food. Christ man, there was possibly more than one occasion when a brother captured whilst fighting for the King was watched over by his brother under the command of Fairfax, or vice versa."

"Who was Fairfax?" interjected Harry bravely, prepared to show his ignorance in order that he might learn.

"He was the General who commanded the Parliamentarian forces at the Battle of Naseby," informed George willingly, savouring these few faint echoes of the role in life which he had thought he had left behind completely.

"That's right," confirmed the Republican soldier, eager to demonstrate that he too had some depth to his knowledge. "Although the Battles of Marston Moor and Naseby were undoubtedly great victories," he continued, assuming that his listeners were of the same opinion, "I think the way he suppressed the 'Levellers' was a disgrace.

Harry wanted to ask about the 'Levellers', but a second thought advised him to hold his tongue. George had heard the expression, but being unsure of his ground, also made no further reference to the radical seventeenth-century movement. Legionnaire Gilbert believed it to be a truism that everybody seeks to conduct his or her argument from a position of strength, and he certainly wasn't the exception that proves the rule, therefore, despite his humble circumstances, initially he sought to gain the ascendency. To prove himself equal by striving to be better than the man presently in control of his life was important for his self-esteem. Only later did he come to appreciate that victories gained in the short term do not necessarily lead to the successful attainment of long-term goals. For the present, even his desire to stay alive was subsumed by his eagerness to elevate himself by diminishing his opponent in this contest of minds.

"I can see perfectly well," he countered, "that there are indeed similarities in that we as Englishmen have been fighting on opposite sides, but the circumstance of our having become your prisoners is merely a coincidence, and I can tell you that it only happened because we were about some business too far in front of our lines, business which with the benefit of hindsight strikes me as having been rather foolish."

"I agree," interjected Harry. "If we hadn't gone to fetch mud we would be dead, or we would have retreated with the other survivors to sleep tonight in the bosom of our adopted family. I doubt that we would have become your prisoners."

George turned to look at Harry with a silently questioning expression, for he needed a few moments to work out whether his friend had made the comment in earnest, or if he was being deeply ironic. After several seconds of intense scrutiny, George returned the focus of his attention back to the soldier he was trying to enlighten, his quest being to reveal the error of that individual's ways.

"Although this war we're engaged in is being fought in Spain, its significance is much wider in scale than is defined by geographical borders. Indeed, so far reaching are the ramifications of this conflict that they can be described as being almost global. We are Englishmen and we are your prisoners. These are incontrovertible facts, but we could just as easily have hailed from one of any number of countries, and we could just as easily have been captured by Americans, French, Spanish, or whatever, given a different time and place in the context of this war. By the same token you might march on to be killed or taken prisoner by Italians, or Germans, or even the Irish."

In mentioning the enthusiastic participation of contingents from Britain's nearest neighbour on the nationalist side, in a jocular way George drew attention to their proven fighting qualities.

"Look what an Irishman did to Harry's teeth, and we were supposed to be on the same side. Go on, give the nice man a big smile Harry," ordered George; and responding unquestioningly Harry complied, thereby revealing his loss as a result of pugnacity. "Compared with this conflict," added George, his voice and manner returning to their former seriousness, "the English Civil War was a parochial spat. Victory for our side in this campaign, and in campaigns to follow, will see the eradication throughout Europe not only of the canker which is Jewish-controlled Capitalism, but also a few dangerous myths."

"Such as?" questioned the former miner.

131

"The democratic lunacy which would encourage us to believe that all men are created equal for a start," answered George. "Didn't Darwin tell us that all life on this planet progresses by means of evolution and that within any given species only the strongest and fittest survive to pass on their genes," he asked rhetorically, jumping forward in time as he sought to bolster his argument with ideas first promulgated in the nineteenth century. "What's more," he continued, "in his theory of inherited characteristics Darwin also explained why life in a biological sense is like it is."

"Christ man!" exclaimed George's adversary, unthinkingly resorting to his favourite epithet as he became increasingly incensed by the assault on his ears. The Legionnaire's words were anathema to him. "What sort of world do you think we would end up with if that dog-eat-dog mentality were to hold sway and become the accepted norm. Before long all those not conforming to a stereotype determined by Franco, Mussolini, Herr Adolf, or some other tin-pot dictator seeking apotheosis, will be eliminated, their machine-gunned corpses thrown into mass graves without ceremony, with as much thought given to their disposal as is given to an accumulation of household rubbish. Christ man! Do you suppose that a human being can be held responsible for where he or she emerges from the womb. From what I've heard in Nazi Germany they've established a pecking order, a league table determined by race with guess who at the top; not you as an Englishman that's for certain; so why do you want to lick Aryan boots?"

"I believe your prophecies to be fanciful," said George, wondering where in such a league the English might appear. "I certainly wouldn't want people to be killed willy-nilly simply because they were Jewish or in some other way racially inferior. There's a big difference between exterminating undesirable elements in society and preventing further reproduction. A programme of enforced sterilisation for those racially inferior, and generally for people of low intelligence and questionable behaviour, would solve society's problems within a generation as the weak fade away and the strong march on to a glorious future. And as for us, for the likes of Harry and I, the struggle for a new world order starts here. You mark my words, the battles fought here on the Ebro, in Asturias, in the high sierra of Andalucia and in the streets of Madrid, will point the way ahead not only for the Spanish people, but for Western civilisation."

"Will you keep the noise down over there, some of us are trying to get some sleep," called a voice from the darkness.

"It hasn't been an auspicious beginning to your struggle," responded the Geordie in a volume lower than he had spoken thus far. "For you personally I mean," he added contemptuously.

With that parting shot the republican soldier called a temporary halt to the discussion as he rose to his feet and stepped over what remained of the wall at the front of the house to answer a call of nature. His prisoners, though never out of his sight, were now able to communicate with each other in private, and Harry took full advantage of the opportunity to remonstrate with his friend about tactics.

"I think that you're getting through to him," said Harry. "But a fat lot of good it will do us if you antagonise him so much that he contrives a way to shoot us in the back for trying to escape."

George needed no further explanation as to where Harry thought he was going wrong, but as yet he didn't quite grasp how far Harry was prepared to take his policy of appeasement.

"You think that I might be pushing him over the edge?" asked George in a whisper. "It's amazing how agitated some people become when the basis on which they have lived their lives is undermined by the ruthless probing of a greater intellect."

"What you say is probably true," said Harry dismissively. "But it seems to me that it is better to lose a battle and win the war, and not the other way round, assuming that your discussion is the battle and our continued existence is the war."

"Point taken," said George thoughtfully, before adding somewhat naively. "What sort of game-plan did you have in mind? What do you suggest?"

"I suggest," answered the Londoner as their guard adjusted his clothing, evidently with some difficulty for being encumbered by his personal weapon, "that until you see the error of your ways and alter the thrust of you argument accordingly, you let me do most of the talking." Turning his head towards the approaching figure stepping back into the frame that was the rubble-strewn farmhouse floor, with obvious concern Harry asked, "Do you really think that if the fascist parties gain and hold on to power across Europe, that there will be mass executions of the type you described?" Without waiting for an immediate answer he continued, "George and I were just remarking that we could never condone such carnage, such evil; for evil is what it would be, wouldn't it?"

Chapter Fourteen

Flying at 250 knots – just under our top speed – The Daimler Benz engines purred beautifully as we approached the golden dunes of the Danish coast a few miles to the north of the Thyboren Kanal. Despite the weight of an extra man, the fact that we weren't carrying a payload meant that we had been lighter than usual on take-off, though we were, of course, considerably more cramped. Ten minutes into our journey, each man had made himself as comfortable as possible for what I'm sure each of us hoped would be an uneventful trip. Dieter Katz, my co-pilot, and I had the best seats, and I relaxed into mine as I let the aggravation of recent hours drain from me.

Ernst and the Abwehr man had installed themselves into the bowels of the aircraft, so to speak. Without risking the muscles in my neck, I could be almost certain what each of them was up to at that precise moment, for I had a clear mental image of Ernst setting his compass points on the relevant chart as Leutnant Kaiser reached down through the half-open bomb-bay to make fine adjustments to the especially installed cameras. I continued peering through the flight-deck window directly ahead, unable to take my eyes off a point along the strand where the sun glinted upon the water, where light of dazzling intensity came into being as a mass of ephemeral, aquatic snakes performing a frenetic dance. For several moments, as we drew ever nearer, I beheld the spectacle in a state of hypnotised wonder, and it took a tap on the shoulder from Dieter to break the spell and wake me from my reverie. He had seen something which had excited his curiosity, and judging by his facial expression, much more vibrantly than the natural phenomenon which I had been observing had aroused mine. My co-pilot was grinning broadly as he pointed with the thumb of his left hand to the sight of special interest which he had beheld on the aircraft's starboard side. I leaned over as far as I could crane my neck to peer down at the beach below, and saw nothing to write home about, merely a wavy line marking the high water-mark, and beyond that, nothing until the first fields began but sandy dunes and wisps of grass. Whatever was there, and so far Dieter was saying nothing about the spectacle which he obviously didn't want me to miss, would only become visible to me on our present course were I to get up out of my seat and conduct my surveillance of the ground to starboard at a much narrower angle. After ensuring that Dieter was flying the aircraft, I did my best not to rock the boat, as it were, as I leaned between his upper body and the controls. I was pleased to discover that my hasty manoeuvring was worth the effort, for there, lying face-up in a hollow amongst the dunes on an otherwise deserted stretch of shore, two nubile women were sunbathing topless, evidently making the most of what could easily be the year's last spell of fine weather. Presumably they were Danish, but they showed no flag. Indicating to Dieter that I was very pleased to have had my attention drawn to the display of female pulchritude, I thought it would be good for morale if the others in the back were to be made aware of the sight which had amused and delighted Dieter and myself. Returning to my seat I summoned the others on the internal net to come forward for a visual treat. The thought crossed my mind that our guest from military intelligence might not appreciate our Luftwaffe ways, but in the end I decided to trust him not to report me for deviating unnecessarily from our mission, a course of action I would soon need to take if we were not to lose sight of our lovely young ladies forever.

"What is there to see?" asked Ernst, leading the way forward.

"Look down below to the right," I instructed, "and hold on."

The fact that I was once again in control of the aircraft became immediately obvious as I banked sharply to starboard, tipping the standing occupants of the flight deck towards Dieter. My intention was to circle these visions of loveliness, these subjects of our future sexual fantasies once only, for although I knew that the extra fuel we carried extended our range by fifty per cent, I didn't want to squander our supply frivolously. The essential manoeuvre resulted in three pairs of eyes peering lasciviously through glass which more than once needed to be wiped clear of exhaled breath. Any lingering doubts I may have had regarding the complete integrity and unity of my crew were soon dispelled when Leutnant Kaiser asked if it would be possible to land the Dornier on the beach. In response to my negative reply, the good Abwehr man came up with an alternative suggestion, which involved his baling out here and now, before it was too late. Noting that the height registering on the altimeter oscillated between just under and just over fifty metres, I made the comment that at this height he might as well leave his parachute behind, that it was probably safer to jump without one. The Abwehr man emitted a sound indicative of someone giving a proposition serious consideration. No longer able to see for myself, I heard from the ribald comments of my colleagues that the buxom beauties on the beach, far from being intimidated by our presence, had stood to wave enthusiastically, thereby revealing their charms. Our circle complete, I levelled the aeroplane and headed towards the sea. Our fun and games were over.

"I've got a new heading for you Kapitan," informed Ernst from behind me. "Go straight on 240 degrees until we reach the mouth of the Tees River. Then turn to port on a setting of 200 degrees. That should bring us within sight of the first of our targets before noon."

"Danke Ernst," I said. "Turning to port on 240 degrees."

I noticed that Dieter gave one last look at the beach diminishing by the second before he turned to scan sea and sky in a wide arc ahead.

"Climbing to three hundred feet," I added, easing the controls back gently to gain the small increase in height I thought necessary for safety.

Our original flight-plan had been to join a formation of 'flying-pencils' on a bombing mission to York, parting company with them as soon as we reached the British coast. The logic behind Krupp's plan was that there could be safety in numbers. I wasn't so sure. A large number of aircraft flying in echelon formation was bound to show up on the enemy's radar, and very soon after they would present a juicy target for marauding fighters, particularly as our Schnellbombers were without an escort of Messerschmitts. On the other hand, an aircraft flying alone over enemy territory, as God willing we would be shortly, would provide an easy kill if spotted by a patrolling Spitfire or Hurricane. Weighing up the situation as we headed out over the North Sea – or the German Sea as it was known even to the British in bygone days – it seemed to me that the events, unpleasant and ridiculous as they were, which had led to our delayed take-off and consequent solitary journey, could yet be to our advantage. My analysis of the situation was that the formation an hour or more ahead of us would act as a honey-pot to every waspish fighter the Royal Air Force could get off the ground, leaving us, or so I hoped, with a relatively easy run in to target. I realised that if the scenario I envisaged were to come to pass, as perhaps the devil in me secretly hoped, that many a crew with whom I had become acquainted over the years would perish. The thought I kept to myself was rather somebody else than me. Altruism in life or death situations is not my strong point. In my opinion our best chance of getting back in one piece was to sneak in under their radar, do the job, and leave without the RAF becoming aware that we had been. My thoughts were interrupted by a familiar crackle in the headphones, followed by a sound which to my mind was reminiscent of waves breaking on a pebble beach. These sounds were a prelude to our being hailed by Aalborg Control Tower.

"Hello Turmfalke (kestrel) two-nine, hello Turmfalke two-nine, this is Turmfalke Control, are you receiving over?"

Before I had a chance to respond Dieter nudged my arm, and, smiling broadly, warned me to be on my guard.

Speaking above the noise of the engines he said, "They'll probably want to know why we've been flying around in circles. The two women on the beach were probably Feldgendarmarie (military police) working under cover."

Dieter was known for having a dry sense of humour. Once again I heard our call sign being summoned. This time I responded promptly, disregarding my colleague's advice.

"Hello Turmfalke Control, this is Turmfalke two-nine receiving over."

"Hello Turmfalke two-nine. I have a message from Sonnenstrahl (sun-ray) for you. Message reads: good views of water closets will get you out of the midden. Good luck!"

Unable to think of anything suitably cryptic or witty in reply, I responded simply: "Hello Turmfalke Control this is Turmfalke two-nine. Thanks to Sonnenstrahle for the incentive. We'll do our best to comply. I am suspending all routine transmissions until 1400 hours. Turmfalke two-nine out."

By that time I reckoned we would be half way across the North Sea on our way home and out of trouble, and judging by the last radio message, out of trouble in more ways than one. Maintaining radio silence was an additional precaution our people took on missions of this type, the aim being to prevent detection by unfriendly ears tuning into our frequency, whether deliberately or by chance. In the main, the flight across the water was uneventful, the only distraction being our sighting of a lone steamer steering down the coast about ten kilometres from shore. At a considerable distance she was heading towards us as we crossed her course. It had been the sharp-eyed Leutnant Katz who first espied her. Without question he was the most cavalier member of my crew whenever the prospect of attacking an opportune target presented itself, and today was no exception. Knowing that without bombs we would be unable to blast the ship out of the water, he nonetheless suggested that we put in an attack with our 20 mm cannon and 7.92 mm machine-guns, of which we were armed with four of each. I rejected the idea out of hand, as Dieter no doubt expected. I think he would have been taken aback if I had agreed. The reasons for my reticence were entirely logical, for not only did I wish to conserve ammunition in order to give us a fighting chance in any forthcoming aerial encounter, but I thought the target not worth the effort. I surmised that the vessel was a collier transporting coal from the northern coalfields to the capital. Such was the legacy of my geography lessons at school. My hope was that the ship's crew weren't as vigilant as Dieter, and that we hadn't been seen. If the crew were wide awake and had spotted us, then my next hope was that their aircraft recognition skills weren't up to scratch. We flew on regardless. At that moment Ernst appeared at my right shoulder, informing as he stooped slightly in order to scan the horizon, that we should sight the coast of Britain any minute. Needless to say, none of us would ever have described Britain as being Great, though in later life I changed my attitude completely. Suddenly there it was, a stretch of coastline emerging from the haze, remarkable for the way sandy beaches curved towards the headland either side of a river estuary.

"Congratulations Ernst, that must be the Tees River ahead, wouldn't you say?"

I posed the question as my eyes focused on the area of bright sunlight reflecting from the water at the river's widest point.

"I believe so, but there's a rather unusual structure spanning the river a little way upstream I was told to keep an eye open for. When we catch sight of that I'll be one hundred per cent certain that we've got the right river."

We flew directly over the lighthouse standing at the southern tip of the estuary, and then on over a village comprised entirely of huts. Small fishing boats bobbing languidly at wooden jetties gave some indication of the purpose served by the sheds. A number of fishermen, having seen the black crosses on the underside of our wings, ran for cover. A few remained in the open where they had been hauling nets. These gestured brazenly in our direction, but ignoring their defiance, onward we flew. Further upstream we saw beneath us the grimy assemblages of heavy industry, the greater part of which looked to be remarkably intact and functioning normally. I wondered why we hadn't flattened the area.

"Keep your eyes skinned for fighters," I warned, stifling a yawn as I looked above and to the sides.

Every so often the effects of having had little sleep came over me suddenly, and I had to adopt simple strategies to stay alert. Sometimes I would shake my head vigorously. On other occasions I pinched my skin so that it hurt. For his part, my partner in crime seemed to be coping quite well, but he had probably taken the opportunity to snatch a few minutes sleep during our flight across the sea. Katz made a comment which I didn't quite hear, but I believed his remark to have been about the weather. The climatic conditions were undoubtedly of interest to me. For the duration of the flight from Aalborg till now, we had flown above a calm sea under a canopy of clear blue sky. Evidently that weather was changing, but so far not to our detriment. Directly ahead there was variable cloud cover, as could be observed in the billowing cumulous rising from a cloud base of approximately one thousand metres. The good news was that we would be able to evade attack by losing ourselves in a mass of vapour. If there were any bad news on the horizon it would be that the cloud might thicken and the weather deteriorate to such an extent that it would be difficult, if not impossible, to get the imagery of the dams we needed. I knew their location to be amid high ground. For the present, however, I was completely optimistic about the mission, and this despite my fatigue.

Suddenly, pointing with the index finger of his right hand directly ahead whilst tapping me on the shoulder with the curled fingers of the other, Ernst exclaimed with the excitement of success, "There it is!" Then after a pause he asked somewhat pensively, "But what is it?"

Notwithstanding the elegant symmetry of the structure, the object which Ernst was pointing at was a strange configuration of metal comprising a stanchion standing approximately twenty to thirty metres high either side of the river. These supported a conjoining section of girders along the top, from which was suspended – presumably, because we were unable to discern the cables – a platform capable of transporting people and vehicles backwards and forwards across the river without being a hindrance to shipping.

"It looks ingenious to me," I observed. "The practical product of some exceptional creative thinking," I added, pompously. "It combines the attributes of a ferry with the structure of a bridge."

"Well, it's good enough for me. You had better turn onto the second of those two headings I gave you Kapitan," Ernst advised.

"Verstanden!" I replied. I'm turning to port on 200 degrees. Leutnant Kaiser," I called to our Intelligence Officer, "come and have a look at this."

I thought it worthwhile his coming forward to get a glimpse of the unusual piece of engineering a few kilometres ahead, although it was soon, or so it would seem, to veer round to the right. It may be that in consequence of what he was about to see our next mission would be to bomb the thing. Whether or not it was destined to be destroyed, another consequence might be that once we had won the war, similar structures might span Germany's mighty rivers.

"What do you think of that thing sticking up from the river?" I asked our Abwehr guest as he ventured forward from where he had been tinkering in the bomb bay, indicating the structure that was soon to be hidden by our starboard wing.

"I think that it would make a really good target," interjected Leutnant Katz enthusiastically.

"I see," said Leutnant Kaise. "On first sight it would appear to be a remarkable piece of engineering, particularly useful where space to build a bridge of sufficient height to allow shipping to pass is limited. The concept is not new of course. Nevertheless, perhaps we could take a closer look on the way home."

There was a danger that the Leutnant's words might lull me into a false sense of security.

"We'll see," I replied, responding in a manner similar to that adopted by my father whenever as a boy I asked him if we could do something or go somewhere later, particularly when the likelihood of my wish being granted was almost nil.

"Achtung! Achtung!" shouted Dieter. "Two aircraft patrolling at two o'clock, way above us," he added, emphatically putting an end to our discussion of ancillary espionage pursuits.

"Back to your seats gentlemen," I ordered, for having raised my eyes to glimpse the sector indicated by Leutnant Katz, I was able to pick out, amid a large area of blue sky surrounded by clouds of varying shades of grey, the sun glinting on the glass of two aircraft flying in close formation on a parallel but opposite course to our own.

My escape and evasion plan was to head for the nearest mass of nebulousness, an expedient which necessitated my making a steep climb and veering farther to port than our original course setting. I was immensely grateful that the cloud cover was as it was, for once we were immersed, as it were, by the swirling vapours, we would be safe.

"Do you think that they saw us?" I asked Dieter as soon as the world around us had turned monochromatically opaque.

"I don't think so, but I can't be certain," my comrade replied. "They certainly gave no indication that they had, judging by the way they maintained their height and course."

"What type of aircraft were they?" I asked, unable to come up with a likely nomenclature for the shapes which I had only fleetingly glimpsed.

"Those chunky, two-seater jobs – Beaufighters I think they're called," Dieter replied.

We emerged from the cloud after no more than a minute to find ourselves once again bathed in bright sunlight, the shadow of the Dornier passing presently over cultivated fields interspersed with narrow lanes leading here and there to farm buildings. My immediate concern was to ascertain whether or not we had the sky within view to ourselves, and after searching as much of the firmament as was practically possible, I was relieved to discover that we seemed to be alone, a realisation which Dieter was happy to confirm. My hopes were that the Beaufighters – if that was what they were – had been on their way to conduct a routine patrol of the coast, and that we wouldn't see them again. We flew into another vaporous mass, this time routinely. At this higher altitude I had no worries about the possibility of our crashing into the side of a hill, although I was aware that we were now probably a noticeable blip on an RAF radar screen. Following our first sighting of the enemy, my earnest wish now was to get the job done and turn for home. Some of my earlier optimism had dissipated, and I was becoming a little fraught, a nervous state which I attributed to fatigue rather than fear. Of course it didn't occur to me that I might be deluding myself. I began to take deep breaths as a means of regaining my self-control. Upon next emerging from the opacity of cloud I noted that the terrain ahead and below was too rugged for agriculture, at least of an arable nature. Evidently this higher ground like wilderness did serve a useful purpose, however, for clustered and easily discernible among the vast tracts of heather were sheep in large numbers. I called to Leutnant Kaiser to stand by to switch on the cameras.

"Can you see anything on the ground that might assist with navigation Kapitan?" asked Ernst on the radio, obviously eager for some visual clues to confirm the accuracy of his reckoning.

Before I had a chance to reply, Dieter, who was always quick off the mark, informed that there was a road running along a valley to starboard. Upon learning that the valley and road ran parallel to our present course on a north-east/south-west axis, Leutnant Eckener expressed his delight.

"According to my charts we're approaching Carlton Highdale, which means that Angram and Great Scar Reservoirs should appear off the port wing at any moment Kapitan," our navigator informed.

No sooner had Ernst mentioned the names of the reservoirs, when, as if by magic, they appeared, two great silvery sheets of water held back by formidable dams set in a forbidding landscape, a scene made more daunting now that the golden orb was no longer our companion. The clouds to the south-west looked dark and lugubrious, their precipitation being clearly visible. Appearances can be deceptive, and in this instance the dirty weather seemed to be rushing to meet us, to be heading our way at a speed not that much less than we were travelling towards it. If we were to obtain any useful imagery at all we would need to work quickly. Despite my sense of urgency, I gave the order with good humour, some might say flippantly.

"Kamera! Aktion!" I called, momentarily exchanging the role of pilot for that of a film director, and without diminishing my confidence that the cameras would roll.

"I'm going to make two passes of the reservoirs in opposite directions," I informed the crew, and banking to port so that our heading was now due east, my plan was to loop round and fly over the dams and reservoirs more or less equidistant from either end of each barrage, and from either shore.

This flight-plan necessitated a change of direction approximately two-thirds of the way along Scar House Reservoir as we adhered to the configuration of the man-made lakes. For the second run we adopted a similar procedure in reverse, a course which would bring us back to the start of this first serious phase of our reconnaissance mission. The sortie over Scar House and Angram was completed without incident, and shortly thereafter I turned due south to make for Grimwith Reservoir, thirteen kilometres away. Unfortunately, we had only covered ten of those kilometres when we flew into the band of heavy rain. The rain proved to be persistent, making for conditions which precluded our making further progress in that direction. Consequently, after checking with Ernst, I turned seventy degrees to port with the aim of coming upon Gowthwaite right bang in the middle, and this we did. Once again we made two successful passes in opposite directions before moving on to film the dams to the north at Roundhill and Leighton. Uplifting to our spirits was the fact that by having turned to reconnoitre the last three dams on our list, we were heading away from the worst of the weather, and were presently making our way through that friendly mix of open sky and cumulus, conditions most favourable to our purpose. I felt reasonably satisfied with what we had achieved. We had missed out on getting imagery of Grimwith, Fewston, and Swinsty, but Gowthwaite, Angram and Scar House had been a complete success, as were the two which the Intelligence people considered to be less important, namely Roundhill and Leighton. All in all I thought that we had done a reasonable job, particularly as I had always considered our task to be something of a tall order for a single mission. Now it was time to head for home.

Chapter Fifteen

After asking Ernst to plot a course from the most northerly point of the barrage across Leighton Reservoir to the bar in the Officers' Mess at Aalborg Airfield, and turning on to a heading of sixty degrees in response to the figures he was able to provide in an instant, once again I felt my resistance to the demands of sleep begin to weaken. On this occasion my strategy was to pour myself a cup of black-market coffee from a small vacuum flask I kept close at hand. Ordinarily, the fact that we were flying over enemy territory in broad daylight would preclude my taking any form of refreshment, but I needed to counteract my fatigue somehow, and caffeine is renowned for being an effective stimulant. There no longer being any need for us to hug the ground, I thought it wise to fly at a height at which we would be able to lose ourselves and the enemy in cloud if necessary. The arrow indicating our height flickered on the altimeter near the three thousand metre mark. The time was just after one o' clock in the afternoon, and the sun, being just past its zenith, made its presence felt on the backs of my hands and the tops of my thighs. The land below appeared pleasantly green, but the sea beckoned. After draining the last drops of warm liquid from the cup, I stowed the thermos flask by the side of my seat and resumed my duties considerably revived.

We had been flying for approximately ten minutes when our course took us yet again through a large formation of cloud. On this occasion the most remarkable effect of our entry was the instant removal of the sun's direct heat from my upper limbs. The contrast was chilling. There was never an occasion when I didn't instinctively relax as soon as we were hidden from view. Of course, there was always the remote possibility that our fate would be sealed by a collision, but in these circumstances – flying alone, and so far undetected – that prospect seemed more remote than ever. The damp, cold air flowed over our wings for no more than a minute when we emerged once more into bright sunlight and a surprise scenario that was nothing less than the harsh reality of war.

Death came so quickly. With machine guns blazing, the Spitfire came at us from ahead and slightly to starboard. The attack, the way the deadly aircraft pounced, was reminiscent of a predator that has been stalking its prey, though this thought only occurred to me hours after the debacle I was fortunate to survive. The serendipity which I experienced in being alive, I quickly discovered had not been evenly distributed, for the effect of the Spitfire's burst of machine-gun fire had been devastating, having, in a matter of seconds, taken the lives of my entire crew. I found myself struggling to retain control of an aeroplane the starboard engine of which was burning fiercely. Not surprisingly my realisation of all that had happened had not been immediate, for prior to my being able to make an assessment of the situation I first had to gather my thoughts. This in itself was a difficult enough task when you consider that my mind was a tumult of sense impressions which began with the flashes of gunfire and ended with my scanning the ground for a likely field in which to attempt to land. I already knew that any landing would be of the crash variety. The seconds in-between these two points in time were a whirligig of violence and chaos in which I have a clear mental image of our attacker's grey underbelly, distinct with roundels, sweeping above our heads, but so close that I thought the fighter's tail-wheel would strike our frame. In these same explosive moments I was conscious of glass shattering into umpteen fragments as the deadly rounds penetrated the cockpit, and I was aware also of the near and almost instantaneous thuds, thwacks and pings – depending upon what they hit – as those same rounds lost velocity towards the end of the their violent journey, a journey which I subsequently found had made three men lifeless. In this regard, instinctively I had recoiled with horror when my right arm and leg had suddenly become splattered with blood. Confident that as yet there were still only seven openings into and out of my body, I realised that the splatterings could only have come from Dieter, and upon turning my head to confirm my suspicion, I grimly took note of how his body was slumped in its seat. From a cursory inspection I estimated that he had been hit in the chest at least six times. His head was tilted to one side, resting with the serenity of stillness against a strut holding in place the jagged remains of the cockpit window. It seemed that the flames from the burning engine could easily set fire to his hair, and were this to have happened it surely would have provided for a grotesque finale, yet at the moment when I first perceived that a premature cremation was a distinct possibility, the flames made for a spectacle of almost supernatural awe, as if in death Dieter had been chosen by the gods to ascend to Valhalla to feast with Odin, as if he were on the verge of achieving apotheosis. The thought occurred to me as I glimpsed his ghastly demeanour that all his boyish enthusiasm for the fray had come to nought. A more urgent consideration, however, quickly gained ascendency in the hierarchy of my mental activity, and after calling to Ernst and Leutnant Kaiser, but hearing no word in reply, I decided to try by some deft flying to put out the flames and land the aircraft in such a way that I would be able to walk away in one piece. Forlorn as it might seem, that was my plan. At least now, though steadily losing height, I was able to keep the aeroplane on an even trim. I dismissed the idea of trying to bale out for a very good reason, that being that as soon as I let go the controls the Dornier would more than likely go into a spin before I had a chance to jump clear. Such an attempt, I concluded, would result in my joining Dieter at his unlikely repast. In the real world of blood and guts, a world far removed from the pantheons of gods, what I really didn't want to happen at that moment was for our attacker to return with the sole purpose of finishing the slaughter he had started. Eager to know my fate, I searched the skies for the predatory hunter, and for any of his kind. Finding the sky clear, I experienced a resurgence of hope. I cut off the fuel supply to the starboard engine in the hope that the flames, having been starved of nourishment, would be out by the time I hit the ground. The immediate effect was negligible, but gradually the burning aviation fuel began to diminish in intensity from the apocalyptic conflagration which had presented a vision of a mythological afterlife, to a mere flicker. The number of times I glanced past Dieter's solemn visage was legion, the focus of my attention being on that which I wanted to die. It occurred to me as I struggled to keep the machine level that if I were able to land successfully – and to my mind a successful landing meant my sustaining only minor injuries – it would be better for one of the others to be seated where I was now sitting. The reason for why was that when the 'Tommies' eventually came to sift through the wreckage, they would find nothing amiss and presume that the entire crew had been killed. To find my seat empty would be to arouse suspicion, and as I retained hopes not only of surviving the landing, but also of evading capture and making it back to the Fatherland, I naturally wanted the investigators to believe that there had been no survivors. For the same reasons that I had dismissed the idea of bailing out, however, I also had to dismiss the idea of hauling the dead weight of a man's body and placing it in my seat. It would have been impossible for me to maintain the limited degree of control I had over the aeroplane whilst performing such an onerous task. It crossed my mind that I might be able to organise something to dupe the enemy once I had landed safely. The flames flickering around the starboard engine refused to die down completely, and when I attempted to veer to port, the idea being to expose the burning engine to the full force of the draught generated by my descent, there was no response from the rudder. The Spitfire had effectively destroyed our rectrix.

The thoughts which I had had subsequent to our meeting with disaster were necessarily compressed into a short time-scale, the time it has taken to describe them being much longer. That's how it always is with action of the dynamic kind; and suddenly, the time to think expired completely as the ground seemed to rush up to meet me. The perfect landing-site was not available, nor was there a level field within view. No; the ground on which I might possibly lose the light was an expanse of heather-covered moor. Of course, at the time I had no idea what this area of Yorkshire was called, but later I learned that I had crash-landed on Arden Great Moor, a few kilometres to the north-west of Hambleton Village.

In the immediate reality of the Dornier rushing towards terra firma, for obvious reasons I was grateful for the absence of trees, and after we had come to a stop, for the cushioning effect of heather. Even if the mechanism controlling the undercarriage had worked, there was no point in my lowering the wheels. They would have done more harm than good. Right now, at a height of no more than twenty metres above the ground, my main concern was to keep the aircraft's nose up slightly, so that after the initial impact she would continue to plane along the ground on her belly until the law which states that a body continues in a state of rest or uniform motion in a straight line unless it is acted upon by an external force came into effect to apply the brakes in the form of friction. That impact when it came was more violent than I had imagined it would be, and for a few crucial moments I sought to protect my head by crossing my arms in front of my face. The noise was deafening. It was a barrage of irrevocable destruction as the solidity of Mother Earth proved too much for the frail construction that was my only protection. It was my good fortune, however, that if there were ever such a thing as a text-book crash-landing, then this was it. I can state this with the utmost conviction because when I did eventually manage to extricate myself from the wreckage, compared to the injuries I could have sustained, I managed to limp away from the scene more or less unscathed; also the wreckage, though burning steadily along the entire length of the starboard wing, still bore a slight resemblance to the aircraft which only a matter of minutes before had been almost in pristine condition. The injuries I did incur were to my head and knee. The wallop I received on the back of the head shortly after impact was from the barrel of a gun which had become displaced to become, literally, a loose cannon. The blow to my cranium, though cushioned by my flying-helmet, almost knocked me senseless, and indeed, for a time I was totally dazed, seeing a multitude of stars in kaleidoscopic colours. I'm not sure how I injured my knee, but the pain was quite severe, giving me cause for concern regarding my ability to move across country freely. If the need were to arise I wanted to be able to run.

When the Dornier did finally come to a halt, when everything around me was motionless save for the tongues of flame and the wonderfully hypnotic flight of a lone bird overhead, where its body was silhouetted against the passing clouds, the shadows of which combined with patches of seemingly rapidly moving sunlight to dapple the land; when everything around me was silent save for the crackle of the flames and the rush of the wind as it surged through the heather; that was when I threw back my head, and following hard upon a deep exhalation of breath said, "Thank God!" I thanked God that either as a downed pilot making a bid for freedom, or as a prisoner of war, I would live.

The time for reflection and expressions of gratitude was short. There was still a risk that a fuel tank would explode, and my descent would probably have been observed from the ground. The fact that I had come down in a remote location didn't preclude the arrival of potential captors in a matter of minutes. Judging that there might just be enough time to promote Ernst posthumously to Hauptmann and still make good my escape undetected, I placed my arms around his chest from behind and hauled him from the rear of the cockpit with some difficulty, but that was mainly on account of my knee. My head throbbed as if it were about to burst, but at least none of my mental faculties was impaired. Indeed, I was surprised at how clearly I could think and how quickly I could act.

Whatever mental acuity I possessed, and whatever sense of purpose I demonstrated, didn't prevent me from being shocked by seeing what had happened to my friend. My initial reaction upon finding him lying on his back with his right knee bent acutely to one side so that the boot on that limb crossed the knee of his right leg at a right-angle, thereby resembling a figure four, was one of calm stoicism, but that was because I had not yet seen how he had died. The perhaps glaringly obvious clue provided by the pool of blood beneath a head tilted to one side didn't prepare me for the horror of the discovery I was about to make as I stooped to grab hold of the body. Notwithstanding his beady eyes, the mainly handsome face which had been so alluring to Margareta in Hortens, and probably to a number of other nubile young women before she had come on the scene, when I first beheld it in death, appeared unblemished. Only as I raised Ernst's torso from the deck, and his head dropped forward naturally, did I become aware that the right side of his head and face were missing. A mangled mass of brain caused me to look away in horror and disgust, but at least I didn't drop him. I completed the task as expeditiously as possible, and placed my former friend in what I thought would be a beguiling position. Other than to note that he was dead, I didn't give Leutnant Kaiser a second thought.

"That's good enough to fool me," I said to myself prior to exiting the aircraft through the port-side cockpit window.

From the time when the Dornier had slid to a halt until my feet stumbled through the English heather can't have been more than a couple of minutes. Despite the loss of my comrades, I smiled as I hobbled towards whatever the weeks and months ahead might bring. I smiled in anticipation of the future.

Chapter Sixteen

Arden Great Moor

I had never previously tried to make my way across a heather moor, and before today had never seen such vast tracts of the stuff growing anywhere. If anything, from the ground the vista comprised of great swathes of land stretching towards the horizon was more impressive than the scene I had viewed from the air. Scenery aside, however, my first impressions were not good. These were from the perspective of a man carrying an injury and trying to make the most of the good fortune he had already been granted. It's not easy trying to make progress through the knee-deep carpet of ericaceous clumps at the best of times, but the pain in my knee made the task doubly difficult, and I lost count of the number of times I stumbled to feel the shrub's somehow soft yet wiry tendrils tickle my face. Fortunately my falls didn't add to my injuries. This was because the ground was quite soft, at least in those places where I made its acquaintance. The presence of heather signified that the earth beneath my prostrate body was highly acidic, and primarily it was comprised of that sometimes pleasantly springy, and at other times oozing, black goo, that is the decomposed vegetable matter known as peat. The smell of the ling and peat in combination was distinctive and not unpleasant. Later in life, whilst wandering these same moors for pleasure, I learned how stinkingly noxious peat turned to bog can be. Peacetime pleasures, however, were as yet years away, and my immediate concern was to put a safe distance between myself and the aircraft before, inevitably, the fuel tanks exploded, an event which I expected to happen at any second. I discovered that the best way of covering the ground was to take long strides rather than run, raising the thighs higher than usual. Twice I looked over my shoulder to see what was happening to my machine, and without doubt those two occasions contributed to the overall number of times that I fell into the arms of Mother Earth.

An impression gleaned upon looking back, the sight of Dieter and Ernst sitting as if asleep behind the controls is an image which has come back to haunt me over the years. No other image has affected me in this way. It was as if leaving them behind for the last time engendered in me feelings of guilt, for in my own mind I have attributed to their dumb expressions an accusation in the form of questions: "Why did we have to die? Why were you allowed to live?"

The first of the explosions when it came took me by surprise, and this time I dived to the ground deliberately, pressing my body into its welcoming softness in an attempt to make as flat an outline as possible, but only after I had first turned about so that my head was the part of me nearest to the conflagration. Mainly I positioned myself in this way so that I would be able to observe the spectacle. It would seem that curiosity had got the better of me. I estimated my distance from the aircraft at that moment to be approximately seventy metres, and over that distance I didn't believe that my head being two metres farther away from the source of danger would matter in the slightest. Events were to prove me right, for none of the burning debris and exploding rounds of machine-gun ammunition hit me, and nor do I believe that any of the potentially lethal projectiles came even close, though in respect of the latter I'll never know for certain. One thing that I was certain of was that the noise of our descent, crash-landing, and subsequent near total destruction of the Dornier, would have been heard for miles around, and now that it was safe to move again, move I should.

It was, however, with some reluctance that I hauled myself up out of the heather to begin my odyssey in earnest. The reasons for my disinclination were both psychological and physical. I had found being prone in the heather to be a more comfortable experience than I would have imagined it to be, and the brief respite from strife provided by the ling tempted me to tarry longer. From a psychological perspective, I have to admit that after the traumas I had just experienced, a part of me wanted to give up there and then, to lie down in the heather in the autumn sunshine until somebody came to take me prisoner. At least as a prisoner of war I would be given food and shelter, and no doubt eventually I would have the companionship of my peers. Fortunately, I was able to overcome my disinclination by summoning up that resolve and tenacity of spirit which had been so effective in seeing me through hardship in the past, and I set off once more across the exposed wilderness that is this part of Britain.

I was thinking on my feet, literally. I knew that our intended course in flight had been on a heading of sixty degrees, and that in being forced to land I had not veered widely from that setting. Without needing to check the compass in my pocket, from the position of the sun I also knew which way was east. It goes without saying that I knew Britain to be an island, and that to walk in a straight line in any direction would bring me to the coast. I reasoned, however, because by aiming to go east I would be heading for home, that that was the direction in which I should travel. What I would do when I reached the coast would depend upon the circumstances I found when I got there, but I had it in mind to stowaway on a ship bound for a neutral port, or commandeer a fishing boat at the point of a gun.

The only weapon I had at my disposal was my pistol. I had no map, no food, and no water. Obviously I would need to forage. These were my thoughts as I struggled through the heather.

After having picked myself up off the ground, I had about doubled my distance from what was left of the Dornier when my thoughts, and my progress, were interrupted by the sound of voices. They seemed to be coming from somewhere over my right shoulder, and though when I looked in that direction as yet I could see no-one, as a precaution I dropped down into a hollow in the ground, making full use of the cover the natural flora provided. I was grateful for the fact that my flying jacket and trousers did not clash, so to speak, with my present environment. Their respective shades of brown and grey didn't make for ideal camouflage, but neither were they likely to give me away.

"Crikey! Look at that!" distinctly I heard a voice say.

The astonished individual had spoken loudly, as if the person he was addressing was some distance away. Raising my head by merely a few centimetres, I peered through the topmost growth of the heather, trying to identify who, and pinpoint where, the speakers were. The pitch of their voices indicated youth. Mild for the time of year, the breeze wafted gently against my face and carried the vocal sounds towards me. Whether unfortunately or fortunately – it was as yet too early to say – the breeze also brought ever nearer the rain clouds which had thwarted our mission over Grimwith reservoir, and the sky in the direction I was now looking had darkened considerably. The arrival of what would probably be the first of many 'crash inspectors' on the scene prompted me to draw my pistol and cock it. I did this in the knowledge that if in these circumstances I ever had to fire it, the game would be up for sure. Nonetheless, I considered my weapon to be a useful deterrent. Suddenly a dark human form came into view on the skyline, and as soon as he appeared he stopped. I watched him turn around as if to respond to, or encourage, a friend following in his footsteps. That person I could not yet behold, but if he or she was more or less the same age as the person in view, then the first people on the scene were children of about twelve years of age. Sure enough a second boy appeared soon to catch up with the other.

"What is it?" asked the newcomer innocently.

"It's a Jerry plane," called the boy in front, his voice clearly expressing the excitement of discovery, "or what's left of it."

Obviously, as the second boy drew level with the first, the volume of whatever was said between them diminished, and I was no longer privy to what they were saying. Dressed in short trousers and pullovers, the presence of the boys didn't make my chances of getting away undetected any better than they would have been had they been adults dressed in uniform. If anything their youthful sharp eyes and ears would be better able to pick up on an unnatural sound or movement, and obviously I wasn't going to shoot them. No; aware that shadow, shape, shine, silhouette and movement are the factors which might reveal a fugitive in the wild to the eyes of merely human pursuers (tracker dogs provide for an extra challenge), I decided that I had no choice but to stay where I was, till nightfall at least.

The curious pair approached the wrecked Dornier with caution. Here and there the debris flickered with flames which would soon expire. For about ten metres in my direction the ground was smoking too, and in places the ling also burned. It wasn't burning fiercely. Indeed, compared with most fires it was quite pathetic, but the disturbing thought occurred to me nonetheless that I might be forced to make my bid for freedom under cover of smoke rather than beneath the cloak of darkness. The boys' movements became more circumspect the closer to the crashed plane they got, and in observing their big adventure I thought of the things my friends and I got up to at their age. Of course, none of us had been so lucky as to stumble upon the wreckage of an enemy aircraft, but we too had had our moments of danger and excitement. It occurred to me as I observed the youthful pair of curious onlookers that essentially there was no great difference in appearance and natural behaviour between these two boys and the boys at home or in Denmark. The main differences, exemplified in Germany by the wearing of the swastika on shirt sleeves and standing to attention prior to giving a straight-arm Nazi salute whenever a teacher entered the classroom, were unquestionably the result of conditioning. The boys approaching the wreckage, demonstrating their increased trepidation the closer they got, gave the impression that it wouldn't take much for their caution to turn into panic, at which point I would surely see them turn tail and run. They appeared by their actions to be free, either to be brave, or conversely, to be fearful.

Personally, to deter them from getting too close, I hoped that fear would gain the upper hand. Not only was I concerned about what might happen to them physically if a few more bullets were to fly in any direction, but also that they might become mentally scarred for life were they to find the charred remains of my erstwhile colleagues. For a moment I entertained the thought of breaking cover and telling them to stop, but before in my case sentimentality and foolishness gained the upper hand, a gruff voice did the job for me.

"You two, stay right where you are," the stern voice commanded almost at the same time as the man who had shouted the order came into view.

Judging by his silhouette on the skyline the chap who had just appeared was a little portly and mature in years. His outline indicated that he was wearing a cap, and that in his right hand he carried a shepherd's crook. These appendages led me to believe that he was a local farmer. He used the crook to assist his progress through the heather. When he dropped down from the crest of the moor to draw near the boys, I was able to note a few additional details. I could see that he was wearing civilian clothes which consisted of a maroon pullover beneath a jacket of the sporting kind. I though it odd, bearing in mind where we were, that he was wearing a tie. The group of three soon became four when they were joined by the easily identifiable figure of a British policeman; a 'Bobby' was the word I came to use when I became more fluent in colloquial English. I continued to observe as the quartet held a discussion which resulted in the boys turning back the way they had come, and the adults, after an inspection of the wreckage at close quarters, each retrieving a panel with which to beat the volatile heather. The boys didn't disappear from the scene completely, but at what they thought, or at what one of the adults had deemed and told them was a safe distance, they sat down to watch developments. Clearly there was no chance of my leaving my shallow hiding place till nightfall, which, after looking at my watch and checking the position of the sun, I estimated to be in about three hours.

Moving my arm with the slow deliberation of a snail, I placed the Luger on the ground beside me and then took my bearings of the terrain farther removed from the plateau which, compared no doubt with its former desolate emptiness, had suddenly become a hive of activity. In the direction where the sun was preparing to take leave by creating shadows of ever increasing length, the trees of a deliberately planted conifer forest poked their pyramid-shaped crowns above the horizon. In the opposite direction, in the direction in which sooner or later I would be heading, the upper reaches of two hills – the first revealing a series of bumps against the sky, whilst the second was smooth and rounded and resembled a beached whale – were bathed in the golden light of an exceptional October afternoon. Bearing in mind my worm's eye view, elsewhere in my field of vision the topography was gently curved

153

open moor. Apart from staying hidden, there being little of a practical nature which I could presently consciously do, I folded my arms in order to provide my head with a modicum of comfort and fell asleep.

The next time I opened my eyes I was startled by a movement close by, so close in fact that I thought that I might be discovered by being trod upon as opposed to my being merely seen. My immediate response was to reach for my gun, placing my hand upon the grip at the second attempt, for with my eyes on the ominous dark shape almost within reach, I had searched for my pistol blindly. Once fully awake and alert to the reality around me – a world which was so very different from the one in which I would have hoped to have found myself waking, yet at the same time a world in which I was extremely fortunate simply to be – I realised that the sizeable creature nearest to me was nothing more threatening than a sheep. I soon realised that it was the nearest of a small flock that appeared to be free to roam the moor at will.

I had woken to rain falling steadily, and rather than my being disgruntled by the rivulets of water trickling down my face, I found the sensation to be refreshing. It was too dark for me to see the hands of my watch, and that fact alone indicated that I had been asleep for a number of hours: I estimated between two and three. It was the twilight hour, the hour of velvet shadows.

Once I had ascertained that my horned neighbours posed no threat whatsoever, I turned my attention to the more intense activity in and about the remains of my former aeroplane. From what I could make out from the scene before me, it appeared that the boys, and the man whom I had thought a farmer, had left. They had been replaced by a greater number of steel-helmeted soldiers: I would say no less than ten. Occurring as I watched, two of their number picked up a stretcher, and, at the direction of their officer, set off across the moor towards a truck and a jeep which were parked in front of the conifer forest. Evidently there was a track there suitable for wheeled transport. In respect of each vehicle, the headlights were on and the engine was running. Whoever, or whatever, was on the stretcher was covered by what looked like a sheet of tarpaulin. I presumed that it was the body of a member of my crew that they were taking away, and naturally I wondered whether it was Ernst, Dieter, or Leutnant Kaiser whose departure, presumably en route for a Christian burial, I was watching.

At the distance I was from the activity, I thought it sufficiently dark to be able to slip away unnoticed, but I was in for yet another surprise, for off to my left, no more than thirty metres away, a soldier was standing guard. I only became aware of his presence because he chose at that moment to light a cigarette, and the flame from the match that he held in cupped hands eerily illuminated his face as he tilted his head forward to ignite the tobacco. Once again I had the gods of serendipity to thank for not deserting me, for had the soldier not drawn attention to himself at that precise moment, I would probably have blundered into him.

I had no idea how many guards had been posted and where, but I assumed that there were others forming a perimeter, the radius of which was my, and my nearest enemy's, distance from the wreck. Even though the latter had given away his position, I couldn't accuse him of being negligent in his duty. After all, his job was merely to keep souvenir hunters at bay, and that on an island whereupon the only enemy troops were prisoners of war. The fact that he was so blatant about his little inhalations of pleasure indicated to me that he had probably been given permission to smoke. No; it had definitely been my luck and not his dereliction of duty which had prevented our becoming acquainted.

In view of my latest discovery, a change of plan was needed. My decision now was to wait another half hour until darkness had descended completely. Then I intended to increase the distance between myself and the crash site by heading north for the first kilometre before turning towards the coast. Meanwhile, I kept a watchful eye on the dark silhouette of the soldier standing guard. His ominous presence was also defined by a helmet, poncho and rifle, the weapon being slung from his shoulder. He was a shade darker than his own personal backdrop of sky, and in present circumstances could be more easily pin-pointed by the glow of his cigarette each time he inhaled. My main concern was the possibility that in order to keep warm, or simply from a desire to stretch his legs, or out of boredom, he might choose to walk in my direction and, were I not to take evasive action, step on me. Fortunately he maintained the same position for the entire time that I watched, and eventually, when I thought that the night could get no darker, I set off on my lengthy crawl, each time reaching forward to plant my fists gently but firmly in the peat prior to using them as anchors enabling me to haul the rest of my body in the right direction using my arms as levers. Progress was slow but sure, and necessarily conducted as a quiet secret known only to myself. My efforts to remain a non-entity to the British authorities were assisted by the notorious British weather and a few hardy sheep.

When I thought that I had crawled far enough, and the undulation of the moor was such that all activity relating to the crashed Dornier was hidden from view, as on the last occasion that I checked by looking over my shoulder, slowly I raised myself up from the ground. Resting both hands on one thigh I kneeled for several moments, watching, listening, and then cautiously I rose to my feet to stand upright for the first time in hours. From head height I was able to discern the glow of lights, but nothing more, and after rubbing and shaking the stiffness from my legs, I set off walking in the direction I had originally intended to go.

The elation I felt upon getting away and being able to move freely soon dissipated as the daunting nature of the task I had set myself loomed large in my mind. The fact that the going was physically hard also sapped my spirits, and in rain-soaked darkness I was still on the open moor. I may have been cold and wet, but at least the few hours' sleep I had managed to have in comfort of an unusual kind, would stand me in good stead, or so I thought. On top of everything I was hungry, hungry enough to eat a horse.

After I had been wading through the sea of heather for about half an hour I dropped down a short measure on to a track which was easily wide enough to accommodate a vehicle. Unfortunately from my point of view the route of compacted rubble cut across my compass heading more or less at right angles. It goes without saying that to have followed it in either direction would have led me off my intended course. I checked my compass. The green fluorescent arrow pointed into the darkness a little to the right of the track, and by so doing allowed me to extrapolate the way east. For a few moments, and for no other reason than itinerant ease, I was tempted to follow the track in a southerly direction, but on the premise that such tracks were made for people to follow, I reasoned that my chances of meeting a member of the recovery party were too high, and so with some reluctance I set off once more into the arduous unknown.

It wasn't long before I began to wonder whether I had made the right decision, for suddenly the ground fell away beneath my feet, causing me to lose my balance and roll a dozen or so metres down the slope skirting this side of the plateau. By the time my too hasty progress down the hill had come to a halt, I was cursing under my breath. I still had the presence of mind not to blaspheme aloud. For the umpteenth time that night I picked myself up from out of the damp flora, the difference this time being that I was definitely out of sorts. Only the fact that I would have to put in a considerable effort to climb back up the slope deterred me from regaining the one and only track in the whole of Britain about which I had a scintilla of knowledge. After all, I reasoned after I had regained my footing and gathered my thoughts, there would be many options available to me were I to be approached, the most obvious being to move a little way off the track and lie down in the ling until the problem posed by people, be they on foot or in vehicles, had passed. My advantage, or so I hoped, was that everyone else on Arden Great Moor that night would be feeling fairly secure for being unaware of the enemy in their midst, the fugitive skulking nearby. My considered decision, however, was to leave that particular moorland track behind and push on down the hill into a wooded valley.

Once I had climbed over a wall to enter the woods, the change in my environment was dramatic, and at first I felt quite at ease weaving my way between the tree-trunks and ducking beneath the nether branches. My impression now was that the climate at this lower altitude, in this valley sheltered by hills, was much more hospitable than on the plateau, and the canopy of densely packed pine needles no doubt helped in keeping some of the rain off me. The ground presently beneath my feet was soft and springy and in the main a pleasure to walk on, though it hardly needs saying that a forest at night is not without hazard. In this domain that was provided by fallen trees and broken branches. Despite the fact that I thought it highly unlikely that anyone else would be foolhardy enough to be walking in the forest, in the dark, and in this weather, I cringed each time a twig cracked – in my opinion ten decibels too loudly – beneath my boot.

I had been walking through woods interspersed here and there by tracts of rough ground for well over an hour before I finally succumbed to temptation. By this time all sense of ease had gone. It was worse than that, for my physical and mental strength had all but deserted me when I emerged from the trees on to a forest trail. Not only was I drenched from the rain, but my feet were squelching in my boots. I had tripped and fallen whilst wading through a stream. What's more, an unanticipated branch had almost poked out my eye, whilst others of less aggressive cut and thrust had merely scratched my face. I was feeling, and no doubt looking, the worse for wear. The temptation to which I succumbed was to follow the forest track even though I knew it would lead me off course. The fact is I couldn't face setting out once more into the wilderness. Of course, without a map I had no idea where I had been and where I was going, but years later I plotted what I thought had been my course down from Arden Great Moor and on almost into Hambleton Village. I will never be absolutely certain of the way I came home that night, but I believe my route to have been through High Wood, Green's Wood and Ellers Wood.

It was in Green's Wood, as I believe, that I fell into the stream which I'm sure was none other than the River Rye near to its source. It was on the far side of the river – in Ellers Wood – that I gave up on my cross-country quest and turned south to follow the track. What a relief it was to follow a contour rather than work against them. I continued to head south through the woods until I came to a bifurcation near to Broach Well, at which point I made the decision to turn left rather than to go straight on, and for no reason other than that it was my inclination. Indeed, from a teleological perspective, and on the

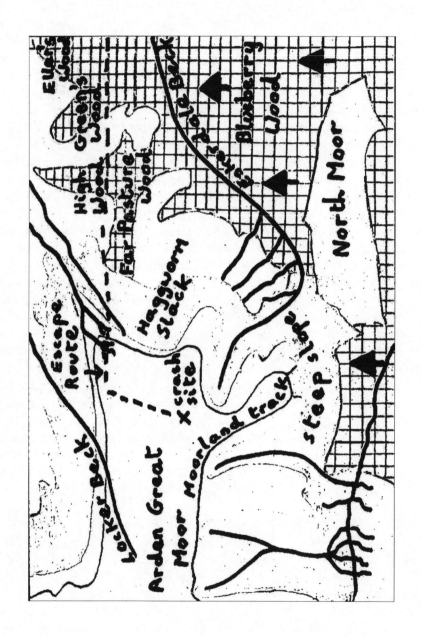

basis that in this instance the ends justified the means, apropos of my navigational choices, none of the decisions I made that night was wrong, though I can well understand that to a rationally minded and dispassionate analyst, focusing merely on the best way of getting from A to B, a few must appear absurd. It's relatively easy to make judgements in the cold light of day, and even easier with the benefit of hindsight, but being lost in the dark in the state that I was, from the time that I first entered the woods, all my decisions were instinctive.

From Broach Well I had only been walking a matter of minutes when I began to suspect that despite my being on a different path, I was effectively doubling back the way I had come. When, therefore, the opportunity presented itself to alter course yet again by turning sharp right, I took it. Disappointingly, or so it felt at the time, the path leading me in the direction I wanted to go was only about three hundred metres in length, and I had no choice then but to turn north or south again. I turned south. This path led me round the slope of a hill so that I could easily have walked down into the deserted, rain-soaked streets of a rustic village. It was Hambleton Village.

My instinct advised me not to enter into the throng of buildings, but to follow instead the path which continued round the hill. At this juncture the rain began to pour with a vengeance, so that I began to feel that the weather gods were going out of their way to make me feel totally despondent. They were on the verge of succeeding. I had been following the path leading away from the centre of the village for only a short while when I noticed the outline and dark mass of a solitary cottage, the chimney of which looked at present to be level with my feet. Separate from the house, several metres nearer to me, I could just make out the dark shapes of two outbuildings, one situated in each corner of what was probably the garden. Emboldened by the solitary location and the apparent absence of any human habitation, and chastened as I was by the weather's greater inclemency, I decided to take a closer a look. Once again, aware of the need to make as little noise as possible, I moved with extreme caution. There being no obvious path leading down to the hedge denoting the boundary at the rear of the property, I turned sideways to the hill as I made the short descent. At each step I dug my foot into the long, wet grass to ensure that there was no mishap to cause a disturbance. These actions exacerbated the pain in my knee, but in that regard I remained stoical. The absence of a path did not preclude the presence of a gate. It wasn't long before I was standing in front of the ramshackle portal, the height of which was level with my groin. Suddenly, from the shed to my left came sounds indicative of life, sounds which I instantly recognised to be the rustling of feathers. I stood listening for what seemed like an age, though in the time measured by clocks the interval was no more than a minute. The relentless rain was acting as both driver and protector. My initial reaction upon hearing the effect nightmares have upon chickens was to reach for my gun, but before my hand had got anywhere near it, I arrested the movement. It didn't take long for the coop to return to silence, and when all was quiet to my left, I turned my attention to the second and larger of the two sheds, the structure visible above the hedge to my right. Invitingly the door was partially open, though I was prevented from even attempting to look inside from my present vantage point simply because the hinges were on the side nearest to me. The door had to have been secured from swinging to and fro' by something, so I assumed that it had to have been by a hook. The question I asked myself was whether I should accept the invitation or move on to endure further hardships. The thought didn't enter my head that the open door might be a trap. The temptation to take an hour's respite out of the rain proved too great to resist, and I opted to take shelter, my intention being to be on the move again before first light.

After inspecting the gate to determine whether it was locked, I decided that the best way of overcoming this particular obstacle was simply to stride over it. Raising my legs one after the other like a rather ungainly Sally Bowles strutting her stuff on the Berlin stage, I acted thus because, although nothing resembling a lock presented itself to my touch, I discovered that the gate had been secured with wire. I manoeuvred in silence, but that didn't prevent me from pausing for a few moments once I was in the garden to confirm that nothing and no-one had stirred. From where I was now standing the house looked dangerously near. In another three strides I was squeezing between the door-frame and the half-open door, and then, at long last, I was out of the rain.

My eyes were accustomed to the darkness, but that didn't mean that they were of much use as I tried to gauge the layout of the shed and its contents. Consequently my actions were not unlike those of a blind man feeling his way between the display cases in a shop selling fancy-goods. My aim was not to behave like a child playing blind man's bluff. Moving about in the confined space of the shed demanded more of me in terms of concentration than I had needed to demonstrate earlier, when extracting myself from under the far from watchful eyes of the sentry, for any mistake now would surely cause a clatter. The first sensory message to be interpreted by my brain had travelled a long way. It was that the floor beneath my feet was concrete and not wood. In one sense this was to my advantage, and in another to my detriment. The advantage was that there was hardly any reverberation at each footstep. The disadvantage was that were I to lie down to rest, from experience I knew concrete to be harder on the bones than wood, and provides less insulation from the cold. My mainly tactile explorations informed me that I was inside a building which was kept neat and tidy, and that most of the items stored therein had been placed on shelves, each shelf forming part of a metal rack standing flush to the wall. Some of these items I was able to identify quite easily. I estimated, for example, that there were approximately half a dozen tins of paint. The tin I picked up was nearly empty. Farther along I curled my fingers around a glass object which a moment later I realised was a jar filled with nails. My heart missed a beat when, as I reached to replace the container without a lid, my fingers brushed against a second jar forcibly enough to make it wobble, but fortunately not so extremely that it fell to the ground to smash into a myriad shards and scatter numerous nails. In short, generally speaking the contents of this shed were no different from those you would expect to find in a garden shed at home, in Streisund. Nevertheless, this realisation didn't prevent me from being pleasantly surprised when I placed my hand upon a pile of hessian sacks. They were stacked in the bottom right hand corner of an array of shelves situated to my left when my back was to the door.

In getting to grips with the coarse material, I knew in an instant the treasure I had found, for my sense of smell was working in tandem with my sense of touch. There was no mistaking the pungent odour emanating from the jute and dust combined. I felt fairly confident in my assumption that once upon a time vegetables had been stored in the sacks, and as there were about a dozen of the latter in total, I thought they would now make for an excellent bed, all things considered that is.

Continuing – because I had no choice – to work in complete darkness, I laid half the number of sacks on the floor, overlapping them in such a way that my improvised mattress was only just bigger than my body, in length and width. By accommodating myself on the straight and narrow, so to speak, my plan was to install the maximum thickness of sacking beneath me from the material I had allocated to the task. The remaining sacks, initially at least, I intended to use as blankets. It was while I was arranging things according to this plan that a more ingenious idea came to mind. The flash of brilliance was that I would leave as they now were the mattress of sacks I had just arranged, but instead of using all the remainder as blankets, I would use at least one of them, and possibly two, to make a sleeping-bag. Thinking of how much warmth my body would generate when enclosed in hessian, with yet more sacks above and beneath me, I thought it perfectly feasible to undress completely. After ripping asunder the closed end of one of the sacks, thereby allowing me to poke my head through so as to enable me to breathe, I began to undress. Starting with my feet, I stripped until I was completely naked. It was quite an effort to remove my boots. I would have liked to have been able to stuff wads of newspaper into them, but as far as I could tell none was to hand. Instead I placed my boots side by side on a shelf, their leg-openings facing outwards the better able to be dried by whatever air was circulating. My jacket, trousers and pullover I contrived to hang from the shelves, from sharp corners and other protuberances. My shirt, underpants and socks I stuffed into the sack into which I crawled feet first. I had hopes that by the time I got up to leave these items of clothing would be less damp than they were presently. My penultimate act before I pulled the last four unlikely blankets over me, was to pull the sack which I had designed to keep my upper body warm down over my head. Upon lying down I found that the hessian tickled in several places, but once the dust had settled, I was really quite comfortable. I placed my gun and compass so that they were within easy reach. After setting the clock inside my head to wake me a couple of hours before dawn, to the rhythmic dance of the rain beating on the roof I looked forward to at least five hours' uninterrupted sleep.

Chapter Seventeen

Cascada de la Selva

If what differentiates us from every other living creature on the planet is our ability to enunciate and transcribe our thoughts and feelings in the structurally complex code that is language, then it follows that for the vast majority of human beings the words they utter are bound to have a considerable bearing on their respective lives. A charismatic leader rises to power and, either for good or ill, makes a speech that sways the crowd. Then are we persuaded to love our enemy, or, in imitation of the plebeians exhorted by Mark Antony, we may run amok clamouring 'Revenge! About! Seek! Burn! Fire! Kill! Slay!' On the other hand, however, we may consider ourselves to be at the farthest extremities of the ripple effect engendered by the speeches of Emperors, Kings, Queens, Presidents or Ministers, and that the language of our little, hum-drum lives is regularly more banal than eloquent; yet no matter how simple the syntax, who does not each day seek to scold, to soothe, to persuade, to encourage, to deter, bringing to light but a few of the many acts associated with human interaction, and the hardest of men may be moved to quote poetry when playing the mating game, or at the birth of his child, or at the death of a parent, or an old friend, a comrade.

The conversation involving George Gilbert, Harry Herbert Osborne and their Geordie captor amid the rubble of the ruined farmhouse a stone's throw from the River Ebro was not without consequences, and those consequences were not what either George or Harry wanted, for two weeks after their initial capture, the former legionnaires found themselves aboard a truck in a convoy of trucks which had just turned off the road to enter the prison in the town of Cascada de la Selva, in the province of La Mancha, or so they were told.

The journey from the front had been something of a mystery to the former Legionnaires, for seated opposite each other nearer to the cab than the tail-board, the only vista to view had been over the knees of their fellow passengers, and that had consisted in the main of the receding road and the first of two trucks following behind. There were four vehicles in the convoy, all serving the same purpose. For most of the journey most of the prisoners aboard the second truck – George and Harry included – had been sitting with their bound hands resting on their knees, their eyes staring blankly in front of them as each man reflected on the events which had led them to this sorry state, and as each man gave some thought to the bleakness of his future. Only when the truck had been driven over the occasional nasty pothole had the collective solemnity and contemplation been broken. Then, as one or two individuals struggled to regain their place on the bench after picking themselves up off the floor, a chorus of angry voices had cursed the driver in at least half a dozen tongues. Led by an officer sitting alongside the driver of the lead vehicle, there were four guards to each truck, and following orders they had positioned themselves in each of four corners. On George and Harry's truck, at each sudden furore leading to an outburst of expletives, with remarkable syncopation instinctively each guard had moved a wary index finger from the trigger-guard to the trigger of his rifle.

To enter the precincts of the prison, the convoy would have to pass through a gate-house which consisted of an outer and an inner gate, the idea being that one or other of the gates was always secure, thereby making escape via what was arguably the weakest point in the prison's defences as difficult as it could possibly be. Built into a wall about ten metres high, the gatehouse beckoned its inmates from a distance of say fifty metres from the main road through Cascada de la Selva, and it was along this little side road, encroached upon by stubble fields on either side, that three of the four trucks waited patiently with engines running for the first vehicle to complete the entry procedure.

The impression which George had formed of the town in passing through, an impression based then on the merest of glimpses, was that it wasn't a place to inspire the soul; not that he thought he would have much opportunity to experience whatever cultural delights might be on offer. In passing he had been able to see the doorway steps and lower levels of the dirty stucco walls. The only signs of life had been the bare feet belonging to a couple of children. George presumed that when he had espied them the urchins had been sitting side by side on the step in front of their door. The little he had seen of the houses had looked drab and dingy, and belied the imagined idyll conjured by the name – Cascada de la Selva. In English the name means Cascade of the Forest.

From the perspective of the prisoners-of-war a less desirable sight-seeing trip was difficult to imagine, but as they were in the vicinity, the best view of the town for the men in all but the first truck in the convoy, the truck which had already gone through the outer gate, came when the drivers parked their vehicles by the side of the road leading into the prison, for whilst awaiting their turn to enter, for the first time it was possible to make a visual survey of the town from a static position.

"What did you say the name of this place is?" asked Harry as he leaned forward the better to be able to see over the tailboard; and as George was of the same inclination, a clash of minds occurred, but only in the sense that there was a clash of heads.

George winced and then scowled, but because he had been trained as a teacher, he was able to demonstrate sufficient self-control to be able to curb his language. Harry's reaction was to smile inanely. It took George a few moments to recover before he felt able to answer Harry's question, first in Spanish, and then in English. Upon trying again, but this time keeping their heads a few careful centimetres apart, the captive Englishmen gazed beyond the trucks parked in line astern, and thought of freedom as they observed the townscape. From this viewpoint the vista was considerably more impressive than the street scenes they had glimpsed whilst on the move. Rising prominently from the surrounding plain was a tiered hill, around the base of which a small number of strategically positioned towers stood several metres taller than the walls that linked them. From the level able to be seen above the wall to the flat-topped summit, shade was provided by trees planted specifically for that purpose. The most prominent specimens, however, and easily identified, were the funeral cypress trees standing proudly against the cloudless sky. Being quite linear, the shade they provided was necessarily narrow. Atop the hill, and dominating the view to such an extent that every other building, though it be of architectural merit in its own right, seemed a paltry thing in comparison, stood a white-walled palace of considerable grandeur.

"Who do you think lives in the castle then?" asked Harry of his friend.

"How should I know," replied George with some exasperation. "Perhaps it's the Franco family home."

All further discussion of the scenery prompting wishful thinking was curtailed when it was the turn of George and Harry's truck to enter the gatehouse. Once the formalities of getting into prison were behind them, the trucks lined up from right to left in a quadrangle of sorts, this being the largest open space available within the prison walls. On George and Harry's truck, and presumably on each of the other vehicles, the guards seated within easy reach of the mechanism unbolted the tailboards, which they then let drop with a clatter. This pair of guards then jumped down each to take up a position where there was a sizeable gap in the line of permanent custodians already formed up ready to receive the new intake. The latter were standing with their backs to the wall holding their rifles at the ready. The main discernible difference between the two was in the style of headdress. The itinerant guards were dressed in forage caps, whilst by way of contrast the permanent staff wore hats which were peculiarly Spanish, and which resembled giant wing nuts. Urged on by gestures and shouts of 'Vamos' and 'Fuera', slowly, encumbered by an inability to separate their wrists, in total eighty new prisoners-of-war shuffled towards the dubious light. Some jumped down like athletes. Just as many demonstrated caution by sitting with their legs dangling over the end of the truck prior to launching themselves awkwardly into space to drop hardly any distance at all. Those that had been ensconced in the darker recesses of the canvas-topped vehicles for the duration of the journey, blinked upon emerging into the glare of bright sunlight. Aimlessly the prisoners coalesced into small groups while the guards looked on impassively. Despite there being no physical barrier, and no line painted on the tarred surface to instruct implicitly, 'Cross me if you dare', there appeared to be an understanding on the part of Cascada de la Selva's new residents of what constituted no-man's land. When the time came for Harry to disembark, he sought to encourage a rapid adjustment of his eyes to the intensity of light by rubbing each in turn with the back of his hand. Whether he had wanted to or not, the consequence of the delay was that he had no choice but to jump, pushed as he was by the man directly behind him. The burly Londoner was fortunate to land on his feet, albeit with a jolt which jarred the base of his spine. Moreover, he almost sent George flying in the direction of the gun barrels. Harry's initial reaction was to turn and raise his fist in the direction of the individual who had effectively dared to nudge him into space, but seeing as he looked up an expression of innocence on the face of a fellow prisoner, a sly, scurrilous 'hombre' if appearance is to go by, who by a shrug of the shoulders and a slight motion of the head, indicated that he too had been pushed, and then behind him the features of one of the two guards still aboard grinning malevolently whilst aiming the muzzle of his rifle at Harry's head, the Londoner thought better of it.

Whilst milling about with time on their hands, most, if not all, of the prisoners took the opportunity to weigh up their surroundings. Built of brick the colour of sand, the building which presumably for an indeterminate period was going to be home for George, Harry, and their kind, was a daunting and formidable structure standing, to judge from the rows of barred windows, three storeys high. To the left of the prisoners when their backs were to the line of guards, a building of smaller dimensions jutted out from its corner of the prison walls. A remarkable feature of this building was that the windows were without bars, and consequently George assumed that no POWs were detained there, and that the building was either an administrative centre, or an accommodation block for staff. It was while his attention was focused on this obviously functional edifice that George caught sight of someone whom he thought he recognised. From a room on the second floor the man who might not be a stranger to the Yorkshireman was looking down and watching him. For George the reflective quality of glass served to make identification difficult, and then he was distracted when Harry tapped him on the shoulder to point out the inward-leaning coils of barbed wire running along the top of each wall.

"There doesn't seem to be much chance of getting out over the top," said Harry as George turned to look in the direction indicated.

"Not unless you happen to be a champion pole-vaulter," commented George wryly, before adding by way of an afterthought, "And you happen to have a pole."

Following this comment George returned his scrutiny to the figure he had seen in the window, only to find that there was nobody there.

"If you think the wire looks bad, take a look over there," advised an unmistakably familiar voice.

The voice belonged to George's intellectual sparring partner, the Geordie who had managed to convince the former members of the Spanish Legion of the error of their ways, either that or, as was probably nearer the truth when conceived by the inner workings of George and Harry's minds working in devious collusion, that it was better to be expedient than rigidly honest in sticking to one's principles, and change sides there and then rather than relinquish their freedom for the sake of a suddenly less appealing ideology. The diminutive Scot had taken some convincing, but had been won over in the end. What neither George nor Harry had given a thought to, on the momentous occasion of their transferring their allegiance from Generalissimo Francisco Franco Bahamonde to Captain MacDonald of the British Battalion of the 12th International Brigade, was the possibility of their being captured for a second time, this time by the side they had volunteered to fight for in the first place. The counter-attack had been devastating. Captured wearing the uniforms of their former enemy, the Brigade's newest recruits had effectively jumped out of the frying pan into the fire.

Their Geordie comrade drew their attention past the gatehouse to the opposite end of the prison from the building which the former teacher had taken to be the administration centre. The points of interest which had been indicated to Harry and George were three posts, each standing a few metres apart from its nearest neighbour.

"Christ man, I bet that's where they carry out the executions; you know, tie you to a post to be shot by a firing squad."

"Do you really think that's what the posts are for?" asked George innocently.

"I can't think what else they might be used for," muttered Harry calmly, projecting by the tone of his voice that here was man who was unafraid to face the facts, no matter how stark they might be.

"Christ man! Our lives won't be worth that much in here," Geordie added, snapping his thumb and index finger together to demonstrate their paltry value. "Christ man!" he continued excitedly, "I wouldn't be surprised if they thought better of giving us a bed each for the night and started the proceedings here and now."

His pessimism knew no bounds.

"I don't think that that would be a wise move on their part," responded Harry, assuming the didactic tone so often used by George in his effusions upon life, love and war.

He waited for the expected prompt.

"Why not?" asked Geordie as if to oblige.

"Because, my Durham dunce, they would have a riot on their hands, and although they would do for a significant number of us, there's a slim chance that we might be able to kill the guards and take over the prison. It's amazing to think what eighty men might be capable of when they realise that not to take action would be an invitation to certain death."

It seemed to his audience that Harry had spoken with the Wisdom of Solomon. His playful insult, taken in good heart by the Geordie from Durham, was an indication of how times had changed.

"Yes; it would be much more practical to lock us all up, and then lead us out three at a time to be shot," remarked George as he continued along the track left by his friend's train of thought, terminating somewhat ruefully with a predictable but diurnally changing schedule, "Probably at dawn."

He didn't travel far, for the musings of the speculative trio on the prospect of meeting their maker within the prison walls were interrupted initially by the relocation of the transport, and then its final departure. In response to an order voiced by their officer, the guards that had arrived in the transport climbed back aboard, but only after they had first searched beneath the body of each vehicle for hangers-on, daredevils hell-bent on escape. Evidently nobody had thought it a viable option.

Once the trucks had left, a request was made for the most senior officer to make himself known from the throng of bedraggled prisoners. After a few moments pause, during which time a likely candidate was sought by all and sundry, even by the officer who eventually stepped forward, who should that be, who should emerge from the mass of bodies but Captain MacDonald. Subsequent to his revealing his credentials, so to speak, he was asked to bring his men to order. To an accompaniment of ironic shouts of welcome and a series of warnings bellowed mainly in Spanish from several of the topmost cells, Captain MacDonald, hardly revelling in his new appointment, boomed out his first order. This he did in a volume that belied his physical stature. The words of command were for the men to form three ranks. A sight to make a Guards Drill Instructor cringe, the men shuffled into the required formation, and in so doing prisoners Gilbert and Osborne found themselves standing side by side on the extreme right of the front rank, their attention focused on the officer facing them calling the tune, the man who had given them a second chance, such as it was.

At this juncture neither of the traitors to their original beliefs, bearing in mind the language difficulties, had had the opportunity to try to convince their captors that their presence in republican guise was really a big mistake, and that they should be welcomed with open arms back into the fascist fold. Without, however, having yet given utterance to their thoughts, both felt that the opportunity might soon present itself. The question was should they take it. After all, for such calculating minds as George and Harry's to change sides yet again, and probably with the full knowledge of those that had latterly befriended them, constituted a rung on the ladder of amorality to which they had not expected to descend. What's more, they had formed a genuine affinity with a small number of their fellow countrymen. Forged in the experience shared by Britons fighting abroad, this bond between enemies might well be easily broken were it to be put to the test, but it existed nonetheless. Finally, there were practicalities to consider. To reveal to their new masters that really they were on the same side, and that for the past couple of weeks they had been working under cover, would more than likely result in their being sent back to the front for a cause they were much more reluctant to die for than of yore. It goes without saying that unsettling conversations about the likelihood of their having to face a firing squad provided for a weighty counterbalance to any nascent sense of camaraderie or re-orientated loyalty. After witnessing the macabre faces of many a violent death at close quarters, George and Harry's earnest wish now was to live. With that selfish ambition uppermost in mind, ready to respond to Captain MacDonald's next words of command, for the time being they watched and listened.

Upon observing, approaching from the direction of the smaller of the two prison buildings, a group of officers dressed in the mainly olive green uniform of the Spanish Legion, Captain MacDonald began to take his responsibilities seriously, and gave the order which brought the men under his command to attention, albeit a little slovenly. Three of the four Spanish officers looked remarkably alike in that they were of the same height as the Scotsman, but unlike him they had each chosen to decorate their facial features with a moustache. Another difference was their swarthy skin. The fourth individual was not only much taller, but also fair skinned. He appeared to have achieved only a modicum of success in keeping his head down when the bullets and shrapnel were flying, for like a badge of distinction he wore a patch over his useless right eye. He was missing his left arm to boot. Wearing the insignia of a Lieutenant Colonel, guards and prisoners were his to command. Needless to say his own officers and men responded to his orders more or less willingly, whilst the remainder demonstrated varying degrees of reluctance. The Spanish officers were smartly dressed in brown, knee-length boots which accentuated the billowing cut of their trousers. They were in shirt-sleeve order. In the fashion-parade of headgear, each officer was wearing an olive-green forage cap adorned with gold braid, one end of which was a tassel dangling from the hat's peak. George was thinking how smart they looked compared to the Scottish Captain, though the latter's bedraggled appearance was explained by the fact that he had been wearing the same uniform for weeks, as had most of the prisoners. Until that moment the Yorkshireman had been waiting for something to happen with only moderate interest, but his focus sharpened considerably when the realisation dawned that the individual who had been watching him from the upstairs window and the officer standing in the shadow of the one-armed Colonel were one and the same. More startling still was the realisation that it was none other than el buen mayor, the officer who had been his Company Commander in the dim and distant past that was a fortnight ago. The change of environment and el buen mayor's now spruced appearance had served to obfuscate his identity to the astonished Englishman, but now that the penny had dropped, so to speak, George was absolutely certain of his man. Even as the Colonel was addressing the prisoners, uttering short phrases which were then translated into English by a subordinate, George dared to whisper to Harry about his discovery. This was a mistake, for just as daring to hold a private conversation whilst on parade would be taboo in all but the most rag-tag of armies, el buen mayor was going to have none of it. He glared at the culprits as he called for silence in the ranks. Then, after apologising to the Colonel for his outburst, he proceeded in part to imitate the actions of the prisoner who had incurred his wrath and whispered a few words into the Colonel's ear. In response to the information which el buen mayor had just imparted, the Colonel too cast his good eye in George and Harry's direction, withering them with a look of disdain verging on disgust.

No sooner had the Colonel finished speaking when el mayor strode towards George and Harry with menacing intent. He stopped a metre in front of Harry and adopted a stance which spoke volumes of his frame of mind, and which gave an insight to his character. He stood facing the Londoner with feet spread wide apart and a clenched fist placed on either hip. He scrutinised his quarry, and then, without changing his stance, turned his look of condemnation upon the next man in line. Just as George and Harry were certain of him, now he was sure that these were the same two individuals upon whom he had trained his binoculars only minutes before the opening shots were fired in the Battle of the Ebro.

"Comrades Gilbert and Osborne if I'm not mistaken," he said, his moustache elongating a little as he proffered a smile of the sort which didn't bode well for the men over whom he had absolute power.

"Legionnaires Gilbert and Osborne Señor," corrected George sharply, the right course of action having revealed itself by events.

"Legionnaires my foot!" barked el mayor, palpably incensed by the effrontery of the claim, so much so that he lashed out at Harry with the back of his hand. "Sois traidores a la causa (you are traitors to the cause)," he thundered, and he took a step towards George to mete out to him punishment of even greater severity.

George's head reeled as el mayor's fist made contact with his temple. The Spaniard had still not delved into the works of Pyrrho of Ellis, but as a considerable number of days had passed since his suspicions had been initially aroused, he was now absolutely certain that these two prisoners were guilty of the worst kind of treachery, and that there was no need to suspend his judgement further.

"On what grounds do you make these allegations Señor?" asked George, bravely.

Now that he had recovered he was standing ramrod straight and looking directly ahead, as was Harry. El buen mayor, being a little confused by the idiomatic language, couldn't quite correlate his interpretation of 'grounds' with 'allegations', but he fathomed the gist of the question nonetheless. For the Castillian officer the question vividly brought to mind events on the day of the attack, and unfortunately for the Britons the picture book of images included his being knocked unconscious whilst taking a pee. The ignominy of it! His conquistador antecedent must have turned in his grave, if he had a grave. The pain from being hit on the head by flying debris may have gone completely, but the memory still hurt, so much so that the macho Spaniard felt compelled to punch Harry in the stomach. Fortunately Harry saw the clenched fist coming his way moments before it struck his abdomen, and he had sufficient time to tense his stomach muscles and take the punch with the minimum of discomfort. For el mayor the occasional act of violence proved cathartic, and now that his anger had been released, he deigned to answer the question.

"On the day when your communist friends attacked across the Ebro, you deserted your trench to inform them of the precise location and strength of our positions," he said accusingly.

"No Señor; that's not true: we were simply going to fetch mud."

Upon hearing George's steadfast denial, once again the Legionnaire officer's anger got the better of him, and he prepared to strike the provocative prisoner. It was the intended victim's good fortune, however, that el mayor's pugnacious zeal was deflected from its purpose by the Colonel's voiced impatience and sense of propriety. After putting straight his hat, el mayor made a significant gesture for the benefit of the hapless Britons, though the meaning of 'benefit' in this instance was limited in the extreme, and applied merely to his willingness to put them in the picture about their immediate future, for the information imparted was not good.

Chapter Eighteen

Cascada de la Selva

The prison at Cascada de la Selva had been built before the war primarily as a facility to house the criminal fraternity sentenced by the courts in Madrid, but that didn't preclude the incarceration of felons from as far away as Cadiz in the south and San Sebastian in the north from being sent down to make the austere cells their home for any number of years. Up until the opening salvoes of the conflict that became known to history as the Spanish Civil War, a smattering of Spain's regional accents could be discerned, contrasting with the predominant Castillian; and though on occasion it was also possible to give an ear to the other distinct Iberian languages – namely Basque and Catalan – within the prison walls, to hear languages that were truly foreign to Spain was extremely rare.

Not so now of course; now that to a man the prison's civilian population of robbers, rapists, and murderers had been given the opportunity to atone for their crimes by volunteering, in a manner of speaking, to fight for the fascist cause. In consequence the cells had been emptied to make way for the blackguards, as perceived by Generalissimo Franco's staff, that were the republican prisoners-of-war. Included in that number were a couple of individuals of dubious caste.

Formerly Legionnaire, but presently Comrade, Gilbert was physically exhausted from having been made to stand to attention for over an hour. Harry had suffered equally. George was feeling despondent as he stood outside the cell he had been allocated. He watched with mute resignation as one of the two guards that had escorted him from the quadrangle and along the comparatively cool corridor that ran from end to end along the ground floor of the building, inserted the right key into the lock. Similar corridors ran along the second and third storeys. The key in question was located on a ring of about a dozen keys secured by a chain to the guard's belt. The depth of

George's moroseness can be judged by the fact that for the first time since he had met up with Harry, he began to perceive the Londoner not so much as a friend with whom he had shared many a perilous adventure through thick and thin, but as a malign spirit, or a jinx perhaps, who had been, and continued to be, the source of many of his troubles. In searching for a scapegoat to blame for his present predicament, he thought ill of Harry for persuading him – George Gilbert – to come to Spain in the first place. Significantly he didn't at all presently consider that his enthusiastic willingness to take part in the adventure might be to blame, (for it seemed that an object to blame must be found), and that he had acted of his own free will, without the slightest coercion. What he really despised Harry for at this time, however, was for coming up with a plan – a plan that held sway – to change sides when the going got tough. By acceding to the spirit of expedience, probably for the first time in his life George was ill at ease with himself, to the point of self-loathing. The heavy metal door, in which there was a window no bigger than a post-card positioned centrally more or less at eye-level, was slowly swung open. Upon receiving a far from gentle nudge from the second of the two guards, George was strongly encouraged to enter.

Prisoner 216 Gilbert (he had been given a number to be used by prison staff) had expected his new abode to be austere. What he hadn't expected was for his new home to be squalid, and it was the squalor which took him aback. In the corner facing him as he entered was the metal frame of a bed, single of course, on top of which a mattress was folded in half, thereby sandwiching two neatly folded blankets. If the stains on the side of the mattress which was visible were anything to go by, then what might be revealed when he rolled back the tainted soft-furnishing designed for sleep would probably be just as, or even more, prevalent. There were no pillows. The floor was blue linoleum, which was not only being eaten away at the edges, and in one corner in particular, but was also pitted with the burn marks of countless carelessly discarded cigarettes, this despite there being a sign at either end of the corridor informing, verbally and graphically, that smoking was 'prohibido'. Pushed against the cream-coloured walls in the corner opposite the bed was a Formica-topped table, the corners of which also showed signs of abuse and disintegration, perhaps from having been thrown about in fits of rage. Tucked under the table was a tubular metal chair, which looked sturdy enough. The smaller contents of the cell consisted of a chamber pot presently stowed under the bed springs, and an ashtray, which was atop the table. George's increasing familiarity with his new environment added greatly to his feelings of self-pity and dejection, feelings which could not be dissipated by such light as there was filtering through the stained-glass window – stained in the sense that its presence would have defiled rather than adorned a church or cathedral. Beyond the grimy, toughened glass were the iron bars. This fenestration to stay clear of if possible, being above head height, would at least allow George to glimpse a heavenly body through the grime, be it sun, moon, or star. At that moment George's cursory inspection was interrupted when he was spun round by a firm hand on his shoulder. The hand belonged to the guard who had opened the door. Upon turning George found himself facing the other hand holding a clasp-knife with the blade pointing towards him.

"You are a very lucky man to be given such a nice room free of charge, verdad?" said the guard as he cut through the cord which had bound prisoner 216's hands together.

The guard gathered up the severed bindings and stuffed them into his pocket. George would have been surprised if the man in the funny hat had been anything other than mocking, and normally he would have responded in like manner, just to show that he wasn't going to let them grind him down, so to speak. On this occasion, however, his response was restrained and without edge, for he merely asked in which cell they had locked-up Legionnaire Osborne. Neither of the guards would say, and smiling inanely, or like people privy to an important secret they could not be made to tell, they slammed shut the heavy steel door behind them, and left prisoner 216 to stew in his own perturbation, or alternatively to meditate in peace.

George unfolded his mattress, and after removing the blankets was pleased to discover that the stains now revealed were not nearly as bad as he had imagined, and compared favourably with those which were now hidden; or was it the case that after no more than five minutes had elapsed he had already grown accustomed to the somewhat fetid conditions of his immurement. After spreading one of the two blankets over the mattress, and replacing the other still folded, his next exploration involved grabbing the chair from under the table to relocate it to beneath the window. By standing on the chair he was able to see through the odd patch of clear glass perforating, as it were, the greater surface areas of grime, to a world beyond the iron bars. Disappointingly, this new perspective offered little of interest in that it consisted of nothing more than the barbed-wire topped wall and the hard surface between it and the cells, all of which were the more depressing to observe for being cast in shadow. All that was visible beyond the exterior wall was the presently featureless cobalt blue sky, in which for as long as he looked, neither a bird nor a cloud passed to break the visual monotony. The time George spent gazing was probably not as long as he thought. To his consternation, when finally he had grown tired of looking at nothing, he made as if to step down from the chair, but wasn't successful in the quick assessment of ratios required for the effective distribution of force, and thereby caused the chair to slip sideways before it was sent crashing into the table. George, using language of the sort that wouldn't have seemed out of place in barracks, and certainly wasn't out of place in prison, swore loudly as he jumped clear to land on his feet without injury. An unforeseen but beneficial consequence of the commotion was the expression of concern it elicited from the adjacent occupied cell.

"Are you alright in there?" asked a voice which to George's ears was only vaguely familiar for being muffled.

"Yes; I'm fine," replied George, thinking it unnecessary to explain what had happened. "Is that you Geordie?" he asked tentatively, hoping that the reply would confirm his suspicions.

"How did you know?" was the interrogative answer, followed by a similar request to be informed: "Is that you George?" Geordie asked.

Once their respective identities had been established both men immediately felt less isolated, and in consequence George's spirits for one began to rise. The effort required by each man to be heard was considerable. Their conversation could be likened to speaking to neighbours through the walls of a semi-detached or terraced house.

"What's your pad like?" asked the man from farther north than Yorkshire.

"Pretty grim," answered the Yorkshireman, and upon asking the same of his neighbour, he couldn't help but smile when he heard the former miner's caustic words.

"It's not bad, provided, that is, you don't mind sleeping on a mattress that smells of somebody else's vomit. Christ man! What I'd give for a bottle of brown ale is nobody's business."

"Me too!" responded George, though he realised as soon as the brief statement of solidarity had left his mouth that he was being disingenuous, and what he really would have offered a month's pay for was a pot of tea and a jug of milk.

Without removing a single item of clothing or footwear, he flopped on to the bed and stretched out on his back to gaze up at the ceiling, where for the first time he noticed that a light was embedded. A number of broken springs in the mattress became immediately apparent, and he had to adjust his position more than once to avoid a buttock or thigh coming to rest on the sharp point of a prong, a wire with the potential to pierce his skin. He let the back of his head rest in the clasped palms of his hands, and the sensation of feeling the coarse fibres of the blanket against his knuckles was not unpleasant, and the smell of old wool went a long way towards masking the other more obnoxious odours. George would have liked to have been left with his own thoughts for an hour or so, but he felt that he had to show generosity of spirit to the man who was likely to be the one and only source of friendly conversation for the foreseeable future, and so he resolved to respond as openly and as honestly as possible to every question that Geordie put to him.

"Do you know where they've put your friend Harry?" Geordie asked.

The erstwhile miner's more conspicuous traits of character were that he was naturally inquisitive and inclined to be friendly.

"None whatsoever," George replied. "Though I suppose he can't be far away."

In the protracted silence that followed both men began to grasp in an emotional sense how their conversations were to be conducted. This level of understanding was facilitated by the knowledge that they were already acquainted, and therefore could easily bring to mind the image of the other person. Eventually a perfect equilibrium was attained, its existence proven by the fact that neither felt compelled to maintain a conversation for the sake of it: neither felt ill at ease when silence returned after speech. When approximately ten minutes had elapsed, yet more sound waves filtered through the walls in the form of words.

"What's the name of that place you come from in Yorkshire? Is it Hamble something or other?"

"The village is called Hambleton," replied George succinctly.

"Do you have a wife and kids waiting for you in Hambleton?" Geordie asked, putting an unnatural emphasis on the name of the village.

"I have a wife but no kids," George replied, and then, in a voice so quiet that it would have been impossible for anyone else to hear, he added, "At least I believe I still have a wife."

"What's her name?"

George really didn't want to be put in mind of the life he had left behind in Yorkshire, and so after informing his fellow POW that his wife had been christened Martha, he made an excuse for curtailing their conversation for the present, stating that he would be better company after he had closed his eyes for an hour or two. In the silence that followed he drifted off into that recuperative unconscious state that is sleep.

Martha's husband had no idea how long he had been in the land of nod, but having been awakened by the resounding steps of jack-boots approaching along the corridor, he didn't think that he had been asleep for long. The shadows may have lengthened, but it was undoubtedly the afternoon on the day of their arrival. Aware that the key had been inserted into the lock, George called out to his neighbour by name.

"Yes; what is it?" responded the committed republican.

"How long would you say it has been since we last spoke, since you asked me about my wife?"

"About half an hour," came Geordie's reply.

With alacrity George got up from the bed. He had it in mind to meet whoever came through the door on equal terms, as far as that was possible. The guard opened the door as far as its hinges would allow. The same individual who had locked George up was the first to enter. The second guard followed hard on his heels, and he too was already known to George, as was the third person to join the rapidly burgeoning crowd – el buen mayor. The two guards stood with their rifles pointing at George's stomach. They were ready to fire from the hip if provoked. Prisoner 216 Gilbert scanned the expressions of all three Spaniards in the hope of being able to divine events about to unfold. He gleaned little from the men holding the rifles, for in this context their countenances were those of mere functionaries responding to el mayor's orders, and as such they were expressionless. The Major's face, however, spoke volumes, and what George saw written in those dark, malevolent eyes was a tale of disappointment and frustration. This was a tale George gained satisfaction from reading, for quite irrationally he jumped to the conclusion that the Spanish officer had come to release him; and in a sense he had.

"When I heard footsteps in the corridor I thought the guards might be bringing me my supper," said George, the loud rumbling in his stomach making it known to everyone present that it had been a long time since he had eaten.

Only he knew for certain that the last morsel to have passed his lips had been ten hours ago at breakfast, and even then the amount of food consumed – a slice of tortilla and a crust of bread – had been meagre.

"Cada cosa a su tiempo," responded the Major prior to repeating himself in English, "All in good time. If you must know I'm not happy that the Colonel has ordered you to be moved to a better cell."

Letting his words work their magic, the Spaniard reached into his pocket. George felt emboldened enough by the special treatment he was being shown to shout a fond farewell to his friend from the land of the prince bishops.

"I'm sorry Geordie, but I'm going to have to love you and leave you, if you get my gist."

"Oh! Why's that?"

"They're upgrading my accommodation," George replied.

"Silencio!" ordered, on his own initiative, the guard with the keys.

The Spanish officer withdrew from his pocket a piece of black cloth – a blindfold no less.

"Don't worry," said el buen mayor reassuringly. "You have to put this on for security reasons."

"Of course," responded George, and so optimistic was he that his life was about to change for the better that he gave his jailors considerable assistance in making his eyes useless.

Only when the blindfold had been applied, and George had been happy to confirm that he couldn't see a thing did the guards bind his hands, this time behind his back. Once again el buen mayor sought to reassure George with mellifluous words.

"This is necessary for the sake of appearances you understand. We can't have the other prisoners thinking that you are getting preferential treatment," he said.

At first George was surprised and confused by the suddenly felt sensation of being forcibly bound, but el buen mayor's words were as effective in assuaging George's fears as a mother's invariably are the first time she sends her son through the school gates. The Major reinforced the consideration he had expressed to George by speaking harshly in Spanish to the guards, telling them that there was no need to be so rough when their present business was no more than a charade. With the aim of giving the prisoner every opportunity of making sense of the carefully aimed rebuke, he enunciated the Castillian words with deliberate clarity. On his part George believed all that had been said to him by the Major simply because he wanted to believe it. The alternatives didn't bear thinking about. Calmly the quartet left the cell, and the man with the bunch of keys locked the heavy steel door behind them.

"Some people have all the luck!" shouted Geordie as a friendly farewell.

"What? Oh yes!" called back George, turning his benighted head towards the sound.

The guards, having shouldered their rifles, mirrored each other's grip on the prisoner. They were holding him by his upper arm and wrist. George willingly moved as they directed. Emanating from a source clearly visible to those with power to see, from further along the corridor the man bereft of his sight could hear other voices, other footsteps, and the inevitable slamming of a cell door. George couldn't be absolutely certain, but he thought he had heard Harry's distinctive voice ask if there was a wash basin and running water in his new abode. George smiled to himself at the thought. That was it: it had to be: the only possible explanation was that Harry and he were indeed being given preferential treatment prior to being taken back into the bosom of the

Legionnaire family. His illuminating analysis was interrupted by the effort required for the group to pass through two sets of doors. These he could remember and picture quite clearly, having passed through them with eyes wide open when going in the opposite direction only hours before. Soon after, George became aware of the subtle changes which told him that he was no longer inside the building, but once again breathing God's unfettered air. Most noticeable was the way that air caressed his face whilst at the same time stimulating his olfactory sense with the smell of freshly baked bread. He remembered how ravenously hungry he was and thought of asking how long it would be till supper, but he decided to let events take their course on the basis that his hunger would not be eradicated any sooner for the knowing. "Cada cosa a su tiempo," he even muttered to himself, reiterating el buen mayor's words. When George and his escort finally halted, prisoner 216 Gilbert was manipulated to turn ninety degrees to the right before the guards released their grip. George imagined that his blindfold would soon be removed and his hands untied. Instead, he was told by el buen mayor that the Colonel wished to say a few words to him, and for that reason for the time being he should remain silent and stand to attention. George did as he was told. Harry, however, standing a little way off had heard it all before, and though he was unable to see, and therefore identify, the prisoner who had been brought to stand alongside him only yards away, he presumed the individual to be none other than his friend and comrade-in-arms. For him the penny had dropped, and he couldn't resist breaking the spell of deceit.

"Well George," he said, turning his blindfolded eyes in the direction he believed his friend to be. "It looks as if they're about to shoot us."

At that moment, for George the realisation dawned that never again would he see the sun.

Chapter Nineteen

Zealand, Denmark

When Hanne, having, at the umpteenth time of trying, got through on the telephone to somebody at Aalborg Airfield who was prepared to tell her exactly what she wanted to know, had heard that Turmfalke two-nine had failed to return from its mission, she had felt her body go numb from head to toe. At the time she made a point of trying to remember every detail of the strange and unwelcome physical sensation which she realised was her emotional response to the news which she had more than half expected to hear. After taking on board the salient facts, she had conducted this remarkable piece of self scrutiny and analysis whilst at the same time paying a modicum of attention to the words being spouted down the line, words which had sought to console the shocked listener by suggesting that rather than allowing feelings of grief and self pity to hold sway, she should instead feel pride in the knowledge that her boyfriend – a Teutonic knight if ever there was one – had been captured or killed on a mission the successful completion of which would have enhanced the glory of the Fatherland. Despite the attempt to inspire, Hanne had felt nothing of the kind, and many of the words spoken in German had gone in one ear and out the other. It was as if her knowledge of the language had diminished in an instant, and as it was she who had instigated the inquiry a week after she might have expected to hear from Hans had he returned safely, she felt no inhibition in putting down the receiver in mid-conversation. All this had happened three weeks ago, and in a sense it was fortunate for Hanne that Hans had, either wittingly or otherwise, left her a legacy which was not only demanding of her faculties, but fraught with danger. The venture in which she had now enthusiastically become embroiled had gained dynamic momentum when Astrid's Jewish friend Sara, recognising that there was probably a great deal of substance in the warning which Hanne and Astrid had passed on, had agreed that it would probably be a good idea for the Melchior family to pay their distant relations in Angelholm – a small town near the coast approximately twenty kilometres north of the Swedish port of Helsingborg – a visit. If getting the Melchior family's acquiescence to leave Danish territory had been relatively easy, the planning involved in how to put their strongly recommended foreign holiday into effect had proved more difficult, aside an obviously naive and rather comical false start. It was the courage, tenacity and thought required which enabled Hanne to subsume her feelings for Hans until such time as she would be able to put recent events into a wider perspective, and it was as a consequence of her courage, tenacity and thought that she presently found herself seated on the train pulling out of Helsingør station on what she thought would be the final stage of her odyssey to assist her Jewish friends before she returned to pick up the pieces of her normal life.

Hanne was seated in the immediate vicinity of strangers. The railway carriage was of the type which has pairs of seats facing each other, and although she had travelled across Denmark by train and ferry in the company of five people whom she knew, none was presently in her little enclave. The idea not to appear to be travelling as a group which would be conspicuous because of its size was Hanning's, the café proprietor who had eventually revealed himself to the young women in his true colours – as a member of the resistance.

Hanning was seated next to Mrs Melchior facing in the same direction as Hanne; that is with their backs to the direction in which they were heading. They were in the next precinct, but one. Her view blocked by the back of his seat, Hanne could just make out a little of the right side of the café owner's head. The arm, foreshortened somewhat, and thumb of the hand that were holding a newspaper, completed the image of the unlikely resistance fighter's dextral side. The headlines informed of fierce fighting in North Africa. Farther along the carriage, on the opposite side of the centre aisle, Astrid and Sara sat together facing the engine. By looking slightly askance it was possible for either party to make eye contact with Hanne, but so as not to elicit the slightest sign of recognition, Sara focused her attention on the magazine she was reading, whilst Astrid gazed at the passing scenery. They were playing the security game in earnest. Directly behind Sara, so that they were sitting back to back, was Mr Melchior, his Homburg protruding prominently above the headrest. On what was destined for the parents to be their last train journey on Danish soil, everything thus far had gone according to plan.

Hanne smiled to herself as she too turned her attention to the arboreal and pastoral scenes flashing by the window. Upon passing through a sizeable tract of forest, she had tried to penetrate with her eyes deep into its innermost mystery, but was distracted in this innocuous but psychologically significant activity by her own reflection in the window. The sight of her self-indulgent expression caused her to stop smiling abruptly, lest her fellow passengers close by should think her a simpleton. The reason she had been able to smile – in her opinion inanely – at a time when her feelings, though somewhat confused, were undoubtedly more sombre than light, was because she had brought to mind at that moment Astrid's and her original plan for getting Sara, and, as it turned out, Sara's parents, out of the country. Their potentially brilliant but inevitably flawed plan had been to hire a sail boat in one of the smaller ports along the east coast of Jutland. They were soon to discover that with, on average, less than an hour's sailing experience each, that this would be an impractical, and therefore hazardous, mode of travel, and especially so when the distance they would have needed to sail was approximately eighty kilometres. The young women had gone so far as to hire a boat for a trial run after convincing a ruddy-faced fisherman in Ebeltoft (the name of which, perhaps a little incongruously for a town on the coast, in English means 'Apple-orchard'), that they were reasonably competent sailors. Needless to say they had soon realised that they weren't as skilled as they had thought, and although they had managed to make some progress at the outset, unfortunately for the gullible owner, the three women in a boat could only manage to make landfall across the picturesque bay that is Ebeltoft Vig, where a group of German soldiers were enjoying some free time playing football on the beach, time referred to in military parlance as rest and recuperation. Ingratiating herself by incorporating into her speech and body language all the flirtatious subtlety and feminine wiles she could muster, but without resorting to anything which might subsequently cause her to feel ashamed, Astrid had proceeded to persuade a couple of interested individuals in knee-length shorts to sail the dinghy back for them. Upon receipt of their promissory word the trainee fugitive and her accomplices left the scene to return to Ebeltoft on foot, the women's respective psyches bathed in the almost visible glow of satisfaction at having done all they had thought was necessary to return the craft to its rightful owner. Their sense of relief even supplanted their feelings of disappointment at having failed in their mission to become expert sailors in an instant. The day after their original idea had been tried, tested, and found wanting, the female trio had sat down to consider the problem with a greater degree of resolve. Astrid it was who had emphasised that what they were about was hardly a game, and that they needed to be cautious and thorough in all that they did, and when it came to matters of security, meticulous. By this time, having been certain of her man for some weeks, she had brought Hanning into the picture, and with his contacts in the resistance movement, his contribution would prove invaluable.

After a journey lasting just under half an hour, the train which had begun its journey in Helsingør pulled into Hornbæk station, where about half the people in the carriage occupied by the meticulous six made ready to disembark. During the kerfuffle generated by people reaching for items of luggage and donning their coats, Hanning, having folded his newspaper and placed it under his arm, turned around and projected towards Hanne the warmest of smiles and a barely perceptible nod, gestures which told her that everything was still tickety-boo, and that they were to alight from the train in accordance with their plan. The order of disembarkation which had been agreed at the final clandestine meeting held in Hanning's café, was for Hanning and Mrs Melchior to leave the train first, followed by Mr Melchior, who in turn was to be followed by Sara and Astrid. Hanne had volunteered to bring up the rear. This arrangement was progressing better than envisaged by virtue of the fact that about an equal number of other passengers had interposed themselves between the individuals and pairs that collectively were involved in an escapade the importance of which, in the sense that it would be a prequel for others, could not as yet be appreciated fully. Indeed, the courage of their endeavour cannot be understated, for by choosing to take heed and respond positively to a warning which had to be at least questionable for it having been given by one of the invaders to his infatuated girlfriend, Sara's parents in particular were not unaware that their present actions might lead precipitately to an unpleasant fate, perhaps one more lamentable than if they had decided to stay put and do nothing. In their late fifties, neither Mr nor Mrs Melchior was gravely concerned about what might happen to each of them if things were to go sadly wrong over the next twenty-four hours, but whenever they considered their daughter's safety, which ever since the occupation had been most of the time, the level of their anxiety was almost unbearably high. Not being naturally inclined to adventures involving subterfuge, everything they were presently about had been driven by Sara for their benefit. From their perspective, they were only too willing to be driven, or led, for the sake of their daughter's future. Not one of them had the slightest inkling that they were in effect the advance party of an exodus of thousands, an exodus that would see somewhere in the region of ninety-five per cent of Jews living in Denmark escape The Holocaust. Mr and Mrs Melchior would have been struck dumb at the thought.

At Hornbæk Hanning was to look for a man wearing a blue, corduroy cap waiting near to the station exit. He would be standing with his hands behind his back clutching a newspaper folded in a manner not dissimilar to Hanning's, the sole difference being that as a mark of recognition to his contact the traveller from Aarhus was to carry his periodical under his arm. It was the stuff of spy stories, both real and fictitious. No sooner had Hanning stepped off the train on to the platform than he espied the man he was looking for. The man from Hornbæk, being a tall, barrel-chested figure with a complexion as tough as a narwhal's skin, stood head and shoulders above the crowd, and that made his corduroy cap easily discernible. A moment later, however, it became apparent to Hanning that not everything was as it should be. The fisherman was standing with his arms folded across his chest. In his close vicinity the only newspaper in sight was being read by one of two Wehrmacht officers, figures that couldn't be more easily recognisable attired as they were in their field-grey uniforms, high-peaked caps and shiny, black, knee-length boots. Each officer was wearing a belt with a pistol-holder.

Hanning, who was the only member of the party to be aware of the arrangements which had been made with the resistance movement in Zealand, had to assess the situation and make a decision on how best to proceed in a matter of seconds. What's more, he had to make that decision alone.

The procedures involved for meeting the contact were known only to Hanning because of concerns about security, and though this had been questioned by Hanne and Astrid on the basis that the remainder would be left completely in the dark if anything untoward were to happen to the man whom they now looked up to for seeing in a different light, knowledge of those procedures was not disseminated.

Smiling down at Mrs Melchior as if nothing were amiss, Hanning offered to carry her suitcase for her, and following her willingness to relinquish this burden, Hanning, still with the newspaper under his arm, achieved a state of perfect equilibrium by carrying a suitcase in each hand, the other being his own. He declined an offer by Mrs Melchior to let her, in return, carry his newspaper for him. His mind raced as he considered the possibilities that the presence of the German officers and the apparent redeployment of the newspaper that was not his heralded. He wondered as he joined the queue to hand over his ticket, whether he should take it upon himself to abort the mission completely, or at least postpone it. He was still in two minds as the railway employee said, "Tak!" to him. It seemed that he had no choice but to follow on the heels of Mrs Melchior as steadfastly she made her way towards the station exit, where stood, certainly from Hanning's perspective, the enigmatic welcoming committee. The fact that by this time the two members of the resistance movement who had never before met, were each aware that the other was a bird of a feather, so to speak, might, under the circumstances, have led to a few indiscreet nods and winks as Hanning and the man from Hornbæk sought to exchange a few silent questions and answers in the form of looks which might have aroused the suspicions of an observant third party. In the final analysis, however, neither Dane had much to worry about, for the German officers were too absorbed in the news from North Africa to be concerned about what the man from whom they had borrowed the newspaper was doing behind their backs. Pressured as he had been just as the fifteen-ten from Helsingør had pulled into the station, Hanning's contact hadn't been about to put himself in a difficult position by denying the young officer's request. For his part Hanning continued to act as if everything was going according to plan.

The man from Hornbæk, after allowing his gaze to rest just a little longer than might be expected when eye contact is made between strangers, to rest on those knowing and friendly eyes that approached his with equal import, turned towards his sworn enemy and, demonstrating the kind of familiarity which can only emanate from a person who has nothing to fear or hide, he tapped him on the shoulder. Needless to say, in some respects the man from Hornbæk had fallen back upon his thespian skills, skills which until this moment he wasn't at all sure he possessed. The German officer knew at once whose hand it was, and upon turning an enquiring face towards the fisherman, was about to apologise for having appropriated his property for longer than he should have, when the formidable Dane held up his hand for the officer to desist. At the same time he explained in his mother tongue that the people he had arranged to meet had not turned up, that he was about to leave, and that it was alright for the officer to keep his newspaper. He added that he had read most of it earlier in the day. The fisherman's utterances were hardly textbook Danish, and at least half of what he had said was lost on the young officer, who found the language easier to understand as the written word. Fortunately for all concerned his aural comprehension was ably assisted by his fellow officer, whose knowledge of the lingo was evidently sufficiently accomplished for him to be able to interpret the fisherman's words correctly. Within earshot of this conversation, Hanning felt a surge of relief when he realised that the circumstance which had given him so much cause for concern, was nothing more than one of life's little cameos, the sort of thing which cannot be anticipated when planning an operation.

The Germans smiled at the giant of a man standing beside them and expressed their thanks. Surprisingly perhaps, the officer who had been tapped on the shoulder was pleased that the Dane had acted so informally, for deep down he was of a disposition which wanted to be liked by the people he had helped to subjugate. Without more ado the fisherman left the station, confident that all the members of the disparate group he had come to meet would follow.

Leading the way was Mrs Melchior, whose bustling resolve to proceed straight ahead when the direction was obvious, was not without its comical aspect. When uncertain of the way she would pause to look up at Hanning over her left shoulder, and he would indicate the direction with a nod. It didn't take her long to work out, as they trekked through the narrow streets of the fishing hamlet, the history of which stretched back half a millennia, that the twists and turns they had made exactly matched those of a man walking approximately twenty metres ahead of them, a man remarkable for his size, and for the fact that he was wearing a blue, corduroy cap. Mrs Melchior, as a Jewish matriarch for the present may have relinquished much of her authority, and not an inconsiderable amount of her autonomy, by allowing strangers to take responsibility for the safety of her family, but that didn't mean that she was blind to everything going on around her. Trusting of her acute female sensitivity, she had not failed to notice Hanning's heightened sense of anxiety in the railway station, but had put that down to the daunting presence of the Wehrmacht. Since then she had worked out that it wasn't by chance that they were following the man in front, and that he was operating as their guide. Only once on their journey from the station did Mrs Melchior turn around to check that Hanning and she were being followed, and in so doing she was reassured to discover that shadowing them about twenty metres behind, in close proximity to a pair of middle-aged women, was her husband, and that a similar distance behind him, were her daughter and Astrid. Hanne had yet to appear from around the corner at the end of the street. Mrs Melchior, though aware that there were going to be many trials to endure and overcome before she and her family could even begin to feel secure, was pleased nonetheless that thus far everything seemed to be going according to plan. Once again she asked Hanning if he would let her carry his newspaper, and as he had no further need of it, this time he relented.

"That's a weight off my mind," said Hanning as he handed over the periodical, all the while keeping a close watch on the movements of the man leading the way.

"We must be a great burden and a worry to you," rejoined Mrs Melchior with a generosity of spirit which enabled her to appreciate that these individuals, these newfound friends, were risking their lives so that she and her family had a feasible chance of a future, and they weren't even Jews. "I just want you to know," added Mrs Melchior in the same quiet tone which the seriousness and magnitude of the situation demanded, "that I'm sure that I speak for my husband and daughter when I say that irrespective of what happens, whether things turn out for the good, or for the bad, we are extremely grateful that you are doing this for us."

Hanning said nothing in reply, but merely looked at Mrs Melchior with an expression which effectively communicated that it was an honour to help, notwithstanding the risk he was taking.

They walked on in silence into the thickening twilight, the rapidly increasing darkness prompting the man from Aarhus to quicken his, and in consequence, Mrs Melchior's pace. He didn't want to lose sight of their guide.

Wherever they were being led had to be near, for in the gaps between the buildings they could see, directly ahead, the harbour quay. The cold, inhospitable waters of the Kattegat were visible in the same way that a photographic negative reveals, that is by the greater intensity of darkness. The sounds that could be heard were of that same water lapping against the hulls of small boats, and above the heads of many a listener could be heard the plaintive cries of two or three defiant gulls. The air was fragrant with the smell of the sea.

The fisherman in the cap no longer discernible by its colour switched on a torch as he entered a maze of narrow alley-ways that criss-crossed to form a grid in the veritable shanty-town of fishermen's huts, a lattice of space that was navigable with ease only to an experienced few. Needless to say the act of following was made considerably easier by the presence of a guiding light, notwithstanding the fact that the distance between each compartment of the human train, bar one, was now only five metres. The crucially important exception to the train being complete was the absence of Hanne, who as the last carriage, so to speak, and through no fault of her own, had inadvertently become uncoupled, ultimately leaving her no choice for a time but to follow a track of her own choosing.

In an occupied country, where the new masters have imposed and established their authority by force of arms, the problem for an attractive woman walking out alone is that she is seen as fair game by the lowliest ranks of that occupying force, as a potential date in the amorous sense of that word. With no other intention in mind than to ingratiate themselves, therefore, a pair of patrolling Privates had detained Hanne almost as soon as she had stepped out of the station, and as the one and only reason for detaining her was to make an attempt at courtship, with genuine affability the soldiers went through the motions of checking Hanne's papers. The documentation proving her identity, being genuine, was not a cause for concern. What could have been a problem, however, had she not given some thought to this eventuality beforehand, was the requirement to provide a plausible explanation as to what she was doing so far from home. Obviously she couldn't fall back upon the truth. Instead she resorted to her practised cover story, a tale which she was able to deliver under pressure with naturalness and apparent sincerity.

In point of fact, the story which Hanne had come up with back in Aarhus was so good, so plausible that when she narrated it to her friends, Astrid and Sara gave the creator a round of applause, and asked if she had any objection to their using the story if either or both of them were stopped for questioning. Flattered somewhat that her ingenuity was so appreciated, and after coming to the conclusion that one or all of them could be about to apply for the same course, Hanne had expressed no objection, and more importantly, neither had Hanning. Hanne's cover, and the story she had set about telling the naively optimistic German soldiers checking her papers, was that she intended to enrol on an art appreciation course at Aarhus University after Christmas, and as part of her preparations she had come to Hornbæk to discover what it was about the village that had, in the last century, attracted such eminent artists as Kristian Zahrtmann, P.S. Krøyer, Viggo Johansen, and Locher. Hanne found herself becoming quite effusive about her subject, and asked the soldiers if they were familiar with the works of any of the people she had mentioned. When, as she had expected, the soldiers replied in the negative, in a didactic sense she began to dominate the discourse to such an extent that the two young men excused themselves from taking any further part in Hanne's impromptu al fresco lesson. After handing back her papers and wishing her a pleasant stay, they bade the blonde swot adieu.

Hanne's feelings as she watched the soldiers walk hurriedly away, were those of a woman who has just achieved notable success. After all, it's not every day that so many recently nascent skills are put to the test, and in so doing she had emerged triumphant, confident in her ability to act, to teach, to lie. These skills, she analysed, appertained mainly to the role she had assumed as a student of fine art; as an undercover operator intent on completing her mission she perceived herself to be the real thing. The minutes of savouring success soon passed, and as she stood watching the prowling soldiery go through the same procedure with a woman who had just emerged from the station, and who, at least from a distance, could have been her doppelganger, Hanne's sense of achievement began to lose its lustre. Without a clue as to the whereabouts of her friends, consternation and panic became manifest. Hanne's immediate urge was to run, not from a desire to escape, but in the hope of catching sight of Sara and Astrid before they disappeared round a corner not yet visible to the secret-agent becoming more disillusioned by the minute. Hanne had enough presence of mind, however, to walk rather than run, for the more dynamic action would, more than likely, have aroused suspicion. Twenty metres from where she had been detained, she turned the first corner and felt a churning sensation in the pit of her stomach, for her friends and accomplices were no longer in sight. Hanne struggled to act rationally and not allow her mind to be ruled by capricious thoughts, notwithstanding the fact that one of those thoughts seemed remarkably rational for the realisation it brought, specifically that perhaps she wasn't such a cool secret agent after all. The more than slightly distraught woman from Aarhus made steady progress towards the harbour and the shanty-town of fishermen's huts into which she hoped, and in fact sensed, that the others had gone.

Meanwhile, realising only when it was too late to do anything about it, at least for the time being, that Hanne's carriage no longer formed part of the train, the others had followed their guide through the maze of huts until they arrived at a door held open by a second fisherman, a man who in all probability was also a member of Holger Dansk. Hanning's first impression of the ghostly figure whose face was only partially illuminated by the light cast by a candle burning within, was that here was a man presently susceptible to, and intent on keeping out, the cold.

The man in the corduroy cap led the way inside the hut which had been selected as a safe-haven because of it being one of the larger wooden buildings in the shanty neighbourhood. Primarily it was used for stowing gear and drying fish, but had been cleared of most of that paraphernalia for the mission in hand. Facing each other along the internal walls of the hut were benches which could be used as beds. If the people in residence were six feet tall or less, then it was possible for two people to sleep on either bench, and those fortunate few to have already experienced the restful comfort the benches provided, had slept with their feet touching, or almost touching, in the middle. The individual the larger man had brushed past, continued to hold open the door with one hand and beckon the new arrivals with the other. At the same time, for the purpose of generating warmth, he performed a little dance which involved stamping his feet alternately. This man's head, which was extended by a hat with a bobble on top, was sunk into his hunched shoulders. In passing, Mrs Melchior joked that he needed to get some blubber on his bones, and if it were only possible she would be only too willing to transfer a hefty portion of hers.

It was only after the company of worthy conspirators had gathered that Astrid and Sara, being as yet the only people in the know, to have any intimation that Hanne was missing, could reveal their concerns to all and sundry. Hanning's initial reaction was one of disbelief, and what he couldn't accept with equanimity was the fact that the young women hadn't informed him sooner. He was more than a little exasperated with them, and more than a little anxious for Hanne.

"When did you first notice that she wasn't behind you?" questioned Hanning, his tone totally devoid of a café-owner's servile politeness.

"I glanced behind me just before we made that first turning into the warren of paths between the huts, and was aghast to discover that Hanne was nowhere in sight. It was getting quite dark by then, but that didn't prevent me from being able to recognise the few people that were out and about as total strangers. Naturally, after grabbing her by the arm, I gasped my discovery to Astrid, and there and then we decided to keep to the original plan for the simple reason that to do otherwise could have put in jeopardy the entire enterprise."

"That's right!" added Astrid in support of her friend, just as she had done on more than one occasion when Hanne and she were being reprimanded at school. "We couldn't have very well called out to you, and to have run after you would have been just as foolish."

Her tone was defiant, barbed. The group of five new arrivals plus one formed a standing circle in the centre of the room. In the hope that the missing person might appear at any moment, and despite the fact that he was feeling the cold, the fisherman in the hat with a bobble remained outside, looking along the path between the huts as he held the door slightly ajar.

"Oh dear!" exclaimed Mr Melchior as he placed his suitcase on the floor between his feet, "I do hope nothing untoward has happened to the poor child. Perhaps," he postulated as he regained his full height (which didn't alter the fact that he was still the shortest man in the room), "she has been taken by the Gestapo."

This comment motivated Hanning to alter his tone, to assume again the role of confident leader able to overrule his emotions, and not as a fraught individual with obvious misgivings. His next words were therefore meant to project optimism about the prospects of bringing Hanne back into the fold within the hour.

"Hanne's a resourceful and intelligent young woman," said Hanning, and lowering his head slightly to look directly into the eyes seeking reassurance, eyes that were presently set to implore like a puppy-dog's beneath Melchior's shining head with its furrowed brow, he added, "I'm sure she'll come to no harm."

"What's your missing friend's full name?" asked the taller fisherman of Hanning.

"Hanne Hjelmsleve," interjected Astrid emphatically, "and if you're going back to look for her, Sara and I are going with you."

The big man from Hornbæk looked intently at Astrid, and with a voice which resonated so deeply that if it were heard and the speaker remained unseen, so that that same voice sounded as if it had originated in the ether rather than a human larynx, and therefore could possibly be mistaken for the voice of God, he said, "You are all to stay here." Less portentously he asked, "Was she the woman carrying a check-patterned holdall, the checks being black and grey if I remember correctly?"

"That was observant of you," commented Hanning.

"It pays to be at times like this," responded the fisherman curtly.

"Are you taking the piece?" enquired the man holding the door. "I can get it for you in a trice."

He was referring to a pistol which had been removed from the lifeless body of a German officer some time back, this after the officer in question had been despatched by the Dane when the giant was feeling less than gentle. Indeed, after stealthily approaching from behind, the hunter had killed his prey using only his bare hands.

"Leave it where it is," the big man ordered. "I don't think I'll need it."

The fisherman who had just declined to carry a weapon turned to the people for whom he was acting as guide and got down to a few house-keeping points which, though essentially banal, were crucial for the people in transit to know. After informing their guests that they were not to leave any evidence at all of their stay, the man most definitely in charge apologised for the lack of what today would be described as en suite facilities, but relieved the pressure a little when he pointed out that his comrade, who would be staying with them and in whom they could have complete trust, would show them where to go if they needed to go. His last instructions before setting out on his individual quest were that other than to answer a call of nature, nobody was to leave the hut until he returned, and that with over six hours to wait until high tide, which at Hornbæk was scheduled to be at twenty-six minutes to midnight, they should make themselves as comfortable as possible.

The fisherman's parting words were, "I'll be back as soon as I can, hopefully in the company of Miss Hjelmsleve."

Chapter Twenty

Hambleton Village

In the hierarchy of most comfortable nights spent in circumstances not normally considered conducive to my sleeping soundly, the hours I spent recumbent on a bed of sacks in a garden shed somewhere in England's back of beyond score quite highly. That said, however, and notwithstanding the leaden weight of my fatigue, it took an inordinate amount of time for me to nod off. I came to the conclusion that this had nothing to do with the relative comfort or discomfort of my improvised bed, and everything to do with the images racing through my mind. The majority were mental replications of the momentous events which had occurred in the past thirty-six hours. These meagre additions to the history of the world constituted an epoch in my personal biography, for I can say unequivocally that never before had I lived so dangerously, so intensely, and I reserve judgement as to whether I would ever want to live so near to the edge again. It seemed, as the images passed vividly before my eyes, appearing and disappearing apparently of their own volition, that I had, over the preceding couple of days, experienced everything life had to offer apart from the birth of my progeny and my own demise. Of course I know that in reality there is even more to life than these not insignificant happenings, but that was how I felt at that precise moment. From my having witnessed death at close quarters I was able to form a crystal clear impression that this was a state of being – or perhaps it would be more accurate to state non-being – that I wanted to postpone, particularly at the age I was. One immensely positive thought to enter my consciousness as I lay awake listening to the rain beating down upon the roof that was only vaguely discernible, was that I had been fortunate in the extreme to have emerged from the maelstrom of my recent past still healthy in mind and body. I didn't need to make an in-depth analysis to realise that there were plus signs at every turn, and though these same signs were remarkably effective in counteracting fear, doubt and self-pity, insofar as they were able to perform as substitutes for sheep deliberately brought to mind to be counted, the associated images were counter-productive. Their seemingly random appearance didn't completely relegate me to the role of automaton, for an aspect of the supine slide show over which I retained some control, was in how long I dwelt upon each image.

Upon seeing in my mind's eye my friend's and comrades' lifeless bodies, I revelled in being able to touch with the palms of my hands first my stomach with its bed of soft hair, then the smooth outer flanks of my thighs, and last but not least, that part of the male anatomy which rises and falls in accordance with its pleasure. This tactile awareness of my continued physical existence brought Hanne to mind, initially the memory of our love-making prior to my departure to fly on this mission. The fantasy of her naked form partially covered by slightly dishevelled tresses was a big plus, and, I don't mind admitting, for a short time was the cause of considerable tumescence. A lesser plus to come to mind, perhaps the main purpose of which was to relieve the pressure in my loins by overriding the stimulus provided by Hanne's phantasmagorical presence, was the timely arrival of the Army convoy under the command of Leutnant Schultz. Ernst's and my ride in the captured ambulance was mainly of interest. The incidence of our having become entrapped within its dark interior, though undoubtedly infuriating at the time, made me chuckle at the absurdity of it, and I almost laughed out loud when the image-controller inside my head brought into view, as it were, Major Hofmann, particularly his reaction to the sorry state of his beloved car. Strange as it may seem, the Camp Commandant's splendid ire is the last thing I remember before, at long last, sleep ruled the roost.

My plan to wake before dawn and slip away, without anybody noticing that I had spent most of the night in their midst, went sadly awry. I was still dozing dreamily in my sack sleeping bag when I became dimly aware of the shed door being opened. The rain which I had heard incessantly before sleep, had passed during the night and given way to a day of bright sunshine, though at that time of year the air felt colder for it. Dust unsettled by the sudden movement floated like airborne plankton in a strait-edged plane of intense luminescence. Just as I had noticed when Ernst and I were riding in the back of the ambulance how the light emitted by the headlamps of passing vehicles penetrated the darkness in the form of narrow beams, similar effects were in evidence in the garden shed. The differences between then and now, that place and this, were that the holes and cracks in these walls hadn't been made by bullets fired from a Mauser, and the light which passed through the tiny apertures in and between the timber planks, was visible for more than a few seconds.

Awakened by the creaking hinges as the unknown person was about to enter, it took a few moments for me to substitute the stuff of dreams with perceptions of reality, though for a time which was the most unwelcome of the two hung in the balance. I say this because in the drowsiness of my waking state the strongly backlit figure at the door I identified as a man dressed in the leather garb beloved of the Gestapo, and he had come to question me, me of all people. I knew what he wanted to know before he had uttered a word or had a chance to remove his hat. It was now obvious to me that they had picked up Hanne for disseminating information prejudicial to the interests of the Reich, information which I had divulged to her. The Gestapo man was accompanied by a 'heavy' dressed in the brown shirt and cap of the Sturmabtellung, the notorious Storm Division. I hadn't previously met any members of that insanely zealous gang, though I had discreetly witnessed their methods when they came to remove a family from the house situated across and a little way up the road from my parents' house. That was a few years before the war, and I knew the family to be Jewish. My mother had told me not to get involved, not to talk about it. It was as if that family had never lived amongst us, and the harsh treatment I had seen being meted out had never happened.

It did happen though, and the memory which most often rises to prick my conscience is of their possessions being piled up in the tiny front garden for any passing Aryan to plunder or destroy as the fancy took us.

My last unrealistic thought was that if these characters, these brutes, were to intimate that they had harmed Hanne in any way, I would shoot them both there and then.

My first realistic thought upon waking was that it was hardly likely that the Gestapo and their brown-shirt henchmen were able to operate in England, and therefore the person who had opened the door had to be someone else who wasn't likely to take kindly to me. My first action upon becoming fully awake, therefore, was to reach for my gun.

Demonstrating all the alacrity and manual dexterity you might expect of a man who was now fully in control of his mental and physical faculties, and who perceived there to be an immediate threat to his security, gripping with my left thumb and forefinger I cocked the pistol. In the same instant, with a deft flick of the thumb of the hand which held the pistol-grip, I released the safety-catch. Ready to fire, I aimed the weapon at the unsuspecting figure standing in the doorway. Needless to say the stuff of dreams had dissipated, and in place of my insubstantial inquisitors was a substantial woman. In my urgent desire to take control of the situation the first words I spoke to her were in German.

"Hande hoch!" I ordered quietly, for the last thing I wanted was to bring other family members running to the woman's aid. I repeated the command in my best student English: "Hands up!" At the same time I beckoned with my free hand for the astonished creature to take a few steps forward.

"Please," I said, "you may close the door behind you."

The woman did as she was bid and then turned once more to face me. Now that we had both got over our respective surprises, mine at having been discovered, and hers at having made such a shocking discovery, we each began to rationalise the situation. It occurred to me that this must have presented a greater challenge for her than it did for me. For one thing I was pointing a gun at her. Moreover, I was sitting naked and uncovered from the waist up in an improvised bed of sacks; that and the fact that I had effectively revealed my identity as a member of an opposing tribe rather than as an indigenous gentleman of the road, must also have added to her bewilderment. Naturally I didn't allow this insight to spill over into expressions of sympathy. In point of fact neither of us said anything more for several moments. For me this time was taken up by working out in my head what I wanted to say, and what I eventually said was, "Please, I would like now to get dressed, so if you wish to turn your back to me, you may so do. It is entirely up to you."

The woman did as I suggested. Notwithstanding the fact that I could have shot her dead at a whim, I found the business of extricating myself from the hessian sack to stand naked in broad daylight in the presence of a stranger of the opposite sex to be embarrassing, and it was with nervous haste that I pulled out my still damp socks, underpants and shirt which upon turning in I had stuffed in the sack with me. Apart from a single sock, the individual items of clothing had become enmeshed as one, and though I searched inside the sack for an age, for an age the missing item of footwear eluded me. It only came to light after I had put down my gun to shake free with both hands the sack's elusive content. In an attempt to fill the silence, and to convince my female hostage that she wasn't being held captive by a dolt, I decided to make polite conversation.

"Please, what is your name?" I enquired.

Taking into account the length of time that had elapsed since I made the suggestion designed to save the woman's blushes, it was hardly surprising that she should respond to my question as if I was dressed and decent, and instinctively she made as if to turn towards me. I hardly need say that as soon as she realised that I hadn't made much progress with my dressing, she arrested the movement with a start and a vocal utterance which, though incomprehensible to me, sounded apologetic.

My problem, I realised, was that I could be so concerned about being glimpsed completely naked save for a sock. Attired thus, however, it occurred to me that I couldn't have appeared more comical, less macho, less like an officer in the Luftwaffe.

"My name is Martha Gilbert," the woman replied.

Her voice had a sombre tone, and my first impression of Martha was that here was a woman who lived a life of relentless drudgery.

"Are you going to shoot me?" Martha asked forlornly.

"That depends entirely on you Martha, on how you behave," I warned. Thinking it not inappropriate to introduce myself, I said, "I am Hauptmann Hans Hebbel. I am a Luftwaffe officer, and the Luftwaffe does not intentionally make war on women and children."

I realised, before the last words were out of my mouth, that this statement must at best have sounded hollow, and at worst a damnable lie, but my platitudes could not be retracted.

"Tell that to the people of London, of Hull, of Coventry," said Martha with considerable defiance.

Thinking that it was neither the time nor the place to get involved in a discussion about the conduct of the war, I sought to reassert my authority.

"Who lives in the house with you?" I asked sternly.

"I live alone," Martha replied.

"You may now turn about," I said as once again I placed my pistol on a shelf within easy reach.

It's not that easy to fasten buttons with one hand, or even two hands when one of those hands is holding a weapon. Every item of my clothing to come into contact with my skin felt dishearteningly cold and damp. I'm sure that my captive was aware of the peril she would put herself in by lying to me, but that didn't mean that I could be certain she was telling the truth. I questioned her further.

"What! You mean to say that you have no man in the house. Where is your husband?"

Feeling the cold, I was glad to finish dressing as I put on my jacket. I fully expected my prisoner to tell me that her husband was away fighting in the service of his country, or that he had been killed or captured.

"I haven't seen my husband in four years," she informed. "Not since he took it into his head to go off to Spain to fight for the cause, as he described it."

I was surprised by what I heard, and because the statement was congruous with the manner of its telling, I believed every word. Mrs Gilbert had the look of a woman whose chance of happiness in life had been taken from her, and by events far away, events over which she had no control whatsoever. Her demeanour at first was that of a woman who has been betrayed, undoubtedly by life, and possibly by death. I had picked up my gun only to find that I wasn't sure what to do with it. To have pointed it at her at this juncture would have been too threatening, so I held the weapon loosely by my side, allowing the barrel to point harmlessly at the floor. To fire a lethal round all I needed to do was to raise my arm and squeeze the trigger. I looked at Martha intently, as if by close scrutiny I would gain a greater insight into the personality of my captive, knowledge which might be useful in my bid to escape what in effect was an island prison. From their low point at the incidence of my discovery, based on what Martha had told me thus far, I perceived my prospects for getting away to have improved considerably. My mind was sifting through a host of new possibilities even as I was making my study of Martha's physiognomy.

Mrs Gilbert's skin was undoubtedly past its first efflorescence, or to put it another way, the first signs of aging were becoming more obvious, particularly at the corners of the mouth, in the furrow underlining each of her cheeks and leading down from either side of her nose to stop just above a similarly downward pointing line extending either side of her lips. Her cheeks had dimples in them, and her entire visage revealed a ghostly pallor. I thought of Hanne, and in thinking of her I couldn't help but make a comparison, bringing to mind how beautifully radiant she was the last time I saw her, and, most of the time, how sunny was her disposition. That said, I felt that the woman standing before me could improve her appearance immeasurably with not much effort, and in the first instance all she needed to do was smile. For me to have been able to elicit such an expression there and then would have been to ask a great deal of my powers, at least those I normally bring to bear to influence women, for I didn't much feel like smiling myself. A quality of Martha's which did impress me right from the start, however, was that she showed no sign of fear, and appeared to my eyes as steady as the surface beneath our feet. We continued with our conversation made up of peremptory questions and answers.

"He was with the International Brigades?" I asked, the intonation of my voice clearly indicating my statement to be also a question.

"Most people who didn't know us at that time make that assumption; but no; he and his friend Harry joined the Spanish Legion. They chose to fight alongside their German and Italian allies for a nationalist Spain under Franco's leadership."

"Wirklich!" I exclaimed under my breath, and the exclamation was a signal for entirely new trains of thought to make tracks through my head, ideas based on the possibility that this probably bereft Englishwoman would be more useful to me as a willing ally than as a belligerent foe. For a moment I saw myself as a man from the Abwehr recruiting a network of agents, the first of whom would, of course, be Martha. This last thought was followed by the astonishingly trivial notion that Martha really ought to do something with her hair. She must have read my mind, because she began to preen that part of her body by pushing the sunlit mass of straight auburn strands away from her eyes to reveal more of her face. Up to that point her manner of speaking had been matter-of-fact, but when she said, "I believe Harry and my husband are dead," Martha once again revealed that stubborn determination not to be overwhelmed by emotion, not to appear the slightest bit abject before her armed inquisitor. In my vanity I allowed myself to think that she might be removing the most obvious obstacle to any amorous or romantic advances I might make. I directed our conversation back to present practicalities.

"Why have you come here this morning?" I enquired.

My question evidently bemused her.

"I live here," she replied.

"I mean why did you come to the shed?" I explained, before adding, "You can't have known I was here."

"You're absolutely right," she agreed. "I didn't expect to find anyone in here at all when I came to fetch the basket I use to collect eggs from the chicken-coop," and in so saying she did indeed reach across to a shelf for the one and only basket that was there. "It's something I do daily when the hens are laying, but usually a little earlier than this. The cockerel didn't wake me this morning, and consequently I overslept, which isn't like me at all."

"A 'cockerel' you say. What is this 'cockerel' you are talking about?"

My English was proving up to the mark insofar as making polite conversation and asking a few basic questions were all that was required, but I could be easily thrown by the interpolation of a word or phrase which is not likely to be used generally, and, as you can imagine, such words and phrases abound in every major language. In response to my question Martha rather impressively imitated the raucous call of the male chicken when he's about to strut his stuff.

"Aha; now I understand; das ist ein junger hahn."

Perhaps it was because we had both been through different kinds of hell – mine intense but of short duration; Martha's not nearly so dramatic, but a much more protracted ordeal of waiting without knowing whether the loved one she was waiting for would ever return – that simultaneously we both erupted with spontaneous laughter, and at that moment, in my eyes the woman whom I had perceived from the outside to be suffering on the inside, became transformed. In a matter of seconds she had become more youthful by at least fifteen years, and she repeated my German just as perfectly as she had mimicked the sounds made by the 'junger hahn'. Then, right on cue, the real cockerel began to crow, and for a second time we expressed our exuberance, our somewhat forgetful, child-like joy.

I decided, once I had regained my composure, to escort Martha back to her own house and lie up there at least for the remainder of that day, but I saw no reason to prevent my new acquaintance from letting out the chickens to have the run of the garden, and then collecting their eggs as she had intended. Not surprisingly I half expected to benefit from Martha's endeavours in a way too obvious to mention. To this end, making as if we were allies working together, I strode past Martha and pushed open the door wide enough for me to poke my head out in order to look for signs warning of possible further human interference. I wasn't able, from my present position, crouched with my gun at the ready, to survey the hill behind the shed, but I doubted whether a postman on his rounds or an unsuspecting villager would appear from that direction. To my knowledge the coast was clear.

"Please, you are to go and attend to the chickens and then come back here. Then together we will go to the house. I will keep you covered for the entire time."

I motioned with my hand for Martha to come past in the same instant that I took a step backwards to allow her enough room. Inadvertently on my part, the back of my hand brushed against her right breast, causing a surge of sexually charged energy to jolt my arm. She responded by thrusting her chest forward so that the breast I had touched, notwithstanding the fact that it was covered by the flower-patterned material of a workaday dress and the grey wool of an unbuttoned cardigan, became more prominent. With my eyes focused on that part of a woman's anatomy which beckons infant and man alike by its rounded softness, I was, long enough for Martha to notice, transfixed, momentarily spellbound.

Noticeably pleased with the effect that our slight intimacy had produced, Martha walked off with a spring in her step which I wouldn't have thought was in her ten minutes earlier, and merely to obey my instructions. In next to no time she had opened the door of the shed which housed the chickens and allowed its feathered denizens to emerge. I counted eight birds as they began to disperse around the garden, and though initially I was a little concerned about the commotion they were making, I quickly dispelled my anxiety by rationalising their antics as being perfectly in keeping with the time and the place. Indeed, were the birds to be cooped up for the entire day, or even for a couple of hours longer, the suspicions of any passer-by who knew Martha and was aware of her domestic arrangements, would more likely be aroused. Martha stepped inside the coop to collect the eggs. A few minutes later she reappeared to approach me with the same jaunty step I had observed in her going. After inspecting the contents of her basket in broad daylight, she gave me a smile which revealed to me that she was pleased with that morning's bounty. In our little interplay that was really a battle of sorts, but a battle involving hearts and minds rather than blood and guts, I was beginning to realise that I might not have the upper hand. Half way between the chicken coop and my temporary abode, Martha veered in the direction of the house, and with a slight tilt of the head she gestured for me to follow, as if she were the party giving the orders. Tentatively I stepped out from my hiding-place, and with a watchful eye and a deliberate lack of haste, and my gun discreetly hidden, I followed Martha's bare legs into the house.

Chapter Twenty-One

Hambleton Village

Before I got to know Martha more than superficially I got to know her house. I made my initial tour of inspection not on the basis of idle curiosity or with the purposeful inquisitiveness of a prospective buyer or tenant, but from my need to confirm that apart from ourselves the house was deserted. I also reasoned that a good move would be to get a mental picture of the layout of the place just in case I needed to hide, or make a hasty exit through an unfamiliar door or window. I made this confined journey of discovery in the company of my ambiguous host, and although I didn't have the muzzle of my pistol pressing against her kidney at any time during our guided tour, I wasn't yet prepared to let the weapon out of my hand. In the course of my familiarisation with the interior of the house I couldn't help but make comparisons with my parents' home in Streisund, and the homes of friends, both theirs and mine. This was the first English house I had entered, and although it is usually unwise to make generalisations from such a singular experience, it is difficult to resist the urge to do just that. I found Martha's house to be a shrine to flowers big and bold, or at least their images appearing in repeated patterns on carpets, on the couch and its accompanying chairs, and on the curtains and bed-covers. The effect of seeing so many resplendent pink roses protruding from garlands of leaves was enough to make me feel quite giddy at first. It was quite overwhelming, but that might have been because so soon after my recent travails, I hadn't expected to find myself in the midst of such cosy, domestic comfort. A man whose previous beds have been the open moor and the floor of a garden shed can easily come to terms with poor taste. An impression I formed about the English in that first hour inside Martha's house was that they preferred to live with furniture smaller in scale than that which is normally found in German houses. In Germany an entire wall of the lounge may be taken up by a schrank, an item of furniture similar to a dresser but larger in scale. In Martha's sitting room, where in addition to the upholstered furniture were a number of pieces made from wood that had been highly polished. These consisted of a sewing-table tucked away in the darkest corner of the room, a dining table with both its leaves folded down pushed against the window-ledge, and, most interesting of all, standing directly behind the door leading into the scullery cum kitchen, was a grandfather clock which ticked the passing of time as if the main manifestation of that abstruse concept was its insistently rhythmic sound. I leaned forward to inspect the face of the clock and read the words 'Owston' and 'Scarborough'. I knew Scarborough to be a town on the Yorkshire coast, but if 'Owston' were a place, it was unknown to me. I didn't think it worth my while to make enquiries of Martha with regard to her clock, and was happy to assume that a Mr Owston had made the timepiece in the town renowned in song for its fair. The question I was prompted to ask at this juncture, however, was how far it was to the nearest port, and whether that might indeed be Scarborough. Martha informed me that it probably was, and that the distance from here to there was about thirty miles in a direction which she indicated with her finger. She was pointing through the front room window beyond the stone wall that bordered her garden dominated by its tree, beyond the nearby fields and the distant woods. In looking I became immediately concerned about the likelihood of an itinerant individual passing along the road and looking in to be surprised by the sight of a Luftwaffe officer in full uniform standing next to Martha. Despite, to all appearances, our chatting amiably as if we had all the time in the world, it was too early in the day to be wearing fancy dress, and the game would be up for sure.

"You could reach Scarborough by nightfall if you set off now. There is bound to be at least one boat tied up in the harbour," Martha told me.

I was grateful for this intelligence and believed it implicitly, yet I couldn't help feeling slightly disappointed that Martha had suddenly become so eager to see the back of me. In trying to fathom each nuance of meaning, as might be expected of a fugitive under pressure, I considered the alternative possibility that although she was definitely encouraging my departure, and soon, it was only because she believed that to be my earnest wish.

"Thank you for that," I said in respect of the information about Scarborough, but all the while my mind was focused on the sorry state of my apparel.

There's nothing I dislike more than wearing clothes which have been recently saturated, and which are not yet dry. To cite the cliché that desperate situations call for desperate remedies is not inappropriate, for it was then that I had the thought which could easily have led to my downfall, and which would probably be objectionable to my host. It occurred to me that Martha's husband, having gone to war no doubt with the intention of returning, sooner or later, to the conjugal home, couldn't possibly have taken all his clothes with him, and provided that we were of a similar size, I would be able to borrow a few of his things. The great danger, of course, was that if I were to be captured wearing civilian clothes, I could be accused of being a spy and shot, or hanged, or whatever the powers that be did to undesirable types they were keen to discourage. I knew that we executed their people when they were caught dressed in mufti, so I couldn't expect better treatment in return. That, I thought, would go against the British sense of fair play. Bearing in mind my physical discomfort, I came to the conclusion that the risks involved were worth taking. The dilemma I had was how to put the idea across to Mrs Gilbert. I deliberated as to whether I should use diplomacy or force in getting her to part with her husband's belongings, or at least a few of them.

I had already considered that I would need to take some form of drastic action against Martha before I resumed my odyssey, otherwise there was a real danger that she would simply go to the authorities and inform them of my status and likely whereabouts. She would also be able to provide an up-to-date description of what I was wearing. Following my ruminations on this matter it seemed to me that when the time came the decision I would need to make would be one of three options. Without doubt the most draconian of these was that I should kill her in cold blood at close range. This option had the merit of ensuring my prisoner's absolute silence, but let me make it absolutely clear here and now that I would have found it an easier task to blow out my own brains than execute an innocent woman. A less drastic but nonetheless problematic option was that I could take Martha with me as a hostage. Her knowledge of the local geography and customs could be of great use. On the other hand, however, were she to choose to work against me with the aim of becoming my Nemesis, then that knowledge would be to her benefit and my detriment. The final option, the course of action I had thought most practical and reasonable for all concerned, was to tie Martha to the bed and gag her. I had made the assumption that somebody would find her before she became seriously distressed, and by that I mean on the point of dying of thirst, but not so soon that I hadn't managed by then to have made good my escape by boat. Despite the fact that so many thoughts were crowding my mind, I was, I like to think, able to maintain the insouciant air of a man in complete control. I decided to try gentle diplomacy, aware that if that were to fail, all I had to do was raise my weapon.

"Please," I said, mindful that as concepts determining behaviour diplomacy and politeness are the best of friends, "as you can feel, the clothes that I am wearing are uncomfortable for being so damp, and I wondered to myself if some of your husband's clothes might be a good size for me. After all, you haven't heard from him in four years, and you yourself said that you believe him to be dead."

I let my statement transform itself into a request as each phrase worked its magic on Martha's brain. To my amazement Mrs Gilbert responded positively, even going so far as to warn me that the consequences would be dire for me if I were to be apprehended dressed as a civilian. The warning having been given, she led me upstairs to the master bedroom.

This room, chintzy in style, was the most feminine in the entire house. In addition to the bed, the furniture consisted of two wardrobes, a dressing table and a chest of drawers, all of which were a dust-free white. The wardrobes were set back into an alcove either side of a which, although the metal bits necessary for a fire to be laid were present, looked as if it hadn't contained burning coal or wood for an age. Down the centre of the wardrobe to the right of the chimney breast was the mirror which, as I was to discover later, had last reflected a masculine image four years previously. That had been when Martha's husband George, prior to his departure for London, had practised his Nazi salute. The man who now scrutinised his dishevelled but far from pathetic image reflected in the mirror made no such gestures. I merely raised my head a little so that my chin was prominent as I appeared to look down my nose at myself.

Then, feeling with my thumb on one side of my face and my fingers in close array on the other, I rubbed the stubble growing from the skin on my jaw and cheeks.

Thinking aloud, I said, "You need a shave Hans."

"I agree," commented Martha. "I don't think you would suit a beard. I'm not really keen on men with beards. I've got sensitive skin."

These snippets of information made me pause for thought. First I tried to work out the correlation between what I understood to be a formal mode of dress and the hair on my face, but with the answer beyond my intellectual grasp, I opted to remain confused. It's an exhausting business trying to maintain a conversation in a language which one speaks and understands less than perfectly, and I concluded that the best way to improve my linguistic skill in English was to be selective with my questions. Secondly I wondered whether Martha was inviting me to kiss her. In this regard I took no decisive action, for the time being at least.

"Are your husband's clothes in here?" I asked, my hand already reaching towards the nearest of two shiny brass knobs on the door of the wardrobe in which I could see an image of myself reflected.

Martha made no movement to restrain me, but instead caused me to focus my attention in the right direction by opening the door of the wardrobe which contained the remnants of her husband's clothes.

After browsing with her fingers she made a selection for me, extracting from the plethora that the wardrobe contained, a pair of coat hangers, one made of wire and the other made of wood. From the wooden hanger hung a green corduroy jacket and a pair of brown cavalry twill trousers. Wrapped around the wire hanger was a shirt, the mainly beige brushed-cotton material of which was superimposed with a check pattern formed by two distinct shades of the same colour. The darker shade perfectly matched the trousers and the protective elbow patch on each of the jacket's sleeves. Upon feeling the jacket at the lapel, I began to imagine myself walking along a series of English country lanes all the way to Scarborough, at times raising my imagined rustic walking stick in salutation to any passing stranger rather than risking a strongly accented verbal greeting.

"I think these garments should fit you reasonably well. This is the jacket which my husband used to wear to school. Did I tell you that he was a teacher here in Hambleton?" she posed. "That seems such a long time ago," she added, allowing her head to drop slightly as wistfully she seemingly focused her gaze on the carpet, but truly upon nothing external in particular.

"You didn't tell me this," I answered, laying the clothes I was about to borrow down on the bed as I began to undress.

I left it to Martha's sense of propriety as to whether or not she should turn away, mainly because I had no intention of stripping off completely. I was prepared to accept a certain amount of damp discomfort rather than descend to the ignominy of asking to borrow another man's underpants and socks. I needn't have been so prissy about the matter though, for Martha took it as read that I would want to change my entire attire, and rummaged through the contents of two drawers in the chest of drawers until she found what she had been looking for, specifically the aforementioned smaller items of clothing and a woolly jumper. The dun colours which formed the pattern on the pullover put me in mind of garments which my uncles or grandfather would wear, but I wasn't concerned about fashion to the extent that I was prepared to reject the warmth which the sweater would provide. Its earthy hues also matched the tone of the trousers which Martha had chosen for me. After suggesting that she might like to take pleasure in the bucolic scene overlooked by the bedroom window, my intention now being to change every item of clothing on me, I set about changing my appearance, and indeed my persona if the old adage, 'clothes maketh the man', is to be believed. I had only managed to undo the top buttons of my shirt when Martha, ignoring my suggestion to look away, interrupted proceedings.

"You said that you needed to shave; well you might as well go the whole hog and have a bath," she said.

With this comment she almost succeeded in bamboozling me completely, and yet again I looked at her quizzically as I sought clarification. It occurred to me at that moment that for two people who had just met, and given the unusual circumstances of our meeting, I had spent an inordinate amount of time dressing and undressing in her company.

"I'm sorry," she said, her inscrutability at this time giving way, figuratively if not literally, to a disarming smile as the light of understanding illuminated her face, notwithstanding the fact that the beacon transmitting this light had been my dimness in failing to grasp the meaning of her idiosyncratic speech. "To go the whole hog is an expression we have in this part of the world."

"Bitte!" I interjected. "What does this mean? What is a hog?"

In keeping with the example set by her rendition of the call made by a cockerel, she screwed up her face and proceeded to imitate what most people would recognise as being the noise made by a pig, a porker that was grunting rather than squealing. Once again I laughed out loud at her grotesque mating calls, and realised that just as I had seemingly been in a perpetual state of divestment in Martha's presence, she seemed to have the same proclivity to indulge in animal mimicry. The result was that the tension between us was released once more, and more emphatically than the first time. In this regard the auras we projected were like oscillating waves, the amplitude of which was, despite our mutually perceived roles in our unusual circumstance, being modulated towards convergence. Martha tried to explain as I placed my pistol on the bed, ensuring that the barrel was pointing in a neutral direction.

"To go the whole hog means to go all the way," she guffawed, as if there lurked a hidden meaning behind what to me was still something of a mystery.

"I suppose the literal meaning is to eat the whole pig, a hog being another word we use for pig."

"Aha!" I exclaimed. "Schwein! I think I now understand. To go the whole hog would be not only to shave, but to bathe as well. Is that so?"

"That is so," Martha replied.

"And where will I do this shaving and bathing?" I enquired, rather keenly.

The prospect of my becoming a civilised human being again was very appealing, but I didn't lose sight of the fact that the balance of power between Martha and I would be strongly in her favour once my naked body was immersed. If she was trying to trick me, apart from defecation, there wasn't a situation I could imagine in which I would be more vulnerable vis-à-vis my wily hostage. Once in the bath, wherein no doubt I would be lulled into a false sense of security by the eagerly anticipated sensual experience, it would be the easiest thing in the world for Martha to exit the house quietly and raise the alarm.

"I use a tin bath which I keep in the outside loo," she said, before altering the colloquialism to a word which she thought I would understand. "I mean toilet. Usually I light the fire in the front room and have my bath in front of its roaring flames. The water I heat in pans and a kettle on the range in the kitchen. That I got going when I first got up. You can come downstairs in George's dressing gown. I'm sure there'll be a razor of his somewhere in the house."

Martha returned to separating the hangers in the wardrobe in order to extract a white flannel dressing gown with the initials G.G. embroidered in blue high on the shoulder. She handed it to me and I took it from her, thereby signalling my willingness to go the whole hog, so to speak.

Chapter Twenty-Two

Hambleton Village

"I can help you with those," I said as Martha, having come from upstairs, walked into the living room, her arms burdened by a stack of grey blankets which came up to her chin.

I made this comment having been motivated by what to me was an unfamiliar kind of guilt. For most of the two and a bit decades which had been my life to date I had been perfectly happy, in the domestic sphere of hearth and home, to let my mother work for the benefit of the man and boy in her life, and unless I had been bribed or strongly cajoled, had rarely lifted a finger to help with the chores. Now, sitting comfortably in an armchair with my feet up in front of the fire, my nakedness covered by her husband's dressing gown, I thought the least I could do was offer to help in whatever task Martha was involved.

"That would definitely not be a good idea," Martha replied.

"And why do you think it not a good idea?" I retorted brusquely, my pride having been dinted a little by the offhand rejection.

"Because, my handsome lover," Martha proclaimed, "I'm going to hang these blankets up at the windows to conform to the blackout. It's something I do each afternoon or evening, depending on the time of year, just before it gets dark. It's something we all have to do, and have done ever since you and your friends began bombing our cities."

"If you are remiss in your duty what might happen to you?" I asked, already aware that the purpose of the blankets was to prevent the lights switched on inside the house from shining without, and thereby serving as navigation beacons for our squadrons.

"A warden would be round here as quick as a flash to come down on me like a ton of bricks."

"A ton of ..."

This time Martha didn't give me time to express my confusion. In a way she was becoming adept at educating me in the use of idiomatic language by immediately following up a colourful expression which I was hardly likely to grasp the meaning of with terminology which was much more basic, and therefore for me much easier to understand.

"A man would come and shout at me to put out the light," simplified Martha latterly, articulating each word clearly as if she were addressing a child. "And neither would it do for you to be seen at the window by a passer-by, and certainly not in George's dressing gown."

Martha placed her burden on the floor while she strode into the kitchen to return shortly with a small set of wooden steps which she duly placed at one end of the living room window. No more than a metre high, these she ascended holding in her right hand a corner of the blanket whilst maintaining her balance with the other, which she rested on one of the upright struts holding the glass in place. Even from where I was sitting I could see that there was a hole protected by what appeared to be a brass ring about three centimetres in and equidistant from two edges of the blanket. It was a simple task for Martha to hook the blanket in place prior to her moving the steps to the opposite end of the window, where she repeated the procedure. It may not have been her expressed wish, but as far as I was concerned I remained seated in accordance with implied instructions. My focus of attention descended gently from the deft movement of Martha's hands to her shapely flower-patterned back and posterior to rest for a while on the willowy elongated curves of her calf muscles as she stood with her right foot placed on the plateau that was the top of the steps, and the left on the one and only other tier.

You've probably already surmised that several hours have passed since my morning immersion in front of the fire. Regardless of the fact that to my knowledge nobody had ventured along the road in either direction since I had been in the house, Martha had sought to protect me from prying eyes by placing a lace curtain across the lower panes of the window, a stratagem which was perfectly adequate save that a peeping-tom, or the female equivalent, were to approach the window and observe proceedings by standing on tip-toes, a happenstance which Martha had thought unlikely. Bath nights at home in Germany had always been a pleasure, but not nearly so pleasurable as this morning's ablution, for the simple reason that once I had lowered myself into the water to be soothed physically and mentally, initially at least, by the just about thermally bearable liquid, Martha, having entered the room from the kitchen, had offered to scrub my back. After I had placed the front and back door key, which I had been mindlessly holding in my hand ever since I had locked both doors, down on the floor next to my gun, without further hesitation I succumbed to Martha's kindness.

They say that most people that put pen to paper as authors find it difficult to write convincingly about the sensual intimacy shared by a man and a woman, and increasingly these days the intimacy between individuals of similar sex, but as I seek no accolades in respect of the written word, but am merely an old fogey eager to tell his tale before body and soul part company, I shall refrain from attempting to be a nonagenarian D.H. Lawrence or a similarly aged John Cleland, and leave the details of what came naturally to Martha and I, as it has come naturally to every couple since Adam and Eve, to each and every reader's imagination. In order to make fervidly colourful that which might be drably grey, however, I can tell you that in the hours between Martha gently caressing my spine and my ogling her elevated calves, Mrs Gilbert and I had enjoyed sex three times. Given our circumstances and respective loyalties at the outset, it shouldn't have happened; but happen it did, and sitting in my newly acquired favourite chair, for the first time in my life I felt profound contentment, and for the first time in many a year I felt no desire to wage war or hurt a fellow human being.

"There we are, just about done," said Martha with satisfaction as she stepped down from the steps onto the carpet for the second time.

For an obvious reason the light in the room having diminished considerably, the effect of the flames dancing in the grate as the burning logs crackled and hissed became more dramatic as the two-dimensional decorative flora caught fire with shadows, as did Martha's dress. The main source of natural light now came in through the partially open door leading into the kitchen, where that window was still to do.

"If you really want to help you can put a few drawing-pins down the sides a couple of inches apart. It's not something I do every night, but now that you're here I'm not taking any chances. There should be a box of pins in the drawer of the sewing-table just behind you."

I turned in my seat and opened the drawer to rummage amongst the pin-cushions and bobbins of cotton in almost every colour under the sun in my search for the likely box, but in this corner of the room where the light was at its dimmest, despite stretching my neck I could see nothing of the kind, and no likely contender came to hand. There was only one thing for it, and that was to get up out of my chair and walk around to the table in order to open the drawer to its fullest extent so that I could survey the contents properly. In the process of getting to my feet, however, my injured knee gave way and I fell back onto the chair's thick cushion with an anguished groan, my face undoubtedly contorted by the sudden sharp pain. To draw attention to my suffering I searched for swelling around the patella, but could find nothing out of the ordinary.

"I see," said Martha upon observing my predicament.

"What do you see?" I enquired, my arms outstretched as I applied both hands to manipulate and massage the areas of soft tissue on the inner side of my left kneecap.

"I see a man who makes a woman an offer, but then puts on an act because he doesn't really want to get up off his backside, either that or he genuinely can't because he's not the man he once was, being something of a cripple," she answered provocatively.

There were occasions – and this was one of them – when I thought that Martha's comments were as piercing as daggers, and yet I found this somewhat incorrigible aspect of her personality to be especially attractive, and I believe that this was because at the deepest level of my psyche, my overweening Teutonic pride wanted to be lanced, my ego deflated. If on this basis my attraction to Martha equated to masochism, then surely it was masochism of the noblest kind.

I made a strenuous effort to get up out of the chair, but my attempt was thwarted by Martha's matronly hand pressing down on my shoulder as she went in search of the elusive pins.

"You stay right where you are," she ordered. "It's no effort for..."

She didn't finish the sentence, but instead, as she attempted to pass in order to get round behind me, gave a little yelp of delight as I encircled her waist with my arm prior to drawing her lithe body towards me. There wasn't the slightest resistance as she stumbled over the arm of the chair into my lap, allowing herself, for a few enthralled moments, to become nothing more than a pilot's plaything, to become like a rag-doll with no will of its own. Martha's body didn't remain limp as if lifeless for long, and to put it succinctly, and I hope not crudely, neither did I as she inserted her hand inside my dressing gown and kissed me with all the passion that a woman who had been pining for years could muster. It wasn't long before the garment I was wearing was covering only my back as Martha hurriedly removed her most intimate item of clothing prior to hoisting her dress more than a little and lowering herself onto me with a precision which was both immaculate and exquisite. This was the first time in our love-making that I had effectively allowed Martha to take complete control, and so pleasingly voluptuous were the sensations I was experiencing – as I trusted Martha was too – in the light and shadows cast by the flickering flames, that I felt as if there was no place on Earth I would rather be, that I was indeed in a state of bliss. Following lust's crescendo, our passion sated until the next incipient rumblings, the next vibrations, Martha rolled off me to rest on her side wedged between my body and the arm of the chair. In response to my asking, Martha raised her hips slightly whilst I rearranged my dressing gown. She took the opportunity to rearrange her dress, but left her knickers where they had fallen. They had landed in such a way that they partially covered my pistol where I had placed it on the hearth. It certainly was an incongruous pairing. For several minutes we sat in each other's arms staring at the fire with our heads seemingly conjoined, our respective temples providing mutual support. The focus of my gaze was the clearly visible incandescence on the underside of a large log where it almost merged with its bed of red-hot coals. It was Martha who felt compelled to break the spell.

"It is madness going tonight with your knee in the state it is. I think you should rest here for a day or two and give your leg a chance to heal properly. You're thinking about walking thirty miles either across rough country or on hard roads, neither of which would be good for your knee. You might do yourself some irreparable damage."

They say that forty per cent of what people communicate to each other in person is understood in the context of the circumstances in which they find themselves, and that an additional twenty per cent by virtue of facial expressions and body language generally. If true these figures make the burden of meaning carried by words less onerous than one might at first think. These ratios I thought particularly apt in the languages employed by Martha and I in respect of each other, and though the meaning of words such as 'irreparable' was lost on me, I usually got the gist of what Martha was saying, and I was improving with practice. In this instance there was no doubt in my mind that Mrs Gilbert wanted me to stay longer; as to how long she had in mind I had as yet no idea, but I little thought that I would stay forever, and I'm sure she didn't either.

"It might be better to lie low for a couple of days," I said wistfully after ruminating for a while on the significance of Martha's words.

The ponderous reticence and ambiguity of my reply, far from being a sop to satisfy or placate this woman's needs and desires, was a genuine expression of my own uncertainty regarding which now would be the best course of action to take. I had it in mind still to go, but the question I now considered was how long to postpone my departure.

I knew for certain that I wouldn't be leaving this night, that I would gainsay the tentative plans I had formulated earlier that day.

"Do you know," said Martha, unknowingly interrupting, and effectively eliminating, the inconclusive schedule that was my train of thought, "weeks can pass without my having a single visitor, and if it wasn't for the fact that I have to go out to work and meet people, I would hardly know there's a war on. I have to go to the village store for my rations of course: they're essential; but I can choose for myself whether or not I listen to the news on the radio."

Martha paused as she considered how best to put into words her earnest wish.

"Wouldn't it be marvellous Hans, if you and I could live our lives in perfect seclusion, completely divorced from this world of death and destruction?"

The notion that Martha had a job hadn't occurred to me. This particular item of news came as an unwelcome surprise for no reason other than that I thought this addition to an already difficult equation complicated matters considerably. I had heard and understood all that Martha had said, but I was presently disposed to dismiss her fantasy of our living together happily ever after in a rural idyll. Instead I concentrated my attention on the practicalities involved in Martha going to work.

"What is it that you do?" I enquired, disengaging our crania as I turned my gaze from the fire to look into the gateways of Martha's soul for those telltale signs which differentiate truth from lies.

I may have been sitting comfortably, but in matters relating to my personal security, notwithstanding the bond created and strengthened by our physical intimacy, by sex, I remained suspicious, ever vigilant. Eager to demonstrate her openness, her honesty, Martha proceeded to provide me with a disquisition centred on her working life since her husband George had left home.

"I don't think that George would have gone to Spain if he hadn't been victimised at school," began Martha solemnly. "I didn't do any paid work when my husband was a teacher. I didn't need to because he was the breadwinner. There was a kind of tacit agreement between us – an unspoken understanding to put it more simply – that my role in our marriage was to look after him as soon as he walked through that door. My work was to cook, to wash and mend clothes, and to keep the house and garden neat and tidy. For my own simple pleasures there were tea parties to attend or host, and umpteen charitable events to organise. For years we trundled along nicely in this fashion, and although latterly it became increasingly difficult to keep our political beliefs to ourselves, beliefs which I am sure are not out of tune with your own, I don't believe that we ever rubbed anybody up the wrong way – that is to say, I don't believe we upset anybody because of them."

Once again I was grateful for the elucidation expressed as an afterthought. Interrupting her explanation, Martha extricated herself from my hold to get up out of the chair and poke the fire. There weren't any logs to hand, and the metal bucket which had contained the coal was empty. This action completed she returned to my side, where she gently but firmly raised my right hand and arm so that she could return herself and them to their former positions.

"I'll need to fetch a few more logs in from the shed shortly," she said, a little forlornly, as if the reduction in heat being generated in the grate were a physically radiant metaphor reflecting the transformation in the matrimonial lives she was about to describe.

My interested silence compelled Martha to continue with her story.

"The fact that George was under a cloud – in serious trouble – following the girl's accusations – accusations which were false of course – inevitably reflected badly on me..."

My curiosity aroused, I had been about to enquire about the nature of George's alleged transgression, but a spark of intuition provided the answer before I had framed the question.

"This is a small community, and everybody knows everybody else's business. At least that's how it used to be before the war; this war that is. When George went off to fight for the nationalists in Spain, I found myself out on a limb, not only in the sense that I live in a fairly isolated cottage, but socially as well. People didn't exactly shun me, but I did find that I was spending more and more time on my own. In the end I realised that I enjoyed my own company so much that I became resentful when an acquaintance did call unexpectedly."

During the course of her narrative, Martha had fixed her gaze on the glowing embers, but suddenly she turned to look at me with a concerned expression.

"I'm not boring you, am I Hans? Are you able to understand all that I'm saying? I know that I have a tendency to go on so once I start. It's probably because I don't speak to anyone for days on end that when I do have the opportunity to bare my soul, the floodgates open."

Overlooking my failure to understand fully the reference to portals and inundations, I merely said, "Please; it would be helpful for me if you could speak more slowly; just a little."

Martha smiled benignly and resumed her discourse, mouthing her words more or less at the same rate per minute as she had done before I had asked her to speak more slowly.

"Following George's departure and prolonged absence, eventually I found it necessary to get a job to make ends meet... I'm sorry... to put food on the table and coins in the meter. By this time our savings had gone, and I discovered that the only work I could get was up at the big house on the far side of the village. The house is called Hambleton Hall. You might have seen it on your travels. You would know if you had. With twelve bedrooms the place is huge. The people I work for are called Lord and Lady Gowerdale. It's just domestic work... you know, the sort of thing I used to do for nothing when I worked for George."

Martha paused for a moment as she reflected upon the words she had just uttered, as if she regretted their temerity.

"That's unkind of me really; after all, it was my choice to be a housewife, and I was not unhappy in my past life. What I mean to say is that the work I do for the Gowerdales is no different from what I did – and still do – at home. What's more, Lady Gowerdale is kind to a fault, and I often come home of an afternoon with a jar of honey or a brace of pheasant... that's two... shot by Lordy or one of his friends. Another perk is that her ladyship lets me borrow books from their library. It was she who recommended the book I'm reading at present. It's upstairs on the bedside table. The book is called, '*Thus Spake Zarathustra*'. The author is a fellow countryman of yours I believe."

"Ah! I know this book. It was written by Friedrich Nietzsche. I too have read this work. Do you enjoy this knowledge?"

"It's a little heavy going for me," Martha replied.

Getting back to the subject of Martha's employment, I made a comment which sought an answer. "But you were not at work today."

"It's funny the way things turn out; funny strange that is. If I had gone to work this morning events would have unfolded differently, so differently that we might not have made love, and that would have been a pity: I'm sure you would agree."

To emphasise the pity inherent in this mysterious alternative history, the sensual woman resting in the crook of my arm shifted her weight slightly so as to kiss me first on the forehead, then on the tip of my nose, and finally on the mouth. Indeed, things were warming up nicely when to my surprise and consternation Martha drew back abruptly and scowled.

"I have to be at work by six tomorrow morning," she informed. "There'll be more than one fire to rake out and lay before breakfast. I should be back soon after one though, if I work my normal hours that is. The reason I didn't go in today was because the Gowerdales have been away for a long weekend, and I wasn't needed." Adopting a more ponderous tone of voice Martha repeated an earlier remark. "It's funny the way things turn out," she mused.

There followed a protracted silence during which time I considered the significance of Martha's comments for my own decisions on the morrow. About my staying the night not an affirmative word had been spoken, but I knew that Martha was already instinctively aware where I would spend the ensuing hours, and that her present anxiety – for I could read her face like a book written in German for kindergarten children — was the result of her dwelling upon the possibility of our parting company, either that or the likely problems which our continued rapport might bring.

"I'm getting cold," I said, elevating my concerns for my own physical well-being over and above those generated by nebulous speculation.

"I'm sorry!" exclaimed Martha. "I'll get some logs from the shed right away," she responded practically, jumping up from the chair with alacrity, the kind indicative of a sense of guilt following an oversight.

Reaching out with my hand to grab hold of hers, I looked up at Martha the log-lady with imploring eyes and said, "Leave the logs for another day. Let's go to bed."

It didn't surprise me when she acceded to my wish.

Chapter Twenty-Three

Hornbæk, Denmark

"Somebody's coming," warned Astrid in a voice which was surprisingly loud for a person who was supposed to be in hiding.

Her audience was the group from Aarhus – Hanne included – and the resistance operator who in Mrs Melchior's opinion needed to put on weight. They were all close enough to have heard Astrid were she to have spoken in more subdued tones. The operator acting as guide had asked those under his tutelage to address him simply as David, though whether this was his real name was open to question. Nonetheless, to be the namesake of the biblical hero renowned for killing Goliath seemed entirely appropriate for a diminutive man who was fighting for a nation which is small in area and population compared with the mighty juggernaut of a neighbour which had invaded in 1940. David, together with everyone else hiding in bushes no more than thirty metres from where the Kattegat's saline waters gently lapped the shore, looked across the curvature of the bay towards the promontory which hid from view the lights of Hornbæk. He gave an instruction for those over whom he had some influence to keep calm and perfectly still. The air was clear and tranquil beneath a gibbous moon and the crepuscular canopy pin-pricked by stars. The timeless motion of the sea as wavelet after wavelet unfurled produced sounds which were soporific for being so rhythmic. It was not difficult to make out the two figures which had appeared suddenly at a distance of a couple of hundred metres. One of the pair was carrying a powerful torch, the beam of which for a few moments shone erratically, as if the torch-holder had stumbled. Then, from the viewpoint of the hidden watchers, the beam steadied as it scanned the undergrowth skirting the shore. The threat posed by these two individuals was bad enough, but even more alarming was the fact that they had with them a dog. The animal must have been sniffing about in bushes close to the shore on the far side of the promontory, at some distance behind its master.

To the Danes in hiding this was a reasonable assumption to make, simply because the dog's presence was detected initially by ear when it had barked in response to the human voice calling it to heel.

"Tell me if I'm wrong, but I don't think that was a Danish bark I just heard," said David to the others lying prostrate on the sandy ground either side of him. "And I don't think those two are fishermen."

"It's a German patrol," said Hanning, giving voice to their fears as he turned his head to look past Mr Melchior and his wife in an attempt to gauge the reaction of their guide and mentor in the darkness of their hiding-place barely touched by moonlight.

"It could be the same pair that detained me," interjected Hanne from the extremity of the line of prostrate bodies farthest from the approaching figures.

"They didn't have a dog with them did they?" questioned Sara from her position of shoulder-rubbing proximity to Hanne.

"No; but they could easily have got one since," Hanne responded, irked somewhat by having to state a possibility which she thought obvious.

"Quiet!" aspirated David severely while keeping his eyes on the enemy patrol, and then, thinking that he had perhaps been too peremptory, with an emollient smile he added, "Dogs are reputed to have excellent hearing."

The thought which had crossed the would-be giant killer's mind when he had uttered his harsh command was that it might have been better if his superior in the organisation had not found Hanne so quickly, for in David's humble opinion, thus far she had proved herself to be something of a liability. In his eyes she was a blonde stunner who had almost got herself arrested, who had certainly got herself lost, and who was now eager to demonstrate her talent as a chatterbox. Immediately subsequent to this unkind assessment of Hanne's character, however, when he considered what she had recently been through from a different perspective, his attitude softened, for he realised then that she had been through quite an ordeal. This dreadful ordeal was within a few words of becoming a far from cherished memory when the fisherman in the corduroy hat had found her wandering, more than a little fearfully, between the rows of huts. This friendly giant had made that fear horrendously palpable when he had reached out from the shadows to grab Hanne from behind, the better to be able to seal her mouth with his hand. Fortunately for Hanne her violent arrest had been conducted with the best of intentions, and she was quickly released after the big man had spoken reassuring words into her ear.

The fisherman in the blue bonnet had latterly introduced himself as Henrik, but in the next breath he had in a way teased the people from Aarhus by stating that they wouldn't be wise to believe that that was his real name. He it was who had given David instructions to lead the escapees and their helpers to their present location. It had been necessary to make the hour-long trek through the woods which skirt the coast to the south of Hornbæk because of the untimely arrival of a German E-boat into the harbour. Consequently the plan for the Melchior family's escape had had to be changed almost at the last hour. The fishing vessel which would take the party to Sweden was preparing to leave port, ostensibly for a night's fishing, under the casual scrutiny of the Kriegsmarine. After putting out to sea, *The White Bird* as she was called, would return to shore without having cast its nets in order to become fishers of men and women. Needless to say the presence of the German patrol would likely scupper the entire operation, and there was a danger that the group waiting ashore, after having been sniffed out by the dog, would be apprehended.

"What time is it?" asked David of Hanning, but it was Mr Melchior who, after consulting his silver fob watch secured to his person by a silver chain, was first to answer.

"I make it a quarter to eleven," reported Melchior as he lovingly fondled one of only a handful of small treasured possessions which he had been able to bring with him.

"That's what I make it," added the Aarhus café-owner quietly.

"What time are we to expect the boat?" asked Hanne of anyone who cared to answer.

"High tide is a little after eleven thirty; so any time between then and midnight," David replied, making a conscious effort to talk and act as if nothing were amiss, though the degree of tension he was suffering, in body if not in mind, can be judged to be high on the basis that he snapped a live twig he was holding without his realising that he was applying the slightest pressure.

"Perhaps we should give ourselves up before somebody gets hurt or killed," suggested Mrs Melchior, a comment engendered by her pessimistic belief in what might happen if they didn't, and her optimism in what might happen if they were to emerge from the bushes with hands on heads submissively.

"Don't talk such stuff and nonsense," ordered Mr Melchior, sternly for having nonetheless spoken quietly.

"Yes; be quiet mother," added Sara in support of her father.

For the next several minutes the seven pairs of eyes peering from heads raised just above ground level watched the unwelcome figures approach haphazardly along the strand bathed in moonlight. The man – who was presumed to be a soldier – had switched off his torch, and had resorted instead to throwing pebbles into the sea for his dog to chase. By this time the trio of two men and their canine companion had narrowed the distance between them and the clandestine Danes to about a hundred and fifty metres. They were to come no closer.

"They're heading back!" exclaimed Astrid, her obvious delight startling the others as she broke the long silence.

"Are you sure?" asked Hanning, at present unable in the silvery gloom to determine in which direction the patrol was heading.

"Absolutely," replied Astrid emphatically. "I can tell by their size relative to that broken branch they stepped over a few minutes ago. Keep watching and you'll see them step back over it."

She was almost wholly right, and the detail in which she was wrong hardly mattered. Only one of the pair retraced his steps more or less exactly, whereas the individual throwing projectiles had veered closer to the water's edge in order to be able to throw his stones further into the Kattegat, his aim being to provide their best friend with more strenuous exercise.

"Let's hope they keep going all the way back to town," said David. "What's the time?" he enquired.

If anything he was more agitated now than he had been five minutes earlier. This he put down to the renewed hope which welled up inside him, and because the success or failure of their enterprise as yet teetered in the balance. The focus of their attention being elsewhere, initially there was no response from the men who had previously checked their watches. It was not that they were so absorbed in observing the patrol's moonlight flit that they failed to hear David's question, it was simply that Hanning had left it to Melchior to respond and Melchior had left it to Hanning. A further prompt was needed.

"David wants to know what time it is father," said Sara helpfully.

"Oh! Does he? Yes; of course he does," spluttered Mr Melchior as he sought to bring the face of his fob watch into such light as there was. To gain maximum illumination he had to stretch his arm and tilt the watch face towards the moon, and then he had to crane his neck to see the hands and numbers. "Five past eleven," he said to David, who by this time had adopted a kneeling position.

The earliest *The White Bird* was scheduled to appear was twenty-three thirty, and the main cause of David's concern was that she might come into view from over the horizon to approach the shore before the patrol had left the beach either side of the promontory and returned to base. Without radios there was no way of communicating with Henrik, who happened to be the fishing boat's skipper. Apropos of the crew, for this mission there was only Henrik's son Karl, who had just celebrated his eighteenth birthday. On a trip of this kind it was better, as far as humanly possible, to keep matters within the family, and to keep the numbers involved down to an absolute minimum. David waited for what he thought was a lengthy interval before he asked the hour again. When told somewhat curtly by Mr Melchior that only ten minutes had elapsed since the last time he asked, the man seeking knowledge took all that was said to him to heart. For in addition to his being provided with the snippet he had asked for, he was proffered advice to the effect that perhaps he should demonstrate a little more patience, and with regard to events over which he had no control, he would be better served by putting his trust in God. Significantly David made no further requests to be apprised of the hour for the rest of that long night, and made a pact with himself to get his own watch repaired – the watch passed down to him by his deceased father – at the earliest opportunity.

No sooner had the patrol disappeared around the promontory when the entire group began to move restlessly so as to stimulate the flow of blood, partly to dispel the numbness brought about by having constricted for too long an ankle or an arm, and partly to stave off the cold. Hanne's teeth chattered as she began to shiver. This natural response to her body's low temperature she made a deliberate effort to accentuate, as if she wanted to make it absolutely clear to her confederates that she was suffering badly. In her position at one end of the line, the right side of her body had been exposed to the cold night air for the entire length of time that they had been in hiding. Imitating the actions of a seal, Hanning slapped his hands diametrically against the sides of his body. Initially in murmurs, conversations were instigated which for a time nobody thought unacceptable, the preponderance of comments expressing dissatisfaction, specifically with regard to the Danish climate, the war, and last but not least in being the object of invective, Herr Adolf Hitler. Exponentially increasing in volume of their own accord, these moans and groans were approaching a dangerous crescendo when the event which, latterly at least, had been hastily planned for occurred.

"Listen!" ordered David in a normal voice, thus bringing to an end the diatribes. "I'm sure that I heard something. It struck me as being the sound of an engine out to sea."

It came as no surprise that *The White Bird* – if indeed it was she – was heard long before she was seen, for the plan was that she would approach the shore showing no lights. In compliance with David's instruction for all and sundry to shut their mouths and open their ears, so to speak, each conspirator for the cause of freedom set about testing the maximum range of his or her auditory sense. For several moments nobody heard anything out of the ordinary above the gentle reverberations of a breaking wave, and even David began to have doubts that the sounds he had taken to be the Melchior family's floating passport to freedom had been real as he began to give credence to the thought that his mind had been playing tricks on him. The seconds passed, but their passing didn't amount to half a minute when the chug of a diesel engine was heard, more distinctly this time, so that not one of the people listening intently failed to hear. The unmistakeable mechanical noise informed the people ashore that the craft steadily approaching could be no other than a fishing boat, and David for one was ninety per cent certain that the vessel was *The White Bird*. Concerned that the enemy patrol which had turned back towards Hornbæk might have been alerted by the nocturnal activity close to shore, David turned his gaze towards the very tip of the promontory around which trouble might reappear at any moment. Fortunately none was forthcoming. At a distance of approximately four hundred metres a boat with two masts came into view. She would undoubtedly have been visible at a greater distance had not, a few minutes earlier, what ostensibly was the only cloud in the sky covered the face of the sun's reflector, thereby removing from the face of the Earth its eerie luminescence, its silvery sheen. For those with a proclivity to interpret such happenings, this was a good omen. Nobody was complaining that for a time – and what an important juncture in the proceedings which would soon lead to the success or failure of the mission it was – that the business they were about had suddenly become more discreet.

Like children eager to greet a favourite relative striding down the garden path bearing gifts, the Melchior family and their friends arose as one and set off walking briskly towards the water, but they hadn't gone more than a few paces when David called a halt. The thought had suddenly occurred to him that if the boat coming towards them, and towards which they as a group were on the point of breaking into a run to meet, were other than what he believed it to be, and they were being lured into a trap, then it would be better if only one person were to be caught for certain, thus giving the others a chance – albeit a slim one – of escape. He saw himself as the natural choice to test the water in more ways than one. After providing a brief explanation of his reasoning, the cautious fisherman set off alone in the opposite direction to his charges, who returned to their hiding-place where they remained standing, and where they were to remain until such time that they received the signal, or word, that the coast was clear. Realising that he was going to get more than his feet wet in the very near future, upon reaching the water's edge, David removed his socks and shoes prior to rolling up his trouser legs above the knees. The waters of the Kattegat were icy cold as the waves repeatedly covered his insteps to swirl around his ankles prior to receding. Standing alone on the shore, his right hand holding on to his shoes by their heels, a sock stuffed inside each, in the increased darkness created by the moon's effacement, David intermittently scanned from the promontory, around which he half-expected the enemy to appear in considerable numbers, to the boat which he fully expected to be their salvation. Watching and waiting, he rocked gently backward and forward, shifting his weight from the ball of each foot to the heel, and then back again. More than once he curled his toes into the squelching sand, straightening them soon after to ease the tension.

The White Bird was typical of fishing boats built in Denmark in the late thirties. Put together in the town of Struer in the west of the country, her dimensions and tonnage were such that she was unable to float in water less than three metres deep. The corollary of this crucially important detail was that she had to stand out to sea at least fifty metres from the beach at high tide. The change in the noise emitted by the two-cylinder diesel engine told David that she had reached that point on her journey, and in the instant that the cloud which had restricted the amount of available light suddenly became less effacing, he was also able to discern that her bow was pointing in the direction in which she would soon be heading, towards Sweden. Of course, the skipper, Henrik, didn't expect any of his prospective passengers to swim out to *The White Bird,* and it was for this reason that his son Karl, who though presently much sparer and more rangy in build than his father, was likely to grow into a carbon copy of his dad, clambered into the dinghy which he had secured to the port side of the fishing vessel. The young man had already placed four paddles into the inflatable craft. The totality of this nautical equipment had been procured from the Wehrmacht in exchange for a consignment of cod. The thinking behind deploying so many paddles was that although by use of a single paddle it would be relatively easy to beach the dinghy, with eight people aboard the return journey was likely to be more problematic. At least three of the escapees or their minders from Aarhus were going to have to work this part of their passage. Once Karl was safely ensconced aboard the smaller craft, he untied the rope and was away without a parting word to his father, who nevertheless shouted after his son, "Good luck!"

Karl had only omitted to bid his father adieu because he was concentrating so intently on the task in hand. It was a task for which he had gladly volunteered. Once he had got the handling of the dinghy to his liking, and felt that he was in control, Karl rode the swell towards the shore, dipping his paddle into the briny, first to the left, followed by a couple of plunges to the right, actions perpetrated not so much to gain forward momentum, but rather to deter the inflatable from slewing round awkwardly so that the bow and he were facing the wrong way. For Karl there was no mistaking the figure on the shore awaiting his arrival, though David did look a little peculiar in the sense that he resembled, with his rolled up trousers and shoes in hand, a melancholy soul about to take a midnight stroll along the strand rather than a heroic figure involved in dangerous work. More or less at the same instant the two young men each raised a hand in greeting, but it was David who spoke first.

"You couldn't have timed it better," he said, wading into the water as the dinghy hurtled the last few metres. "If you had got here any sooner the chances were that we would have alerted the entire garrison," he added truthfully. "Half an hour later and you would have probably found our bodies lying dead from exposure," he joked.

"What did the Vikings do in all weathers?" asked Karl as he leapt with the vigorous agility of youth to make a splash in his waders prior to assisting David in hauling the inflatable over wet sand, an action which he pursued until that point of equilibrium had been gained whereat the rear of the dinghy was afloat, whilst the front end was well and truly beached.

"You can see perfectly well that it's me standing here like a ninny and not a member of the Gestapo," replied David after letting go his handle of rope, incredulous that Karl was being so pedantic in sticking to pre-arranged procedures.

"I didn't make the rules for this operation," responded Karl confidently, so come on, play the game. What did Vikings do in all weathers?"

"They bathed on Sundays," said David, concluding that it was much less bothersome to give the correct response than it would be to argue further against what he believed to be the present absurdity of pronouncing it.

"That's more like it. Where are your people?" the young man enquired as he stooped to hold on to the inflatable to prevent it floating away.

"They're hiding in the bushes over there," David replied, and prompted by his own words, he turned in the direction of the darkly silent, unrevealing boscage, and with an arm which would have appeared foreshortened from that direction, waved for his charges to approach. Whether it was because his signal had not been seen, or if seen, whether his expectations, in contrast to his patience, were high that the people from Aarhus would move with a sense of urgency now that the final stage of their odyssey was nigh, it seemed that for an inordinate length of time nothing happened.

Eventually David turned to look over his shoulder at the younger man and said, "Perhaps they really have died of exposure."

"You had better go and get them," advised Karl authoritatively, his overbearing attitude towards David at this time perhaps being derived from the status inherent in being the boat-owner's son.

In other circumstances David would have probably reacted defensively to this assumption of power by the youngster, and no doubt given Karl a piece of his mind, but given the magnitude and perilous nature of their enterprise, he set off to gather his flock as was suggested, but not before he had placed his shoes and socks on the floor of the dinghy with the instruction to Karl, the undertaking of which had very little chance of success, that he was to ensure the footwear stayed dry. Perturbed by his recent confrontation, the barefoot fisherman muttered adjectival expletives to himself as he concentrated upon where he was placing his feet in the soft, dry sand away from the sea's farthest encroachment, for the last thing he wanted was to injure himself by stepping on an object which was sharp, and perhaps rusty. Moon-blanched for as far as the eye could see, mainly the beach was pristine, but that didn't preclude the sinister presence of a foreign object which had possibly been washed ashore to lie in wait like a partially-hidden landmine. Indeed, so intently did David reconnoitre the ground ahead of him, his former fear about who or what might appear from around the promontory was quite forgotten, and he gave not a glance in that direction. His self-absorption with regard to pedicure was so complete that he didn't even notice that his charges, they having made the correct assumption upon seeing their man approach, had come forward to meet him half-way. Sensing that David's mind was presently working on different levels, none of which incorporated the shadowy figures coming towards him, it was Hanning who spoke, penetrating in order to dispel the dichotomy which had been tugging away inside David's head.

"Are we good to go?" asked the Aarhus café-owner.

It came as no surprise to Hanning that his question seemed to startle the individual to whom it was directed, bringing the latter down to Earth with a jolt from his internally-directed blinkered orbit. That said, however, David's response was equally startling, and not only to Hanning.

"What did Vikings do whatever the weather?" the Hornbæk man asked humourlessly.

"David, what on Earth are you talking about? You've been with us all night," said Astrid. "Apart from when you sent us back whilst you went to check that everything was as it should be; but you haven't been out of our sight in all that time. What have you done with your shoes and socks?"

"They're in the dinghy. I gave instructions to Henrik's son, Karl, that I would have his guts for garters if they got the slightest bit wet," he lied.

Sensibly David didn't persist with the presently unnecessary game involving secret codes, but turned towards the waiting dinghy with a beckoning gesture to follow which this time everybody saw, and which everybody obeyed. Upon arriving at the inflatable he advised on the order of embarkation. After first wading into shallow water to rearrange the paddles so that they were not such an obvious encumbrance, he demonstrated an appropriate level of respect for age and gender by picking up Mrs Melchior in his arms to place her with the least amount of inconvenience to herself into the dinghy, but only after he had first obtained hers and her husband's permission. Mrs Melchior made a comment about how she had dreamed about being carried off by a young man, and this young man, she made a point of mentioning, was evidently stronger than he looked. Mr Melchior and the others followed in an orderly fashion, filling the dinghy to capacity. A few chose to sit, but most chose to kneel. After a heave and a shove by Karl and David, working in perfect unison if not in perfect harmony, and ably assisted by Astrid and Hanning manning the oars, that is to say half the complement of paddles, the dinghy began its return journey to the mother-ship waiting patiently offshore. Needless to say, when the two Hornbæk fishermen leapt aboard, they too reached for the wherewithal to assist propulsion.

A few groans could be heard, a consequence of the inevitable splashing.

The journey back to the fishing boat took approximately twice as long as the shore-bound passage, but more importantly than the greater length of time it took was the fact that everything had proceeded without a major mishap. Indeed, the one and only minor mishap was that David's shoes and socks had got wet, but for that he had only himself to blame. By seeking a more comfortable position in which to conduct his struggle with the sea he had inadvertently drenched them. For this personal misfortune he decided that he couldn't, with any justification, vent his spleen on Karl. This part of the voyage across the Kattegat was in the main conducted in silence. It was as if all on board had been mesmerised by the gently pitching motion, had been hypnotised into muteness as soon as the sea, now foamless, welled about them with the profundity of aeons. Standing by the mainmast aboard *The White Bird's* looming hull, and easily identifiable to his prospective passengers by virtue of his substantial frame and corduroy cap, Henrik called down to Karl to come alongside and secure the inflatable astern, where a short ladder disappeared into the briny, three of its rungs being totally submerged. Approaching to assist with the potentially hazardous business of transferring people from boat to boat at sea, Henrik first reached down to take from Karl the dinghy's forward rope – which he duly secured – and then the dinghy's aft line – with which he did likewise. Once the two craft were side by side and relatively stable, once again Mrs Melchior was asked if she would lead the way. This time she was ably assisted from above and below by three pairs of hands as Mr Melchior and Hanning dispelled with decorum by kneeling to provide Mrs Melchior with additional support and lift by placing a hand on each of the lady's hips and buttocks. If she felt at all embarrassed she showed no sign, and was soon lifted like a child onto the deck of the larger vessel.

"There you are Mrs Melchior," said Henrik, "safe and sound aboard my little beauty. There are a couple of flasks in the wheelhouse if you feel steady enough on your feet to go and help yourself to a mug of soup."

"Shame on you for thinking such a thing," responded Mrs Melchior whimsically, leaving the friendly giant who towered over her momentarily perplexed as to what he had been thinking that could possibly have been so shameful.

Holding on to a secure fixture or fitting wherever she could, Mrs Melchior made for the wheelhouse, planting each foot firmly on the oak deck with greater concentration than more than likely she would ever need on land. Ladies first, and to a man having rejected the offer of helpful palms, one by one the others climbed up from the dinghy onto *The White Bird's* deck, soon to join the Melchior family's matriarch for a mug of soup. Henrik and Karl held a short discussion as to what they should do with the dinghy, deliberating on whether it would be better to haul the inflatable aboard or tow it. An important consideration was that they would probably want to use the craft again within the hour. Despite the fact that the more practical option was undoubtedly the latter, for the sake of appearing as fishermen were they to be sighted and stopped by a patrolling E-boat, they manhandled the dinghy out of the water and stowed it on deck between the mizzenmast and the stern. When they were almost ready to get under way the skipper came to what he believed was a necessary decision. It was a decision which he knew would be deeply resented by his passengers, but not, he surmised and hoped, to the extent that they would feel themselves to have been incited to mutiny.

Chapter Twenty-Four

The Kattegat

The decision which the skipper in his wisdom had made, and which he envisaged would cause considerable consternation amongst his passengers, was to detain them in the hold for as long as he deemed necessary. At this juncture he really believed that they would be below deck for no more than an hour. Henrik was pleasantly surprised, however, when his order for certain individuals to descend into the bowels of the boat was greeted with only murmurs of resistance, and these were voiced mainly in respect of the need to demonstrate yet again more than a modicum of physical dexterity by making use of the ladders. Those brought to bear for the purpose, for the simple reason that they were the only set on board, were redeployed from the port side of the boat. It may have been because the people from Aarhus were aware that by taking this deemed necessary precautionary measure they would soon be reunited with their meagre luggage – the weekend bags and holdalls which it had been considered reasonably safe, or a risk worth taking, to smuggle aboard in Hornbæk – that they were prepared to put up with the noxious smell left behind by umpteen former catches. Moreover, they too believed that their malodorous ordeal would be for an hour at most. In searching for a positive perspective from which to view their new predicament, this after all who had been designated to go below had got below, Hanne pointed out that down here the air was tangibly less chilled, and that for as long as the hatch remained open they would be able to observe the stars, the illusion of their passing.

Measuring twenty-two metres from bow to stern, and four and a half metres in the beam, *The White Bird* was one of the larger boats working the Kattegat, and presently devoid of fish, the hold was quite spacious. After shuffling aimlessly for a minute or so, or purposefully ambling about the better to get a feel for the boat's dimensions, eventually the Aarhus people settled down, some to do as Hanne had suggested, craning their necks as they sought to identify this or that constellation with at most only half the configuration in view at any one time, while those choosing not to get involved in star-gazing either sat with head on their neighbour's shoulder, or with jaw resting in cupped hands. The posture described latterly, and assumed by Hanning and Melchior, depicted a weary glumness. At this hour of the morning, bearing in mind all that the good conspirators had been through, it was plain to see that fatigue was beginning to affect behaviour. The seating in the hold consisted of several empty wooden boxes which had been put there specifically for that purpose. If their usual purpose wasn't immediately obvious, it soon became so, thanks to Hanne's little find. It was whilst lifting up one of these makeshift chairs that she let out a little squeal, a shrill cry generated by her sudden repugnance of something cold and slimy striking her wrist before whatever it was slid over the back of her hand to fall to the floor with a barely audible plop. Of course, once the wheels and cogs inside her brain had begun to turn, or more realistically, the neurotransmitter-generated impulses had leapt in this context across a myriad synapses in an attempt to rationalise the unpleasant experience, she quickly put two and two together to come up with the only possible answer. She was on board a fishing boat, and they were in the hold where the netted fish were stored, ergo, she concluded, the creature which had sullied her skin was in all probability a fish. Lo and behold, when she looked down into the darkness which almost hid her feet she was able to discern the silvery glint of a significantly motionless sprat, one that was obviously dead. Hanne did not deign to retrieve the lifeless creature, but instead kicked it to one side, succeeding in making effective contact only at the second attempt. Her lack of a certain skill elicited a mildly derisory comment from Hanning; something about her not giving up the day job if her ambition was to play centre forward for Denmark.

Ten minutes after everyone was seated as comfortably as it was possible to be under the circumstances, the change in the rhythm and level of noise emitted by the Hundested engine made it resoundingly clear that *The White Bird* was under way. Fuelled by cooking oil for the simple reason that diesel was more difficult to acquire for being in short supply, particularly to civilians, it was obvious that the engine was no longer idling, but was being asked to work.

The White Bird was making eight knots without sail. She was showing bare poles as they say in maritime circles. Significantly she was showing her navigation lights, but the decision to do so had been contentious. It had been put into effect only after there had been an animated discussion involving the entire crew, specifically the three Hornbæk men. In this instance David and

Karl were in complete agreement and had argued in favour of running without lights. Their persuasive powers did not prevail. Henrik, though a minority of one, as skipper of the boat had the casting vote in this empery which had little time for the discursive machinations of democracy. He had been prepared to admit that he had been remiss in not having given the matter a moment's thought beforehand, and though he had been prepared to give an ear to his son's and David's argument, in his own mind he was absolutely certain that the safer course was to proceed as if they had nothing to hide, and that entailed showing navigation lights. The skipper backed up his determination by pointing out that if they were to be stopped for showing no lights they would be boarded and searched for sure. He didn't need to point out that the consequences of such an eventuality would be dire for them all. In keeping with his stratagem of operating as if *The White Bird* was a fishing boat going about its normal business, he gave instructions to his underlings to be ready to lower the nets over the side at a moment's notice. Standing alone in the wheelhouse, peering into the argentine darkness beyond the lifebelt harnessed to the bow, Henrik was able to go over in his mind the merits or otherwise of the many decisions he had made thus far, and although he would be the first to admit that there had been a hiccough or two, on the whole he was satisfied that he had made the right choices. Once the Melchior family had been deposited safely ashore in Sweden, he thought, for the journey taking the pretty blonde and her friends back to Aarhus they would be able to show as many lights as a Christmas tree, the thought of which inspired him to consider that it might just be possible to have then a little celebration, a party no less. With this prospect taking shape in his mind, becoming more clearly defined by the minute, Henrik opened the door of the locker located on the deck to starboard beside him. He took out his holdall and checked inside to see how much schnapps there remained in the one and only bottle he had brought with him. For a time the big man, whose capacity for strong liquor was renowned for being prodigious, was sorely tempted to open the bottle which he had inspected and take a swig, but mindful that David and Karl were working on deck tending to the nets, and that for either one of them to enter the wheelhouse and find him imbibing spirits would be deemed as setting a bad example, he showed considerable restraint and resisted the temptation. There would be a time to let their hair down, of that he was optimistic, and in the not too distant future.

The skipper's optimism was in an instant transformed to its opposite, however, when Karl wrenched open the wheelhouse door with such force that he caused his father consternation, such was the older man's concern for the durability of his boat, in particular the wheelhouse door's hinges. The younger man, his features expressive of fear verging on panic, began to speak of what he had seen.

"Dad! Dad!" he exclaimed, echoing the epithet in a voice which for him was more high-pitched than usual.

His manner of speaking was shrill, piercing. Henrik's thoughts of knocking back a mouthful of the heart-warming spirit were dispelled to oblivion as he turned to follow with his eyes the direction of Karl's outstretched arm and pointing finger. He saw, at the same moment that he heard, the object of his son's distress.

"There's a fast boat approaching off the port beam. I think it's a German patrol. It's coming straight for us. What are we going to do? We can't put up a fight. We don't have weapons."

Each of Karl's bullet points hit home. Despite being initially alarmed by the far from welcome news which his son had imparted, Henrik quickly took control, first of himself, and then of the situation. With only one course of action available to him as Captain, as the man responsible for the safety of everyone on board, he decided that now was the time to commence fishing. He reduced speed to enable the nets to be lowered over the stern more easily.

"I told you we shouldn't have shown any lights," said Karl turning to look in the direction of the vessel bearing down on them.

Approaching with the throttle wide open, by this time the E-boat's powerful engines were clearly audible above the chug of the civilian craft, and they were getting louder by the second. Henrik, realising that this wasn't the time to argue the toss with his son on this illuminating subject, gave instructions for the hatch above the hold to be closed. He realised that the people down there would be plunged into total darkness, but there was really no alternative. If they were to be boarded by members of the Kriegsmarine, the chances were that their ordeal would not be for long, and if, either by God's Grace or a remarkable piece of serendipity, *The White Bird* was allowed to go about her business of catching fish unmolested, then there would be nothing about which to complain. Henrik made a graceful downward gesture with the palm of his hand, a gesture which was perfectly congruous with his spoken instruction for Karl to keep calm.

"They'll have field glasses trained on us as we speak, and they're bound to pick up on any sudden, unnatural movement. Whatever you do, don't rush. Now go and do what I've asked you to do."

By the time Karl had set about closing the hatch the people in hiding below knew perfectly well that something was amiss. The young man merely peered into the hold for a second to say to the array of faces staring up at him with ghostly pallor that a German E-boat was approaching and that they were to keep calm, and that if they were boarded they were to keep absolutely quiet, perfectly still.

A moment later the only thing to become absolute in the hold was the darkness, and in its midst the overall level of fear began to rise. This disquietude was not evenly distributed, and it was the person who was perhaps least affected by trepidation who reinforced Karl's parting words.

"You heard the man," said Hanning, "I think we should make ourselves as comfortable as possible again and do exactly as we have been told. And if it helps," he added, "It wouldn't do any harm, and it might do a lot of good, to offer a prayer for our deliverance; that would be a silent prayer of course."

Discernible to each other only by sound and touch, the people from Aarhus settled down once more to abide with their innermost thoughts and fears, and though it was impossible to perceive the facial features of the person who was closest, it was impossible not to be aware that the atmosphere of fear which had been in evidence at first had given way to a collective feeling of resignation and composure. It was as if each person were gaining strength from a kind of lateral osmosis, the salient power of which had been Hanning's invocation to silent prayer. This mystical power, being circular in motion, gained in intensity with each quiet revolution. Before long the only sounds to be heard were the susurrations of several people breathing. This was the quiet before the storm.

In this instance the tempest did not come in the form of a sudden change in the weather, nor, as was distinctly possible, did it materialize in the form of gunfire, explosions and death. The eruptions which came to pass were much more basic for being biological, and as such are not an uncommon experience for people unused to being at sea. Seemingly held by the power of the patrol boat's searchlight, and in response to having been hailed by megaphone, Henrik had cut the engine. His boat was now at the mercy of the swell, and this enabled the capricious and unpredictable motion of the sea to wreak its nauseous havoc. It was ironic that the first person to throw up was Hanning, and his vomiting made it clear beyond doubt that the spiritual calm he had been able to impart to others was not matched by an ability to control the grosser parts of his being, specifically the content of his stomach. He turned to be sick in an empty corner, the involuntary retching of his gut subsuming his previously pressing concerns beneath a newly dominant feeling of disgust. In a lull between the first and second phases devoted to the expulsion of food only partially digested, Hanning entertained the thought that he no longer cared about what might happen to him. This defeatist attitude, however, did not prevail, for his next thought was the realization that his bout of sea-sickness would be of short duration, whereas to be made to stand against a wall in front of a firing squad would lead to a state devoid of self-willed animation, and this he would rather postpone indefinitely.

Hanning's retching had osmic consequences, for the smell of vomit even masked the smell of fish. Whether the circumstances of the majority of people in the hold had in consequence changed for the better was doubtful, and for one person in particular they certainly had not. For Sara too had felt the briny's churning motion working to produce a similar effect in her stomach, with the likelihood of engendering a response not dissimilar to that being demonstrated by Hanning.

More than once she had felt the urge to stand and make for a clear space in which to puke, a space as far away from her friends and family as it was possible to reach in the seconds that would be available to her. On each occasion that she had begun to make a move, however, she had felt the nausea subside, and so each time had allowed her body to relax. Unfortunately, Sara's condition was not improved by the extra stimulus Hanning was providing. By having no choice but to smell and listen to the rather messy and malodorous splats indicative of their perpetrator's discomfort, the odds soon weighed heavily in favour of Sara joining him. Upon feeling yet again a sudden surge of biliousness, she knew that this was going to be the real McCoy. She leapt up from the box on which she had been sitting, and in her haste to clear a path she stood on an instep which she was able to identify as Hanne's by the tone of voice inherent in the cry of pain. Supporting herself with outstretched arms and splayed hands pressing against the wooden partition serving as a bulkhead, Sara joined in the repulsive cacophony. Hanne, Astrid and the senior members of the Melchior family, though they continued to sit in stoical silence, were nonetheless aware that within the next few minutes there was the very real prospect that they would be apprehended, or worse.

While this unpleasant upheaval was going on below, the crew topside was behaving with the level-headed sense of purpose one would expect of fishermen that had nothing to hide. Henrik had stowed his holdall back in the locker without having replaced the bottle of schnapps. This he was keeping to hand.

At speed, the E-boat made almost a complete circuit of the fishing boat, chopping up the water as effectively as a sudden squall. The military craft had steered around *The White Bird's* stern prior to cutting across her bows. She came alongside the larger boat in such a way that the bows of the two vessels were pointing in opposite directions. It was impossible for the crew of *The White Bird* to see the layout of the E-boat; such was the bedazzling power of its searchlight.

This didn't prevent the fishermen from trying to catch a glimpse of what was going on aboard the sleeker, faster, and more menacing craft riding the swell at a distance from *The White Bird* of no more than thirty metres. None was successful. All had to look askance and shield their eyes. If they had been able to redirect the searchlight beam, however, or switch it off completely, they would have been able to discern that a dozen sailors lined the port side of the E-boat's deck, all of whom were holding machine-pistols at the ready. Manned also were the twin twenty-millimetre and the single twenty-millimetre cannons, the barrels of which were pointing directly at Henrik's wheelhouse. The E-boat's three Daimler-Benz engines purred.

"Identify yourself and your crew, please Captain?" boomed a megaphone voice in German.

Henrik was able to speak and understand some German, but he responded in Danish nonetheless, stating, at the top of his voice, his own name and the names of each member of his crew. He added, on the assumption that the Kriegsmarine Captain had seen *The White Bird* cast off and get under way, that their home port was Hornbæk. His assumption was correct.

"You are late getting started with your fishing Captain," the German officer commented, the silent pause which followed indicating that he wanted to know the reason why.

"We've had a problem with our winch, but I think we've managed to fix it," Henrik bellowed, adding as an inspired afterthought, "I was just about to pour myself a little schnapps to keep out the cold of a Danish night. Would you and your second-officer care to come aboard and join me Captain? You might bring us luck."

There was an intermission in the verbal exchange as the E-boat Captain was provided with a more or less accurate translation. There being no reason to suspect that the fishermen were up to no good, the officer politely declined the invitation and wished Henrik the best of luck with his catch in his absence. In keeping with the spirit of projecting, in a friendly manner, the spirit of national pride, he pointed out to the civilian that it took a German drink to keep out the Danish cold. Without more ado the E-boat's engines began to roar and she powered away in the direction of the Oresund, the body of water beyond the narrow strait between Helsingør and, on the Swedish side, Helsingborg. Travelling at about thirty knots, it didn't take long for the kriegsmarine vessel to put sufficient distance between it and *The White Bird* to enable the latter's crew to breathe a sigh of relief.

Henrik, who had just stepped back into the wheelhouse, was soon joined by a young man who was grinning as if he had just won a thousand kroner at cards.

"Dad, that was brilliant, truly brilliant. You're invitation to the Kraut to join us for a drink was inspired. Are we getting under way?"

"All in good time," responded Henrik with a nod of the head in acknowledgement of his son's high praise. "It wasn't a bad piece of bluffing was it?" he added, handing Karl the bottle of schnapps. "Call David over here to join us and I'll tell you what's going to happen."

"Yes sir!" exclaimed Karl as he clicked his heels and gave a normal salute, his antics being more in play than mockery. Imagining that the sole reason for the delay was to allow each of them to take a swig of the stimulating spirit prior to starting up the engine and making for land, for Sweden, with unbridled enthusiasm he called, "David, come and get a mouthful of this;" and in so saying he held up the bottle as a visual incentive.

By this time Sara and Hanning had stopped retching and removed themselves from the immediate vicinity of their regurgitations. They had apologised to the others for having spoiled their boat trip, Sara being particularly solicitous with regard to any injury she might have caused to Hanne's foot. Hanne, for her part, wasn't being totally truthful when she told Sara that her foot was no longer hurting in the slightest. The smell in the hold was unpleasant in the extreme. Surmising from the sounds he had heard that the German navy no longer posed an immediate threat, Hanning considered it safe to call to the men aloft with the aim of alleviating the predicament of everyone trapped in the hold alongside him.

The call for assistance could not be retracted, but Mr Melchior expressed the thought that the Germans might have put a couple of people aboard before their vessel had departed, and for that reason perhaps it would have been wiser for Hanning not to have drawn attention to himself. Mr Melchior's hearing was not what it once was, and he hadn't been privy to half of what Hanning had heard. The man who was being rebuked, and as he thought, without good reason, felt his face become flushed with a sudden surge of emotion. He was thankful that his darkly erubescent cheeks were visible to no-one, and he gave no consideration to the philosophical problem this temporary transformation to his visage posed.

"Well it's too late to do anything about it now," he said, directing his words towards the inky blackness a little to his right, towards the source of his critic's words of censure. "They seem to be enjoying themselves up there whilst we have to contend with being cooped up in this fetid hole."

"And who was responsible for creating the stink in the first place?" questioned Melchior, the acerbity in his voice clearly audible to all and sundry below deck.

"Father, that will do," protested Sara from the resting place she had returned to after stepping gingerly so as not to do further damage to people's tendons and bones. "Hanning is only doing what he thinks is for the best, and not just for him, but for all of us."

Her command to her father to desist was made partly because she knew that she shared responsibility with Hanning for having created the noxious odours and did not wish her partner in crime, as it were, to accept all the blame, and partly because she knew how irascible her father could be when tired. There was a long pause, during which time the atmosphere thickened to the extent that it seemed possible to cut the air with a knife. On deck there was subdued elation.

Speaking to his son whilst handing the bottle over to David, who was standing just behind the youngster blocking the doorway, Henrik said, "What we are going to do, for the next hour at least, is exactly what I told that naval officer we were going to do, which means that we're going to lower the nets and attempt to catch some fish."

"But dad, that's ridiculous..." said Karl, though he was unable to voice his opinion fully because of his father's unwillingness to concede.

"Now look son, the skipper of that E-boat is no fool, and it's my belief that he'll be back within the next ten to fifteen minutes, and if he finds that instead of having lowered our nets we're under way and heading for the Swedish coast, he won't know what, but he'll know for certain that we're smuggling something. Believe me," added Henrik, "there's considerable method in my madness."

"That was just what I needed," said David with gusto prior to returning the seriously depleted bottle to its owner.

"There's not much to go round at our party," observed Henrik as he raised the bottle to head height in order to inspect the transparent liquid's new level.

"What party?" Karl enquired.

"Yes; what party?" echoed David.

"Ho!" exclaimed Henrik. "It was just a daft idea I had; but never mind about that now. Karl, go and remove the hatch cover. That shout we just heard was undoubtedly one of our passengers. I should think they're becoming restless. Explain the situation to them and tell them that they're going to have to stay hidden for a while longer yet. David, start to lower the nets."

Without another word both men set off to do as they had been instructed.

Chapter Twenty-Five

Hambleton Village

Three days after ensconcing myself in the little cottage at the outer limits of the, as yet unbeknown to me in daylight, village of Hambleton, once again I was sitting in the armchair in front of the fire that was cheerfully blazing away in the grate. Martha was in the kitchen preparing a hot drink for us both. The grandfather clock behind me, the body and face of which were just within peripheral vision over my right shoulder, had just chimed the hour, so that I knew without looking that it was a little after nine. In keeping with regulations, the blankets were maintaining the blackout in such a way that not a pin-prick of light was able to escape. I knew this because once Martha had hooked the blankets, I had secured the edges, and after using up all the pins this time, had stepped into the garden to check. She had said that I exemplified German efficiency.

Apart from the crackling and occasional hissing of the fire, and the culinary sounds Martha was making, the silence was absolute.

In the three days since my arrival there had been few distractions. At eleven o' clock precisely on the morning of my first full day in the cottage, whilst Martha was at her place of work, a convoy had passed by heading towards the centre of the village. The convoy was led by a jeep and in addition had consisted of three trucks and an ambulance similar to the one in which Ernst and I had travelled, and, to our undoubted embarrassment, had become temporarily trapped. Against the drab, olive green that is the normal livery of vehicles belonging to the British Army, seeing again the red-cross contrasting with its white circle background had brought back memories. Naturally I had thought poignantly of Ernst and the others. Upon letting my curiosity get the better of me, I had stood transfixed in shadow a short distance from the window, but evidently not so far back that I had remained unnoticed. Without parting my lips I had smiled at the officer in the jeep – a

Captain I think – when, upon his looking in at the cottage, our eyes had met. In response to my insincere but apparently friendly gesture, he had raised his swagger stick to touch the peak of his cap. Fortunately for me he had not considered my presence in the cottage to be in any way out of the ordinary and had motored on towards the village centre. None of the drivers of the heavier vehicles had looked my way. I had wondered if the troops these trucks were carrying had been tidying up the mess left by yours truly up on the moor. I had also considered the alternative possibility that they had been looking for the one that had got away. There was no telling.

On the second day, at approximately the same hour of the morning that the Army contingent had passed the day before, I was attracted by the sound of horseshoes ringing on the road, and by equally resonant human voices. This time I had decided that I would remain secreted, and after ever so slightly drawing back the curtain where it would otherwise have touched the living room wall, I had taken a cautious peek at the outside world to see a man and a woman riding side by side on horseback. They were a striking couple, both for the straight-backed discipline of their respective postures and for their attire, his being more gorgeous than hers. The man was wearing a crimson jacket, which had contrasted markedly with the navy blue garment worn by the woman. Her jacket had matched the colour of their riding hats. Adding to the impressiveness of the scene they had presented were the black knee-length riding-boots and cream-coloured jodhpurs each was wearing. Their voices and manner were revelations of absolute confidence Their mounts had been no less impressive, his being a bay with a fine head of about sixteen hands, and hers a grey of equal stature and nobility. Indeed, I had gained the impression that this couple were members of the British aristocracy, guessing that they might even be Martha's employers – Lord and Lady Gowerdale. When I described the couple to Martha hours later she had confirmed that my guesswork had been correct.

On the third day I saw no-one, and felt exceedingly happy when the woman whose prisoner I had willingly become returned from her remunerated duties. Since morning my state of mind had been one of wait and see, but the longer I waited and the more I saw, in my mind's eye if not with my eyeballs, the more I thought it worth my while to do nothing precipitate. This seemingly insouciant conclusion was based on the re-evaluation of my original plan and its chances of success. In the cold light of day I now considered my chances of getting away to be minimal, and I foresaw the future as being years of unremitting boredom cooped-up behind barbed wire. When I compared this most likely of prospects with my present, though perhaps transient, comfort, it was little wonder that I felt disinclined to leave.

A life on the run in all weathers compares badly with hot homemade food and sleeping between clean sheets on a firm mattress. My good fortune in being able to sleep in close proximity to a naked woman who was, sexually speaking, just as ready, willing and able to satisfy me as I believe I was able to satisfy her, made the idea of leaving the cottage seem ludicrous. Of course, there was a distinct possibility, perhaps even a probability, that I would be discovered and captured in my English haven of comfort and tranquillity, and that the outcome would be no different were I, in the next day or two, to be apprehended whilst attempting to steal a boat. It doesn't, however, take a genius in logic to realise that the longer I stayed in Martha's good books, so to speak, the less time I would have to spend sleeping in a hut in the company of a score of other downed pilots, probably all of whom snore. I had felt this way ever since Martha had given me such a warm embrace prior to her leaving for work, so I blame her for my change of heart, though without a hint of malice. In a sense I felt relieved that I was no longer preparing myself for an impossible mission, and this peace of mind, I believe, was the consequence of my clearer perception, of my having had sufficient time to have given the corollaries and possible ramifications of whatever course of action I might decide upon, proper consideration.

I can fully appreciate that to a person reading this history decades after the war had been won and lost, I must appear to be a disagreeable character, or worse, particularly with regard to my relationship with Martha, and how I was prepared to manipulate her loneliness and sense of alienation for my own ends. Well; perhaps my attitude towards her in those early days was calculating and lacking in chivalry, but I would ask all who would judge me harshly to be mindful of how far our European civilisation has come since the cataclysmic synthesis of those dark days. Ask yourself what you would have done if you had been in my shoes at that time. I had been through many ordeals. I had survived the crash-landing and destruction of my aeroplane, seen the bloody remains of my friend and the others of my crew, and endured the misery of being a man on the run behind enemy lines in the worst possible weather. What would you have done? Besides, these were early days in Martha's and my conjoined lives, and the emotional bonds which bind two people together need time to develop, to strengthen. I would also ask you to consider Martha's power to manipulate me to get what she wanted. She isn't passive by nature, and though she may well have been living the life of a lonely spinster when I first burst in upon the scene, after seventy-two hours in her company I realised that she wasn't as vulnerable as I had first thought.

Sitting in her living room on that third day I can say that I was genuinely fond of Martha, and that I would have rather put myself out in some way than upset her, never mind do her harm. With regard to doing harm to anybody, in the belief that armed resistance would be futile if I were to be challenged by the authorities, I had hidden my pistol. It was in the drawer in the chest of drawers in the master bedroom which contained the believed to be deceased person's socks and underpants. In the light, therefore, of my temporary renunciation of violence of the ballistic kind, the plan taking shape in my head was quite different from my earlier strategy, the one centred on escape. Now my plan was to reside in secret and in comfort for as long as possible, or until the end of the war. Given my circumstances, I had thought it wise to give some thought as to when that event might be, and who was likely to win. My mental grasp of the overall strategy behind the conduct of the war, either from an Allied or Axis perspective, was somewhat vague, but after Dunkirk I believed that even the Führer would have had to admit that our campaign to defeat the British had not gone according to plan. Inspired by the stirring speeches of their cigar-smoking leader, Winston Churchill, they were proving remarkably stubborn in not surrendering. Our failure to defeat the Royal Air Force was significant, and our attempts to bring the country to its knees by bombing the civilian population had proved counter-productive. Their determination to resist had increased with each raid. No doubt if I were in a position to express these thoughts to my fellow officers in the mess in Aalborg, I wouldn't be thinking in this way. Peer pressure would have taken precedence over reason. Ensconced in an armchair on this side of the German Sea (you, and indeed now I, usually refer to the body of water separating the British Isles from the continent of Europe as the North Sea) things looked very different. They looked so different in fact that I didn't expect our forward echelons to enter Hambleton Village, or any village in Britain for that matter, at any time soon. In my opinion it was questionable whether they would ever arrive.

They say that knowledge is power, and what I knew was that the Afrika Corps under the brilliant leadership of Generalfeldmarschall Erwin Rommel had been repulsed with heavy losses following our attack on the Alam Halfa Ridge, and that consequently the next attack in that theatre of operations would be by the British. I knew also that Rommel had returned to Germany because of ill-health, and to my mind this augured badly. Of greater concern to me in my undoubtedly peculiar position, however, was the fact that the powers that be in Germany seemed to have given up completely on the idea of invading Britain, so much were their minds focused on the ebb and flow of battle in the East, in Russia. I knew that at this point we continued to hold the upper hand in that campaign, but I had a feeling in my bones that the Russian bear, despite the Red Army's losses in equipment and men, had hardly begun to growl, and that we would come to regret out eagerness to follow in the footsteps of Bonaparte's Grande Armée. The much feared Russian winter was coming. When you add to these forces ranged against us the emerging might of the United States of America, you can understand how I came to the conclusion that my liberation might be a long time in coming. The idea of my taking part in a fly past over Buckingham Palace whilst the Führer surveyed the London skyline from the balcony seemed fanciful to say the least.

My ruminations on a global scale were interrupted by the appearance of Martha holding a mug of steaming hot cocoa in each hand. One of the mugs had a chip on the rim, and this she kept for herself whilst handing the pristine mug to me. She sat down on the rug at my feet in front of the fire and stared into the flames serenely. To make myself more comfortable, I undid the button at the waist of my recently appropriated trousers. This pair of pants might have fitted their former owner perfectly, but I found them to be constricting, particularly after the hearty meal of rabbit and vegetable stew which Martha had prepared earlier. In these timeless moments I too felt contentment, for it seemed that the world and its troubles were elsewhere, and they would never bring turmoil to our halcyon domain.

"Which side do you think is going to win the war?" Martha asked solemnly, without turning her face from the burning ash logs emitting yellow gas tinged with green.

My first inclination by way of answering was to toe the party line, to wave the swastika, to sing 'Deutschland, Deutschland über alles' but I thought better of it and said, "Hauptmann Hans... no; not Hauptmann, but simply Hans Hebbel and Martha Gilbert are going to win the war; and they... I mean we... are going to win the war by surviving; and by getting a divorce from the idiotic ideologies that got the world into this mess in the first place."

My comment evidently struck a harmonious chord with Martha because her face was beaming with delight when she turned her head to look up at me. Her eyes, eyes which at the time of our surprise meeting were devoid of life and empty of hope, looked into mine, scanning from left to right and then right to left like beacons searching in the darkness for that which she had thought was surely beyond her reach. The object of her quest, her scrutiny, was ineffable. She was searching for love. She was moved to speak.

"That's exactly how I feel Hans," she said with unmistakeable warmth in her voice. "Do you think that our chances of survival would be improved if we were to face the future together, or do you believe that we have no choice but to go our separate ways?"

This was undoubtedly a pivotal moment. To use a modern expression, her question may have cut to the chase, but I hesitated in giving my answer, primarily because I wanted to answer truthfully. The fact that she had presumed that there was no-one else in my life I overlooked, for Hanne might just as well have been on the dark side of the moon.

"Well they do say that two heads are better than one," I answered. "And I doubt that whoever spoke those words was thinking that they should be on one body."

I believed that I had answered diplomatically because in reality I was committing myself to nothing, yet the person who in all probability was seeking commitment would find in my statement a great deal about which she could be optimistic. Martha's satisfied look showed that my words had not displeased.

"If I'm going to be around for the foreseeable future, we're going to have to work on a cover story that's plausible, and I'm going to have to get used to responding to a different name; but let's leave all that till tomorrow. By the time you get back from work I will have had more time to think. Now I think it's almost time for the broadcast. Switch on the radio love, and we might learn something about what's going on in the world; but then again we might not."

"It was really clever of you to get it working again," said Martha, raising herself to her knees the better to be able to reach across to switch on the set in the corner which in later years was the home of our television. She switched on just in time for us to hear Lord Haw Haw's far from endearing nasal greeting.

"Germany calling, Germany calling…"

Chapter Twenty-Six

Viken, Sweden

Appearing like the first stars at the onset of darkness, one by one the lights of Viken could be discerned through the mist which had settled in the early hours of the morning close to shore along the Swedish coast. The skipper of *The White Bird* was steering his beloved boat slowly and warily. The last thing he wanted at this stage in the voyage was to founder on rocks which obviously, if such an event were to occur, should have been elsewhere. Henrik had ventured into the fishing port's harbour only once previously, and on this approach he was keeping a careful watch for the brightly coloured buoys which he knew served as warning markers indicating where and where not to go. Daylight was advancing over the land, and protruding above the swathes of mist, Viken's encroaching hills were becoming more clearly defined with each passing minute.

"There it is dad. There's the harbour entrance over there," said Karl, as he pointed with one hand whilst enthusiastically grabbing hold of his father's arm with the other.

The three members of the fishing boat's crew were standing in the now cramped wheelhouse staring a little askance of directly ahead of them at the gap which Karl had spotted between the harbour's two man-made promontories. With the assured skill of a fishing boat captain with years of experience under his belt, Henrik turned the wheel a few degrees to starboard to line up on the harbour entrance. The sea, though far from being a mill-pond, was calm. Aware that there was now little chance of having the bottom ripped out of his boat, the thought occurred to the skipper that he hadn't seen anything of the orange floats resembling footballs which had been in place on the occasion of his first visit. With a shrug of his shoulders he concluded that in the foggy conditions he had missed them completely.

"You can let everybody in the hold know that their ordeal is over," said Henrik, turning to look at his son in a way that spoke volumes.

Described in those volumes was the bond which had been forged between father and son in the face of shared dangers. Certainly from Karl's perspective it seemed that his father had inherited the Wisdom of Solomon. On this voyage the crowning glory of that impressive and exemplary sapience had been his decision to lower the net as soon as the German patrol boat had sped away. For lo and behold the roar of the warship's powerful engines could be heard making a fast approach barely twenty minutes later, and for the second time that night the crew of *The White Bird* had had to shield their eyes from the glare of the searchlight. This time the E-boat had passed directly in front of the fishing boat's bows without the slightest deviation in course or change of speed. By the evidence of his own eyes her Captain was clearly satisfied that the Danes were not involved in any skulduggery. Henrik's little subterfuge had worked to brilliant effect. For it not to have worked brilliantly was for it not to have worked at all. After another hour had passed following the patrol boat's departure for the second time, the fishermen had set about redeeming the net.

In the light of the navigation lights the meshed bundle was hauled from the sea. It had dripped water onto the deck and glistened with silvery bodies, a writhing mass of cod and whiting mainly, with a few flat fish for good measure. Normal practice would have been to release the catch into the hold, but on this occasion, thinking it too cruel an act to consider, for the sake of his passengers the skipper had deviated from routine.

Nevertheless, a compromise had had to be reached, and for the remainder of the voyage to Viken the catch was suspended in the bulging net, where the fish wriggled and writhed and gasped for oxygen until they died.

"It's safe to come up now," called down Karl after he had removed the cover to the hold. "Ugh! What's that smell?"

The young man poked his head a little way inside the ad hoc passenger quarters, but quickly withdrew it again. He had been expecting the sudden appearance of a friendly face, his face no less, to be greeted with warmth and enthusiasm, perhaps even a few cheers, but nothing of the kind was forthcoming. Instead he was greeted with comments barbed with irony.

"It's about time too," said Astrid, who was evidently in some discomfort judging by the way she shifted her weight from one foot to the other: she wasn't sure if she could hold on much longer.

Perhaps it was because that as a mother she had endured the raw physicality of having given birth that Mrs Melchior had shown less inhibition and relieved herself in the darkness, her attitude moreover being that the hold would need to be thoroughly cleansed and disinfected before it would again be fit for purpose. Sealing his nostrils between his thumb and forefinger, Karl realised that David and he would have an unpleasant job of work to do before the day was much older.

"It might be a good idea to fetch the ladder so that we can climb out of this cess-pit," suggested Mr Melchior.

"Yes; of course; right away," said Karl, determined not to let the obvious dissatisfaction of the Aarhus lot, nor the unpleasant nature of the day's job prospects, dampen his spirits, his sense of elation at what they had achieved.

Karl fetched the ladder and lowered it. Item by item the baggage was raised first, each weekend bag and holdall being placed by Karl in a neat pile on deck directly in front of the wheelhouse. Subsequently, one by one, and yet again led by Mrs Melchior, the people in the hold ascended into the chilly air of an autumnal morning. The weariness felt by each person was clearly discernible in their stiffness of movement, and though not a single face amongst them was beaming with good cheer, it was possible to perceive nonetheless that each man, and each woman, was thankful for his or her deliverance.

For a reason known only to herself, but one which can easily be guessed at, Astrid, having ushered the others to ascend the ladder ahead of her so that she was last to emerge, had delayed her departure from the depths. Mr and Mrs Melchior, Hanne, and eventually Astrid, congregated at the bow facing the life belt. They had gravitated to this point so as to get a good view of Sweden as exemplified by the small fishing village that is Viken, little realising that they were impeding the view of the man driving the boat.

Henrik instructed David, who was presently standing beside him in the wheelhouse, to tell the passengers to come to the rear of the boat, where they would not be a distraction. In proceeding to comply with this order David had to squeeze past Hanning who, instead of joining the others to take pleasure in the view, was making for the wheelhouse to say a few words to the skipper. The frustration that had earlier got the better of Hanning had dissipated, and ever since his reason had gained supremacy over his emotion, he was aware that the circumstances of everyone aboard *The White Bird* could, at this precise moment, have been so very different.

"Thank you Captain for a job well done," said Hanning, holding out his hand to the fisherman for the latter to shake. "Well; I'll not be stingy with the accolades, for a brilliant job in fact; though I'm afraid to say that we haven't been the best of house guests, if you catch my drift."

"Don't tell me you were sick down there," said Henrik, slightly alarmed for realising fully for the first time on the voyage just how unpleasant the passage must have been for those kept in the dark for so long. Whilst gripping and then relinquishing the proffered hand he kept his eyes focused on the steadily approaching gap through which they would shortly pass to enter the harbour. The mist by this time had thinned to reveal the apparent reticence of a pellucid sun. By an unknown hand the lights of the town were switched off, and this prompted Henrik to switch off the lights on the boat. The other Aarhus people filed past the wheelhouse as they made their way towards the stern. With nods and smiles they too showed their appreciation to the man who, by the animation of his eyes rather than by moving his head, looked askance at them through the spray-washed glass.

"If we do this run again – and I'm sure we will – I'll make better provision in the hold," commented Henrik apologetically. "Here we go. Welcome to Sweden."

The White Bird chugged into the quiet harbour without mishap, and though Henrik had to spin the wheel hard to starboard upon entering, this was because of the harbour's design, and not because he had suddenly needed to alter course by ninety degrees in response to an unforeseen circumstance. There was little sign of life inside the harbour, amongst the half-dozen or so fishing boats moored alongside the jetties jutting out from the quay. Her back to the Danes, a woman wearing an orange headscarf and walking a black Labrador dog was walking towards the town, and as it so happened, towards the only vehicle in sight. This was a green Volvo P52 parked at the far end of the quay. Upon seeing *The White Bird's* Danish pennant, the driver of the vehicle flashed his lights to draw attention to himself. From here and there, now and then a gull shrieked from a rooftop perch, whilst others of their species chased one another across the sky in graceful arcs of flight, or passively bobbed up and down in keeping with the gentle undulations of the water.

"That must be our welcome committee," said Henrik as he pin-pointed in his mind the exact place he intended to berth.

"They'll be relieved to see us I'm sure," said Hanning. "I wonder how long they've been waiting." Then, turning to look at Henrik, he asked, "How long do you intend to stay in Viken?"

Henrik at that moment hadn't quite made up his mind as to when he intended to leave, but prompted by Hanning's question he decided that it would be propitious to leave at noon.

"If we cast off at midday that should give us time to get you and the two girls, Hanne and Astrid, back to Aarhus at a reasonable hour. I trust you'll be able to put the three of us up for the night," he said quizzically, at the same time cutting the engine so as to let the boat's momentum take her towards the timbers of the jetty that was nearest.

"You don't need to worry about that," said Hanning, steadying himself as the port side of the boat collided with an old tyre which had been put in place to act as a buffer.

"You and your crew are guaranteed a warm welcome in Aarhus: I'll see to that. That's a fine lad you've got there," he added as the attention of both men was drawn to the athleticism of Henrik's son as he leapt onto the jetty.

"Yes; he hasn't turned out too badly; a little too headstrong for his own good at times perhaps," said Henrik in acknowledgement; yet all the while his mind was focused on more practical matters. "Leaving at noon gives us a few hours to clean out the boat and get something to eat in town; a chance to stretch our legs ashore; that sort of thing."

With the confidence that only comes with practice, Karl tied the boat up forward while David stood ready to throw him the rope with which he would be able to secure the boat aft. The waiting Volvo had begun to move, the driver's intention being to approach with the car as close as was practicably possible. It was possible to discern, as the distance between the observers and the object observed decreased, that there was only one person in the car, he, of course, being the driver. The car stopped on the quayside directly in front of the entrance to the relevant jetty. The man got out of the car and proceeded to wave to his prospective passengers before he was standing fully upright. Despite the absence of rain and the prospect of a fine but cool day ahead, the man was wearing a raincoat. Above a neck that was smartly dressed in a white collar and a navy-blue tie, and beneath a wide-brimmed hat, the man's face beamed with pleasure in anticipation of the meeting, and with welcoming goodwill. Evidently this was a friend and not a foe. This was none other than Mrs Melchior's brother, and to ensure that there was enough room in the car he had come alone to pick up his sister, brother-in-law and niece. Once they had dealt with the formalities, he would then take them to their new home for the duration of 'The Alert' (as the war years were referred to in Sweden) in Angelholm.

"If you can come up with the materials, I'll clean up the mess in the hold," said Hanning to Henrik. "After all I am responsible."

"You're on," said Henrik. "Come on, let's see what we can get in exchange for our fish."

Placing his big fisherman's hand upon Hanning's shoulder, he almost pushed the café-owner out of the wheelhouse as the two men set out to help the others step first onto Swedish wood, and then on to Swedish concrete. There could now be no doubt that in the very near future they would be able to step onto Swedish soil.

Chapter Twenty-Seven

Hambleton Village

Allow me to introduce myself. My name is Aage Frederik Hjelmsleve. I was born on the twenty-first of August nineteen hundred and nineteen on the Danish island of Læsø, a fact which I suppose makes me a Leo from Læsø. I've never really shown much interest in astrology, thinking in the main that being able to predict the future for a specific but undoubtedly large group of human beings by observing the movement of celestial bodies in relation to each other was largely mumbo-jumbo. Recently, however, I came across a description of a typical Leo and thought, "Yes; that's me. In my 'grandeur of manner, splendour of bearing and magnanimity of personality' I am a 'monarch among humans as the lion is the king of the beasts'." After giving careful consideration to these characteristics, I came to the conclusion that they reflect my personality perfectly, and that perhaps there's something in this pseudo-science after all. My parents, who had been born and bred on the island, and had lived there all their lives until I had reached the age of ten, had timed my conception well.

Mum and dad ran a small farm not far from the island's capital, namely the small town of Byrum. We used to live in a house which was remarkable (though not on Læsø) for the fact that the fabric of the roof was seaweed and not the thatch which is typical of farmhouses in other parts of Denmark. Another vivid memory I have of my place of birth is of how the girls used to wear national costume on high days and holidays, a tradition which was supposed to have originated in the fourteenth century when Queen Margrethe the first, so the legend goes, was rescued from a shipwreck off the coast. She gave her rescuers a beautiful dress as a token of her gratitude, and henceforth this became the fashion for the island's female population right up until the outbreak of the present conflict.

Shortly before my tenth birthday my parents took me from the salt marshes, woodland, heaths and meadows that covered much of my island to go and live in our new home in Skagen, on the northernmost tip of Jutland. It was my father's intention to leave the land in favour of making a living from the sea. My mother wanted to set up a business painting and then selling her pictures. She had always been of an artistic temperament, and the town was, and indeed still is, a magnet for artists. My parents also thought that the move to a bigger town on the mainland would be better for my education, and would enable me to broaden my mind more easily. Personally I found it much more exciting to go out on the boat with my father at weekends than being called upon to help with milking the cows on the farm we used to have on Læsø. I took to the sea – dare I say it – like a fish to water, and everything in our lives was going swimmingly until the morning of the 9th April, 1940. That was the day when life for the vast majority of Danish people changed for the worse.

At precisely four-fifteen in the morning of that eventful day, and contrary to a non-aggression pact signed a year earlier, Adolf Hitler ordered the invasion of my beloved country. After no more than a couple of hours and the deaths of seventeen of our soldiers, the Cabinet decided to capitulate. I'm sure most people understand why. For those who have some difficulty in this regard, however, I would simply point out that Denmark is a small country compared with its much more powerful, and as it was then, aggressive neighbour to the south; and this comparison applies equally to the populations relative to each other as it does to the number of square kilometres forming the area of each country. To people who would say, on the basis that Denmark has responsibility for some aspects of the island's governance, 'But what about Greenland – Greenland is huge', I would simply say please don't mention Greenland in this context. It should also be borne in mind that following the signing of the mutual agreement not to go to war, Denmark had, so as not to antagonise the Third Reich, deliberately maintained its armed forces at a low state of readiness, whereas, as everybody knows, the war-machine of Nazi Germany was ready, willing and easily able to gobble up its smaller and weaker neighbours. What's more, the peninsular being flat, Jutland would have proved ideal country for tanks, and there were a great number of tanks in the Wehrmacht. No; my sceptical friend, to have put up more resistance than we did at the outset of the invasion would have been futile, and I believe extremely detrimental to my fellow countrymen.

Back in the bubble of my personal ambitions and desires, the microcosm formed by family and friends, news of the invasion when it reached my ears compelled me to make a fateful decision. It was undoubtedly a hasty decision, but on reflection, and taking into account subsequent events, it was not one which I have regretted; though I do, of course, regret the loss of my friend Ludwig, who jumped at the chance to join me in my escapade. Fired by the spirit of youth, and armed with the confidence generated by the strength we possessed as young men, Ludwig and I decided not to put up with mere existence, with having to tolerate the heel of oppression. Instead we chose to make a bid for freedom by sailing to Britain. Our reasons for choosing the British Isles were based on common-sense, for we reasoned that, because of their geographical location, it would be difficult under any circumstances for an army intent on invasion to cross the sea separating the islands from the mainland of Europe, and even more so when the Royal Air Force and the Royal Navy appeared so formidable. There seemed little point in our attempting to escape the yoke of tyranny by going to Norway or Sweden because, we reasoned, it would only be a matter of time before those countries suffered a fate similar to that of Denmark. In respect of Sweden, I know that thus far our fears have proved unfounded, but keeping in mind that we were accomplished strategists only when it came to catching fish, I don't think we made a bad job of hazarding a guess as to how geo-political events would unfold.

Ludwig, who was a couple of years older than me, was the proud owner of *The Skagen Flyer*, and it was in this slow but basically sound old tub that after taking leave of our respective parents we set sail for Britain, arriving at the mouth of the Tyne in the early hours of 12th April. After a few weeks in the north, during which time we established to the satisfaction of the authorities who we were, we sailed for London, arriving in the capital just in time to join the armada of small boats mustered to take part in Operation Dynamo, the rescue of hundreds of thousands of British and French troops from the beaches near to Dunkirk. It was on our fourth run in towards the beach that tragedy struck in the shape of a bomb dropped by a Stuka. Ludwig was killed instantly, but miraculously I survived to find myself floating in the water thanks to my life jacket. After shouting for all I was worth, I was rescued by a boat already crammed with soldiers. I felt fortunate indeed that the boat's skipper had not passed me by.

Despite the fact that *The Skagen Flyer* and Ludwig are no more, I feel immensely proud of the fact that the three of us had managed to bring safely home to England somewhere in the region of one hundred and twenty soldiers. The physical legacy of that final run on the last day of May, 1940, is that I walk with a limp, and am lost without the assistance a walking stick provides. That's what a piece of shrapnel in the leg did for me.

Many of the soldiers we brought home were in a much worse state of repair than me. What's that you ask? To which Regiment did they belong? They were, in the main, from the Somerset Light Infantry. What's that I hear you say? The Regiment known as the Somerset Light Infantry was not in France at that time. The fact that I had, and still have, no idea as to whether the Somerset Light Infantry was in France in 1940 was a weakness in my cover-story which was proving difficult to rectify, mainly because I, Hans Hebbel – yes, by now you have realised that Aage Frederik Hjelmsleve does not, to my knowledge, exist, and never has; and that the events he has described wherein he is the protagonist and hero did not take place – was wary of arousing suspicion by asking questions of a military nature. I had picked on the Somerset Light Infantry to be my band of rescued brothers simply because I had heard of the name, and because here in Yorkshire there was less chance of my meeting with a flesh and blood member of the Regiment who might prove me wrong. Martha had no idea as to which British Army units had been evacuated from the beaches, and for her to find out on the quiet, would have necessitated her going to one of the newspaper offices, either in this county or the one adjacent, to check through back copies for coverage of events which occurred over two years ago. That, Martha informed me, would require our making a trip to Darlington, Middlesbrough, or York. For us to travel to any of these cities would require considerable effort, for the nearest was over twenty miles away. In wartime, and without transport of our own, that was not an insignificant distance from our rural village. To have made such a journey would have taken us a world away from our daily routine. After having given the matter a great deal of thought, I decided to keep the rescue of elements of the Somerset Light Infantry as an integral part of my cover-story, concluding that if I were to be asked to divulge this level of detail the game I was playing would soon be over anyway. Notwithstanding the fact that I had not committed a word of this epic tale to paper, Martha considered my story worthy of a literary award for fiction masquerading as genuine fact.

It was she who suggested, and this she would put into effect at some unspecified time in the not too distant future, that she tactfully draw the attention of others to the presence of my alter ego before we first appeared in public together, primarily to put the idea into people's heads that I was of Danish descent before my distinctly un-English accent could set alarm bells ringing.

In at least one of the many books that I've delved into since my arrival in England, books I've struggled through not only to improve my English, but also to pass the time, I read that the most convincing lie is one which contains a few grains of truth. I quickly realised that in the spy genre, as in real life accounts of escape and evasion such as mine, the easier it is to recount from memory, thereby being able to include an autobiographical flourish or embellishment here and there, the more likely the deception is to succeed. My knowledge of a certain county Regiment's recent history may or may not be flawed, but my mental images of Læsø and Skagen were as clear as sharply focused photographs taken in perfect light. In my alter ego's namesake's company I had spent time in both these places.

Adding to the credibility of my cover story was my ability to speak a little Danish, not perfectly I admit, and though my vocabulary was extremely limited, I possessed enough confidence in my language skills to be able to convince the average Englishman. I didn't consider this to be indicative of brilliance or extraordinary in any way, simply because the English, as everybody on the planet who is not English knows perfectly well, are the world's worst linguists. Even they do not deny it. I'm sure that their belief in the supremacy of the English language has some bearing not only on what they think, but also on the way they think. Despite my bravado, a bad eventuality would be for me to meet a supposed fellow Dane. Then the cat would be out of the bag for sure.

The skill I developed in being able to walk with a limp and the ruse which manifested itself in my apparent inability to cope without a stick are worthy of mention. When you consider that there was nothing physically wrong with me whatsoever, initially my thespian talent was tested to the limit as I struggled to perfect and maintain my self-imposed impairment. Eventually, however, after weeks of practice the role I was playing became second nature to the extent that I found myself limping as soon as I got out of bed in the morning. It also became second nature for me to reach for my walking stick on the occasions that I was about to venture to the chicken-coop or the garden shed. Indeed, so effectively did I adapt myself to the role of being a wounded Danish war hero that I found it nigh on impossible to stop the charade, and here I'm writing about a time long after the war had ended. In the same way that I had had to convince myself that the role I had imagined was plausible, eventually I had to retrain my mind to accept that there never had been a boat called *The Skagen Flyer*, and that a piece of shrapnel from the bomb which had supposedly sunk her had never entered my leg. The strangest aspect of my phantom disability was that when at long last I did pluck up the courage to walk into the village without my stick and with the gait of a person who is able-bodied in every respect, nobody seemed to notice the difference.

If any person did, no mention of the apparent miracle that was my recovery was made in my presence.

At a time nearer to the beginning of my rustic domicile, once the church bells had been rung to celebrate the victory achieved by Montgomery's Eighth Army over Rommel's Afrika Corps, I knew that the writing was on the wall for Hitler and his thousand-year Reich, for the gang from which my divorce, first of my body, and then of my soul, had been engineered by circumstances combined with personal volition. Consequently I experienced none of the pangs associated with a guilty conscience for having decided to sit out the war in relative comfort; and as the weeks passed, and the affection which Martha and I had for each other deepened, I began to feel that the life I had led prior to the night I had spent in Martha's shed had been an illusion. By adopting an alter ego, and then adapting to it wholeheartedly, I was beginning to have doubts that Hanne and Ernst and the others from that nebulous phantasmagoria we call the past had ever existed. Martha's and my days together at this time were an existential progression from the arrowhead or spear-point of which, with regard to our personal perspectives, we did not dare look too far into the future, and from the flux of which we chose not to dwell upon the mistakes we had made in the past. The transformations which had been wrought in our innermost beings had engendered a profound change in the way we perceived the world and humankind. The weak were no longer waiting to be conquered, and nor were the submissive to be enslaved. There had been a sea-change in our politics which, although we were as resolute as ever in our contempt for communism, was perfectly at ease with the principle of live and let live.

On the whole my cover worked well, and gradually my sense of impending nemesis that each day brought began to subside as my alter ego's existence became increasingly established and accepted. I wasn't asked to explain who I was by a British person other than superficially, but I was put under some pressure by a group of American soldiers whom I had the misfortune to meet. It was a case of my being in the wrong place at the wrong time. The irony was that my capture, albeit of relatively short duration, was a glaring example of mistaken identity. I remember the incident as if it had occurred only yesterday.

On a beautiful morning at the beginning of April in 1944, I set out from the cottage to check my snares as usual. I made these simple devices from a length of wire one end of which formed a loop. The other end of the wire I wrapped around a stick sturdy enough to be whacked into the ground. I used to set my ingeniously simple traps on hillsides which were riddled with rabbit holes. The loop, which tightened and constricted when pulled, I positioned to dangle directly over the hole so that any rabbit rushing in or out would be inextricably caught, and its fate sealed in a pot or a pie. I had not eaten the long-eared animal prior to my arrival in England, but I certainly made up for that gastronomic omission subsequently. I enjoyed the strong flavour. Martha was less enthusiastic initially, but so much did she appreciate the additional meat I provided during those years of stringent rationing that she came round to my way of thinking in the end. We both realised that the plenitude of edible game and my skill at catching it were essential components in our being able to live together in the way that we did. For obvious reasons I didn't have a ration card, and Martha's meagre allowance of food which she brought home each week from Yatton would not have been adequate for us both to live on for any length of time. With the meat that I provided, which also was comprised of hare on occasion, and as a consequence of a singular piece of good fortune, the venison provided by a roe dear which I had found dead by the side of the road, we ate quite well; certainly much better than the average British city dweller was able to eat from what I could gather.

In my hunting for game, and rabbits in particular, I effectively practised a form of crop rotation, there being four specific hunting grounds that I used to visit on a regular basis. I would have liked there to have been more, but I didn't find any other likely contenders to add to my mental list, at least not one that was within a reasonably accessible distance from home.

My reason for wanting more warrens was eminently practical: I didn't want to be instrumental in causing a decline in the rabbit population in a given location to the extent that eventually there would be none left for me to catch. It was as I was making my way along a grassy track towards the farthest of my favoured sites that I noticed a number of dark shapes in the wood away to my left, shapes that I was struggling to identify. The track I was on led through a deciduous wood which consisted mainly of oak trees, most of which, judging by their gnarled appearance and size, were considerably older than my parents. The leaf canopy was embryonic, but such foliage as there was filtered the surprisingly warm April sunshine and transformed it into dappled light. Already three miles from home, and wearing one of only two of George Gilbert's short-sleeved shirts that he had left behind, I was enjoying my carefree early morning perambulation through the glorious English countryside; for that's how I had come to perceive my adopted environs, as a landscape that on certain days – and this was one such day – seemed, even to the eyes of this foreigner, to be divinely infused. In my attempts to assimilate English ways and customs, by reading avidly I had learnt, and was still learning, an amazing amount each day, one of my more recent accomplishments having been the learning by heart of those memorable lines spoken by John of Gaunt In William Shakespeare's play Richard II:

'This royal throne of kings, this sceptre isle,
This earth of majesty, this seat of Mars,
This other Eden, demi-paradise...'

Two years ago these words would have been anathema to me, but on this particular morning I found myself whispering their rhythmic cadences as if they were a prayer. I had read, but hadn't gone on to learn that part of the speech which refers to 'stubborn Jewry', but bearing in mind my National Socialist education and conditioning, I was hardly going to be deeply offended by such a statement. The business of defending Jews or persecuting them was no longer relevant to me. Martha's and my philosophy of live and let live had not turned us into saints.

On my way to retrieve the anticipated and hopefully as yet still fur-covered meat ration for the week ahead, I was in a particularly positive frame of mind when I stopped in my tracks, leaned on my walking stick, and studied the black shapes that continued to perplex me. In the dappled confusion, in the intricate interplay of light and shadow created in part by the forest undergrowth, these more or less oval forms were too solid to be natural, and I was about to take the bold step of forsaking my limp to step off the track and venture the ten or so yards (I had found it exceptionally difficult to relinquish the metric system I had learned at school when it came to measuring or judging distance, but I was determined not to stand out from the crowd, and eventually, with perseverance, I succeeded, and now I only ever use miles, yards, feet, and inches), into the forest to take a closer look when I heard a commotion behind me, a noise of heavy but determined movement emanating from the trees growing along the side of the track opposite to that which had thus far absorbed my attention. My immediate thought was that it was a deer breaking cover, and I spun round on my heels expecting to confirm by sight the activity I had determined upon on the basis of the sounds I had heard. I couldn't have been more mistaken, because a moment before I was unceremoniously and aggressively thrown to the ground by the individual who was the vanguard of his group, I caught sight of several – later I determined five – black faces, all of which were looming towards me, and all of which were fractionally covered at the forehead by helmets normally worn by soldiers belonging to the American Army. Dressed in olive-green uniforms, their weapons, easily recognisable because of their wooden stocks, were M1 carbines. Presumably the Yank, who by virtue of his skill in unarmed combat had caused me to drop like a sack of potatoes, had passed his personal weapon on to a comrade to hold temporarily. Fortunately, I managed to withhold the expletive I had been about to utter in German as I felt my feet being swept from under me. If I had thought about giving myself a few moments respite, some quiet time on the ground to gather my thoughts and get my breath back, those thoughts were immediately supplanted as two of the Americans dragged me to my feet. Neither of this pair was the man who had first laid hands upon me. My assailant was standing directly in front of me looking for the world as if he was in charge. I noticed that on the left arm of his combat-jacket was an insignia denoting rank, specifically two inverted black stripes edged and interspersed by material which was the colour of gold. This badge of rank indicated to me that my attacker was a Corporal. Whilst I was being hauled to my feet I noticed that the dark shapes which had first aroused my curiosity were black faces belonging to three more American soldiers. They approached from their rather conspicuous hiding-place, joining their comrades to make a total of eight. The Section's configuration was such that in addition to the two men standing behind me, each of whom was gripping one of my arms, five of my captors had formed a semi-circle a stride or two to the side and behind their leader, who was standing centrally. Held rigidly straight and pointing away from my back, thereby forcing my head and upper body to take a protracted bow, my arms were the source of considerable pain. In this position it would have been impossible to wrestle myself free, for either one, or perhaps even both, of my arms could have been easily broken. I was at the mercy of my captors.

In my painful predicament my first thought was that my cover had been blown, and that it was as Hauptmann Hans Hebbel that I had been apprehended, though why my arrest should have been carried out by members of a black battalion of the United States Army rather than by British soldiers or police was puzzling. Following this line of reasoning, I then thought that at least I had had two years of relative comfort, and in the light of this fact, if I had been able to, I would have shrugged my shoulders to show how philosophical I was about the sudden change in my fortunes. For the time being, however, so as not to be the instigator of my own nemesis, I decided to keep faith with my alter ego.

"Hey man, what's your name?" enquired the Corporal in a melodic voice, stepping forward to check my pockets and other parts of my body, I presumed for a concealed knife or pistol.

Despite this being the first American that I had met face to face, his accent, though strangely incongruous for being heard in rural Yorkshire, sounded familiar, a sort of caricature of the voices from the southern states which I had either heard on the radio or as part of the soundtrack to a film.

In heavily accented English I said, "My name is Aage Frederik Hjelmsleve... Captain Aage Frederik Hjelmsleve of the Royal Danish Navy... Freddie to my friends."

I thought that there might be some small advantage in ascribing to myself a rank superior to that held by the highest ranking of my captors, and equally by assigning myself to an organisation which, in their view, was probably obscure.

"So nice to meet you Freddie," teased the Corporal as he turned towards the others seeking confirmation. "We all want to be Freddie's friends don't we boys?" he added.

In various ways the others expressed their assent prior to each soldier telling me in turn how nice it was to meet me. I wasn't convinced that they meant it. These pleasantries sounded ominous to my ears, and sure enough the drawled salutations proved to be blatantly ironic when the Corporal struck me across the face with the back of his hand. Hard upon impact my head reeled, and for a second or two I saw a multitude of stars, tiny pin-pricks of light in kaleidoscope colours, but with blue predominant.

"What did you do that for?" I asked inanely, directing my voice towards the tufts of grass and dandelions growing in the space between mine and my assailant's feet.

My walking stick lay half on and half off the path, and because each end rested upon higher ground, a length of no less than eighteen inches in the middle effectively formed a bridge for ants. At the moment of my noticing the position of my stick I became smitten by an irrational fear that it would be the easiest thing in the world for one of these jokers to break my stick in half with his heavy boot. The boot in question would need to be driven down with considerable force, but to me more than one of these guys looked mean enough to deprive a crippled war-hero of his means of physical support.

"Because you lied to us man," replied the Corporal, yanking my head upwards by pulling a clump of my hair. "And if you lie to us again, next time I'll use my rifle butt."

"Yeh; and if you're a sea-captain you sure are a long way from your ship," commented the soldier who was gripping my right arm; "And that Royal Dutch Navy you belong to, is that on our side or theirs?"

"I belong to the Royal Danish Navy," I corrected. "And it's definitely on our side."

There were guffaws and chuckles at my expense. A third soldier, whose diminutive frame was partially hidden by his leader's imposing bulk, spoke up in a similar vein from beneath a helmet which looked a couple of sizes too big for the head it protected.

"What sort of ship did you used to drive man?" he asked, prior to providing me with a list of grandiose options: "An aircraft carrier; or a destroyer perhaps; no; I'll tell you what you is, you're a cruiser captain."

For a reason I couldn't quite fathom this mildly jocular banter produced yet more raucous laughter. Indeed, an observer who had arrived late upon the scene might be tempted to think that the ambiance created by our little gathering was far from sinister, and that the proceedings in which I was involved were merely a game. I was beginning to suspect, as well as to hope, that this possibility would eventually manifest itself as fact, and to give some foundation and structure to my newfound optimism I analysed in my head all that had been said in our verbal exchanges thus far.

It was the comment about whether the Royal Danish Navy was on our side or theirs which resounded in my consciousness with the clarity of birdsong or a celebratory bell, allowing me to consider the possibility that in my captors' perception of reality the wickedly nasty Nazi enemy was not among us, and that simply by being in the right place, but at the wrong time, I had inadvertently become involved in some kind of war game. I allowed myself a sigh of satisfaction as this realisation took hold to develop in strength and form until eventually it became the basis of a plan. The situation as I now perceived it to be was that here was a group of black American GIs on a training exercise in preparation for the invasion which everyone knew was in the offing. They had captured a man whom they believed to be an American soldier like themselves, but who was enacting the role of a German spy or operator. It was now my belief that they had no idea that I really was a German, one trying desperately hard to be nobody's secret agent. I decided that the best strategy I could adopt for obtaining my release was to go on the offensive and interrogate them.

"If you don't believe that I am who I say I am, would you mind telling me just who you do think I am?"

My request for information instigated the third bout of hilarity. These boys were really enjoying their day's work. This, I thought, augured well. It was true that the Corporal in charge had threatened to hit me with his rifle butt if I didn't tell him what he wanted to hear, but that was merely a threat, one which I hoped would prove hollow. Indeed, the only harm I had come to thus far had been to receive a slap across the face, but if this lot had really meant business they could have subjected me to much worse right from the start.

"You're the enemy," said the Corporal in answer to my question, the succinctness of his reply being totally unhelpful. Fortunately he was more forthcoming when he added, "You're one of the Special Service Force tasked to infiltrate our lines and act as saboteurs, but if you're anything to go by you guys aren't as good as your reputation would have people believe." Turning his attention from me to the men standing behind him and to his right he said, "He doesn't look so special to me, does he you guys?"

"About as special as a swamp alligator that's lost his teeth," volunteered a wit who had not previously spoken, one who at the same time had perhaps given some intimation that his state of origin bordered the Gulf of Mexico.

The sense of satisfaction was now undoubtedly mutual, though for different reasons. The fact that my true identity had not been discovered, and that I was certain of this knowledge, did not mean, however, that I was out of the frying pan, and some skilful persuasion was yet required for me not to end up in the proverbial fire. In trying to gauge my immediate future, I imagined that I would be hauled back to their Company or Battalion headquarters where I would be kept under guard until some such time that my captors' mistake became glaringly obvious, possibly if and when real Special Service Force captives were brought in, or when the Exercise finally came to an end. In either event the increased exposure would be potentially dangerous, and I anticipated the prospect with foreboding. Nonetheless, I was about to go along with their little game and offer my surrender in the guise of the person whom they had just described, when I heard sounds which were not unfamiliar to my ears, and which were definitely not human. The noise I heard was the measured clip-clop of a horse's hooves. The horse was approaching at a walking pace, and though it was impossible for me to turn my head to look, or lower it to the extent that I would be able to peek between my legs and past the lower limbs of my custodians, it was obvious that the animal was being ridden. The question was by whom. The arrival of the mysterious horse and rider was a greater distraction to my captors than it was to me, though the majority of them were able to see quite clearly who was holding the reins. The figure they beheld must have impressed them because the Corporal commanded his men to come to attention in the instant that he adopted the same respectful stance himself. Raising his hand to the rim of his helmet, the Corporal saluted in the direction of rider and horse, who and which by this time were behind my right shoulder, making steady progress as if they were about to pass. I felt a sequence of sharp pains in my arms and shoulders as I was yanked, in more ways than one, farther to one side. After my forced relocation I looked up to see that the lone rider was none other than Lord Gowerdale dressed in the impressive brilliance of his scarlet jacket and, of course, other items of equestrian apparel. I didn't for one moment believe that my deferential captors had any idea who Lord Gowerdale was, and I sensed that they were paying these military compliments on the basis that it was better to be wrong in one way than another. I wasn't surprised that they found the spectacle to be impressive.

"Ah! Mr Hjelmsleve, it's you!" his Lordship exclaimed. "I see that you're helping our American friends with their war games. Good for you," he said by way of encouragement.

"As much as I might enjoy being slapped across the face and having my arms pulled almost out of their sockets," I responded ironically, "On this occasion my participation is not of my choosing. If they had asked I would have been only too willing to offer my services, but I was pounced upon whilst going about my lawful business... at least I don't believe it to be unlawful... and today that was to check my snares for rabbits."

"I see," said Lord Gowerdale, his facial expression upon learning the truth of my predicament revealing his disappointment at my present lack of zeal for the war effort. His countenance changed to a self-satisfied grin, however, when in his mind he undoubtedly made the comparison between my present situation and my stated intentions. "You seem to be caught in a snare yourself Mr Hjelmsleve. How do you propose to extricate yourself?"

I pondered the meaning of the word 'extricate' and hoped that I had interpreted it correctly. By this time Lord Gowerdale had reined in his horse so that the animal and he were positioned at a standstill a yard or so in front of me. The bay was the same fine specimen of equine power and vitality that I had observed for the first time two years earlier, when his Lordship had ridden past the cottage in the company of her Ladyship. Lord Gowerdale appeared no less resplendent now than he did then, and because this was the closest that we had ever been to each other, I couldn't help but note how handsome he was, his tanned features denoting strength with humour, grace with power, adorned by a neatly trimmed black moustache. The thought occurred to me that this man whom I was presently looking up to was of an age to be in uniform, and I wondered if members of the British aristocracy were exempt from military service, perhaps for reasons to do with inheritance or maintaining the bloodline. I quickly dismissed this idea in favour of a more mundane conclusion, which was that Lord Gowerdale had been exempted on health grounds, though I was hard put to imagine what they might be. I made a mental note, on the optimistic basis that I would soon meet up with her again, to ask Martha why it was that Lord Gowerdale seemed to be living the life of Riley while his fellow countrymen were enduring hardship. I assumed that his Lordship had learned a great deal about me from the same fountain of knowledge which I hoped would tell me more about him. I knew for certain that on more than one occasion he had seen me in Martha's company.

In response to my unwitting benefactor's question I replied, "I think that by simply mentioning my name you may have already done the lion's share of what will be necessary in that regard your Lordship." Turning towards the Corporal, who though still standing rigidly to attention had dropped his arm down by his side after saluting, I said, "These chaps think I'm one of their Special Service Force bods trying to infiltrate their lines."

"The prisoner told us that his name is Aage Frederik Hjelmsleve and that he's a Captain in the Royal Danish Navy. Are you about to tell me that he is who he says he is," questioned the Corporal, adding after a moment's hesitation, "Your Lordship?"

The pause was significant. It indicated that the Corporal, who by this time had given himself an order, unheard for having been unspoken, to stand at ease, was unaccustomed to addressing the nobility, a consequence being that he was somewhat diffident when it came to uttering the appropriate terminology. The fact that he was a black American in a land brimming with quaint customs added to his sense that he and his men, though generally made welcome, were outsiders. For his part Lord Gowerdale was clearly embarrassed to hear that I had gilded the lily a little by having commissioned myself and my boat into the King of Denmark's navy. He expressed this embarrassment by coughing into the tunnel formed by the curled up fingers of the hand he raised to cover his mouth. I had not seen nor heard his Lordship expectorate prior to this incident, and neither did I do so subsequently.

The coughing bout over, Lord Gowerdale addressed the Corporal.

"I know this man as Freddie Hjelmsleve. He lives in a cottage on the outskirts of Hambleton, with one of my employees I might add; but as Mrs Gilbert is a married woman whose husband is away, I'm sure everything is above board there."

Lord Gowerdale looked at me with a knowing expression, and what he knew for certain, it said to me, was that the opposite was true. I also saw in that look which spoke volumes a sense that the man behind the eyes was not about to criticise, and that though there were many differences between us, in his Lordship's view I was a fellow man of the world.

"I can tell you also that Mr Hjelmsleve here is Danish to the core, and that he was indeed a Sea Captain. More importantly, however, this man is a war hero. He evacuated an entire battalion of the Durham Light Infantry from the beaches at Dunkirk, didn't you Hjelmsleve?"

"I don't think it was as many as that my Lord," I said rather sheepishly.

"Dunkirk… That sounds as if it should be in Scotland, but it can't be, because that just wouldn't make sense," said the Corporal, revealing his ignorance not only of European geography, but also of recent British Military history.

With a nod of his head he silently instructed his subordinates to let go of my arms. Rotating each arm in turn I imitated the action of a windmill, my purpose being to loosen the sinews in my shoulders. I looked down at the ground where my walking stick still lay in one piece and then meaningfully back at the Corporal, who took the visual hint. Being only too willing to make amends for his mistake, my former assailant stooped to retrieve my wood support. After handing my stick to me, the Corporal held out his hand for me to shake. This time he really did want to be Freddie's friend. This was a gesture, a genuine peace offering, which I thought it wise not to spurn.

"Please accept my sincere apologies for the inconvenience we have caused you this day," said the Corporal lyrically. "And if there is any practical means whereby I may be allowed to atone for the offences I have administered to your person, be sure to let me know."

"Let's forget it ever happened," I said dismissively.

My erstwhile assailant had begun to sound like a fervent preacher from that part of the United States of America which I later learned is referred to as the Bible belt. Lord Gowerdale meanwhile, convinced that he had brought order to where previously there had been violence and chaos, urged his horse to walk on, looking back over his shoulder to give me a parting instruction.

"Come and see me at the house Hjelmsleve. I might be able to do something for you. Monday morning would be a good time. Let's make it about ten."

"Tusend tak," I said in Danish prior to translating into English, "Many thanks… I'll not be late."

I didn't at that moment give a thought to the possibility that I might just have accepted an invitation to walk into a trap, but later, as I was making my way home empty handed apart from using my stick, I ruminated upon the likelihood of such an eventuality, and came to the conclusion that his Lordship was being sincere. After all, if he did have knowledge of my real identity, he could, I reasoned, have handed me over to the Americans there and then. The downcast soldiers, making valedictory gestures and uttering apologies, turned to follow Lord Gowerdale and his horse. My parting comment had been to advise them that they needed to put in some work on their camouflage. I turned to walk back the way I had come. I had had enough for one day.

Chapter Twenty-Eight

Hambleton Village

By now you may have an inkling that my story is drawing to a close, and you would be right. There are, however, two significant events which I would relate to you, events which I consider to be closely linked though they are separated by over fifty years. To enable you to gain some understanding of these remarkable happenings as they manifested themselves to my percipience, however, let me lead you through the portals of perception gently, so that you too might experience some of the awe and wonder which I felt when these happenstances, and I think particularly the latter, came to pass. In the play called, 'The Tragedy of Hamlet, Prince of Denmark', the play set in my adopted country by your – and I dare say our – divinely inspired poet and playwright, there are a couple of lines spoken by the protagonist that I would ask you to be mindful of as you make this journey with me. The words, 'There are more things in heaven and earth, Horatio, than are dreamt of in your philosophy...' resonate in my mind with the power of thunder and the clarity of lightning.

Compared to my biography prior to my encounter with the black American soldiers on their training exercise, for the remainder of the war my life was an ocean of calm. I kept my appointment with Lord Gowerdale, and was relieved to discover that there was no skulduggery there. On the contrary, I was gratified to be offered gainful employment doing odd jobs around the house and helping with the garden. With regard to the latter it was Lady Gowerdale who kept me busy. It was she who had designed the garden, and clearly this often colourful, always verdant, composition harmoniously poised midway between chaotic wilderness and disciplined order, was her pride and joy.

Inclusive of lawns, flower-beds, vegetable patch, and orchard, the amount of work involved for two pairs of hands was considerable. That work would have been back-breaking in the extreme if a proposal to dig up the lawns and flower-beds at the front and back of the house had been put into effect. Lady Gowerdale, whom I believe had had the final say on the matter, believed that such a course of action would have been tantamount to vandalism. She was perfectly happy with the concept of digging for victory, as long as it wasn't in her back yard. In the light of this judgement the basic layout of the garden more or less remained unchanged throughout the war years and after.

Martha and I were extremely grateful for the opportunity I had been given, and not only insofar as the additional money was welcome, but also because, having passed muster as it were, my being employed at the big house by no lesser persons than a Lord and his Lady effectively deepened my cover. There were, of course, practical difficulties to surmount, not the least of which was how I should be paid, bearing in mind my self-appointed status as a Danish citizen. It was the head-gardener – Lady Gowerdale – who came up with a solution which was brilliant in its simplicity, a scheme which she referred to as 'salary diversion'. The plan was to pay Martha considerably more than she was receiving at present, and this boost to her earnings was to incorporate my remuneration. My being paid under a scheme formalised by this sort of language made me feel quite respectable, almost legitimate. I was perfectly happy with the arrangement. After all, prisoners of war weren't paid. Strange as it may seem, after the war our employers didn't allude to changing this modus operandi, and neither Martha nor I sought to alter the status quo until these members of the landed gentry, these people whom we had got to know well without ever forgetting our respective stations in life by seeking to become overly familiar, eventually sold up and moved on to live in less grandiose surroundings. That was about thirty years ago. Their departure caused a certain amount of upheaval and consternation in our lives because I felt that I had no choice but to formalise my identity, and I went to considerable lengths so to do. It will come as no surprise when I tell you that many of the measures I had to take were dubious to say the least. Without going into too much detail – I don't want to incriminate the people who helped me in this regard – let's just say that I had to make a clandestine trip to Denmark, and that I handed over a not insubstantial amount of Kroner to obtain the necessary documentation to state officially that I am indeed Aage Frederik Hjelmsleve, and to allow me to travel openly instead of my having to be smuggled. I reiterate the question I made at the beginning of my story: what punishment would you mete out to a man in his ninetieth year for making such an admission? I expect you to let it pass without censure.

I would, however, ask you at this juncture to forgive an old man his inability to keep his thoughts in check, for I have allowed them to sprint too far ahead, and I must now take you back to that decade of austerity incorporating the final year of the war and after.

Following the incident with the Americans, and indeed right up until the present for that matter, never did Aage Frederik Hjelmsleve come so close to having his true identity revealed, and this was Hans Hebbel's good fortune. The weeks and months passed, and my British hosts and I began to believe that the war would soon be over, and that an Allied victory, particularly once the June landings on the Normandy beaches had been consolidated, was assured. Martha and I had heard on the radio that the American casualties on that stretch of coastline which had been designated Omaha Beach had been horrendous, and I wondered how many, if any, of my erstwhile captors had survived. In truth, I hoped that they all had, for I bore them no ill will for our confrontation. On the contrary, it was only a week or so after my humiliation at their hands that I came to appreciate that from my point of view all had been for the best, though I could hardly be like Voltaire's character Pangloss and say in the best of all possible worlds. This reasoning began to hold sway as soon as I was given the job at Gowerdale Hall, for if I hadn't been detained as a suspected saboteur, in all probability I would not have met my benefactor and future employer when he was of a mind to hire me. 'There's a divinity that shapes our ends…'

In the wider world the great events which come to be known as history continued to unfold with the deaths of individuals and the deaths of thousands. Paris was liberated on 25th August, and though there were major blips in the campaign to defeat my misguided homeland, specifically at Arnhem and in the Ardennes, in March 1945 allied forces crossed the Rhine to link up with Soviet troops at Torgau towards the end of April. On 30th April Adolf Hitler, the man in whom, for one reason or another, I had initially put so much faith, and whom I eventually learned to despise for having perpetrated such heinous crimes against humanity, and in particular against gypsies, Jews, and homosexuals, killed himself in his Berlin bunker. On 7th May the country in which I had been born and which, prior to my fascist indoctrination, had nurtured me, surrendered, and in the United Kingdom of Great Britain and Northern Ireland the following day was proclaimed as VE day (Victory in Europe). Needless to say there were exuberant celebrations in cities, towns, and villages throughout the land, and Hambleton Village was no exception. It will probably come as no surprise when I tell you that I joined in the general euphoria with as much gusto as those that had genuinely earned the victory. I was motivated to participate in three different ways. First and foremost was my obvious wish not to stand out from the crowd. To have been anything other than deliriously happy on such a momentous occasion would have been to invite suspicion. Secondly, I was profoundly relieved that the war in Europe was over, and in keeping with the belief I had held for the past couple of years that victory for the allies was inevitable, it seemed to me that the sooner that victory was accomplished the better. Thirdly, and I know this must seem trite in comparison, I enjoy a good party as much as the next man, and though I was wary of getting so drunk that I might say something I would later regret – I believe that an appropriate expression in English is to spill the beans – I certainly didn't stay stone-cold sober. Fortunately any embarrassment or scandal I may have caused when I was in my cups paled into insignificance compared to that set in motion by the vicar, who was reputed to have made a pass at Lady Gowerdale. I didn't personally witness anything unusual in this regard, but whether true or false village gossip can travel like wildfire. With Martha by my side I walked home from the Hambleton Inn that night feeling as if I was well established, as if I was an integral part of this community. Rather than scolding me, as she would have done on other occasions, Martha merely giggled when I twice dropped the key to the cottage door, when I succeeded in getting the thing open only at the third attempt.

The end of the war in Europe did not mean, of course, that the killing was over completely. In May 1945 the Burmese capital Rangoon was retaken from the Japanese, whilst the Americans drove their arch-enemy from island after Pacific island, but with heavy losses. With the aim of saving American lives the decision was taken to drop the new destructive force that was the atomic bomb and force Japan to surrender, thereby making an invasion unnecessary. With the destruction, at a single blow, of Hiroshima on 6th August, followed three days later by a similar form of Armageddon being visited upon the city of Nagasaki, the world had entered a new and fearful age, an age symbolised by a giant mushroom cloud forming miles above the point of detonation. The second bomb brought about Japan's surrender on 14th August and VJ Day (Victory over Japan) was celebrated the next day. After a conflict in which an estimated sixty million people had been killed, peace returned to the world at last, but the spectre of a war of almost unimaginable destructive force has remained with our world ever since.

After a war of the magnitude which the Second World War undoubtedly was, revelations of man's inhumanity to man were bound to surface, and none was more disturbing to me as a native German than the deliberately planned extermination of the Jews by the Nazis. At the time I comforted myself with the thought that perhaps Hanne – she whose surname I had usurped – had acted upon my warning and in turn had warned any Jewish friends or acquaintances she might have. For her to have done so would go a long way towards removing a burden of guilt from my shoulders, and would lead me to believe, despite my appearing to have imitated the actions of Alcibiades when it came to demonstrating tribal loyalty, that I hadn't had such a bad war after all.

Someone whom the British authorities thought had had a bad war was the man whose distinctive voice had kept Martha and I informed, and latterly amused, on many an evening in our cosy Yorkshire cottage when the weather was bitterly inclement outside, and that was William Joyce, alias Lord Haw-Haw. Indeed, his propaganda broadcasts must have really got up the noses of the authorities because on the third of January 1946 he was hanged in Wandsworth Prison following his conviction for treason. I for one was sorry to learn of his fate. For years his nasal whine had kept me entertained.

The aforementioned facts relating to the progress of the war and its aftermath are common knowledge to professors of history and the students they have taught. For those people alive today that are old enough to have lived through those turbulent times and were old enough then to be able to comprehend their significance, there will also be nothing in my sequence of events that is revelatory. What is likely to be revelatory, however, is the fact that on the second Sunday in May 1950, Martha and I went to church, there to encounter the first of the two events which caused me to be amazed at the time and pensive thereafter.

To those people that have not previously visited the little church situated on the northernmost bank of the River Rye to the west of Hambleton Village centre, I would say that to make such a pilgrimage is a treat in store, for the church and its setting are a picture, most of the time, of rural harmony and tranquillity. A wooden gate leads from a quiet lane into the graveyard, the solemn beauty of which is enhanced and not diminished for largely having been left to the natural adornments of nettles and buttercups. Outside the main entrance to the church is a Douglas fir, the topmost growth of which I would estimate to be seventy feet above the ground. Unfortunately the tree appears to be dying from the bottom up, and only the top third looks healthy.

The sloping roofs of the church, the chancel and nave of which are said to be Norman, ascend by a single step, as it were, towards the bell-tower, this being, as you would imagine, the sacred building's most prominent feature. Here two bells are housed side by side. On the occasion of my last visit the tower was being encroached upon by the branches of a sycamore tree, but perhaps the tree has since been pruned. Directly beneath the tower some elaborate stone-work frames, and thereby shapes, the enclosed stained-glass as a pair of candles. Quite naturally what appears dark and not particularly colourful from the outside is a scene of vivid colour when viewed from the nave. When I first beheld the scene depicted, the irony that one or other of my family – my German family that is – could have been responsible for the suffering portrayed was not lost on me. The image the glass reveals is a scene from the First World War wherein two stretcher-bearers are carrying a wounded comrade. In the foreground is a seated soldier whose luminous face, whose enlightened eyes, are raised to behold the radiant figure of Christ crucified on the cross. The relevant inscription reads: 'Unto thy hands I commend my spirit.'

When I entered the church that fine May morning I was full of the joys of spring, and was surprised to see that the congregation was slightly larger than usual, and not only by the presence of an individual whom I had not seen before, and whom I later learned was a stranger to the entire village. He was remarkable in that he stood several inches taller than anyone else in the congregation, and in that respect he resembled our vicar, the Reverend Strang. Our eyes met when the stranger turned around to greet Martha's and my arrival with a questioning look. There was something about this lanky man's demeanour, his probing scrutiny, which said to me that his presence amongst us had a specific purpose. He had the look of an errant knight who, after years of strife, and once the task he had been about had been accomplished, would be able to find rest at last.

It shouldn't be inferred from the fact that I had judged the numbers present to be greater than usual that I was a regular churchgoer, but I did go often enough for people whom I recognised, and who recognised me, not to be surprised by my taking a place in the pews. On those occasions that I declined to go Martha sometimes went alone, but in the months leading up to the Sunday in question we had invariably attended services together. I think I can put it down to nothing more demanding than my need to stay tucked up in bed for as long as possible of a Sunday morning as the reason for my non-attendance, as pathetic as that must seem. For whenever I did make the effort to get out of bed and make myself presentable to the world by donning the missing husband's altered suit, more often than not I emerged from the hallowed interior into the churchyard spiritually refreshed, my soul to some extent purified. Of course in May 1950, and for decades after, I had no intention of purifying my soul completely by admitting to the central deceit that I had been an enemy in their midst.

After the nods of acknowledgement and hushed, simple greetings, and the opening hymns and prayers had been sung and said, we sat to listen to the sermon. The Reverend Strang's rangy figure ascended to the pulpit where, despite giving the appearance that he might topple on to the chancel floor were he to sway too excessively or do anything that might affect his balance, he began his oration. From my perspective his position on that particular perch looked incongruous, slightly precarious. I could have more easily envisaged his striding across the moors invoking the wrath of God for empowering human beings with the capacity to behave so often with such crass stupidity. Nonetheless, the sermon the reverend gave that morning pleased Martha and me immensely, primarily for its tone of reconciliation towards the German nation and its people. What astonished us both, however, I'm sure to a far greater extent than it would have done anyone else present that morning, if they were astonished at all, was the dedication of a wreath to the memory of three former enemy airmen whose plane had crashed on the moor eight years previously.

He proceeded to read out the names of my former crewmates with all due solemnity, with a reverence which would not have been inappropriate had the fallen been members of his own parish. My eyes began to moisten as each name mentioned brought images to mind of Dieter and Ernst in life, and in death. The only person's name not to be mentioned was that of Leutnant Kaiser, for having been a supernumerary, conveniently in death he had become me. You can imagine how I felt to hear my own rank and name being commemorated as a dead person. I heard these details as echoes of a past which belonged to someone else, someone farther removed than an alter ego. Martha, who was as surprised as I was by the ceremony taking place, rejected her normal sense of decorum to take hold of my hand, something which she had never in church done before. Our vicar blessed the wreath and then handed it to a woman whom I only knew as Anne. Anne, in her role as churchwarden, carried the floral arrangement of crimson petals set upon a bed of olive-green foliage to the end of the church opposite the chancel, there to lay it on the ledge beneath the window depicting the First World War battle scene. The poignancy of these moments and the significance of this small act of reconciliation were magnificent in my eyes, and I don't mind admitting to the fact that I had to wipe away more than one tear from my eyes with a handkerchief which I borrowed from the woman standing beside me.

Feeling a little unsteady on my feet, and still holding Martha's hand for support, we eventually left the church enveloped in a bubble of silence whilst everyone else was behaving normally for such an occasion. Whilst shuffling towards the door, despite my emotional numbness I listened intently to the various comments being made around me, the more strident of which let it be known that a few were as yet reluctant to follow where the Reverend Strang had led. Martha surreptitiously let go of my hand moments before we were about to shake hands with the vicar who was, as it were, standing sentinel just outside the door. I thanked our reverend warmly, without, I hope, becoming too effusive about a service which was without doubt the most memorable I had ever attended, and would probably ever attend.

For me the day's emotional tsunami was over, but for Martha, who being a woman of considerable empathy, had not been unaffected by my experience, the tide of news which would shortly disturb her equilibrium was waiting to overwhelm her at the churchyard gate, for standing there as bold as a policeman was the suspicious stranger. This individual, who spoke with an accent which even I could recognise as an instrument of what to my ears is that strange mumbo-jumbo which is normal speech farther north, introduced himself as Geordie. After confirming that he was presently addressing Martha Gilbert, and that she was the wife of one George Gilbert who had joined the Spanish Legion to fight for Franco, he told Martha the simple but tragic news that her husband was dead.

The Final Chapter

Forgive an old man his foibles if I have said as much before, but this time I will cite the cliché that time is a great healer not primarily to reveal this nugget of wisdom to the world as knowledge, but to obtain dramatic effect when I tell you that it took precisely two hours thirty-seven minutes for Martha to recover from hearing the then less than tragic news of her husband's demise, much less time you will be glad to hear than it took me to get over my profound sense of loss when she shuffled off this mortal coil. Nonetheless, in adhering to the cliché which is also a truism, the years that have passed since her demise have worked well to assuage my pain. Whether my friends will ostracise me after they have read this composition which is part autobiography, part history, I may soon discover. Alternatively I may consign these pages to the darkness of some rarely opened drawer, and be content in the knowledge that in their writing I have done a good job, for their creation has been cathartic. For it would undoubtedly cause me sadness if I were to be given the cold shoulder the next time I stepped inside the pub for a pint of beer and a packet of crisps, and of course a chat, but I couldn't very well blame anyone who chose to behave in such a manner towards me. To expect people to praise me for my resourcefulness and the successful outcomes of the decisions I made and the chances I took, would, I think, be too much to ask for.

My ninetieth birthday approaches, and though there can be no doubt that the years I have lived outnumber by far the years I have left to me, I look forward to the future with the radiant optimism that comes with having attained a degree of enlightenment. This narrative has been fundamental to that attainment, and the day after I put down my pen after annotating, 'The End', I shall begin a new project. I have as yet no idea what that project will be, but I can tell you two things about it for certain. The first is that it will not be expensive, and the second is that it will be life-affirming, an activity which by keeping mind and body in good working order, will go a long way towards my achieving my later life's ambition, which is to receive a birthday card on the occasion of my one-hundredth birthday from Her Majesty Queen Elizabeth II, who would then be the country's longest-serving monarch.

I have taken a peek into the future, but there remain a number of loose ends from the past upon which I can and ought to shed some light. When I went to Denmark to formalise my new identity in the underhand way I have intimated, I made a half-hearted attempt to find Hanne. I learned that she had moved to Hornbæk to run a hotel in tandem with a fellow who used to own a café in Aarhus. That was the sum total of information I could glean, but I was certain in my mind that she had had two point four children and was perfectly happy. I also felt considerable satisfaction when I learned just how many Danish Jews had survived that tide of evil we now refer to as the holocaust. It may indeed be true that the warning I had given Hanne in the early hours of that fateful morning when we parted company played a significant part in that exodus, and then again, it may not. I like to think that it is true and that it did play an important role. During my visit I was also impressed to learn that after the war had ended, when British troops occupied the country and the Jews ensconced in Sweden thought it safe to return to their Danish homes, that the majority of the latter had returned to discover that for the years of their exile their homes had remained unmolested.

With regard to my own life there remains only one more truly remarkable loose end to tie up, and that is to tell of the second of the two events which to my mind are in some numinous way linked and concatenated by the mystery we call time. The space involved was once again the hallowed precincts of Hambleton Church and its surrounding graveyard.

On 19th June, 2005, which happened to be the day before my birthday, I was returning from a lengthy walk, a perambulation which was a pilgrimage of sorts around Arden Great Moor and the site where I had crash-landed my plane, and was making my way along the footpath which leads close by the church when I realised that I wasn't going to make it home before the heavens opened. I had been keeping an eye on the weather for over an hour, and the relentless build-up of nimbus clouds looming ever darker over the village which was my home and, therefore, my destination, had caused me to quicken my pace, for I knew that I was in a race against time as measured by the minute hand of my watch. I had, of course, walked through bad weather on many occasions, but there was something about these clouds which made their presence more ominous than usual, and I ascribe this to the fact that their menacing darkness was tinged with lurid colour, predominantly green. Sure enough, before I had gained the metal road which passes in front of the church the first heavy drops of rain began to fall. In search of sanctuary, I moved as fast as my still quite sturdy octogenarian legs could carry me, eventually finding shelter under the arch which housed the church door just as the rain began to fall with a vengeance. Fortunately I didn't have to shelter for long before I was espied by a farmer I know. He was in his Land Rover. He offered me a lift back to the cottage. Holding my coat so that it covered my head, my hasty approach indicated my acceptance.

My sense of gratitude at being rescued became profound when I saw on television the next day, and read and saw in the pages of the local newspaper, just how devastating the deluge had been. Not only had the bridge over which I had been transported from the church been washed away, but the building itself had been inundated. Moreover, a great many of the gravestones around the church had been laid low by the power of the flash flood the storm had generated. When I saw the film footage of the devastation I was dumbfounded, but it was a front-page photograph of fallen headstones which moved me most, and I brought to mind an inscription I had read:

'All you who look upon this stone
Reflect how suddenly we were gone;
Death does not always warning give,
Therefore be careful how you live.'

THE END